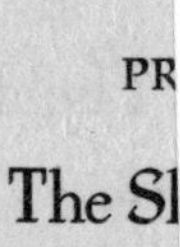

"[*The Shadow's Heir*] showcases the author's impressive ability to create a nicely developed world populated by complex characters . . . I look forward to seeing what new developments are birthed from this author's labyrinthine imagination!"

—*Night Owl Reviews*

"A compelling and exciting story . . . K. J. Taylor has the rare gift for a fantasy writer of knowing how to keep the story moving . . . I am eagerly looking forward to book two in the series."

—*SFFANZ*

"*The Shadow's Heir* forms a great basis for an epic new story, one that I am looking forward to following. I've said it once, but I'll say it again: K. J. Taylor is a talented author who continues to bring us spellbinding stories, and if you aren't already reading her books, then you should remedy that!"

—*Speculating on SpecFic*

PRAISE FOR THE FALLEN MOON TRILOGY

The Griffin's War

"Taylor brings the Fallen Moon trilogy to a satisfying conclusion with a chronicle of pitched battles and political intrigue . . . Strong, realistic characterizations and an intricately conceived milieu make it clear that Australian Taylor is a talent to watch."

—*Publishers Weekly*

"A strong climax to a fabulous trilogy."

—*Alternative Worlds*

continued . . .

The Griffin's Flight

"An intricately plotted story that is full of imaginative characters . . . It is difficult to have sympathy for such an antihero . . . but one ends up unwillingly fascinated with the twists and turns that mark Arren's life." —*Night Owl Reviews*

"Twisty plots are Taylor's strength . . . Readers who value plot above all else in high fantasy will certainly appreciate this book and its predecessor." —*Bookseller+Publisher Magazine*

The Dark Griffin

"A joy to read—rolling prose, tight action . . . and some twisty betrayals." —*The Straits Times Blogs*

"A grim and complex story . . . Taylor's strong vision and firm hand make it compelling reading." —*Herald Sun* (Australia)

"A compelling mixture of intrigue and adventure . . . This is a strong example of intelligent high-stakes fantasy."
—*Bookseller+Publisher Magazine*

"Young yet talented author K. J. Taylor surprisingly weaves an intricate tale, appealing to the senses in a wholly transporting way." —*Portland Book Review*

"[A] dark and intricate fantasy debut . . . Taylor's complex world-building and bloody battle scenes will hook fans of both action and politics." —*Publishers Weekly*

Ace Books by K. J. Taylor

The Fallen Moon

THE DARK GRIFFIN
THE GRIFFIN'S FLIGHT
THE GRIFFIN'S WAR

The Risen Sun

THE SHADOW'S HEIR
THE SHADOWED THRONE

The Shadowed Throne

THE RISEN SUN
BOOK TWO

K. J. TAYLOR

ACE BOOKS, NEW YORK

THE BERKLEY PUBLISHING GROUP
Published by the Penguin Group
Penguin Group (USA) LLC
375 Hudson Street, New York, New York 10014

USA • Canada • UK • Ireland • Australia • New Zealand • India • South Africa • China

penguin.com

A Penguin Random House Company

THE SHADOWED THRONE

An Ace Book / published by arrangement with the author

For information, address: The Berkley Publishing Group,
a division of Penguin Group (USA) LLC,
375 Hudson Street, New York, New York 10014.

ISBN: 978-0-425-25824-8

PUBLISHING HISTORY
Ace mass-market edition / January 2014

PRINTED IN THE UNITED STATES OF AMERICA

10 9 8 7 6 5 4 3 2 1

Cover illustration by Steve Stone; sword © Vertyr/Shutterstock.
Cover design by Judith Lagerman.
Map by Allison Jones.

Dedicated to the real Heath, who has the charm
but not the criminal tendencies (probably)

Author's Note

If you're new to this series, welcome! If you're an old hand, welcome back.

As always, the language the Northerners speak is Welsh. In Welsh, "dd" is pronounced "th."

So, for example, "Arenadd" is pronounced "Arren-ath," "Saeddryn" is "Say-thrin," and "Arddryn" is "Arth-rin." Their surname, Taranisäii, is pronounced "TAH-rah-nis-eye," but it isn't Welsh—Arddryn the elder made it up because she thought it would sound impressive.

Griffish, meanwhile, is pronounced just as it's spelled, since it doesn't have a written form and is therefore spelled phonetically.

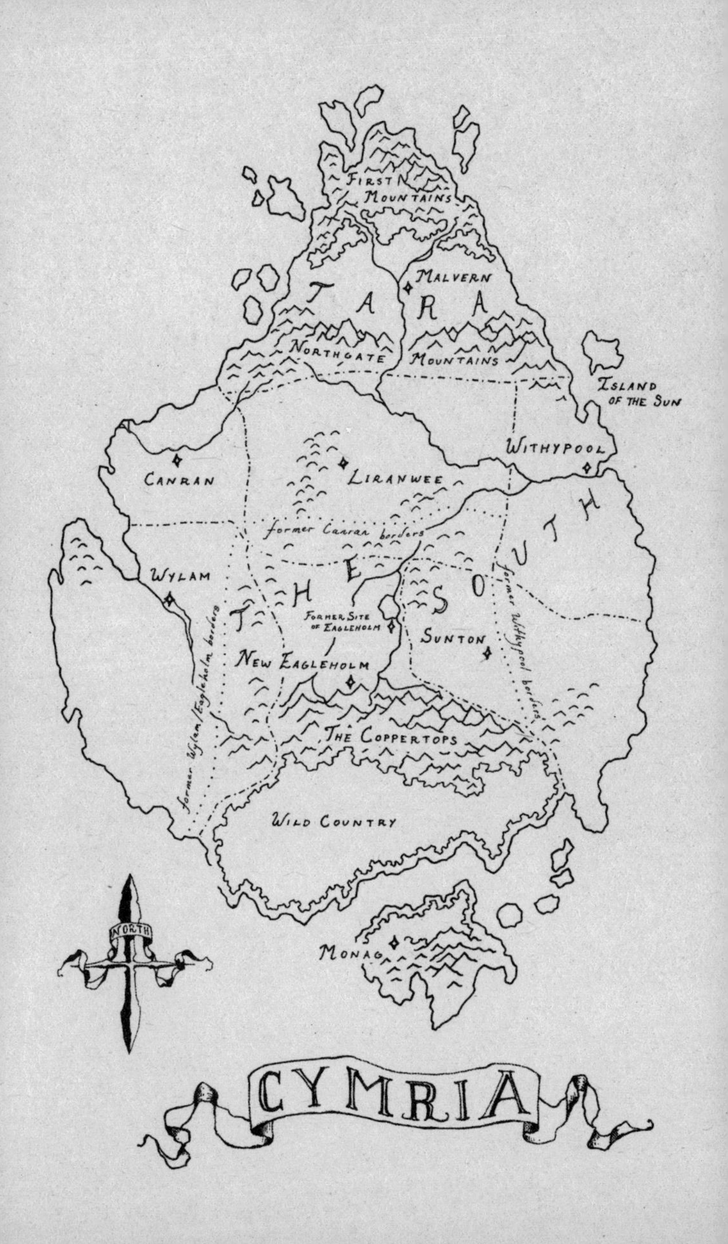
First Mountains
Tara
Malvern
Northgate Mountains
Island of the Sun
Withypool
Canran
Liranwee
The South
former Canran borders
Wylam
Former Site of Eagleholm
New Eagleholm
Sunton
former Withypool borders
former Wylam/Eagleholm borders
The Coppertops
Wild Country
Monag
North
Cymria

Prologue

Looking Back and Forward

The inn had stood by the road that ran between the Northgate Mountains and the city of Withypool for more than twenty years. Travellers on their way between Withypool and the North often stayed there, but the place had been built specifically to serve as a stop-off point for griffiners travelling from Eyrie to Eyrie. Those who could afford it could hire a pair of rooms, one for the human and one for the griffin.

Most of the time, the majority of the inn's patrons were ordinary travellers. But now that had all changed. The Eyries were at war, and griffiners were on the move.

Over the last few months, the owners had seen several of the great lords and ladies come and go, each one accompanied by a haughty and demanding griffin. Some were veterans, travelling to new commands. Others were junior griffiners or apprentices or even untrained nobodies who had only been chosen when extreme circumstances forced unpartnered griffins to drop all standards and claim whatever human was available.

So it wasn't unusual to see plenty of griffiners about, or to see unconventional sorts coming by to take a room. But the pair that had arrived that night still managed to stand out from the crowd.

Not just because the griffin was middle-aged and wild-looking. And not even because her partner was grey-haired despite her youth and spoke and acted as if she had very little experience or patience with other people. Or because she was heavily pregnant.

Mostly it was because the two of them had an entourage.

An enormous one.

The innkeepers had seen them coming from a long way off, and the sheer number of them made them fear the worst and run to hide their possessions, then themselves. But when they saw that the "army" of robed men were unarmed, collared, and following a griffin with a rider, they began to relax.

Sure enough, the griffiner called a halt and came to knock on the inn door, where she tersely explained that she and her slaves would be staying the night. She purchased rooms for herself and her partner and bought food for the slaves, who made camp all along the road and in the field behind the inn. They seemed peaceful enough, but the head of the family that owned the inn privately decided that he would be much, much happier when they were gone.

The silver-haired griffiner seemed completely unflustered and locked herself away with her partner the moment they had both eaten.

In private, the ageing griffin lay down by the fire in her partner's room and idly groomed her wings. Her partner sat nearby, squatting awkwardly in a chair and shifting restlessly from time to time. She touched her swollen belly and winced.

The griffin looked up from her grooming. "When will you lay?"

"Soon." The woman shuffled around in her chair again.

"It is a long way back to the mountains," the griffin pointed out. "There will be no good nesting places for many days."

"I know," said the woman. "I have decided to stay here until I have laid my clutch."

The griffin cocked her head. "You think that you will lay eggs, Skade?"

"I do not know." Skade grimaced again. "Hyrenna, I am . . . not certain."

"You are human," said Hyrenna. "And have mated with a human. Surely you will give birth to a human pup."

"I did not think that we could make young at all," said Skade. "He is not a living man any more, and surely . . . the dead do not father eggs."

"Who can say how this should work?" said Hyrenna. "No human has ever walked without a heart before. But if you did not mate with any other male, then he must be the father."

"He is," said Skade. "I knew I was pregnant before we left."

"Did you tell him?"

"No."

"Why not?"

"You know why not," said Skade. "It is not the way. We say nothing until after the egg is laid and has hatched. An egg counted before then will die. And besides, I am not certain of what I will lay."

Hyrenna clicked her beak. "Arenadd will be pleased when we return, and you show him his young."

"I think he will be," said Skade. "He once told me that he wished he could have a family but did not believe it could be possible."

"And you are his favourite female," Hyrenna added.

"Yes," said Skade. She sounded dispassionate, but inside she was thinking of Arenadd. Her love. Her human love. The only reason she did not care that she had been condemned to live in this body forever. He had sent her away to bring back the slaves to join his cause, but she knew he had sent her in particular to keep her safe. It mattered just as much to him as the freedom of his people. Maybe more.

She hoped that she could bring him their child back as well. But she was uncertain. And afraid, more afraid than she would admit to Hyrenna. She had never been pregnant before and knew very little about how it should be, but part of her told her that this was not right. The thing growing inside her hurt whenever it moved. It almost felt as if it had claws. She had bled, more than once.

She wanted to protect her young, wanted to have Arenadd's child. But part of her was afraid that if she did, then she might not survive.

But it was not her way to share these fears, or any of the fears she might have. She was human in the body now, but she was still a griffin on the inside, and griffins did not show fear. She would bear this out and see her pregnancy through to the end—whatever that end might be.

So she stayed at the inn for the next several days, resting from her journey. Following her instincts, she built a nest for herself on the bed provided, lining it with straw and feathers taken from Hyrenna. The huge, soft bowl shape made her feel better, and she spent a lot of time curled up in it, breathing slowly and wincing from time to time as the child moved inside her.

Outside, the slaves kept up the routine they had learnt during their travels across the country. They ate the rations they'd brought with them and the food their master bought from the inn. When the last of her money finally ran low, they paid the bills in labour—organising themselves into teams that tended the garden, fed the animals, and made any repairs that needed to be made around the inn. Several of them even dug a new well, with all the efficiency of men whose entire lives had been controlled by never-ending labour.

Theirs wasn't the only labour that took place at that inn.

On the fourth day after her arrival, Skade's child began to be born.

She prepared for it in the griffish way, retreating into her nest, where she stayed for an entire long day, struggling alone. Hyrenna, knowing what should be done, left the inn altogether and wandered here and there, watching the slaves at their work.

Skade's labour continued into the evening and then the night, with the child showing no signs of appearing. Despite the intense pain, she made almost no sound at all—but she made enough. The innkeeper's wife, coming to bring her food, heard it and cautiously investigated. The moment she had seen what was happening, she ran out of the room.

Skade was not the only guest staying at the inn that night, and it saved her life. The innkeeper's wife returned with another woman—a woman who carried a bag of leaves and powders, and who sent for hot water and old cloth at once.

If the midwife had come earlier in the day, Skade would almost certainly have driven her away, but by now she was too exhausted to do anything than gasp out a threat, which went ignored.

With help from the innkeeper's wife and two others roped in from elsewhere in the building, the midwife laid Skade out on a table and gave her a draught that dulled some of the pain and helped her to rest. While she dozed, the midwife examined her—feeling her belly and checking the birth canal without embarrassment.

"It's going to be a hard one," she remarked eventually.

It was.

The contractions came again after a short while, waking Skade up, and the birth resumed. The midwife stayed on hand, doing whatever she could to help, and when at last something began to show, she reached in and helped guide it out.

Or began to. As the first part began to emerge—what should have been a head—she screamed and lurched away. The others there came to see what she had seen, and most of them cried out as well. The innkeeper's wife began to pray aloud.

Skade didn't seem to notice. She opened her mouth wide and snarled. Clawlike fingernails gouged the table beneath her, and one last mighty heave moved through her body, finally forcing the thing out and onto the blankets.

It was not a baby.

The thing that Skade had given birth to was something pinkish white and formless, vaguely oval. Veins branched out over its surface, pulsating slightly.

Very carefully, the midwife approached it. Moving as if it might bite her at any moment, she reached down to touch it. It was soft and flexible under her fingers.

"What is it?" one of the others there almost whispered.

"It's warm," said the midwife. "And . . ." She ran her hands over the thing's bloodstained surface, and her eyes widened. "And . . . it . . . it's got a *heartbeat*."

"A what?" the innkeeper's wife stopped praying, and came closer to see. "Are you sure?"

"Yes." The midwife felt the object with more certainty now. "See the veins there pulse? There's a heartbeat making that happen."

"But what is it?" one of the other two there asked.

"I don't know." The midwife prodded it experimentally. "I never saw anything like this before in my life."

"But it's alive?"

"Yes. Must be, with a heartbeat."

They glanced at Skade. She seemed to be asleep, or unconscious.

"How could she give birth to this?" asked the innkeeper's wife, with a kind of wonder.

"I don't know." The midwife gently eased her hands in under the object, as if it were a baby, and lifted it. Instantly, it began to move, squirming weakly in her hands like a grub. To her credit, she didn't drop it, and only grimaced.

"It's alive!" One of the two helpers backed off sharply.

The midwife, however, had begun to look a little more certain. "There's something inside," she said. "I can feel it—look! See there, you can see something pressing from the inside!"

Sure enough, as the innkeeper's wife leaned in to look, she saw the thing bulge and stretch—as if something were trying to get out.

"It's a membrane, that's what this is," said the midwife, putting it down again by Skade's side. "I saw something a tiny bit like this once before—a child was born with a sheet of skin over her face. A caul, we call them. It just peels away. This—this is something like that, I'm sure of it."

"But there's no cord!" the innkeeper's wife put in. "No afterbirth."

"That might come later," said the midwife. "But . . ." She looked at the thing lying innocently by Skade's side. "But if there is a child, it's inside that . . . skin."

"Should we cut it open, then?" one of the onlookers suggested. "It might be drowning in there."

"Maybe—" The midwife took a step closer and reached out to touch the thing.

Skade's eyes snapped open, and she hissed weakly. "Do not . . . touch it."

The midwife stood back and folded her hands to show she was harmless. "It's your . . . child, my lady. There's a membrane on it, and I think it should be removed."

Skade's head lolled to the side, and she peered at the thing. Her hand moved to touch it. She felt it, brushing it with her fingertips, and finally fell back with a sigh. "No. My egg . . . must be incubated in the nest. Do not touch it, or I will kill you."

" 'Egg'?" repeated the innkeeper's wife.

The midwife blinked slowly. "An egg." She half-laughed. "Gryphus take me, she's right. It's an egg!"

"Don't be daft!" said an onlooker. "Eggs have hard shells on 'em, everyone knows that!"

"Bird and griffin eggs do," said the midwife. "But I've seen lizard and snake eggs as well, and they're different. Their shells are soft, like this."

"But people don't lay eggs! It's a mem-thing, like you said. We should open it up, see what's inside!"

The midwife shook her head. "My mother always told me, don't interfere with what you don't understand. I've done my part, and now it's up to the mother to decide what to do. And if she says to leave it, we will. For now, we should put her back to bed and leave her to rest. She needs it."

"I'll help," said the innkeeper's wife.

"And me," said one of the onlookers, reluctantly.

The midwife approached Skade cautiously. "My lady," she said. "We're going to put you back into your bed to rest. We'll put your . . . egg next to you. Don't worry, we aren't going to do anything to it. It's yours."

Skade opened her eyes a crack. "It stays with me. Nobody shall touch it."

"All right, then." The midwife put her hands around the egg, and helped Skade to lift it onto her belly. Skade held it there with both hands, keeping it steady, as the four humans took her up off the table and lowered her back into her nest. She rolled onto her side and pulled the egg with her, cradling it in the curve of her body.

The midwife put a blanket over the pair of them and silently gestured at the others to help her clean up. Afterward, they left together and let Skade sleep.

Skade stayed in her makeshift nest for the next several days and refused to leave the room for any reason. She wouldn't even have eaten if the innkeeper's wife hadn't brought food up to her. As for Hyrenna, she stayed away. Others soon did the same, as Skade snarled and threatened anyone who intruded on her, and—once she recovered—took to throwing things and slashing with her claws. Even the innkeeper's wife had to leave her food by the door and hurry away.

In time, Skade recovered from the birth and was able to walk around her room, but she rarely left her nest, and when she did, she took the egg with her and carried it against her stomach, wrapping it in a blanket. It moved from time to time, squirming sometimes in her grip, and she would murmur and cradle it until it stilled again. She took encouragement from this—the movement felt strong, and that meant the infant must also be strong.

Soon she began to use it as a gauge of how it was growing as well—the infant's wriggling grew noticeably more vigorous and powerful over time. The infant itself grew as well—the ugly shell covering it began to stretch as its contents expanded. Its surface had become dry and cracked, and now it finally began to weaken.

And then, nearly a week and a half after its strange birth, the egg began to come apart.

Skade, dozing in her nest, woke up with a start when she felt the egg moving against her. She sat up and saw fluid oozing down the side. A tear had appeared.

Silent, unsmiling, she sat on her haunches and watched without moving a muscle.

The egg's surface distorted even more, and she could see the infant struggling inside—this time not stopping to rest. Tiny limbs thrust outward, not flailing vaguely now but pushing in a determined effort to escape.

For a while it looked as if it would not succeed, but after a moment's rest, the infant made one last push upward. A wet, tearing sound was followed by a trickle of bloody fluid, and an instant later, Skade heard the first cry of her child.

She reached down at last, pulling away the remains of the egg, and there was her baby, lying in a puddle of blood and slime, tiny hands reaching toward her.

Skade hissed suddenly, loudly, like a cat. "No!"

The child made an ugly croaking sound. Stubby talons curled.

Skade stared a moment longer, her yellow eyes dull with disbelief.

Then she moved away. She climbed out of the nest and stripped off her dress, selecting a clean one from her bags. There was some food left from lunch—she ate it, then squatted down to groom, all the while completely ignoring the creature calling for her.

She packed her belongings and walked out of the room without ever looking back.

Downstairs, she found the innkeeper's wife, who started horribly at the sight of her. "Er . . . milady, I'm sorry, are you leaving . . . ?"

"Yes." Skade reached into her bag, and handed over a small, leather pouch. "This is the gold for you. Now I am going to find Hyrenna and my slaves, and I shall leave."

The innkeeper's wife followed her as she left the building. "But milady . . . your child. Where is it?"

"I have no child," Skade said curtly, and strode away.

Hyrenna was flying overhead and came down to meet her. "Skade, I am pleased to see you. We are leaving now?"

"Yes." Around them both, the slaves were already packing up their belongings.

Hyrenna glanced toward the building. "Your egg?"

"It did not hatch," said Skade, expressionless. "I have no young."

"That is sad for you." Hyrenna raised a foreleg, and slowly scratched her face. "What will you tell your mate when you see him again?"

"I will tell him nothing," Skade snapped. "There is nothing to tell. When I find him again, I shall make new eggs with him, and we will both be proud of our young."

"Yes," said Hyrenna. "That is how it should be. Come now, put on my harness, and we will fly ahead."

Skade did so, buckling on the straps around Hyrenna's head and neck that would provide handholds for her in the air. Once they were adjusted, she climbed on, and the griffin took off with an easy flick of her wings—flying up and over the inn to circle while the slaves finished their preparations and moved off again along the dusty road northward.

1

Queen Laela

The ring seemed to glow golden in the firelight, the gems glittering all over its outside. She stared at it, entranced. Such magnificence, and all for her.

The human turned it over carefully, to let her see it from all angles. "This is one of my finest pieces. How d'ye like it?"

"It is beautiful."

The human only stared at her, nervous and uncomprehending.

Oeka clicked her beak irritably and held out her foreleg. The human understood this and carefully snapped the ring closed just above her knee. It fitted perfectly. Pleased, Oeka offered her other foreleg to receive its twin.

The rings were heavy and felt odd, but she didn't care. She pecked at the gems, cooing softly at their shine. Every other griffin who saw her now would instantly recognise her superiority, no matter how much bigger or older it was. Only the highest of the high could wear rings like these, and she was that.

Oeka huffed to herself, her feathers fluffed. *Only I am worthy,* she thought. *Only I have a human who is a Queen.*

That reminded her—she should go and show the rings off to her human now. She would want to see.

Oeka turned her back on the goldsmith and walked out of his workshop, reflecting proudly on everything that had happened over the last week or so. When the Mighty Skandar had flown away from Malvern, taking his human and Oeka's with him, it had felt like a disaster. Oeka had no way of knowing where her human had gone—the human she had to protect and bring to greatness. For all she knew, her human could be dead.

She had stayed alone in the city, hiding from the traitors who wanted them both gone, hoping endlessly that she would hear some word of where her human might be. But nothing came.

She had watched, hidden on a rooftop, as the traitor prepared to crown herself Queen in place of her missing cousin. Her whole body had trembled with the need to do something—anything—but what *could* she do? Without her human, she was nothing.

But her human had returned. Laela had returned. Alone, ragged, and exhausted . . . but she had returned, and all of Oeka's hopes had returned with her.

Still, she hadn't moved. She stayed where she was, watching to see what would happen. Surely, Laela would die now. Without the Mighty Skandar and his partner, the King, to support her, she would be helpless.

Oeka shook her wings, happy at the memory. She had been wrong, and that was what made it wonderful. Laela had not needed Skandar or the King to help her. She had triumphed that day, and the moment Oeka knew it, she returned to her side at once—ready to be her friend once more.

Laela was Queen now, and all of Oeka's grandest dreams had come true.

I was right to choose her, she thought. *There can be no better human for me. She is the one I deserved, for my strength. The daughter of the Mighty Skandar's human is mine.*

Oeka loped through the streets of Malvern, in the tradesmen's quarter, welcoming the excited whispers of the humans she passed.

"Isn't that the Queen's griffin?"

"It is; I saw her myself, before. That's Oeka!"

Oeka cast a glance at the human who'd spoken. "You shall call me the *Mighty* Oeka now."

With that, she took off to fly over the city—heading toward the Eyrie, and Laela.

In her own quarters, Laela was having problems.

She opened up a clothes-chest and rifled through it, hurling various bits of clothing in all directions. Still not finding what she was after, she upended the entire contents onto the floor and dug through them. Nothing. She swore and stumped over to the dressing-table, which had jewellery strewn all over it. Another search of the drawers turned up nothing.

"Damn it!" Laela hurled a set of underclothes across the room, narrowly missing Oeka as she entered through the archway from her nest.

The small brown griffin ducked. "What is this?"

Laela slumped into her chair. "I got a meetin' with the council in a moment, an' I can't find my *bloody* crown."

Oeka trampled over a gown on her way past the ravaged wardrobe. "Perhaps it is in a place you have not looked."

"Not bloody likely. If it's in this room anywhere, then I'm a muddy goat. Where've you been, anyway?"

"I went to see the ring-maker," said Oeka, and raised a foreleg to show off the glittering golden band.

Laela forgot her sulk at once. "Wow, Oeka, that's beautiful! I didn't know he'd finish that quick."

"You are impressed?" Oeka said smugly.

"Damn right I am. Things've got so many jewels on 'em, I'm amazed yeh can still fly. That man knows his work—I gotta give him extra when I send down his pay."

"The council shall also be impressed," said Oeka. "And their humans. How magnificent I shall look!"

"Very. We gotta go see 'em soon—right after I've found that gods-damned crown. And how long that's gonna take I dunno. It'd probably be faster if I just had a new one made."

Oeka sauntered past her to the bed. "It may be good to have one extra."

"Yeah, so you can wear one, too. Hey, what are yeh doin'? Don't even think about tearin' my bed up again; I'll have yeh skinned."

Oeka shoved the pillow aside and hooked the crown out from under it with her beak.

Laela ran to get it. "Finally! What in the gods' names was it doin' under there?"

"Only you may know," said Oeka. "For now, we have work to do."

"Too right." Laela put it on. "There, how do I look?"

"Your fur must be groomed," said Oeka.

Laela muttered and stomped over to the dressing-table. She selected a comb, and sat down to try to neaten her long, curly black hair.

Oeka watched with amusement. "You have your father's coat but not so much of his nature. He would never have allowed himself to be seen before grooming himself."

"I know. I saw his collection of brushes." Laela growled to herself as she struggled with a particularly stubborn tangle.

"I did not doubt that you were his daughter," Oeka said unexpectedly.

"Eh? What's that supposed to mean?"

The small griffin's dark green eyes gleamed. "I knew that you were his from the moment I saw you. You looked like him, and smelt the same. You and he did not know it yet, but a griffin's senses do not lie."

"Yeh weren't the only one, Oeka. Everyone who saw us together thought we looked the same. I thought maybe that was why he always said I reminded him of himself."

"Perhaps. But when I scented his mind, I knew the truth."

Laela put the brush down. "How d'yeh mean?"

"There were memories in his mind," said Oeka. "Buried. Hidden. Things he kept away from himself. He remembered an old life, before he was *Kraeai kran ae*. He remembered another name. And he remembered a female." Her voice became dreamy. "A human female, one he loved and mated with. A coat of brown and eyes of blue."

Laela's own bright blue eyes shone with unshed tears. "My mother."

"Perhaps."

"So he did love her. Old Bran lied. He never raped her."

"Who knows?" said Oeka. "But my magic tells only truth. Perhaps if he had lived, he would have told you."

"He wouldn't have." Laela shook her head. "He didn't remember. Not until after he . . . after he was . . . while he was dyin' . . . that's when he remembered. It was like he woke up, just before he was gone."

"He was your father," said Oeka. "And that is all that matters. I knew it, and that is why I chose you. Why I stayed with you. And I knew that he had chosen you to be his heir."

"Yeh did? When? How?"

"He told me."

They stared at each other.

"*Told* yeh?" said Laela. "When?"

"When we were in Amoran," said Oeka. "When he became ill. He feared that he might die. He told me, 'Oeka, I know I will not be King much longer. My dead heart tells me. I have no wife, no children. I have no heir. My cousin thinks that her son will succeed me, and I had planned for him to do so. But I do not trust him any more. I trust no-one now but Skandar, and one other.' "

There really were tears in Laela's eyes now. "Me. He trusted me."

"Yes. He told me, 'Laela is like a daughter to me. She is like a mirror of myself. She has my strength, but she is not like me because she still has a heart. The North deserves her. Never tell this to anyone, Oeka. Only remember, and when the time comes, Laela can know. I want her to be Queen when I am gone. She will need your help, as her partner. Give her your strength, as Skandar gave me his.' "

"He knew," Laela whispered. "He knew all along he was gonna die. He was plannin' for it, all that time."

"I believe so. His mind tasted of resignation."

Laela turned away. "I should've loved him. I should've been like a daughter. If I'd only known . . ."

"It is not your fault," said Oeka. "He trusted you, Laela. Now live to that trust. Come. Our council waits."

Laela pulled herself together with an effort. "Yeah . . . guess we should get goin'."

"Our power is not yet safe," Oeka reminded her, as they left. "There are still threats we must deal with."

Laela's eyes narrowed. "I know."

The huge chamber built halfway up the largest of the Eyrie's towers had been known as the council chamber back in the days when Malvern had been ruled by Southerners.

It had kept that name after twenty years of playing host to a new ruler and a new council, but it didn't look quite the same any more. The domed roof had been repainted with a mural of a starry sky and the different phases of the moon in a ring, and the tapestries on the walls below the gallery had been replaced with painted hides and ceremonial spears. In the middle of the floor, ringed by the seats of the council, the special sun-shaped platform for the Eyrie Master or Mistress had been given a new coat of paint as well. Now it looked like a full moon instead—a nice touch, Laela had always thought.

After his conquest of the North, her father Arenadd said that his cousin Saeddryn had wanted to burn Malvern to the ground. Arenadd, though, had overruled her—preferring to keep the city and the Eyrie as the seat for his own government.

Laela was glad about that. She had come to love Malvern, and the Eyrie especially.

"Saeddryn and the rest think this Eyrie is a Southern thing," her father had once said. "But they forgot that we were the ones who made it. The Southerners forced us to build it for them, and now we can enjoy the results."

The council had already taken up position by the time Laela entered, and she eyed them confidently as she made her way toward her rightful place.

At only twenty years old, Laela knew she didn't look much like a Queen, but the truth was that she didn't feel like one, even in the fine gown decorated with gemstones and the thin silver crown that rested on her forehead. She was tall and narrow-shouldered, like her father Arenadd, and had inherited his thick, curly black hair. But her blue eyes had come from her Southerner mother, and her pointed nose had a sprinkling of freckles that stood out against her pale skin. Her rough Southern accent had come from her foster father, Bran, who had raised her in a tiny house in the South. She had started her life as a half-breed peasant girl, and now . . .

She stepped up onto the platform, with Oeka beside her, and saw how the human members of her council bowed their heads respectfully to her. She felt the light pressure of the crown on her head. For just an instant, the sheer scale of what had happened to her in such a short time made her feel dizzy. How could she have gone from a Southern village to this? Queen of her own country? It was the sort of thing that only happened in children's stories.

But, of course, it hadn't been her own doing. She had come to Malvern by herself, hoping to find a new life, and that was where she had met Arenadd. Her father, though neither of them knew it. He had saved her, and protected her, and he had been a father to her even before either of them had discovered the truth. He had made Laela his heir for reasons of his own, and now he was gone, and here she was. It was madness, but it was true.

Laela pulled herself together and turned her attention back to the council.

They were all there. Lord Iorwerth, the Master of War, and his partner, the powerful Kaanee. Lord Torc, Master of Law. The Masters of Trade, Building, Taxation, and Farms were there, too. And finally, there was Lady Saeddryn Taranisäii, High Priestess of Malvern. She stood with her husband Torc on one side, and her partner—the hulking Aenae—on the other.

Laela's mouth tightened. Saeddryn's hair was shot through with silver, and she was weathered with age, but there was a hardness to her, as if she had steel inside her instead of bones. She was like her cousin Arenadd in that respect, and Laela knew that she more than equalled him in ruthlessness.

Saeddryn looked back coolly, through her solitary black eye.

Laela gestured politely at the councillors. "Sit down. I think we're ready to get started."

"Welcome, my lady," Iorwerth said as he obeyed. His look toward her was warm but tinged with uncertainty.

"Now then," said Laela. "First up, is there anythin' anyone wants to bring to my attention? I know the High Priestess has somethin' she wants to mention."

Saeddryn took her cue, standing up almost instantly. She folded her hands in front of her and began very carefully. "As yer reign begins, my lady, there are some things that have t'be . . . dealt with."

Oh, I'll deal with you all right, Laela thought.

"Go on," she said.

"First of all . . ." Saeddryn hesitated. "I respect King Arenadd's decisions as much as anyone, and I'd never dream of goin' against his wishes. But when it comes to the question of ye succeedin' him, there are some things that I want answered."

"We all want them answered," Torc agreed.

Iorwerth and several of the other councillors nodded.

"I'm all ears," said Laela.

"Ye say the King is dead," said Saeddryn. "An' I believe ye. If he were alive, he'd have come back by now."

"He's gone," said Laela. "I swear on me own heart."

"But if that's the case, my lady," said Saeddryn, "where is his body?"

Iorwerth stood up. "It's not that we don't believe ye," he said, glaring at Saeddryn. "I do. But I want the King's bones back here. He deserves a proper burial."

"An' you deserve the chance to see him buried," Laela agreed. "Listen, I care about this too. He was my father, don't forget. I owe him everythin'. An' I promise I'm gonna do everythin' in my power t'find his body."

"None of the griffiners we sent out found anything," said Iorwerth.

"We'll send more," said Laela. "I'll go myself when Oeka's a little bigger." *When I think I can leave my throne an' find it still here when I get back.*

"I'll go an' look," Saeddryn said unexpectedly. "He was my cousin."

Laela liked that idea a lot. "Maybe the Night God'll guide yeh."

"What of my father?" Aenae demanded. "What of the Mighty Skandar? You say he did not die."

"Not so far as I know," said Laela. "He flew away an' never came back. I don't see why he'd come back t'Malvern with his human dead," she added sadly.

"If he did return, he would have a comfortable life for the rest of his days."

Laela knew perfectly well that Aenae's greatest desire had always been to fight his gigantic father to the death. "Of course. When we search for my father's bones, we'll search for Skandar, too. He freed the North as much as my father did."

"There's one other thing I want t'know," Saeddryn interrupted. Her eye narrowed.

"Ask," said Laela.

"How do we know ye really are Arenadd's daughter?"

Several of the other councillors glanced at each other.

Laela laughed weakly. "I would've thought yeh could tell just by lookin'. I look more like him than *you* do."

Saeddryn's lips pursed. "It could be just a coincidence."

"Maybe, but when I told him my mother's name, he knew her, an' he knew that he'd been with her."

"The King's word is enough for me," Iorwerth said stoutly. "His promise and her face are enough. Why would he lie about it?"

Laela faced Saeddryn square on. "He planned to make me his heir even before he knew I was his daughter. The Master of Learning went through his papers an' found documents to prove it. He was gonna adopt me—make me a Taranisäii. He only died before he could announce it—the papers are all signed an' sealed."

"It's true," said Iorwerth. "I saw them with my own eyes."

"So did I," said the Master of Taxation.

"And I," said the Master of Building.

"I would've showed 'em to you, too, but you was off busy at the Temple," Laela said sweetly to the infuriated Saeddryn. "I figured now was as good a time as any." She took a scroll from her sleeve and handed it over.

Saeddryn's single eye scanned the neat writing. Stone-faced, she handed it back. "That's his writing, sure enough. Forgive me for doubtin' ye."

Laela bowed slightly. "It's only right that yeh should be askin'."

"Now, on to a new issue," Torc said. "There's something else we ought to discuss."

"What is it?" said Laela. Beside her, Oeka yawned and lay down on her belly.

"A Queen needs a consort," said Torc. "It's time ye started choosing a husband, my lady."

Laela's heart sank. "I've been thinkin' about it already, don't worry."

"We have a good suggestion," said Saeddryn. "The noblest blood in Tara. Yer own age, too."

"Oh, who?" Laela was suspicious already.

"My son, Caedmon," said Saeddryn. "He's another Taranisäii—it'd be the perfect marriage, t'strengthen our great family."

"Hm." Laela rubbed her chin to hide her panic. "I see yer point. Give me some time to think it over, why don't yeh?"

"Of course." Saeddryn smiled.

"Don't do it," Iorwerth said the instant the meeting was over and he and Laela were alone. He came closer, frowning and urgent. "Marry Caedmon, and he'll be on the throne and ye in a dungeon by the end of the week."

"I already thought of that," Laela said evenly. "I ain't so stupid as I look. Only question is, what do I do instead?"

"Ye could marry *my* son, perhaps."

"He's *twelve*." Laela waved away Iorwerth's protests. "I can't rush into this. Whoever I marry'll change everythin', an' I want it to be for the better."

"Betroth yerself to my son," Iorwerth persisted. "When he's older, ye can marry. My family's a strong one—ties with us would make all the difference. It'd put a lot more people on yer side."

"I see that, but . . ."

"Ye need to be strong, my lady," Iorwerth said. "And ye need to become strong fast. The common people love ye, but ye can't ride on that forever."

"I know." Laela grinned and punched him in the side. "Lucky for me I got my strong right arm here."

"I gave my life to King Arenadd," said Iorwerth, unsmiling. "Not to Saeddryn. He wanted me to be yours after his death, and so I am. I was the King's man once, but now I'm the Queen's, through and through. Ye can trust that as ye trust the Night God herself."

Laela felt humbled. "I always will, Iorwerth. That's a promise."

2

Ravana

Something had to be done about Saeddryn.

Laela paced back and forth in her room, shoulders hunched and face locked into a scowl. When she'd first taken the throne, she had thought removing her father's cousin would be easy. After all, Laela had heard her talk about her plan to steal Arenadd's throne with her own ears. By rights, as Queen, she should have been able to simply throw her in prison or have her exiled.

But Saeddryn had been too quick for her. The very day of Laela's coronation—before she could even return to the Eyrie—the High Priestess had sent her daughter away to wherever her son was already hiding. Laela had no idea where they were now, but she couldn't make herself forget the gleam in Saeddryn's eye when she told her that Arddryn had left Malvern like her brother Caedmon, who had vanished somewhere before Laela had come to the city. She hadn't needed to say anything else; the threat was clear enough. If anything happened to Saeddryn, her offspring would be ready and waiting to avenge their mother. Caedmon and Arddryn were Taranisäiis—there were plenty of people out there prepared to support them rather than this half-breed newcomer now sitting on the throne.

For now, Saeddryn seemed content to smile and bide her time, plotting who knew what with who knew which allies. Even her famously honest husband could well be in on it.

Laela couldn't trust anyone, and whether she liked it, or not she needed to keep Saeddryn where she was and pretend they were a happy family.

For now.

In the meantime, she had a country to run, and only a handful of people she knew could give her the kinds of advice she needed.

Silently, she thanked the gods for Iorwerth. Him she knew she could trust. Her father had trusted him, too, and he'd already proven himself worthy of that trust—he had been one of the people entrusted with the secret document Arenadd had written naming his daughter heir to Tara's throne. When Laela had returned to Malvern and announced herself, he had come to her side at once and supported everything she said.

Ever since that day, he had been her rock, and if she ever doubted him again, she remembered what her father had told her.

Now that's a man you can trust to the ends of the earth. At the time, she'd noticed the way he said it—loudly and firmly, as if it were important. Now, looking back, she knew why. *He was already plannin' for all this. He wanted me t'know who to trust.*

Laela cheered up slightly. She had Iorwerth and Kaanee, and she had Oeka. They were a formidable group of allies—Oeka in particular, in her own way. And there were others, she reminded herself. Maybe not as powerful as those three, but there were others.

I'm Arenadd's daughter, she told herself. *He always said I was like him, an' he could handle anythin'.*

Almost anything.

She shivered and tried to push the memory away. That didn't matter now. She was dealing with people and griffins, not . . . other things.

As if sensing her distress, Oeka appeared at that moment to interrupt. "Laela. I am hungry."

Laela brought herself back to the present. "Me too. Let's go get somethin' t'eat, you an' me."

The Queen and her partner ate together in the dining hall, waited on by one of the only other people in the Eyrie that they both trusted.

Laela grinned at the sight of her. "How's it goin', Inva?"

Inva smiled back nervously. She was middle-aged, her pale Northern skin freckled by the harsh sunlight of the land she'd been born in. Her slave collar had been removed quite a while ago, but the scars still stood out on her neck. The hair that had been cut short was growing back in a scatter of black and silver.

Laela watched her taste each dish before serving it. "Yeh know I can still get someone else to do that."

Inva avoided her eye, the way she'd been trained to do from birth. "It is my honour to risk my life for you, my Queen."

"It's *my* honour to have yeh do it," said Laela. "But I ain't got too many friends in this Eyrie, an' I'd hate to lose one now."

Inva finished tasting the food and laid it out on the table. "My duty is to offer up my life in place of my master's."

"It was yer duty in Amoran," Laela said bluntly, "when yeh still had a master."

"You are my master, my Queen."

"No, I'm yer employer," said Laela. "There's a difference. This time, yer gettin' paid."

Inva only smiled in that mysterious way of hers and poured some wine into a cup.

Inva's silences and rigid manners were often frustrating, but Laela was very fond of the former slave. During her visit to Amoran, where she and Arenadd had gone to free the other Northerners who were still enslaved by the Amorani Empire, Inva had been appointed as Laela's personal slave. After she and her fellows had been handed over to the King, largely thanks to Laela's own efforts, she had been set free like all the others.

Despite that, Inva had still spent her entire life up until a few months ago with a strict set of rules to follow, and so far it seemed she wasn't going to give them up.

The other freed slaves had been given homes in and around the Eyrie, on Laela's orders, and had been given jobs that suited their training. Laela had been amazed to find how well educated some of them were. Inva in particular could read and write far better than Laela could, and in several different languages to boot. She knew her numbers as well, and she had seen plenty of politics thanks to years spent working in the Emperor's court and among his family.

That was one of the reasons why Laela had made her her

personal servant, and her assistant in all but name. Other people in the Eyrie disapproved of her keeping company with a "blackrobe," but Laela didn't care. They could complain when they could give better advice than Inva could.

Her work done for now, Inva sat politely and waited while her mistress ate. She didn't try to make conversation.

That was for Laela to do. "How are the new quarters suitin' yeh?"

Inva smoothed down her skirt. "They are . . . cold."

"Cheer up, spring's on its way," said Laela.

Inva shivered. "This land is a desert of ice. The sun is weak here. Sometimes, I cannot see it at all, and I fear that it will not return."

"This ain't the sun's land, Inva," said Laela. "This place belongs to the moon."

"I know. This is the Night God's realm."

"Yeah." Laela scowled. "Far as I'm concerned, it's *my* realm."

"Forgive me, I did not—"

"Never mind about it; I'm just in a bad mood. So, got anythin' to report?"

"Nothing, my Queen."

"Nothin' is nothin'," said Laela. "I know you. What's up?"

"It is not news, my Queen," said Inva.

"Don't care. Tell me anyway."

"Very well. One of my fellows wishes to meet you."

"Is that all?" said Laela. "Who is it?"

"His name is Ravana." Inva looked uncomfortable. "He is a dangerous man."

"To me?" Laela said at once.

"No. You are his master now."

"I told yeh, I ain't nobody's mas—"

"That does not matter," Inva interrupted. "Not to him."

"Why does he want t'see me?"

"To swear loyalty in person," said Inva. "He claims to have skills that could be useful to you."

"Sounds good to me," said Laela.

Oeka gulped down the last of her meat and deigned to join the conversation. "We shall see him," she said. "Any new ally is worthy to meet us."

"Sure thing," said Laela. "Show us t— I mean, we'll be up in our audience chamber. Show him up in a little while, will yeh? I just need some time to clean up an' get ready."

Inva bowed. "As you command, my Queen."

So far, Laela hadn't felt ready to move into her father's old quarters, but she had been making use of the audience chamber attached to them. It was at the very top of the largest of the Eyrie's towers and round to match the exterior. Lined with beautiful white marble, it featured a platform for Oeka to sit on. A chair placed just in front of it provided a seat for Laela.

Oeka hopped up onto the platform and settled down among the cushions. "I wonder why this slave wishes to see us?"

"He ain't no slave," Laela said sharply. "There are no slaves in Tara any more."

Oeka scratched her flank, unmoved. "This one had better have a reason to disturb us. We have more important matters to think of."

"We'll see, won't we?" said Laela, who was frankly curious to find out. Of course, most likely Ravana just wanted to see her so he could either thank her for setting him free or complain about wanting to go back "home" to Amoran. There'd been plenty of both from the others.

"A little while" was nowhere near little enough for Laela, and she was thoroughly bored by the time Inva arrived with Ravana. However, when she laid eyes on the man who'd come to see her, she sat up at once.

Unlike the other former slaves who'd come to see her, Ravana didn't look the slightest bit nervous or awed. He walked ahead of Inva, moving with long, confident strides, his head held high.

But when he reached Laela's throne, all that disappeared in an instant. He knelt at her feet, bowing his head so low it nearly touched the floor. "Master."

"Get up," said Laela.

He did, looking her boldly in the face but saying nothing— waiting for her to speak first.

Laela examined him. He was tall and lean, like most

Northerners, but thick with muscle in the arms and chest. Like all members of his race, he had black hair—still cropped close to his skull—and jet-black eyes that made his expression difficult to read. He wore a woollen tunic with a low-cut neck that showed several raw red scars on his body, and one of his ears had been half–hacked off.

"Ravana, is it?" Laela said eventually.

He nodded once.

"Inva said yeh wanted to see us."

Another nod.

"Speak, then," said Laela, finally giving up. "Tell me why."

Ravana put his hands together in front of his chest and bowed low. "I am Ravana," he said, in fractured Cymrian. "I am *Hm-Waw'ew.*"

"What's that?" said Laela, glancing at Inva.

Ravana followed her gaze, and said something briefly in Amorani.

Inva stepped forward. "He does not speak Cymrian. I will translate."

Laela gestured at her to continue.

"*Hm-Waw'ew* is a warrior slave," said Inva. "Trained from birth to do nothing but fight. Slaves from our race were prized as fighters. Their masters would use them for . . . many purposes."

"I see." Laela looked at Ravana with renewed interest. "Yer a fighter, then, Ravana."

Inva translated. Ravana smiled, showing several broken teeth. He spoke rapidly in Amorani, showing a hint of what looked like excitement.

" 'I was a valued *Hm-Waw'ew,*' " said Inva. " 'I have fought many battles against the sand-barbarians and the snake-spears. I have taken many hands.' "

Laela kept her eyes on Ravana and began to be more and more interested in him. A fighter was just what she needed.

Ravana spoke on, and Inva continued to translate. " 'In the beginning, I had no name. But I fought for the right and was rewarded. For my ferocity they named me Ravana, the demon of the flaming sands.' "

Ravana gestured at his scars as he continued.

" 'Every mark you see on me is the last mark of a dead man.' "

Laela thought of her father and the terrible scars he hid under his robe. She shuddered.

" 'When the wars were done, I was sold to a noble in Instabahn,' " Ravana said. " 'I was his guard, and I followed him through night and day, protecting him against his enemies. Now I have been sold again. I see my new Master, and she is most beautiful and most powerful.' "

"I ain— I'm not his master," Laela interrupted. "Tell him that. He's not a slave now."

Inva translated, but Ravana only shook his head. " 'You are my Master now, my Queen. I have come here to see you, so that I may offer these hands of mine in your service, as they were meant to be used.' "

"He wants to serve me now, then?" said Laela.

Ravana knelt again. " 'Master. Accept me, and I will guard you as I guarded my master in Instabahn. Make my life your shield. I am yours.' "

Oeka looked up. "A guard for you?"

Laela thought quickly. "Inva, what do yeh think?"

Inva folded her hands. "I have known many *Hm-Waw'ew* in my life. There are no better bodyguards in the world, my Queen."

Laela got up and confronted Ravana. "So yeh want to protect me, is that it?"

" 'I would be beside you always, protecting your life at any cost,' " Ravana said at once.

Oeka had come down off her platform. She walked around the man, examining him disdainfully. "He is big for a human, but still human. What protection can he provide that I cannot?"

"Extra protection," said Laela. "The more the better, I say."

"We shall see," said Oeka, and sprang straight at her, talons outstretched.

Laela reeled away, but she wasn't quick enough. Oeka's front paws struck her in the head and shoulders, knocking her back against the throne. As Laela struggled to rise, the griffin came at her again, rasping aggressively.

"Oeka, stop it! What are yeh doin'?"

Oeka ignored her, and reared up, batting at her with her paws.

Laela meant to step forward and face her partner down, but in that moment something hit her in the midriff and she found herself being pulled away. "Hey—!"

Ravana ignored her. He pushed her behind him and darted forward—running straight at Oeka. Still up on her hind legs, she leapt. He flung himself at her without an instant's hesitation, ramming his head into her stomach. Once she was off balance, he seized her by the forelegs, where they joined her body—jamming his thumbs into the joints.

Oeka screeched in pain and hurled him away. He landed hard on his back, and she closed in, beak open to strike.

But Ravana wasn't defeated yet. He kicked upward, catching her in the hind legs. They folded, and she stumbled sideways. In an instant, Ravana was up and had her by the neck, lifting and twisting it sideways. Oeka struggled, but cringed and held still when he gave her head a painful wrench.

Panting, Ravana glanced at Laela and spoke.

"What'd he say?" she demanded, panic-stricken. *"Inva!"*

" 'Shall I kill her, Master?' " said Inva, appearing from behind the pillar where she'd taken shelter.

"No!" Laela yelled. "Tell him to let her go right now!"

Ravana obeyed at once, dropping his hands passively to his sides.

Oeka returned to Laela's side, shaking her head frantically. "*Kreea'kayee!* That human's grip is stone!"

Laela turned angrily on her. "What in the gods' names was that all about? What were yeh playin' at?"

Oeka sat on her haunches and began to groom herself. "Be still. I would not have hurt you."

" 'Be warned,' " Ravana said. " 'The next one who tries to attack my Master shall die, no matter if it is human or griffin.' "

Oeka watched him, green eyes gleaming. "Laela," she said. "I tell you now that you shall find no better human to guard you than this one."

"He fought you to save me," said Laela—adding more quietly, ". . . an' he won, too." She looked at Ravana, who was kneeling again. "Yeh've proven what yeh can do, Ravana, and I'm impressed. Now stand up an' listen."

He did, and stood to attention as Laela spoke on through Inva.

"There are no slaves in Tara, an' there never will be again. Not so long as I'm Queen. We're a land of free men an' women. We can choose what we do with our lives, say an' think what we want. You're one of my people now, an' that means you're free to do what yeh choose. If yeh choose t'be my guard, I'll be honoured to have yeh."

" 'I do choose that,' " Ravana said at once.

"Good. Yeh'll be paid a proper guard's wage, plus some extra, an' as long as yer with me, yeh get a good place to sleep an' all the food yeh want. If yeh need a weapon or armour or anythin' like that, just ask an' it's yours."

Ravana accepted all this gravely, and when Laela had finished, he only said, " 'As you choose, so shall I live.' "

"All right, then," said Laela, and that was that.

3

A Broken Family

Saeddryn did not return to her personal quarters after the council meeting, even though she was hungry. Hunger sharpened the mind, and she needed to think.

More than that, she needed to pray. The Eyrie might be her home, but it didn't belong to her. Only one place in Malvern was truly hers, and that was where she went now.

The great Moon Temple had been built close to the Eyrie, and its high, domed roof was visible from almost everywhere in the city. It had originally been a Sun Temple—the same one where Saeddryn's cousin, Arenadd, had fought and killed the man everyone had thought was the greatest threat to him.

After Malvern's fall to the Northerner rebels led by Arenadd and Saeddryn, its Temple had not been demolished, but gutted and refurbished as the first Moon Temple anywhere in Cymria.

It had been Arenadd's idea, and, at first, Saeddryn had disagreed. The Night God was meant to be worshipped in the open air, where the moon that was her eye could shine down on her people and witness their prayers. But Arenadd had been insistent. It was time to move on, he had said, time to shed the old ways and go on into the modern age.

"The Southerners think we're savages," he had said when Saeddryn argued. "Too uncivilised to rule ourselves. But we're not, and if we want to survive, then we have to accept that the past is dead."

Persuasive words, but, then, he was a persuasive man. Even Saeddryn had given in to his wishes, and once the new Temple was ready—built according to a design Arenadd himself helped to draw up—she had quickly come to agree with him. It had been the proudest moment of her life when he had named her the new—the first—High Priestess of Malvern.

"You like this new Temple of ours," he had said. "Well, now it's yours."

Saeddryn felt the memory of those days move through her as she walked slowly down the main street outside the Eyrie, with Aenae following closely beside her. Ever since Laela's ascension, the big griffin had kept a close eye on her. He'd been just a youngster back then, when Malvern was freed from Southern rule, and she was young, too, so young, and happier. Everything had been so clear back then, and now it wasn't.

"Why are we going to the Temple?" Aenae's voice interrupted her thoughts.

Saeddryn took a moment to answer. "Because I need to pray." She spoke griffish as a mark of respect though, like all civilised griffins, Aenae understood human speech.

"Prayer," Aenae huffed. "Even after so many years together, I still do not understand it. You speak to another human who is not there—who was never there and does not exist."

"It's good for me," said Saeddryn, who had heard this sort of thing from him before. "It helps me think. Sometimes, a woman needs t'be calm an' still for her thoughts to be clear." She said nothing about finding guidance from the Night God—she knew Aenae would only sneer. No griffin believed in any kind of god; to them it was all human nonsense.

His kind did, however, respect the human ability to think and plan, so Aenae accepted her answer and said nothing else.

The Temple doors were open when Saeddryn reached them, though worshippers rarely went inside except at night. There were important rites to be conducted then, at moonrise, and people liked to come and witness them. Saeddryn would conduct the rituals herself, except when she had some other important business and would leave it to one of the thirteen lesser priestesses.

Despite the fact that it was daytime, the Temple was still dark inside. Its windows, which had once been intended to let in sunlight, had now been blacked out, and the only light came from the lamps.

Saeddryn paused briefly in the doorway to admire her Temple. Even now, its beauty never failed to touch her.

Once, before the war, the people of the North had worshipped in stone circles, on hilltops and forest clearings. But here, in the Temple, it was just the same. The floor was covered in elaborate tile work, showing a textured pattern of grass, earth, and fallen leaves. Pillars stood here and there—not in lines, but spaced irregularly, like trees in a wood. To add to the effect, they, too, were tiled, in shades of brown and silver, like bark but with a touch of the ethereal to it. Silver lantern holders jutted from their sides, shaped like curling branches, and the blue-glass lanterns that hung from them gave off a dim, tinted light.

Above, the ceiling was painted to look like the night sky, with careful reproductions of the constellations. And, at the far end, under the dome itself, there was the circle.

Thirteen standing stones, each one the height of a man, grouped around the altar and the statue that stood over it.

Saeddryn took it all in and smiled to herself.

"Truly, it is astonishing what humans make," Aenae said quietly.

"Aye, it is." Saeddryn walked on toward the altar, savouring the fact that all this beauty belonged to her.

The Temple was deserted, except for a young novice priestess who was sweeping the floor around the standing stones. She wore the silver robe of any Temple initiate but cut less finely than that of a full-fledged priestess, and she looked up nervously when Saeddryn arrived.

"Milady, I wasn't expecting—sorry—"

"Get away, Teressa," Saeddryn snapped back, impatiently waving the girl away.

The novice took the hint and hurried off.

Left with only Aenae for company, Saeddryn went to the altar, her single eye fixed on the statue that stood over it.

It was of a woman, carved out of white marble. She wasn't much taller than Saeddryn, but still imposing, her stone face stern and cold. She had been carved with almost no clothing at all—a mantle of some kind hung over her shoulders, leaving her nearly naked, with her breasts exposed. Some had protested over that, but Arenadd had insisted.

"That's what she looks like," he had said, and nobody argued.

For herself, Saeddryn liked the way the statue looked. It reminded her of her mother, Arddryn, and even of herself. Because, like her, the Night God only had one eye. A black gemstone had been set into the statue to represent it, while the other was a silver disc, representing the full moon.

Saeddryn smiled up at the statue and tapped the patch that covered her own missing eye. Then she knelt.

In front of her, the altar was carved from a single block of grey stone. A sharp silver knife lay on it, and now Saeddryn picked it up. She stabbed the point into her thumb and smeared the blood onto the altar, murmuring the ritual words.

"With this offering of true Northern blood, I call to ye."

She waited for a long moment after that, calming her mind and collecting her thoughts. Then, when she felt ready, she took a deep breath to begin her prayer.

"Saeddryn!"

The voice cut across her, instantly breaking the spell of the Temple.

Saeddryn's eye narrowed, but she ignored it and breathed deeply again. This was more important.

"Saeddryn." Footsteps came up behind her, and the voice grew louder.

Saeddryn stood up sharply, and turned. "Can't ye see I'm trying to pray here?" she snapped.

The intruder hesitated. "I'm sorry, but it's important."

Saeddryn sighed. "Fine. What is it, Torc?"

Her husband rubbed a hand through his hair. "It's not like you to pray in the daytime."

"I've got plenty to pray for right now if ye hadn't guessed," said Saeddryn. She eyed him with a hint of caution—it wasn't like him to come into the Temple at all. It had always seemed to make him uneasy.

"I know you do," said Torc. "Saeddryn . . ."

"What?"

"You've got to stop this," said Torc. "Stop antagonising the Queen. You're going to get yourself into trouble. You'll get *all* of us into trouble."

"We're already in trouble," Saeddryn growled back. "In case ye hadn't noticed. We're in deep trouble. Not just ye and me, but our children as well. The whole North is in trouble, for that matter—what did ye think I was prayin' for?"

"It doesn't have to be," said Torc. "Yes, Arenadd's gone, but we're still here, and we can keep protecting our people. But this—what you're doing isn't the way to do that."

"It's exactly what I have to do," said Saeddryn. She curled her lip at him. "D'ye think a real Taranisäii is going to take orders from a half-breed? A bloody Southerner?"

"It doesn't matter," said Torc. "She's Arenadd's daughter, and she's our Queen, and if you keep on trying to get in her way, then it's only a matter of time—"

"She's not his daughter!" Saeddryn shouted, so suddenly that he started. "Are ye insane, Torc? Him, with a Southerner? He couldn't have children—ye saw what happened when he tried! She's an imposter. A liar."

"No, Saeddryn," said Torc. "She's real. And even if she weren't, he adopted her. You saw the documents proving it. He wanted her to rule after him, and that's all there is to it. And I for one still care about Arenadd's wishes, even if you don't."

"Arenadd's wishes?" Saeddryn repeated. "Don't be stupid, Torc. I know he set ye free, but the man was a drunk and half-mad by the end. He was the Shadow That Walks—the Night God's avatar—but he wouldn't even come in here for any of the rituals. That Laela's not his true heir. He put her on that throne to spite us, Torc. That's all."

"He trained her," said Torc. "She proved her worth more than enough in Amoran—making the alliance with the Emperor, bringing the slaves home. She did just as Arenadd would have done. What's wrong with that?"

"No, Torc," said Saeddryn. "She's a ursurper. Our son should be King. He was born for it, trained for it."

Torc looked troubled. "I know that, but after what he did—"

"Oh, it was Arenadd's own fault," Saeddryn growled. "The pair of them, falling out like that over a *woman*, for gods' sakes. Ye'd think they were a pair of boys."

"Stop it," said Torc. "That's enough, Saeddryn. I did what I could to protect Caedmon, and you, but if you keep this up, then there won't be much more I can do. Push the Queen too far, and she'll have you arrested."

"An' how will she do that?" said Saeddryn. "Send ye after me? Master of Law? Don't make me laugh."

"Then she'll have you killed," said Torc.

"She doesn't have it in her," said Saeddryn. "I'm not arguing about this any more, Torc. That girl is in our way. She's in Caedmon's way, an' the Night God's way, an' she'll die for it. If I can't get her ousted by the people, then I'll kill her myself. That's a promise."

"And what if she strikes first?" asked Torc, showing no surprise over his wife's declaration. "Have you thought of that?"

"If she does, I'll leave," said Saeddryn. "Caedmon will need me, an' Arddryn as well."

"And me?" said Torc. "What will *I* do? You know I never wanted to get involved in this, but if you do anything, they'll come after me, too."

"Run, then," Saeddryn shrugged. "If ye can. Ye are Master of Law, aren't ye? The guards will look the other way. Make a plan, but don't tell me what it is. It's better if I don't know where ye go to hide."

"Fine," said Torc. "But Saeddryn . . ."

She glared at him. "What?"

"It doesn't have to be this way. You know it doesn't."

"It does," said Saeddryn. "Arenadd's gone, so now it's up to us to do the Night God's will, and she doesn't want that little bitch on the throne. An' if ye won't do this for the Night God's sake, then do it for yer children. What sort of future will they have, with that half-breed ruling here?"

Torc looked away. "I wish . . . gods, I wish Arenadd were still here. If we could only talk to him, find out what he was really thinking . . ."

"He wouldn't have told us," said Saeddryn. "He didn't trust me any more."

"But he trusted me." Torc looked up at the ceiling high above, where a round hole had been made to let the moon shine in. Just now, it let in a thin shaft of sunlight, which touched his head and highlighted the grey hairs there. "Where is he, Saeddryn? What happened to him?"

"It's been months," said Saeddryn. "Wherever he is, he isn't coming back. It could be he faked all this. Fled the country an' left us behind. Or the half-breed's story is true, an' he's dead." She turned to look at the statue, with its single, glittering eye. "Wherever he is, it's up to us now. We're the only true Taranisäiis left, an' the North's future is in our hands."

Torc followed her gaze. "Yes," he said softly. "It's up to us. Arenadd is with the Night God now."

"*With the Night God, now . . . the Night God now . . . he's with the Night God . . .*"

The words echoed in the Temple, and out of the mortal world, into a place of absolute blackness and freezing cold. Faith carried them there, into the ears of the only one who could hear them.

In the empty void where she lived, the Night God listened and did not smile. *He is with me now,* she whispered.

Pale and bare and primal, she looked down at the crumpled figure that lay at her feet.

You are with me now, she said.

There was no ground visible here in the void. Everything in every direction was black and featureless. Still, Arenadd was lying down, on a surface colder than ice.

The last shards of pain had not yet left his body. His mind swam. He vaguely heard the god's words, but barely understood them. He could feel himself shaking violently.

Will you stand now? the Night God asked.

Arenadd heard her now, but he said nothing. An instant later, the pain hit him again. The memory of his body jerked and spasmed, and a faint groan escaped him.

Will you stand, Arenadd?

Arenadd curled in on himself, like a dying animal, trying vainly to protect himself from an agony that could not be fended off. His teeth clenched, and he tried not to cry out.

Will you stand?

The pain faded again, and Arenadd slumped.

Speak to me, the Night God commanded.

Arenadd would not look at her. He stared away, at the darkness, and mumbled a word.

"Laela . . ."

No, Arenadd, the god's voice said sharply. *She is gone now. Forget her.*

Now Arenadd tried to get up. He dragged himself into a kneeling position and clutched at his head with both hands. Even here, the fingers on his left hand were twisted and crippled, and they shook. "No," he gasped. "No, she's not . . . she's not gone. She's out there. I'm gone. I'm the one who's gone. I'm . . ." He screamed as the pain ripped into him again. *"I'm gone!* Dead! Dead and gone, dead and . . ."

Stop this, the Night God said sharply. *You cannot escape into madness again. Face reality. Rise, and stand with me, where you should be.*

"No," Arenadd moaned. "I can't. I won't." He curled up again, on his side with his back to her, and mumbled to himself. "There is no Arren, Arren is dead, there is no Arren . . . there is no Arenadd. No, no, Arenadd's gone, he's dead and gone. Laela watched him die, and cried for him, she did . . . there is no Arenadd . . ." His babbling broke off into another scream, and he started to convulse.

STOP THIS! The Night God's voice rose higher, and sharper, cutting through the madness in his mind and putting a stop to his crazed wanderings. *Come back to me.*

Arenadd jerked again, silent now, and finally went still.

"Let me go," he whispered. "Please."

No.

"Then let me be mad," he said. "Let me go insane. I can't take it any more, I can't . . ."

No, the Night God said again. *You betrayed me, and you have been punished. Now you will stay with me, and we will watch over our people together.*

Arenadd didn't dare move, or even look at her. "For how long? How long . . . master?"

Forever.

Arenadd smiled his old humourless smile, which was now twisted by pain. "The gods . . . the gods are the slave collar that never comes off. The collar that doesn't clamp onto your body, but your soul. I should . . . I should write that down. I always did have a way with words." He laughed weakly.

Rise, the Night God insisted.

This time, Arenadd obeyed. He pulled himself to his feet, and walked shakily to stand by his master's side. His mind had already begun to clear, and despite his efforts to hold on to it, the madness drained away, forcing him to face the cold reality around him. He was dead, bodiless, and imprisoned for his treachery. He had turned his back on his master, and now he was paying the price. Laela's life for his own.

He stayed beside his master, grim and silent, and together, they watched the aftermath of the argument in the Temple. Torc and Saeddryn parted ways, both visibly troubled. Torc left the Temple, but Saeddryn stayed to pray. Soon, the words of her prayer reached into the void for both of them to hear.

Arenadd tugged on his pointed chin-beard. "What a joke," he mumbled. "Praying for guidance. From you. I want to go mad again."

I told you once that I hear every true prayer, said the Night God. *Now, you see the truth of it.*

"Oh yes. Saeddryn always loved to pray," said Arenadd. He looked out at the small figure of his cousin, and his scarred face twisted again, this time with a mixture of equal parts malice and suffering. "Fool," he hissed.

Her faith in me will guide her, said the Night God, ignoring him. *She will do as I wish her to, even without hearing my voice as you did.*

"Laela will stop her," said Arenadd. He knew he shouldn't speak like this; he was only tempting her to torture him again, but he didn't care any more. Nothing that happened to him mattered now.

The Night God did not look at him. *My will shall be done, and Saeddryn will do it. The half-breed will die, and she will die soon.*

Arenadd stared at her, with an expression of hopeless bewilderment. "Why?" he asked softly. "Why are you doing this? Why do any of this? What did Laela ever do to you, or anyone? Why does she have to die? Why did any of them have to die?"

I am the god of the North, said the Night God. *The god of all Northerners. And I will not allow a half-breed Southerner to rule my people. The North will be ruled by its own people, under my blessing. And once the half-breed is gone, and the rightful ruler is on his throne, the South will fall, and Cymria will belong to my people.*

"Power?" said Arenadd. "Is that all you care about?"

It was all that you cared about once, said the Night God. *And all of Cymria knows it.*

"Yes, yes," Arenadd muttered, turning away. "The Dark Lord Arenadd, all power-hungry and cruel. I'm everybody's favourite bedtime story for scaring the kids. But you're a god. Why do you even care?"

Because my people are all that matter to me, said the Night God. *They will be free. The half-breed will be destroyed. That is my will.*

"Oh yes?" Arenadd spat. "And how will you have it carried out, without me to run around doing it for you?"

She stared at him, her moon-eye blank and bright, and told him.

Arenadd listened, and his own eyes widened. "Oh no. Oh, gods, no. Laela . . ."

The Night God said nothing more after that, but the two of them continued to watch the affairs of the living, and, in time, he saw Laela again. His daughter, alive and ruling after him, just as he had planned. But for how long?

And even though he knew it would make his master angry again, even though he knew it was hopeless, Arenadd kept his eyes fixed on her and whispered the words he wished she could hear.

"Kill her, Laela," he whispered. "Kill her now, before it's too late."

4

Laela's Move

Having Ravana as a bodyguard made Laela a little uncomfortable at first—something that wasn't helped by the fact that he clearly disliked Oeka and didn't like her getting too close. But before long, she came to appreciate having him around and to feel safer as well. He kept everyone and anyone who came to see her at a safe distance—close enough to talk comfortably but far enough to be out of stabbing distance. He would search every room before she entered it, to make sure it was safe, and had loud arguments with Inva in Amorani over which one of them would taste the Queen's food. In the end, they agreed that they would *both* do it, and Laela privately decided that mealtimes were a lot more entertaining when they began with her two attendants fighting over who would sample each dish first.

Every night, Ravana would stand guard outside Laela's bedroom, apparently disinterested in using the quarters she had provided for him. If he ever slept at all, she never saw him do it—he was with her every waking moment, and she never left her bedroom without finding him by the door. It didn't seem to bother him at all.

The rest of the nobility all seemed to dislike him the moment they laid eyes on him, which gave Laela some childish satisfaction. In the meantime, though, she had more important things to worry about, and with Ravana by her side, she felt confident enough to make a move.

* * *

Saeddryn stayed close to Aenae, as she always did these days, and eyed the Queen cautiously. "What can I do for ye, my lady?"

They were in one of the courtyards between the towers, where a little garden provided herbs for both the kitchens and the infirmary. Laela sat down on a stone bench and gestured at Saeddryn to do the same. "I got somethin' to ask about."

Saeddryn stayed on her feet. "Ask, my lady."

"Before the King died, I was bein' instructed about the Night God," Laela began carefully. "It was always the plan that when the time came, I'd be put through the womanhood ceremony an' made a proper Northerner."

"Yes?" Saeddryn's tone was neutral.

"My instruction's done," said Laela. "It's past time that ceremony was carried out, don't yeh think?"

"So it's being said."

"The full moon's comin' soon," said Laela. "The Wolf's Moon. That's the time when I oughta be put through the ceremony an' given the tattoos."

"That's a matter for the Wolf priestess," said Saeddryn.

"I know. But you're the High Priestess," said Laela. "The Moon Priestess. Yeh know perfectly well this can't happen unless yer there to oversee things."

"Perhaps." A slight smile showed on Saeddryn's face.

Laela's own face hardened. "I need this, an' as Queen I expect to see yeh do yer duty the way my father would've wanted. Go back to the Temple an' organise it. Do it today."

"Is that an order?"

"Yeah, it's an order." Laela resisted the urge to slap her. "Listen, Saeddryn—I'm Queen now, understand? An' there's not a damned thing yeh can do about it. I'm prepared to let the past be the past an' just move on. I want to let yeh be, an' I will if yeh don't give me a reason not to." She softened her voice as much as she could, almost pleading now. "What I want is the same as what you want. Peace for the North—Tara, I mean"—she corrected herself—"an' happiness for its people. There's no reason why we can't work together for that, Saeddryn. We're both Taranisäiis, ain't we? Let's be the way we should be. Tara needs us to be workin' together. Help me do it, Saeddryn."

Saeddryn listened impassively. "Ye sounded like yer father, Laela. He'd've been proud."

"Thanks." Laela couldn't help but feel good about that.

"I . . . too . . . care about Tara," Saeddryn went on. "I've only ever wanted the best for us. I fought beside yer father in the wars, an' I remember it every time this eye twinges. I gave it up t'help our people, like my mother before me."

Laela looked steadily at her, waiting to see what she would say next.

"Understand," Saeddryn went on, "all I've ever done was for Tara. All my life, that's how it's been. I serve the Night God now, an' she an' me are the same that way. We're both one-eyed, an' we both love Tara before life itself."

A memory rose up in Laela's mind, of a cold, ice-white face with a blank hole where an eye should be. *Kill her, Arenadd. Kill her now.*

She shivered, and hatred made her throat tighten.

"I fought in Tara's name," said Saeddryn. "I fought for the Night God, as I still do. An' for that reason, I will not let the ceremony happen."

Laela fought to keep calm. She picked a sprig of griffintail from the garden bed behind her and shredded it slowly while she spoke. "I'm Queen of Tara. Queen of all darkmen. I can't rule unless I'm really one of them."

"Perhaps, but I will never let ye become a woman in my Temple. The Night God does not want ye, Laela."

Kill her, Arenadd. "Don't make me do this, Saeddryn. I swear, don't make me do it."

"A half-breed can never be in the Night God's heart," Saeddryn said flatly.

Oeka rose, tail lashing. "Do not insult my human, traitor."

Aenae hissed at her, but the dark brown griffin didn't back away, and he didn't risk making any other move.

"It's not my decision to make," said Saeddryn. "A half-breed belongs to no god. If this ceremony went ahead, the Night God would be angry. Terrible things would happen."

"Terrible things'll happen if it doesn't," said Laela. "An' trust me, they'll be happening to you."

"Is that a threat?"

Laela stood up and looked her in the eye. "Yeah. It's a threat. Good job on spottin' that one, eyepatch. Yeh might think yeh know about the stars an' the phases of the moon an' what tattoo goes where, but I got the real power here, an' trust me—push me too far, an' the Night God ain't gonna save yer sorry hide."

Saeddryn bared her teeth. "How *dare*—?"

"Oh, I dare all right." Laela flung the shreds of herb aside. "I dare. Girl I might be, an' half-breed I might be as well, but I'm still King Arenadd's daughter, an' if yeh give me one good reason, I'll deal with yeh the way he should have. An' trust me . . . that wouldn't be pretty. But I'm sure yeh coulda guessed that part."

Saeddryn bowed stiffly. "My lady."

Aenae stayed behind as his human walked off. He took a threatening step toward Laela and Oeka. "Be warned," he snarled. "Touch my human, and you shall die."

Oeka spread her wings, hissing. "You and your human shall do as you are commanded. It is not you who rules this Eyrie, Aenae."

He raised his own wings, feathers fluffed out until he appeared to double in size. "You do not frighten me, hatchling. I could kill you with a single talon."

Oeka lowered her head and closed her eyes. An instant later, Aenae flinched and backed away, shaking his head dazedly.

If griffins could smirk, Oeka would have done it now. "You have felt my power before, Oh Mighty Carved-From-Tree-Stumps. What you felt then was the slightest touch, and my magic increases by the day. Challenge me again, and you shall feel your own mind burn away from your skull."

Aenae had had enough. Defeated but still bristling with rage, he turned and loped after his human.

Laela couldn't find the enthusiasm to snigger at the big griffin's humiliation. She slumped back onto the bench and rubbed her forehead. "Gods damn it. I knew she was gonna say no."

Oeka, still full of bravado, tore a deep hole in the ground with her talons. "They must be killed," she said. "Both of them. And soon."

"No."

"The longer they live, the more trouble they will bring you, Laela. Kill them now, before it is too late."

"It's too risky. If she dies, everyone'll know it was me. There'd be riots. An' she's got her son an' daughter all ready an' waitin' to take revenge—she made sure I knew it, too."

"If you do not kill her, she will kill you," said Oeka.

"If I ain't careful enough, maybe," said Laela. "I need her around for now."

"You do not," said Oeka. "For now, she is a nuisance and a danger, and she is already beginning to stand in your way."

"Don't worry about that, Oeka. I got a plan." She turned to walk back into the Council Tower. "C'mon. I'm gonna go have a word with Inva."

That night, after dinner, Oeka and Laela retired to their quarters. Rather than go to bed, Laela followed her partner into the adjoining room that housed her nest and walked out onto the balcony. It had no railings and was meant as a platform for Oeka to take off from.

Oeka accompanied her human into the open air. "Is something wrong?"

Laela was looking out over the city. "Just came out here to see the view."

Oeka followed her gaze. "My vision is weak at night."

"Beautiful, though, ain't it?" said Laela. She twined her fingers in her hair, looking almost dreamy. "My city. Look at them stars."

Oeka did. They didn't look any different than usual. Bored, she sat on her haunches and began grooming her wings.

"Just think," said Laela. "Them stars are shinin' on places I never been. Places that belong to me. My lands, from here all the way to the mountains."

Silence.

"I never would've thought this could happen," said Laela. "Me, a Queen. I was born a half-breed peasant who couldn't read, an' now look at me." She chuckled. "Funny ole thing life, ain't it?"

"I would not have thought that I would have a human who

was a Queen," Oeka said eventually. "Though I knew I was destined for greatness. My powers would bring me nothing less." She cocked her head toward Laela. "I feel them grow. Every day, I sense more and more. I scent thoughts, emotions, intentions. I learn to interpret those scents, and they tell me many things. Soon, I shall scent more than even that."

"Wish I could do that," said Laela.

"You do not need to," said Oeka. "I shall tell you what I know." She leant toward her human, air whistling through her nostrils. "I smell . . . uncertainty. But I smell another . . . something strong . . . you are pleased." She stiffened. "Triumph. I smell it. It is growing stronger."

A slow grin had spread over Laela's face, and she put a hand on her partner's feathered shoulder. "Yeah. But yeh don't need powers to guess that. Look."

Oeka turned her head, looking over the city again. Icy wind blew in her face, entering her nostrils. "I smell smoke. I see . . ."

"Yeah. See it?"

A dull red glow had appeared down among the lights of the city. It pulsated slightly, like a heart, and above it a column of smoke darkened the moon.

"Fire!" Oeka exclaimed.

"Yeah." Laela rubbed the griffin's head with her knuckles. "Pretty, ain't it?"

"The city is in danger. You should do something."

"Don't need to. Saeddryn says the Night God don't want me around—why should I care that her precious Temple's burnin'?"

"The Temple . . ."

"It's made of stone," Laela said carelessly. "It'll be saved. Can't say it won't be damaged, though. What a shame."

"You did this," said Oeka. "You had the Temple burned."

"Now why would I go an' do somethin' like that?" Laela tucked her hair back. "Seems there's a woman we brought back from Amoran what doesn't like the Night God much. Got it into her head that Gryphus is the real god. An' we all know Gryphus burns what makes him angry. If only the maniac hadn't got her hands on a barrel of lamp oil an' the key to the back door. Oh well, too bad."

Oeka's tail twitched. "I see."

"They'll catch her soon enough," said Laela. "But she won't stay in prison long enough to talk. I'll have her executed straight off. Terrible crime, blasphemy. Meantime, if Saeddryn wants my money to fix the Temple, she'd better start singin' the song I want to hear."

Oeka looked down on the red glow. "Truly, you are your father's chick."

"I'm gonna be as dangerous to my enemies as he was," said Laela. "But unlike him, I ain't lettin' *her* win. He left that to me."

Saeddryn had gone to bed early that night, wanting to be well rested by moonrise, when she would have to conduct the nightly ceremonies. Normally, the High Priestess would live in or close to the Temple itself, but she was a griffiner and owned some of the finest living quarters in the Eyrie. Her husband had shared them with her once, but that had been a long time ago. Now he had his own rooms, closer to where he worked. Saeddryn couldn't sleep at all any more, unless it was alone.

She curled up under her furs, frowning slightly as she drifted off. On her bedside table, a sprig of drying pine spiced the air. Lately she'd been having more trouble sleeping than usual, and the smell helped to soothe her. It took her mind back to an older time, when she would leave her home in the village and slip away into the mountains to be with her mother.

Old Arddryn had always greeted her daughter formally—Saeddryn didn't remember a time when she had smiled to see her. It was the ice, she used to think. All that ice and stone in the mountains. They got into a person's soul.

Saeddryn never blamed her mother for that inner hardness, never resented it. War took something away from a person, and years of despair took even more.

I've become her, she thought sadly in the darkness. *Old, one-eyed an' bitter in the soul.*

And maybe, like her mother, she would be killed by Arenadd's betrayal. His weakness.

Saeddryn fell asleep with that thought, and it seeped into her dreams—tainting them with old fears, old resentments.

Arenadd. Her cousin. So handsome. So strong. So far away. Everything she had wanted and always been denied.

He smiled at her, but it was a wolf's smile—a cruel smile. *All you wanted,* the smile said.

Saeddryn realised there were people all around, hundreds of them. They were cheering, shouting, throwing themselves forward in joy. *Cheering for me,* she thought, *for me, for me . . .*

Then she realised she couldn't move. She was trapped, frozen in a block of ice, watching as Arenadd walked away into the adoring throng.

The dream twisted, and a rush of confused sensations tangled themselves around her. Cold, so cold. *Moving* cold, cold clutching at her, embracing her, muttering and moaning in her ears, and she was helpless, sick inside with the knowledge. *Isn't this what you wanted?*

She woke up retching, confused by the sound of knocking outside.

"My lady! *My lady!*"

Saeddryn sat up, blinking. Her ruined eye ached horrendously, and she put her hand over it. "What? What's that . . . ?"

Light poured into her room, and a shadowy figure came with it. "My lady—! I'm so sorry, but something's . . ."

Saeddryn snatched up her eyepatch from the bedside table and got up, still wearing her woollen night-gown. "What's going on?" she snapped. "This had better be important, or I swear—"

The young woman who'd disturbed her was too distressed to bow. "It's the Temple! Saeddryn, it's burning! The Temple's burning!"

Saeddryn gaped at her. "What? What d'ye mean it's . . . ?"

"It's bad, my lady. Very bad. They're trying to put it out, but I don't know . . ."

Saeddryn felt as if someone had reached into her chest and tried to rip her heart out. *"How?"*

"Deliberate, my lady," the messenger gulped. "They already caught the one who did it."

"Who was it? *Who did this?*"

"I'm not sure. Garnoc has her down in the cells—they'll be questioning her now."

Saeddryn was already pulling on a gown. "I'm going to go see this myself."

"Yes, my lady. Should I go tell the Queen?"

Saeddryn stopped. "She hasn't been told?"

"Not that I know. I came to ye first."

"Go an' tell her, then," Saeddryn growled. *But she already knows.*

She dressed as quickly as she could and almost ran into Aenae's nest to wake him.

The big griffin rose, huffing irritably. "What is this?"

"It's the Temple," Saeddryn said. "The half-breed's made her move."

"What of the Temple?"

Saeddryn closed her eye for a moment. "She's had it set on fire."

Aenae's wings opened. "*Our* Temple?"

"Yes." Saeddryn's fists clenched.

Moving quickly and efficiently, Aenae unhooked his harness from the wall and tossed it at her feet. "Put this on me. We must go there at once."

Saeddryn obeyed, and, within moments, she was on his back, and he was taking off.

The air was freezing outside, the night sky brilliant with stars. But they were all outshone by the terrible glow down in the city. Saeddryn saw the smoke blacken the moonlight, and her heart gave another, brutal wrench.

As Aenae flew down toward her beloved Temple, she began to see the full horror of what it had become. The tower behind the dome had become a pillar of flame, red and orange tongues stretching high into the sky. The dome itself, made from stone, was veiled in a huge bank of smoke, and below it the windows threw ghastly orange light over everything.

It's the wrath of Gryphus, Saeddryn thought irrationally. *The Night God has abandoned us for accepting a half-breed as our ruler. My Temple . . .*

Aenae landed outside the front doors. They were hanging open, and a group of priestesses were clustered outside, watching helplessly.

They ran to meet their leader.

"I'm so sorry, my lady," one said. "There was nothing I . . . if only . . . oh Night God . . ." She broke down in sobs.

Saeddryn stared stonily at the burning building. Not much

was being done to save it—because there was nothing humans could realistically do against a fire of this size. Around it, people were climbing on rooftops, desperately throwing buckets of water over thatch to stop it from going up. At least there didn't seem to be much danger of the fire spreading—there was a decent amount of open space around the Temple that had managed to stop that. A few small patches had spread, though, and people were fighting those instead.

The priestesses, many of them actually trembling with the shock, kept close to Saeddryn—silently asking for her protection and help.

"Who did this?" she asked eventually.

"Blasphemer," the Bear priestess spat. "One of the Queen's Amorani blackrobes. I caught her while we were escapin'."

"Did the Queen send her?" Saeddryn asked, very quietly.

"No," the Crow priestess said at once. "She'd never be stupid enough. The blasphemer was a madwoman. She babbled on about how Gryphus made her do it, said he came down from the sky an' commanded her."

"What she said doesn't matter," said Saeddryn. "We need to find out—"

"No-one lies that well," the Crow priestess muttered. "No-one."

They stood in silence for a long time, too stunned to do much beyond try to comfort each other without words.

Even Aenae looked shaken. He circled, like an anxious dog, keeping close to his human but obviously unsettled by the flames.

Something crashed and broke inside the Temple, and the fire flared up briefly. Saeddryn jerked away in fright, her hand groping for support. Aenae was there at once, and she leant on him, pressing her face into his neck. "I can't take this," she whispered to him.

Aenae stilled. "I will stop this," he said. "Go to your friends."

Saeddryn moved away from him, proudly refusing the help of the other priestesses. Aenae took a few steps toward the fire before hesitating, bathed in its light. He was a handsome griffin, with his father's black and silver mixed with his mother's grey and autumn brown. His eyes, though, were an extraordinary silver-blue, narrowing against the glare from the fire.

He stood very still, apparently thinking, and then prepared himself—subtly altering his stance to make himself firm and steady with his paws well on the ground. His wings lifted slightly and his tail twitched. Then, suddenly, it stopped.

Aenae's whole body became stock still, and a moment later he lifted his head, opened his beak wide, and unleashed his power.

Blue light poured out of him in a torrent, forming a column like a concentrated jet of water. It punched straight through the Temple doors and into the heart of the inferno.

For several long moments nothing changed. Aenae, unmoving, poured his strength into his magic, which continued to rush out of his beak and throat without slowing. The fire raged on.

Then it faltered. Slowly at first, then faster and faster, the angry orange of it began to fade. The smoke thinned, and the flames licking around the windows receded. Above, the tower crumbled and came crashing down, but the fire that had consumed it had died down. When Aenae finally closed his beak and slumped onto his belly, the Temple was still burning—but only a little. The worst was over.

Saeddryn finally dared to go to her partner's side. "Aenae, are ye all right?"

He turned a glazed eye toward her. "My own power. Great enough." The eye closed.

The Wolf priestess put a hand on Saeddryn's shoulder. "He's not . . . ?"

"He's just resting. Leave him be." Saeddryn looked up at the blackened shell of the Temple. "He's saved it . . . or part of it. An' we'll rebuild it," she added. She raised her voice. "We'll rebuild it! Our Temple will come back, greater than ever before—I swear it on the Night God's holy name! An' the one who did this will feel her rage—but not before she's felt ours."

Yes, she thought privately. *Whoever "she" might be.*

5

Riven

The council met in the small hours of the morning, as the sky outside began to turn grey. It was a messy and undignified affair—nearly all the councillors were bleary-eyed and had obviously dressed in a hurry. The griffins were irritable and kept shifting in their places, eyeing each other distrustfully.

Only Laela and Oeka looked calm. The Queen wore a beautiful black gown with a gold sash sewn with jewels, and the crown rested neatly on her head. She probably had had even less sleep than everyone else, but she looked possessed by some energy that kept her alert. Beside her, Oeka was as glossy and quietly smug as always.

The mere sight of them made Saeddryn sick with hatred. She had intended to approach the situation as calmly as possible, but when she saw the half-breed standing there, radiating triumph, it was too much.

She ignored all protocol and spoke out before everyone was in place. "My Temple is destroyed. I demand justice."

From the way the councillors reacted, it was obvious that they all supported her. Saeddryn felt some of her confidence return. "Who did this? Who's the filth that committed this crime?"

"Calm down," Laela smoothly advised. "The poor lunatic was caught. I've just had a report from Commander Garnoc."

"I know that!" Saeddryn spat. "I want t'know *who*! Who is she?"

"One of our people brought from Amoran," said Laela. "Went by the name of Tyria, or so I'm told. Seems she converted to worshippin' Gryphus. Got all sorts of mad ideas. Garnoc's men have been trying to get information out of her, but she ain't sayin' much that makes sense. Looks like the whole thing was just a sorry accident. But don't worry—she'll be dealt with."

"Enough about that," Torc interrupted. "Our Temple is in ruins, no matter why it happened. What are we going to do about that?"

"Rebuild it, of course," said the Master of Building.

"Yes, an' I'll be happy to provide all the fundin' yeh need," said Laela, while looking straight at Saeddryn.

Saeddryn gritted her teeth. "I'd expect nothing less."

"Well of course," Laela smiled sweetly. "Anything to help out my dad's beloved cousin. Now then, I'm sure our friend the Master of Buildin' Stuff here can start organisin' everythin' the moment the sun's up."

"I certainly can," the Master of Building said stiffly. "As soon as I've rounded up the manpower."

"An' I'm sure we can rely on yeh for that," said Laela. "Fundin's up to me, an' I'll see what I can do. Of course," she added, "all this means there'll be some trouble with my womanhood ceremony. An' me an' Saeddryn were just plannin' it yesterday an' all." She shook her head sadly.

"I'm sure we can find somewhere else, my lady," said Iorwerth.

Laela looked thoughtful. "I'm sure there are other sacred places that might be right for it. Lady Saeddryn, what d'you think?"

Saeddryn's eye burned. She opened her mouth to say no—to *shout* no. To curse the half-breed for the traitor and blasphemer she was. But an inner voice stopped her. It was the same voice that spoke up sometimes, when she was in trouble. The voice of reason. It was always the voice of her mother.

Stop. Think.

Saeddryn made herself breathe calmly. She bowed slightly and fixed a respectful look on her face. "My Queen," she said. "I know a perfect place."

The others there looked curious.

"Go on," said Laela, watching her through narrowed eyes.

Blue eyes. Bile rose in Saeddryn's throat. "Yer own father went through his manhood ceremony under my mother's eye. But not here. His ceremony happened a long way away, high up in the mountains. Once, those mountains were the only place we could live free. There's a place there that's more sacred than our Temple ever was."

"The Throne!" Torc exclaimed. "Of course!"

"Taranis' Throne!" said the Master of Trade.

"It's said great King Taranis himself was crowned there," said Saeddryn. "King Arenadd became a man there." She allowed herself a smile. "I was married there. What better place could there be for a Queen to have her womanhood ceremony?"

"It's perfect!" said Torc.

Saeddryn bowed again, hands clasped over her stomach. "What do ye say, my lady? Come to the Throne with me, an' learn what it is to be a darkwoman. The Night God will embrace ye, an', at last, yer soul will be whole."

Oeka stirred. "And we shall see our territory while we travel there."

Everyone looked at Laela.

"Sounds like a plan," she said eventually.

"It's settled then," said Saeddryn. "Now if ye don't mind, I should go. I'm an old woman, an' I need my rest."

"Don't let me keep yeh up," Laela said graciously.

Saeddryn left, exalting silently. It was all so easy. The mountains were a harsh place, the harshest in Tara. They had claimed many lives in the past. Anyone who went there unprepared, anyone with an inner weakness—anyone not worthy to be in those mountains would be claimed by them.

And Laela would be next. Saeddryn had no doubt about that at all.

As she left, the High Priestess was too frayed to notice the scarred shape that watched her from the shadows.

Nobody saw Ravana, and he liked it that way. At least, people saw him, but they didn't *notice* him. He was used to it. Growing up as a slave from birth, he had always been seen but not noticed. Slaves were supposed to be invisible—noticed only when they failed to do their work the way they should.

Ravana didn't mind. To him, life had always been about pleasing somebody. It didn't matter who gave the commands, or what they were, as long as somebody did. Ravana needed a master. It was what made the world make sense to him. When he had a master, everything came down to two simple rules. He must please his master, and everything he did must be to protect that master.

Being unseen only made following those rules easier. During the meeting that morning, he stayed close to Laela and watched everything that happened around them both. Nobody looked at him or tried to speak to him.

The fact that he could not speak their language made those around him assume that he couldn't understand anything. He was stupid in their eyes, and mute as well. Ravana didn't care. It was just another weapon he could use to defend his master. People were careless around him, they didn't try to hide their feelings. They assumed he would be oblivious.

But Ravana was not stupid, and he did not need language to know what he needed to.

He watched the council talk, and once again his gaze fell on Saeddryn in particular. Since the beginning of his service to the Queen, he had seen the High Priestess many times and had seen how they were to each other. Saeddryn was insolent; she would look the Queen in the face—even shout at her. Ravana knew for a fact that she had threatened her more than once. It was all in how she moved, how she looked at her.

Ravana did not like that. It infuriated him to see such disrepect to a great and powerful ruler like this Queen he served. It confused him, too, that the Queen had not had the old woman's tongue torn out. None of his previous masters would have let her go unpunished.

He thought about it for a long time, day after day, turning the problem over in his mind. Normally it would not be his concern when someone was rude toward his master, but he had become convinced that this Saeddryn was a threat to the Queen, and that was something that could not be tolerated.

In the end, he asked Inva to explain.

"The old woman is the Queen's relative," she told him. "She plotted to take the throne before our Queen took it from her. The Queen cannot risk killing her, or there would be an uprising."

Ravana's brows lowered. "So this woman is an enemy to the Queen?"

"She has not tried to attack her, but she is insolent and will not do as she is commanded."

"Then she's a rebel," Ravana said.

Inva lowered her voice even though nobody listening could have understood what she was saying. "The Queen is afraid that one day the High Priestess will try to kill or overthrow her. The royal griffin believes the same, and has urged her to strike first."

Ravana said nothing to that, but his suspicions had been cemented, and on the day after the Temple burned, and he saw the pure hatred in Saeddryn's eye and heard the false change in her voice, he made up his mind. This woman was a danger and must be plotting something already. It was madness to leave her alive, and he, Ravana, must fulfil his duty and protect his master by removing this traitor at once.

He did not ask the Queen for permission or wait for her to give him the order. That wasn't necessary. Matters like this were for him to deal with; the Queen was too high and dignified to even speak of those things.

Even so, remembering that this was a land where things were done differently, Ravana took one final precaution. On the evening after the burning of the Temple, he waited until the Queen had finished what she had been doing and motioned Inva over to translate for him.

"Master." He knelt.

The Queen looked down on him and spoke.

" 'What is it that you want, Ravana?' " Inva translated.

"To ask a question," said Ravana. "Only one question."

The Queen replied, and Inva nodded. "You have permission."

Ravana looked up. "Do you trust me to protect you in all ways, Master?"

The Queen looked a little puzzled, but then she smiled.

" 'Completely,' " Inva said.

"Then do you give me your permission to do all that I must do to protect you, Master?"

Laela nodded sternly.

"She trusts you, Ravana," Inva said.

There was a gleam in his eyes. "Thank you, Master. I will obey."

The Queen lost interest after that, apparently thinking there was nothing left to talk about. She was right. Ravana had heard all he needed to hear. He had her permission—no, her *command*—to act.

Most of his plan was already prepared. He knew most of the Eyrie by now, and his memory for directions was excellent. He had used his newfound wealth to pay one or two of his fellow Amorani-speaking servants for their help. They had gathered the information he needed—the whereabouts of the High Priestess' home, and a description of its interior.

Armed with the knowledge, Ravana began to plot. Rigid and silent, he stood outside the Queen's bedchamber that night, and thought. Everything was in place now, and the sooner he acted, the better.

He had persuaded Inva to employ a second bodyguard. The newcomer wasn't as good as Ravana, but he was strong and well trained and would be enough to keep guarding the Queen while Ravana was away.

Ravana felt the hilt of the dagger touching his chest. *Now.*

He relaxed out of his guarding stance and nodded to his colleague. "Stay. I check hallway." He said it in the fractured Northern he had learnt, and the other guard nodded back.

Ravana left his spear leaning against the doorframe and slipped away.

The darkened corridors of the Eyrie were utterly silent at this hour. The lamps had been snuffed, and there were no other guards about. In this foolish country, only the Queen herself had her own guards. Ravana was glad—it would only make his work easier.

He moved quickly, counting the doorways until he reached the one that must belong to the High Priestess. He had passed it many times.

The door was locked, but Ravana had come prepared. A piece of twisted wire opened it in no time.

He pushed the door open only the tiniest amount. His bribes had greased the hinges, and they didn't make a sound. Ravana slid through the impossibly small gap and closed the door behind him.

It was even darker beyond.

Ravana flattened himself against the wall and waited. He let his senses expand, eyes adjusting to the darkness, ears opening to the slightest sound. He could feel the slightest breeze coming in through the griffin nest adjoining the bedroom. Just ahead and left of where he stood, soft breathing told him exactly where the traitor slept.

Still, he waited. His night-vision was excellent, and he knew just what to look for. Long experience made it even easier.

There! He saw the faint glisten of moonlight on hair.

Step by step, he moved closer to the bed, until he was standing over it. His hand went into his tunic and brought out the dagger, and he removed the leather wrapping around the blade with extreme care. The blade had been coated in poison, and the slightest cut could kill him.

The High Priestess stirred and mumbled in her sleep. Ravana tensed. It was now or never. It didn't matter where he struck, so long as the blade penetrated. He aimed for the traitor's upper body, and struck.

The blade hit something soft, twisted sideways and embedded itself in the mattress. Quick as a weasel, Ravana recovered and struck again, but before the dagger could complete its movement a scream broke the night. The High Priestess had rolled away from him, and she was up and stumbling away from the bed. Ravana cursed and vaulted over it.

He was too late.

Something huge reared up, taking shape in the archway that led to the nest. Griffin!

Even then, Ravana did not give in. He ignored this new threat and went after Saeddryn. She was old and slow, and he cornered her and caught her by the hair. His fingers were slick with sweat, but his mind was dominated by only one thought. *Finish it! Finish now!*

It was his last thought.

Huge talons hit him, in the midriff. The blow was so

powerful that it lifted him up and smashed him into the opposite wall. He never even had time to scream.

In the silence that followed, Saeddryn picked herself up. Her head ached viciously, and her heart was fluttering enough to make her sick. She stumbled over to the lamp and lit it with a cinder from the fire.

Aenae was already beside her, but neither of them said a thing. They stood together, both breathing hard, and looked down on the intruder.

Ravana lay up against the wall where he had fallen, his body twisted so far that it looked like two half bodies put together the wrong way around. Aenae's talons had gone so deep that only his spine was left to hold him together.

"The half-breed's favourite guard," Saeddryn mumbled. "He wanted . . ."

"He hurt you," Aenae said. "You are bleeding."

Her hand went to her forehead. It came away sticky. "Just my hair. Thankye, Aenae."

It was a perfunctory thanks, but neither of them expected anything else.

"So the half-breed has made her move," said Aenae.

His look toward Saeddryn was expectant. She nodded with difficulty. "The time's come t'do things yer own way now, Aenae. Go an' get yer harness, an' I'll get dressed."

He waited until she had barricaded the door, then disappeared into his nest. When he returned with his harness dangling from his beak, Saeddryn had put on a plain set of clothes—leather leggings and a warm tunic lined with fur. She took some money and a few pieces of jewellery from a drawer and stuffed them into her pocket.

Finally, she went to the fireplace and lifted down a sickle. It was weathered, and the tip had been broken off, but the blade was still sharp.

"Oh by the holy Night God's eye, how I've missed ye," Saeddryn murmured, and tucked it into her belt.

Aenae had been waiting impatiently. Saeddryn hurried toward him and put his harness on.

"Will your mate be safe?" he asked.

"I warned him about what could happen," said Saeddryn.

"He knows what t'do when the time's right, an' I trust him t'do it. Now, let's go."

She climbed onto her partner's back. Aenae snorted aggressively and walked off through his nest. He paused to take a drink from the trough, then charged out onto the balcony. Without slowing, he launched himself from the edge and into the sky.

Saeddryn, hanging on tightly, felt something she hadn't expected to feel and hadn't felt in a long time: excitement. She had grown tired and angry, after too many years of doing nothing but talk and look after the Temple. Now the Temple was gone, and her time spent in Malvern, playing the game of politics, was over. Now it was time to play a new game, one she had played in her youth and never realised how much she had missed.

War.

6

Under an Ugly Sky

Inva brought Laela the news next morning, before she had even eaten. She had already noticed Ravana's absence, and she sat in stunned silence as Inva told her, quickly and tersely, what had happened.

"Ravana has been found in the High Priestess' room. He is dead."

Laela's throat tightened. "How?"

"By griffin. Nobody doubts that."

"Aenae," Oeka hissed.

"Why was he in there?" said Laela.

"To assassinate the High Priestess." Inva said it without any hint that she was guessing.

Laela swore. "Are yeh sure?"

"There was a dagger by his hand," said Inva. "And I knew that he would try already."

"How? Why? I never told him to do it."

"No, but it was his duty to protect you, my lady. His kind are trained from birth to do all in their power to defend their master—even if that means to kill someone they believe is a threat."

"What?" Laela yelled. "How in the gods' names am I gonna run this place if people who're meant to be workin' for me go an' do whatever they want? I never told him to do nothin'!"

Inva flinched. "But you did give him permission, my lady.

Yesterday, he asked for your leave to do whatever he felt was necessary to protect you. He took you at your word."

Laela twined her hair around her fingers and wrenched at it. "Fine," she growled. "What else happened? Is Saeddryn dead?"

"No. The High Priestess and her partner are both gone from the city."

Laela snatched up a vase and hurled it at the wall. Before the pieces had finished falling, she lifted her face to the ceiling and screamed. It was a loud, indecipherable bellow of pure fury. Oeka stood up and added her own voice, but not even she could drown out the Queen's rage.

Inva backed away, almost crouching in fright.

The sound took a long time to die away.

Shoulders heaving, Laela pointed at Inva. "Go find Iorwerth. Bring him, an' Garnoc, an' everyone else what knows fightin'. Send 'em to the council chamber, an' don't let them stop to pack. But before that, go an' tell the guards to go arrest Lord Torc. Lock him up an' don't let him out of anyone's sight. Any man what lets him get away loses his manhood. *Move!*"

Inva nodded once and ran out.

Laela sat down and massaged her temples. "Burn in Gryphus' fires, Ravana. An' may Saeddryn go with yeh."

Oeka didn't blink. "What shall you tell the council?"

"I'm gonna tell 'em the truth. It's war."

"And Saeddryn?"

"She's dead. I'm puttin' out an order. Anyone meets her an' doesn't kill her is a traitor."

"Can you guess where she has gone?" said Oeka.

"Gone to find her brood, that's where," said Laela. "She must've been plannin' this from day one. Now she thinks I've made a move, she's gonna do what she did before. Rebel."

"She will die for it," said Oeka. "I shall watch her die with pleasure, and more so if I am the one to have made that death."

"I didn't want this t'happen," Laela moaned. "Gods damn it all."

"We shall win," said Oeka.

Laela gave her a look. "That so?"

"Yes," the little griffin said firmly. "We shall win because I am with you, and I shall never be defeated."

"That's what I wanted to hear, right enough." Laela stood up. "C'mon. Time to do it your way, Oeka."

"War?" Lord Iorwerth looked distressed.

Laela nodded, unsmiling.

"But surely—I can understand why the High Priestess fled. She must have thought ye wanted her dead, and no wonder. But that doesn't mean—"

"It does," Laela interrupted. "Listen, all of yeh. Saeddryn's wanted my throne for years. Why did yeh think King Arenadd left? She was plottin' against him. He already knew. That's why he named me his heir; to be ready when the time came."

"But why did he run?" Garnoc demanded. "He could've squashed her like a fly."

"Because he knew if he stayed an' fought her, it'd mean war. He didn't want to fight his own people, Garnoc. He told me, 'I built this Kingdom, an' I'm damned if I'll help tear it apart.' I left her alone for the same reason—thought I could negotiate. I needed her on my side, an' I thought if she knew I could arrest her if I wanted, she'd do everythin' to make me happy. I was wrong, an' now Ravana's forced my hand. She wants me gone the way she wanted my father gone, an' if it comes to war, then so be it. I'll rise to that."

"She's right," said Iorwerth. "Saeddryn never thought Queen Laela had the right to rule, an' she'll fight to change it. We all know what she's like."

"She always resented King Arenadd," Garnoc muttered.

"And loved him," said Iorwerth.

There was an awkward silence.

"Loved him?" said Laela. "What d'yeh mean? I never saw her smile at him once."

"He was meant to marry her," said Iorwerth. "Not many people know that, only some of the old guard. Her mother always told her never to marry any man except a Taranisäii. When Arenadd came, she expected to marry him. But he refused her, see? Turned her down for this other woman who came with him."

"Skade."

"I knew *her*," said Iorwerth. "Dangerous woman. Had a

face like a hatchet. Nobody really knew where she came from. Acted like she hated everyone."

"Except the King," said Garnoc. "He was the only one she was kind to."

"Some say he never loved anyone but her," said Iorwerth. "After she died, he was never the same."

"But Saeddryn never forgave him," said Garnoc. "She never stopped believin' it was her right t'be his Queen even though she'd married Torc by then. Where's Torc, anyway?"

"I sent guards to pick him up," said Laela. "He should be locked up by now."

"Unless he's left too," said Iorwerth. "I wouldn't be surprised."

"Garnoc, go an' find out," said Laela. "Guard him yerself if he's in the cells. Iorwerth—stay here."

Garnoc left smartly.

"Now then," Laela said, to Iorwerth. "Time to start makin' plans."

A hiss broke into the conversation, and a griffin rose. Kaanee, Iorwerth's partner, hulking and battle-scarred.

"Now is the time to fight," he rumbled. "The traitor should be afraid that I am here in Malvern by your side."

Laela bowed to him. "I know everythin' yeh did in the war, Kaanee. The King told me. He said once that he never would've won if it hadn't been for you." In fact, Arenadd had said no such thing, but that was beside the point.

Kaanee held his head high. "The Mighty Skandar's human was most wise. Do not be afraid, Queen. I shall win your war as well."

Oeka puffed up. "*I* shall win, Kaanee. Do not forget who is the most powerful griffin in Malvern."

Laela cringed, expecting an attack.

Kaanee, however, only chirped in amusement. "You are young, little griffin, and have discovered your gift too early. Arrogance does not win wars, but be assured that if it did, you would be our champion."

Oeka bristled. "You may be old, but you have not yet learnt all you should know. I shall teach you."

Kaanee faltered under the mental blow, but he didn't back down or strike back. "You are powerful in magic, but weak in body," he rasped. "And the more you use your power, the more you shall be weakened. Have you thought of what would happen if you attacked one in front while another was behind and another to the side? You would die, and fast. Can your all-powerful gift strike more than one enemy at once?"

Oeka looked away. "Soon I shall have that strength."

"And what shall you do, then, little one? Magic is not the only weapon a griffin possesses. Do you know where to strike to break another griffin's neck? When an enemy holds you by the leg, how shall you break free?"

Oeka said nothing.

Kaanee sat on his haunches, satisfied. "So you see that you do not know everything, Mighty Oeka."

Silence. It lasted so long that Laela was about to start talking to Iorwerth again, but then Oeka broke it.

"You are right, Kaanee," she said. "I know less of fighting than you. Therefore, I command you to teach me."

Kaanee's wing twitched. He looked honestly surprised. "If I am not too old and weak, perhaps I could teach the all-powerful Oeka."

"Teach," Oeka said. "We shall begin at once, while our humans plan."

"That's a great idea," said Laela.

Both griffins ignored her. Without waiting to say anything to their partners, they left the council chamber together.

"That was unexpected," Iorwerth said.

"I'll say!" said Laela. "Never saw Oeka go all humble like that before in my life. Humble for her, anyway. That's the closest yeh gonna get. Now, let's get to work."

While Laela and Iorwerth were in the midst of their discussion, Garnoc came hurrying back.

"Lord Torc's escaped, milady."

Iorwerth groaned.

"Escaped how?" said Laela.

"He was gone when they went to get him, milady. Someone must've tipped him off. The warrant's been put out, an' I've got guards searching the city."

"Didn't expect anythin' else," Laela sighed. "He ain't stupid."

"I don't reckon he had anything to do with it anyway," Garnoc added. "Him and Saeddryn were barely speakin' any more, an' he was far too loyal to the King."

"Yeah, loyal enough to think I killed him," said Laela. "Bring him in, Garnoc. Even if he ain't in on it, he's the hostage we need." She nodded to Iorwerth. "We're done for now. Go an' give the orders. An' find Kaanee, for gods' sakes. Send a message the moment there's news."

They parted quickly and went to work.

Laela's first priority was a simple one: send out griffiners to every town and city in Tara, with orders to intercept Saeddryn. Her offspring had to be in one of those cities, and if she wasn't going to join them, they at least should be arrested.

But Laela wasn't really expecting Saeddryn to head for the cities. Her real destination was far more obvious than that. The High Priestess had led a rebellion before, and now that she was about to do it again, there was only one place she would feel safe to begin.

The Throne.

Kaanee was her first choice to fly there. Just Kaanee, and a second griffin to help. Iorwerth could stay behind. She needed his help, and Kaanee would fly much faster without him. Of all the griffins in Malvern, Kaanee was the strongest who was loyal to her. Other than Oeka, of course.

As she strode up the ramps toward her audience chamber, Laela found herself feeling energised in a way she hadn't been in a long time. Her father had once told her that he was someone made for action, and now she began to think that she might be the same. Politics took too much talking and too many lies. Laela had never been much good at either. But when it came to acting fast and aggressively—that was when she felt alive.

Being extremely angry helped.

Her audience chamber was empty, aside from a pair of guards at the entrance and Inva, who was busy cleaning a stain off the floor.

"I got servants to do that, yeh know," Laela said on her way past.

"I am your servant," Inva said, without looking up.

Laela shrugged and pushed the door to Arenadd's bedroom open. Inside, it was just how he had left it, down to the unused bed and the faint smell of wine in the air.

A lump ached in her throat. She wasn't sure if it was grief, or fear. This was the place where she had first met her father—or at least the place where she had first seen his face. She remembered that night clearer than anything else in her life. The sheer terror was clearest. That moment when her new friend had uncovered his face, and she had seen the signs. The long scar under the eye. The crippled fingers. All the marks of a man who had been killed a hundred times over but refused to die.

She shuddered and opened the wardrobe. She almost laughed when she saw the contents: at least a dozen black robes of different designs, some plain, some decorated with embroidery or lined with fur. There were no other clothes in there, other than a few pairs of boots and some folded trousers.

She didn't know why she could have expected to find anything else. Her father had never worn a single garment that wasn't a robe. He was famous for it.

Laela flicked through the robes, still fighting back laughter. They were all beautifully clean and well made, and though they were obviously inspired by the uniform of a slave, they'd been tailored as elaborately as the finest of noble outfits. King Arenadd might have been cold-hearted and bloodthirsty, but he'd always been very meticulous about his appearance.

Laela stopped abruptly and flicked back to the last robe she'd looked at. She frowned and lifted it out.

"What the—?"

While the others were pristine, this one was practically in rags. One sleeve had been torn off at the shoulder, and there were holes big enough to put her hand through. In many places, the thick wool was stiff with something that might have been mud—but she had a horrible feeling that it wasn't.

"Why in the world did he keep this one?" she said aloud. "It ain't even clean."

She shrugged and put it away. There were enough nasty things in her father's wardrobe already, so to speak, without looking for more.

Remembering her original purpose, she sought out one of the thicker robes, which had a fur-lined hood, and put it on over her gown. It was cold outside. That, and she had a point to make.

Laela closed the wardrobe and went to the bed. On the wall behind it, the sickle hung. She lifted it down carefully and felt the blade.

Touching it made her feel sick. She knew how many murders this sickle had committed. But still, it was her weapon by rights, just like the Kingdom. Queendom.

Sickle in hand, she returned to the audience chamber.

Oeka was there, with Kaanee. "And here is the Dark Lady!" she said, sounding almost cheerful.

Kaanee's tail swished. "If your eyes were not blue, I would think that you were your father," he said.

Laela grunted. "Yeh look like yeh had some exercise, Oeka."

The small griffin was breathing hard, and her feathers were ruffled. "I have learnt. Now speak, Laela. What have you and Kaanee's human planned?"

"We're sendin' griffiners to the cities," said Laela. "They're gonna try to catch Saeddryn, or at least they'll take her kids in. Iorwerth's organisin' that already. Kaanee—I got somethin' to ask yeh."

"I am listening."

"The Throne," Laela said bluntly. "I want yeh to go there. Choose another griffin to take with yeh, but you're the one I want."

"You think the traitors will have gone there," said Kaanee.

"Yeah, I do. It only makes sense. An' you're the best one to go catch 'em, Kaanee."

Oeka huffed to herself.

"I'd send yeh, Oeka, but we need yeh here to lead, don't we?" Laela said.

She looked pleased. "That is true. Kaanee, do as my human commands."

"I cannot," said Kaanee.

Oeka bristled. "You refuse to obey me, Kaanee?"

"I cannot do as I have been told," the older griffin said calmly.

"Why not?" said Laela.

"Come, and I will show you why."

There was an archway in the wall, added during Arenadd's time to allow Skandar to fly straight into the audience chamber. Kaanee went to it, shouldering aside a tapestry, and stepped onto the little platform beyond.

Laela came to join him, and saw immediately what he had meant. The sky had turned slate grey, and a huge bank of pure white cloud had drifted in over the horizon.

"There is a storm coming, and a strong one," Kaanee said. "No griffin can fly far."

As if to emphasise the point, thunder growled over the city. Lightning flashed not long afterward.

"Damn it!" Laela stomped back into the audience chamber. "The ole slag's gonna get an even bigger head start on us now. Here's hopin' she gets struck by lightnin' along the way."

"Aenae left before dawn," said Kaanee. "He will reach safe haven before the storm strikes."

"Great. If anyone needs me I'll be down the practice yard, killin' straw dummies." Laela stormed out. Oeka followed at a more leisurely pace.

The storm drew in while Laela practised. Down in one of the courtyards between the towers, a patch of dirt had been fenced in and equipped with archery targets and dummies made from bundled straw. It served as a decent enough training yard.

So far Laela had been taught more about hand-to-hand combat than archery, so she went to work on the dummies with her sickle. It still felt clumsy in her hand; she had had plenty of lessons, but not as much practice as she really needed, and she'd never used a weapon in a real-life fight before.

Not that she really had practice on her mind.

Thunder crackled, louder and louder. Lightning flashed on the sickle, and Laela launched herself at the nearest dummy. Ignoring any notion of strategy or using the moves her father had taught her, she hacked at it with all her strength. The sickle caught on the bindings holding the straw together and flicked out of her hand.

Laela gave an incoherent yell of rage and started to kick the dummy. Above, the storm gathered its power, and the wind and the icy rain gave her a feeling of invincibility. She kicked the dummy again, harder, then started to punch it.

Laela might not have been an expert swordswoman, or an archer, but if there was one thing she knew how to do, it was throw a punch.

Oeka arrived during the midst of her tantrum. She came on foot, thanks to the storm, and stood by the base of the nearest tower to watch. The wind had picked up alarmingly and kept lifting her wings away from her back, but she ignored it and stared blankly at the raging Laela.

Eventually, when the Queen of Tara stopped to rest, Oeka came toward her. She stumbled a little when the wind hit her, but went straight to the dummy. Ignoring Laela completely, she rose onto her hind legs and tore the straw head off with her talons.

"Show-off," Laela growled.

"There is no shame in showing strength," Oeka said. "Be calm, Laela. This upstart can be beaten."

Laela was panting. "That so?"

"Sooner or later, he will come to Malvern," said Oeka. "And when he does, I shall break his mind like an egg."

"Yeh can do that?"

"By that time, nothing shall be outside my power."

"Let's hope. Thing is—" Laela broke off and ducked her head as a spat of rain hit her. The dusty ground underfoot turned dark in quick patches, and an instant later the real downpour had started. Oeka ran for cover at once, leaving Laela to snatch up her sickle and follow.

Sheltering in the doorway to the tower, Laela peered out. The parts of her hair that were still dry whipped around in the wind. The rest stuck to her face. She pulled it away and looked out at the storm. "My gods, look at it. I ain't seen one this big in yonks."

"It is nature's reminder," said Oeka from behind her, where it was completely dry.

"What d'yeh mean, Oeka?"

"Our magic comes from nature," the small griffin explained. "We alone, of all creatures, have the gift to control that magic. Even the cunning human does not have that gift. But when nature rages, it is a reminder to us that for all our magic we can never be as powerful. If there is a storm in the sky, even one that is too weak for danger, a griffin will not fly."

"Sounds like nature's a god to yeh," said Laela.

"No." Oeka snapped her beak. "There are no gods. Nature *is*, and demands nothing. Death is the punishment for those who will not give it caution." Moving carefully, the small griffin came to Laela's side and looked out at the sky. "See, there," she said.

Laela followed her gaze. "What're we lookin' at?"

"There is a griffin in the sky," said Oeka.

"What? Where? *Flyin'?* Now?"

"So I can see."

It took a long time, and the darkness made it difficult, but eventually Laela spotted it. A winged shape, not too far from the Eyrie, struggling to fly. So she assumed—the wind threw it around, whipping it this way and that like a cat playing with a feather.

Laela cringed. "Poor thing ain't got a chance."

"The fool who flies in a storm dies," Oeka said coldly.

"Now that ain't nice," Laela snapped. "For all we know, he couldn't find shelter in time. This thing came on fast."

"Not so fast that he could not have gone to ground," said Oeka. "If he must die, then so be it."

"Let's hope he ain't carryin' a message for us or somethin'. C'mon, let's go up higher an' get a better look. I want somethin' to eat, anyway."

They headed into the tower and upstairs. The dining hall had a large window, and Laela opened it to look out while the servants brought food. She saw the poor griffin again eventually—closer to the Eyrie now, and, incredibly, still struggling to reach it.

"He's gonna get struck by lightnin' at this rate," Laela murmured. "Poor bugger."

When the food arrived, she carried it over to the window to eat it, unable to resist being caught up in the anonymous griffin's survival. More than once she saw the wind grab the poor creature and hurl it off-course so violently she thought its wings must have been broken. But every time, the griffin doggedly righted itself and kept on coming. Eventually, it came close enough that she could make out talons and feathers, and she began to hope that maybe it could reach the Eyrie after all.

She was wrong.

The griffin passed over the outer wall and came in among the towers. Then another gust hit it in the flank and, with terrible ease, slammed it into the wall of the nearest tower.

Scrabbling and flailing at the stonework, the griffin slid downward, then fell away, straight downward. For a moment, Laela thought it had recovered when the wings peeled open, but they only slapped uselessly at the air until the griffin had fallen out of sight.

"Poor bastard. Poor, poor bastard."

Oeka looked up from her lump of raw meat. "The fool has met his end?"

"I dunno." Laela turned away from the window. "He was still movin' when he fell. I think he might've survived. I better send someone to look."

"Do not waste your time," Oeka said, and went back to her meal.

Laela ignored her and summoned a servant. "There's a griffin what just fell at the bottom of the livin' quarters tower. Go let people know, will yeh? I want someone to go see if he's all right an' bring him inside."

"Yes, milady."

The worst of the storm had passed by midafternoon, but the rain kept going steadily. None of the griffins in the entire Eyrie would agree to even go outside, no matter what they were offered in the way of rewards or threats.

Laela had to settle for picking out who would go—with Oeka's help, of course—and giving them their orders for when the weather cleared. After that, the two of them spent more time with Iorwerth, making plans and choosing strategies.

Despite all that the time felt completely wasted to Laela, and as the rain pounded stubbornly on the Eyrie roofs, she felt herself growing more and more frustrated. She had Oeka and a pair of bodyguards, but without Ravana, she felt vulnerable in a way that showed her just how much she had come to rely on him. Oeka wasn't much help either; she was so calm and apparently unconcerned about the situation that she only succeeded in making Laela angrier—and more so because Laela knew full well that complaining about it would just start an argument she would lose.

Toward nightfall, she gave up on trying to make herself feel better and slouched off to see if she could find out what had happened to the griffin that had been caught in the storm. It was partly idle curiosity, but it should keep her mind off things as well.

Finding the griffin wasn't easy. She headed for the storage tower, stopping everybody she met along the way to ask if they knew anything. Nobody seemed to have a clue, until a guard she spoke to said, "I helped bring it in, milady."

"Alive?"

"Yes, milady. I think its leg was hurt, but it walked inside more or less."

"Where is it now, then?"

"We put it in a spare storeroom, milady, just t'rest. It's down on the bottom level, milady."

"Ta." Laela put her hands in her pockets and headed downward. Another guard along the way confirmed the griffin's location and led her to it when commanded.

The injured griffin's temporary home was indeed a storeroom, one used for old crates. Discarded packing straw was piled everywhere.

Laela wrinkled her nose as she entered. "Smells of cabbages in here. Thanks anyway—off yeh go."

The guard left, and she took a torch from the wall in the corridor and went into the storeroom. Oeka, spitting like a cat at the stench, refused to go in after her.

The griffin lay curled up in the straw with his back to Laela, but he stirred and lifted his head when she came closer. Yellow eyes gleamed and blinked slowly.

Close to, Laela could see that the griffin was indeed male, his jet-black ear tufts damp and limp. The rest of his feathers were mottled grey and reminded her of the sky outside.

Laela bowed slightly to him. "Hello. I've come to see if yer all right."

The griffin's head had lowered again. For a moment, he looked as if he were ignoring her, but then he began to move. Slowly, painfully, one front paw folded under his chest and the other grabbing at the floor, he dragged himself around to face her.

Laela hurried around him to compensate. "There's no need to move. Yeh can see me here."

The griffin watched her silently. Now that she could see his face properly, she thought he looked very odd. His forehead, just behind the beak, bulged upward, and his skull was rounded rather than flat-topped like a normal griffin's. His beak, greyish pink in colour, was unusually small and matched the slender forelegs.

"My name's Laela," Laela told him regardless. "Queen of Tara."

The griffin's eyes closed, and he made a sound like a sigh.

"I saw yeh hit the tower," Laela persisted. "I sent people to bring yeh in. Are yeh all right?"

Finally, the griffin spoke. "Thank you. I'll live." The voice sounded odd; it was slower and richer, less flat than an ordinary griffin's.

"That's good," said Laela. "Now listen. I wanted to ask yeh, what were yeh doin' comin' here, an' in a storm, too? Is there news yeh got for me?"

The griffin looked her in the eye—such an unusual thing for a griffin to do that Laela actually took a step back. "I was trying to find this place, and the storm caught me by surprise."

"Yer lucky, then," said Laela. "But why were yeh tryin' to come here anyway? Do yeh have a human?"

"No." The griffin paused. "But I did come here to talk to you, *Aee-ya*." This was how all griffins pronounced Laela's name.

"What about?" she said at once.

"What is this fool saying?" Oeka's harsh voice interrupted. The little griffin sauntered in, stepping delicately around the grubby straw.

The grey griffin raised his head and looked warily at her. "My name's *Kee-ya-oh*," he said.

Oeka rose up and smashed her talons into his face, hard enough to draw blood.

"Hey!" Laela made a grab for Oeka, but quickly changed her mind. "What was that for?"

"If you dare speak to me this way again, you shall die," Oeka snarled, ignoring her.

Kee-ya-oh, if that was his name, said nothing.

"Now speak," Oeka said. "Why have you come here? You are not from this territory."

Silence.

"Tell me, or die," the little griffin said. "You are humanless, and deformed, and should be glad I have not killed you already."

"Don't be like that!" Laela butted in, by now thoroughly alarmed. "He's done nothin' wrong."

The force of the mental blow sent her reeling. "Silence!" Oeka hissed. "This is not your concern, human. Move away."

It had been a long time since Laela had been this frightened of her partner. She said nothing and stepped back to stand near the door.

Kee-ya-oh didn't need any more threats. He looked up, blinking away blood. "I didn't mean to offend you."

"Fools are not welcome in my home," she said, unmoved. "Now tell me. Why have you come here? Do not lie; the truth cannot be hidden from me."

"I came here to find a human."

Oeka snorted. "Go away and choose a commoner. No human here is lowly enough for a misshapen creature like you."

Kee-ya-oh closed his eyes. "Not to choose. I'm looking for a woman called Skade. Is she here?"

"Skade?" Oeka arched her neck in surprise. "That human is long dead."

"Dead . . ." Kee-ya-oh slumped onto the straw. "But did she leave someone? Family?"

"None," said Oeka.

"Her mate," Kee-ya-oh persisted. "She had a mate."

"Yes. The King Arenadd, who was the human of the Mighty Skandar. He was Skade's mate."

"Where is he?" Kee-ya-oh struggled to stand up. "Is he alive?"

"No." Oeka glanced at Laela. "That human died as well, not long ago."

Kee-ya-oh slumped back onto his belly. "Then I came for nothing."

"I'm his daughter." Laela risked coming closer.

The grey griffin's eyes opened. "You?"

"Yeah, me. I'm Arenadd's daughter. He left me his Kingdom. Guess the news ain't spread far."

Slowly, and laboriously, Kee-ya-oh stood up. He kept his injured foreleg off the ground, and used his wings to balance. He looked at Laela, sizing her up like prey or an enemy to fight. "You?" he said. "Arenadd's daughter?"

"That's right."

"But you're a half-breed!"

"Filth!" Oeka launched herself at him.

Kee-ya-oh batted her away with his injured leg. Then he sat on his haunches and did something so shocking that even Oeka backed away smartly.

He started to laugh.

Griffins didn't laugh. They were incapable of it. But Kee-ya-oh did it now. He made an ugly hacking, wheezing sound, and at first it sounded almost like choking. But it was laughter, more or less, and Laela was completely bewildered.

"We are leaving now," Oeka said in disgust. "This one is mad."

Laela had no intention of arguing. She backed out and followed her partner out of the room.

Kee-ya-oh paid no attention. He laughed on, not seeming to even notice that they were leaving. As he shook himself, feathers came loose from his chest and drifted down into the straw.

7

Half-Breed

A day passed, and the weather cleared. Kaanee and his fellow griffins set out immediately, leaving Laela and Oeka to their work.

Laela knew that, until she had more information about Saeddryn's whereabouts and some idea of just what the High Priestess was up to, there wasn't much that she herself could do. She and Iorwerth had decided not to make any formal announcements yet; there was no telling how the people would react. A warrant had been put out for Torc's arrest, for unspecified crimes, and, in the meantime, Iorwerth and the woman who was both his assistant and wife began to sketch out various strategies for defending the city. Laela made sure to involve herself in this and took the opportunity to learn as much as she could about the sort of leadership she would need in wartime. Iorwerth was more than happy to help.

As for Kee-ya-oh, the misshapen griffin didn't show himself anywhere in the Eyrie as far as Laela knew. The only thing she heard about him at all was a vague rumour that he had died, but she had too many things on her mind to worry about it too much. She didn't even mention him to Oeka, let alone ask the small griffin why she had treated him so viciously. That was a road Laela instinctively knew wouldn't lead anywhere good. The whole incident had been a powerful reminder of just how arrogant power had made her partner—and how much more dangerous that had made her become.

More than once, Laela remembered the horrible jolt in her mind, and silently thanked the gods that Oeka was on her side.

Another day passed, as tensely as the one before it. Laela had the entire priesthood arrested and interrogated—nonviolently, to begin with. She doubted any of them knew anything, but it paid to be careful. None of them had anything useful to say, and she debated for a long time before doing what she did next.

She had the Wolf priestess brought up from the dungeon to the audience chamber.

The woman arrived, looking pale and very frightened. Two guards stood on either side of her, and she wisely stayed still and said nothing.

"Tell me yer name," Laela said, without ceremony.

"Gwenna, my lady."

"Yer the Wolf priestess, right?"

"Yes, my lady."

"Good. Now listen up, Gwenna." Laela stood on her platform, hands on hips. "By now yeh probably know why yeh spent today locked up. Am I right?"

"The High Priestess . . . left," said Gwenna. "I swear, I didn't know—"

"That's enough. My father's cousin an' her partner left without permission. They ran away because they committed high treason, an' they knew I had every reason to have the both of them killed. They're outlaws now, an' anybody who helps them gets to die the same way."

"I didn't do anything, I swear I didn't." Gwenna looked close to tears. "I didn't know what she was going to do—"

"Of course yeh didn't know," Laela cut her off. "If yeh did, yeh wouldn't have hung about. Now listen. I'm convinced yeh ain't guilty, an' I got no right to keep yeh locked up. I'm offerin' freedom, but in return for somethin'."

The priestess breathed in deeply. "I'll do whatever ye need, my lady."

"That's what I wanted to hear. What I want's simple. I'll set yeh free, along with all yer friends, an' I'll rebuild the Temple right away, give yeh all the money yeh need. In return, I want yeh to give me my tattoos. Make me a proper Northern woman."

Gwenna winced. "But, my lady, only the High Priestess—"

"I know. Which is why I'm askin' you—High Priestess Gwenna."

Her eyes went big. "What? Me? But—"

"Saeddryn would've picked her successor when she was ready, but by runnin' away, she gave up her power," said Laela. "My father made her High Priestess, an' now I'm gonna do the same thing for you. Be my High Priestess, Gwenna. Serve Tara—by serving me."

Gwenna faltered. "I . . . I would . . . the other priestesses have to agree . . ."

Laela could see she'd already won. "Go speak with 'em, then. Explain the situation, an' I'm sure they'll see things your way." She favoured Gwenna with a smile. "Just fancy. Yer very own Temple, made just the way yeh want. A place on the council, an' a chance to help decide how Tara's run. An' maybe, just maybe, there's a griffin out there somewhere, just waitin' for yeh."

Gwenna looked close to tears again, but not the same kind as before. "A griffin?" she whispered. "For me?"

"They only choose the highest an' the best," Laela said. A master stroke. She gestured at the guards. "Take all the priestesses to the council chamber. Let 'em alone there as long as they want, to make their minds up. They ain't prisoners any more. An' treat my new High Priestess well."

They nodded and escorted Gwenna out of the room as politely as possible. She wandered off between them in what looked like a trance.

Once they were gone, Laela cackled. "Heh heh heh. Did yeh see her face? Gobsmacked. I bet she came in here expectin' a death sentence or maybe banishment."

"What if the others do not agree?" said Oeka.

"They will," said Laela. "They've got no choice. I gave her the carrot an' implied the stick well enough that I didn't need to use it at all. An' I won't have to, either."

Oeka stared blankly at her.

"I mean I didn't have to use threats." Laela grinned. "She knows if she says yes, she gets everythin'. If she says no, she gets a lot worse than nothin'. As for the others, they'll come around. They'll be jealous they ain't the ones gettin' promoted, but they'll get the new Temple, an' somethin' way more important: my protection. Without it, they're dead."

"You are right," said Oeka. "Humans will always choose saving their own lives over loyalty to their friends."

"Not as much as you lot do, but often enough," said Laela. "Often enough that this'll work. Those who decide to get all heroic an' noble, they get to feel somethin' a lot worse than guilt. My boot, kickin' their arse out of Malvern."

Oeka flicked her tail. "I am hungry."

Laela had been hoping for some sort of praise, but there obviously wasn't any on the way. She heaved a sigh and left the room.

Along the way to the dining hall, Inva appeared to catch them up. "My lady!"

Laela slowed and glanced back at her. "Hm? What is it?"

Inva ducked her head. "News, my lady. Good news."

"Did Saeddryn die or something?"

"Ah . . . no, my lady. But Lord Torc has been arrested."

"Great. Garnoc's lot got him, then?"

"No, my lady. A man in the city heard about the warrant and hunted Lord Torc down himself. A messenger just brought me the news."

"Torc's in the dungeon, then?"

"Yes, my lady. The one who brought him is waiting."

Laela considered. "All right, then, bring him up to me in the audience chamber. Might as well have a word now."

Oeka had heard every word. "*Shyaa!* Why can this human not wait until we have eaten? Is he so important?"

"There's more to life than food," Laela said sharply. "An' there's more to it than just worryin' about yerself all the time. Besides, I want to know where Torc was hidin', an' if anyone was helpin' him."

"I will eat now," said Oeka, unmoved.

"Fine." Laela threw up her hands. "I'll have someone bring yeh up somethin' dead if it's that important. My gods."

Oeka ran to keep up with her. "You do not understand. I must eat to make myself strong. My magic feeds on my energy, and if I do not eat, it will hurt me to use it."

"Don't use it so much, then."

Oeka snorted through her beak. "Perhaps next time you are in danger, I should take your advice."

"Oh, quit actin' like a little kid. We got work to do."

They had to wait in the audience chamber long enough for

Oeka's food to arrive, and the small griffin tore into it the moment it was on the floor in front of her. She hadn't said anything during the wait, busying herself with grooming instead.

Laela ignored the sulk, and paced around impatiently. "I'm gonna spend half my damn reign in this damn room. Gimme a fight or somethin', I'll take it. Ugh."

Oeka had finished eating and had apparently gone to sleep by the time Torc's capturer was brought in.

Laela strode forward to meet him, took one look at him, and stopped dead.

The stranger bowed nervously to her. His age was difficult to guess at, and he was . . .

Ugly, maybe. No, not ugly. More sort of . . . odd. Somehow not quite right. His nose was pointed, and a good part of his face was hidden by a ragged black beard. His hair was black, too, and looked as if it hadn't been brushed . . . ever. Somewhere under the tangle were a pair of overlarge yellow eyes.

Strikin', Laela thought. *He looks strikin'. An' filthy.*

The man had a gangly, awkward frame, and he walked a little stiffly. As he turned partly to the right, Laela saw that he had what looked like a hump on his back.

She shrugged off her bemusement and nodded to him. "Welcome. I'm Queen Laela. They tell me yeh brought in Lord Torc."

The stranger smiled at her. "That's right. It's good to see you again."

No "my lady," Laela noticed. No bowing, either. She immediately took a liking to him. "Again, eh?" she said. "Can't say I remember yeh, an' I think I would. But don't worry about that. What's yer name?"

He laughed—it sounded slightly wheezy, but genuine. "You don't recognise me? I hoped you might."

Laela peered at him. "No, I don't think so."

"We met just a few days ago, you know. I wasn't feeling too well, but I'm better now. Thank you for coming to see if I was all right."

Laela raised an eyebrow. "Sorry, yeh ain't making sense yet. Where'd we meet?"

Oeka had stood up. "What is this filthy thing?" she said. "He smells of dead rats."

Laela was very, very glad she was speaking griffish. "Uh, this is Oeka. I should have said so before—sorry. She says—"

The stranger looked down at the aggressive griffin, who just about reached the level of his waist. "I see *you're* no different toward humans as you are toward griffins, but you don't look any bigger from here."

He said it in perfect griffish.

Laela gaped, then glared. "All right, that's enough. Who are yeh, an' why do yeh speak griffish?"

Oeka was already advancing on him. "Do not ask. I shall tear the information from his head."

The stranger threw an appealing look at Laela. "You really don't recognise me?"

"No. Now tell us the truth."

He held up his hands—they were big and clumsy, and the nails . . . "It's me, Laela," he said. "Kullervo."

"What? What are yeh talkin' about? I don't know nobody called that."

Kullervo looked at the floor, in a way that seemed familiar. "Well . . . I don't look the same now. Can't pronounce my name through a beak, either. Always comes out sounding like *Kee-ya-oh*."

Oeka had stopped. "I *knew* that I knew him!" she exclaimed. "The scent, the feel of the mind . . ." She made a disgusted noise. "This is magic that was never meant to be."

"All magic is *meant* to be," Kullervo said sharply. "And doing what you do to other people's minds without permission sounds far more wrong to me."

Oeka gave him a murderous look, but, surprisingly enough, she didn't attack him.

Laela finally found her voice. "Wait. Wait. I don't believe this. Are yeh sayin' that *you*—you're that griffin? The one what flew in the storm? *That* griffin?"

"I am," said Kullervo. "Was." He flexed his arm. "It still hurts when I move it. But it'll get better." He smiled nervously.

Laela sat down and massaged her forehead. "I can't take this. What are yeh, then? A griffin what turns into a human, or a human what turns into a griffin?"

"Both," said Kullervo.

The idea was just too bizarre for Laela to take in. "I never knew there were griffins . . . people . . . like that."

"And there should not be," Oeka interrupted. "A griffin's magic is not meant to be used on himself."

"But that's how I am," said Kullervo. "I didn't choose it, but I accepted it. Nobody can do anything else with who they are. Including you."

His voice was soft and persuasive, and Laela nodded without even thinking. "Yer right. Fine, well—" She stood up. "If that's how it is, then so be it. I seen weirder things in my life. So, Kullervo, they said yeh caught Lord Torc. How?"

"Yes." Kullervo looked relieved. "I took some time to recover, then changed. It happens slowly, and I haven't done it too many times. But when I'd made myself human again, I took some clothes and food and listened to people talk. I found out about you, and what happened with this Saeddryn. I wanted to do something for you in return for your help, so I went into the city and caught this man I heard you wanted."

"How'd yeh find him?" Laela asked.

Kullervo shrugged and smiled. "I have a very good sense of smell in either shape. And I suppose I've just always had a knack for hunting. I found him hiding in a cellar, alone. I think he was planning to leave the city as soon as things quieted down."

"Yeh didn't hurt him, did yeh?"

"No, just scared him very badly. With this ugly face, it's not hard."

Despite herself, Laela chuckled. "Yeh did me a great favour, Kullervo, an' I'm grateful. What can I do for yeh to say thanks?"

"There's only one thing I want," Kullervo said. "I want to stay here. Let me help you."

Laela frowned. "How? What else can yeh do for me?"

Oeka rasped to herself. "Send this freak away."

"I can be useful," said Kullervo, ignoring her. "I can fly long distances as a griffin, and be a messenger or a spy as a human. I can fight in either shape."

"We do not need him," said Oeka.

"Hm." Laela rubbed her chin. "My father always said the best way to rule a Kingdom is to always keep useful people around. All right then, Kullervo—yeh can stay."

He grinned. "Thank you—"

"But—" Laela held up a hand. "But first, prove how loyal yeh are. I can't trust everyone what just says they're loyal."

"I brought Torc in."

"Anyone lookin' for money might've done that. I want yeh to do somethin' else."

"Anything," said Kullervo. "Name it."

"Good. Go find Saeddryn."

Kullervo looked shocked. Oeka looked pleased.

"Yeh say yer a hunter, so hunt *her*," said Laela. "She's the one I really want."

Kullervo bowed. "Give me a map and some food to take, and I'll leave tomorrow."

Laela didn't let Kullervo leave immediately, instead giving him a spare room to stay in and arranging for him to be given some clothes and the opportunity for a bath.

"An' I want yeh to come eat dinner with me tonight," she added.

He looked surprised. "Me, eat with you?"

"I'm interested in yeh," Laela said bluntly. "I want to know more about yeh and where yeh came from. It'll be better'n just eatin' with Oeka. She doesn't talk when she's at her food."

"I'd be honoured."

"Great, see yeh then, then." Laela hesitated. "Uh . . . what do yeh eat? Anythin' special I oughta know about?"

"I like meat," said Kullervo.

"Er . . . d'yeh want it raw?"

He wrinkled his nose. "Cooked, please. What do you think I am, some sort of animal?"

Laela reddened. "Sorry—"

Kullervo broke the tension with his wheezy laugh. "Heh! Don't worry, it was just a joke. I'll eat whatever you do."

Laela smiled. "All right, I'll send someone to get yeh when it's time. See yeh later."

"You like this one," Oeka said when he had gone. "I smell it," she added accusingly.

"He's nice enough," said Laela. "An' he's direct. That's somethin' I don't find much these days."

"He is unnatural," said Oeka. "Ugly."

"*Why* are yeh so bothered about that?" said Laela. "What've looks got to do with anythin'?"

"He has no shape of his own," said Oeka. "He is not human, or griffin. Be cautious, Laela. One with no true shape has no true mind."

"What's that meant to mean?"

"I cannot sense him. I smell nothing from his mind. The shape is wrong."

"Hm." Laela rubbed her neck. "If he ain't givin' yeh anythin', then it must be up to me to do the readin'. That's why I asked him to dinner. The more we know, the better."

"I agree."

"An' speakin' of that, it's time we had a chat with ole Torc."

"I shall help you," said Oeka. "It is time I used my powers again."

"I'll be glad to have yeh there." Laela sighed. "This ain't gonna be nice at all."

Laela brooded on her way to the dungeon. She didn't know Lord Torc well enough to *like* him, but she had always looked on him as a good man, and she knew he had a strong sense of justice. She also knew about how he and his wife Saeddryn had drifted apart, through no fault of his own as far as she could tell.

She knew his personal history fairly well; he was an orphan, and had been a slave up until the age of thirteen. Then he had been lucky enough to meet a fellow slave who turned out to be Arenadd himself, who had been waylaid on his way to the North and sold. After Arenadd had escaped with Skandar's help, the pair of them abducted every single slave in the area, including Torc, and ran away. During the journey, Arenadd set the slaves free, and Torc had been adopted into the Taranisäii family by Caedmon, the old man he had later named his son after.

Torc eventually met up with Arenadd again and had joined in his fight to take over the North. Sometime during the war, he'd married Saeddryn, and had gone on to become an important member of Arenadd's court.

Now, years later, after a long journey to become so much more than he'd been born as, Torc Taranisäii was imprisoned once again.

It put a bad taste in Laela's mouth. She hoped that she wouldn't have to hurt him. *Please gods don't make me hurt him. Not my own family.*

"Rulership comes before everything," said Oeka. "Even family."

"What?" Laela stopped. "What did yeh say?"

The small griffin passed her. "You must be strong, Laela. Remember, there are more important things here than your feelings."

"Yeh knew what I was thinkin'." Laela hurried after her. "Tell me yeh didn't just hear what I was thinkin' . . ."

A guard ushered them into Torc's cell. It was bigger and much more comfortable than most, intended for wealthy prisoners. There was proper bedding, and even a writing desk. Torc was standing in the middle of the floor. He started when the Queen came in but didn't move.

"Stay outside," Laela told the guards. "I got enough protection." When the door had slammed shut, she turned to face Torc. "Sit down, will yeh, so we can talk. Don't worry; yer in no danger. Trust me, Torc, I want to help yeh."

He didn't sit. "Where is my wife?"

"I was hopin' you knew, my lord," Laela said. "I thought since yeh ran off like that, you probably knew more than I did. Sit down, I said."

Oeka had come closer and circled around Torc; he glanced down at her and reluctantly sat on a stool. She positioned herself behind and to the left of him, and sat on her haunches, silently flicking her tail. Torc didn't dare look at her.

Laela took the desk chair. She adjusted the crown she had decided to wear today. "Now look," she said. "I'm gonna be direct. Where did Saeddryn go?"

"I don't know. She never told me."

"So yeh saw her, then? Before she left?"

"No." Torc shifted on his seat. His eyes were red. "I warned her that you were going to try to have her killed. But she wanted to stay here and do whatever she could while she still had the chance. She promised that the moment she knew for certain that she wasn't safe any more, she and Aenae would leave."

"An' in the meantime, when yeh heard she'd gone, that'd be time for you to leave, too."

Torc nodded. "I was going to leave the city when it was safe."

"To go join yer wife," Laela said immediately.

"No," Torc said, just as quickly. "We agreed not to tell each other where we planned to go. If one of us was caught, we couldn't betray the other. Torture me as much as you want; I don't have anything to tell you."

Laela's eyes flicked toward Oeka. The small griffin inclined her head, *yes*.

"Where d'yeh think she would've gone, then?" said Laela.

"Somewhere safe," said Torc. His bloodshot eyes narrowed. "Somewhere *you* and your assassins couldn't find her."

"Listen, I never sent that man," Laela said sharply. "He decided to do it himself. He was out of control."

"So you say." Torc sneered. "I've told you the truth, how about you do the same for me, half-breed?"

Oeka hissed in his ear. "Tread carefully, traitor. I can crush your mind like an insect."

"I told the truth," said Laela. "Lyin' ain't somethin' I'm good at. What's Saeddryn plannin'? Where are her children hidin'? Answer me quick, Torc."

"Arddryn and Caedmon chose their own destinations, just like their mother."

"An' what are they gonna do there?" Laela leaned in close. "Did they tell yeh *that*, my lord?"

"No."

"But yeh can guess, can't yeh?" said Laela. "Yeh know what Saeddryn *wants* to do, don't yeh? Don't think I'm stupid, Torc."

"Bring you to justice," he spat. "You're a murderer and a usurper, and probably a spy for the South as well."

Laela stood up as Oeka snarled. "I'm your Queen, Torc, an' if yeh say anythin' like that again—"

Torc jerked upright. "There'll only ever be one ruler for me, half-breed, and it's not you. King Arenadd is my master, no-one else."

"He's gone, Torc. He ain't comin' back. I know it."

"Because you killed him!" Torc yelled. He pointed at her face. "You killed him! You seduced him, you tricked him, you made him leave his own Kingdom, then you murdered him and stole his throne!"

Laela was about to shout back at him, but she faltered when she saw that there were tears on his face. "I didn't kill him, Torc. I swear I didn't. I never killed anyone in my life. Believe me." Her voice broke. "He was my father. He saved my life, gave me everythin'. How could I want him dead?"

"You're not his daughter," Torc said. "You're a filthy half-breed."

"Look at me," said Laela. "*Look at me!* Look at my face, damn it! He's in me, Torc. All over me. My face, my hair, everything."

"My King would never touch a Southern woman," Torc snarled. "Never."

"But he did. He loved her an' killed her. I'm sorry, Torc. I never made it happen, an' there's nothin' I can do about it. He made me a half-breed, an' he made me Queen. That's just how it is."

Torc had gone quiet. He was shuddering, Laela saw. Oeka had put herself between the two humans, her wings raised to make herself look bigger. She said nothing but faced Torc, threatening to attack if he moved.

At last, Torc raised his head. "Where is he?" he asked, forlornly. "Where is the King? What did you do to him? Please just tell me. I'm begging you."

Laela softened. "Saeddryn was trying to take his throne, Torc. He knew it. He planned for it. When she tried to kill him, he took me and left."

"You're lying. He wouldn't *do* that."

Torc hadn't denied what Saeddryn had done, Laela noticed. "Yeh knew she wanted to take over, didn't yeh?"

Torc looked away. "She wanted to be Queen. She deserved to be. Deserved better than me. She's a hero. She should have had a hero for a husband. Not me."

"But he wouldn't have her," Laela said.

"No. He loved Skade, not her. Skade was all he cared about, even after she died. And Saeddryn had me instead. I would have stood aside and let her be with the King, but she wouldn't let me. She said he would never marry her, no matter what happened."

"Is that it?" said Laela. "That's all there is? She wanted to steal his throne away just because he wouldn't marry her?"

"No. She never really wanted to rule. She only wanted . . ."

"Wanted what?" said Laela.

Torc stared at the floor. "She was afraid of him. She grew more and more afraid all the time. I think . . . I think she could sense what was different about him. Most people couldn't, but she could. I could, sometimes."

"What d'yeh mean?" said Laela. "Sense what?"

"He wasn't really human," said Torc. "He was something else. Something the Night God sent. A chosen warrior, meant to protect us and hold us together." His voice was awed, almost worshipful. "That's why he never aged."

"I know," said Laela.

"But it was easy to be afraid of him," Torc went on, as if he hadn't heard. "Sometimes . . . when he was there, the air felt cold. *He* was cold. I touched his hand once, and I shivered. And his lovers, all dying. He couldn't be one of us, not on the inside. He had death in him, not life. Saeddryn knew it."

"An' she couldn't bear it," said Laela.

"She was wrong," said Torc. "He was our friend, not our enemy. But sometimes, you forget. Now, we remember. I want him back. We need him back. Tell me where he is, half-breed. Tell me what you did to him. Please."

Laela couldn't stand to look at him any more. She turned her back, and tried to control herself. The memory was strong in her mind, too strong. *Oh, gods, don't make me remember. I don't want to remember.*

"Please," Torc said again, behind her. "Just tell me."

"I know what he was," said Laela, without turning around. "He told me. He let me touch his neck. I know he didn't have a heartbeat. An' I know that the Night God was his master. He told me that, too."

"Why?" Torc demanded. "Why tell you? Why trust you?"

Laela turned around. "I asked him that, an' he told me why." She smiled sadly. "Because we were both outcasts. The half-breed an' the heartless man."

"You're nothing like him," Torc spat. *"Nothing."*

"That's right." Laela lost her smile. "I ain't half as nice."

"Why did he run away?" said Torc. "Tell me that. He wouldn't run from a fight."

"He ran because he didn't want to fight no more," said Laela. "He knew there'd be civil war, an' he didn't want t'have to tear up what he made. He left that to me an Saeddryn," she added bitterly.

"Then where did you kill him?" Torc asked sharply.

"I didn't kill him," said Laela. "Are yeh stupid? D'yeh really think a little half-breed like me could kill *him*? The Dark Lord? The one no weapon could kill? He wasn't *mortal*."

"Then he's alive?"

"No. He's dead now."

"How?"

Laela hesitated. He wouldn't believe her, but she knew there was only one story she could tell. Anything else would make her the murderer.

She gave up and plunged ahead. "Only one thing could kill him, an' that's what made him. The Night God. She killed him."

Torc stared at her. "What?"

"She killed him. I saw it. She came down to us, all covered in light. She was angry with him. Said she told him to go invade the South, an' he didn't do what she said. He still wouldn't do it. He said he was tired of fightin', wanted peace for his Kingdom. She wanted him to kill me, but he wouldn't do that either. He wouldn't kill his own daughter. He turned on her. An' then the Night God killed him." Laela closed her eyes. "She said he was no more use, an' then she . . . reached into him, pulled out somethin' . . . all black and misty. Then she just threw him away, like garbage, an' left." A sob broke free. "I . . . I stood there an' watched his bones break an' all his old wounds open up. I held him in my arms, an' he died. There was nothin' I could do."

Torc said nothing for a long time. He looked bewildered and upset. "I don't believe you. That's just a lie . . . blasphemy. The Night God wouldn't . . ."

"How d'you know?" Laela snapped at him. "How do *you* know what she does? Have *you* seen her? Heard her voice? How d'yeh *know*? Yeh don't know, Torc. Yeh don't know nothin'. Yeh don't know how evil she is."

"Go away," Torc rasped. "I won't listen to this any more. Go away, half-breed. Your time is coming. The Taranisäiis won't accept someone like you pretending to be one of them. The Night God will strike you down."

All of Laela's pity for him disappeared. "Fine. Stay here, then. An' hope like mad that I don't find an excuse to give yeh a chance t'see the Night God yerself soon."

She stalked out, fighting back her own anger and tears. Outside in the corridor, she took a few moments to control herself and walked away rapidly, tight-lipped.

8

The Man-Griffin

"I shouldn't've talked to him like that," Laela mumbled later.

"No, you should not have," said Oeka. "He is a prisoner, not a friend!"

"He's family." Laela felt too wrung-out to be angry. "I was upset. I thought . . . if he saw me like that, heard the truth, maybe he'd understand."

"Blind hate understands nothing," Oeka snapped. "I smelt it on him like a rotting dog. You have learnt nothing."

"Not true." Laela raised her head. "I know how Saeddryn's thinkin' now. An' I know what she's gonna be tellin' people so they'll do what she says." She scowled.

"That is something, at least," said Oeka. "But Torc must know more. Have him tortured."

Laela felt queasy and said nothing.

Other than the interview with Torc, things were going well. The priestesses had finished their talk in the council chamber, and Gwenna had come to Laela to formally accept her offer. Laela had responded by immediately giving orders to the Master of Building to start designing a new Temple. In the meantime, a team of workmen had been organised to demolish the remains of the old one. The new High Priestess would be heavily involved with the rebuilding, along with her fellows. It should keep them busy for a while. Things were going smoothly.

For now, Laela could afford to relax and spend some time

with Kullervo. Hearing his story should help take her mind off things.

The shape-shifter arrived in good time, but when he walked in, she didn't recognise him for a moment. He'd washed and combed his hair, and more importantly had shaved off the beard. Without it, he looked much smaller and far less wild.

Laela stood up to meet him. "Well don't you look neat."

Kullervo grinned at her. "I couldn't eat with a Queen without tidying up first. How do I look?"

She inspected him. Under the beard was a young man, probably younger than herself. His black hair and pale skin made him look more or less Northern, along with the lanky, wiry build that made him look awkward. The hump on his back made him look even more awkward, but she was puzzled that he didn't hunch at all.

Kullervo caught her eye. "I know." He sighed. "It's the hump, isn't it?"

Laela started. "No! Yeh look fine. Them clothes fit yeh well."

"There's no need to be embarrassed," he said kindly. "Look." He pulled up the tunic that covered his back and turned around.

"Holy gods!" Laela said involuntarily.

Two long, spindly limbs sprouted out of Kullervo's shoulder-blades. They looked like enormous grey-pink fingers, covered in ugly red pits.

"My wings." Kullervo covered them hastily. "Sorry. I didn't mean to scare you. The feathers fall out when I change, but I can't make them go away."

"It's all right." Laela coughed. "Just gave me a shock. C'mon, sit down an' let's eat."

He took the seat she indicated, laughing at the look on her face. "I'd better not show you the tail."

"Yeah, I think I've seen enough." Laela considered a moment, then took a seat opposite Kullervo instead of her usual place at the head of the table. He blinked, and smiled.

They didn't speak while the food was served, but sat and watched each other. The stares weren't hostile, only curious, as they sized each other up.

"Go on, then," Laela said when they had begun eating. "Tell me about yerself."

Kullervo picked up a cup. He did it clumsily; the last joint of each finger was covered by a long talon. "I'd have trimmed them, but they won't grow back fast enough, and I'll need them soon," he said. "What did you want to know about me?"

Laela tried not to stare. "One thing I'm curious about is how yeh were born. I mean, were yeh born human, or griffin?"

"Both." Kullervo shrugged.

"All right then, who were yer parents? Human or griffin?"

"Both." He smirked.

"That ain't helpin', Kullervo."

"All right, I'm sorry." He tapped his talons on the table. "It's just . . . not easy to talk about."

"Oh. I'm sorry. Don't tell me if yeh don't want to. I'll ask somethin' else."

He frowned, coughed, then looked directly at her. "No, I'll tell you. It's simple enough. And it'll show you why I want to help you."

Laela listened.

"My mother was a griffin," said Kullervo. "When she was young, she committed a terrible crime. As punishment, another griffin changed her into a human woman. While she was in human shape, she took a human lover. I don't think they ever thought they could have children, but they did. She gave birth . . . but not to a baby."

Laela scratched her head. "What'd she give birth to, then?"

"An egg." Kullervo smiled slightly at her expression. "She cared for it, like any mother griffin would. But when it hatched, what came out was me."

"Human or griffin?" Laela was fascinated.

"Both." Kullervo lost his smile, and for the first time she saw lines of pain around his yellow eyes. "The egg hatched into something hideous. Deformed. Human head, griffin wings. Human legs, griffin talons. Fur and feathers, but no beak. A child stuck halfway between two shapes."

"Couldn't yeh change back then?"

"No. I was so horrible to look at that people were afraid of me." Kullervo said it quite matter-of-factly. "There was no way to tell what to feed me, or anything."

"What did yer mother do?"

"What every griffin does if her hatchling is deformed. She abandoned me and never talked about me ever again. I was dead to her, for the rest of her life."

"That's awful!" Laela said. "How could anyone do that to her own kid?"

"It's the griffish way," Kullervo said.

"It is," Oeka said from the floor. "Deformed hatchlings are no use and cannot survive."

"But I did," said Kullervo, without anger. "I was lucky."

"Lucky how?" said Laela.

He smiled again. "I had wings, and I was born in the South. People there believe that a winged man is a sacred messenger sent by Gryphus. When humans found me, they decided they should look after me. If they did, Gryphus would bring them good luck."

"Where did yeh grow up?" Laela asked.

"Many different places," said Kullervo. "When I was a year or so, old the people who found me took me to a city called Withypool. I survived there; people would pay to look at me. Scholars wanted to study me. Even some griffins wanted to look at me, to decide if I was one of them or not."

"What happened after that?"

"It took a long time for me to learn how to walk," said Kullervo. "The bones in my legs and my back weren't right. But I did it in the end. I lived in the fighting pits. That's where I got my name."

"What, they didn't give yeh a *name*?" Laela said.

"No. I was just the griffin-boy. Griffin-man, eventually. I remember an old woman who called me 'Griffy.'" Kullervo chuckled. "But I wanted a proper name. In the fighting pits, they told me about a famous griffin who defeated a powerful fighter even though he had a crippled leg. He was a great warrior all his life even though he could barely walk. I liked that story, and so I named myself after him. Kullervo."

"It's a good name," said Laela.

"I like it," said Kullervo. "I didn't stay in Withypool, though. I wanted to."

"Why'd yeh leave, then?"

"There was a plague," he said. "People were dying everywhere. I didn't know if I could catch it; I never did, though. The people who cared for me died, and so many others. So I left. And then, one day . . ."

"One day what?" Laela prompted.

He laughed softly. "My magic woke up."

"Yeh mean like how a griffin's . . . ?"

"Yes. When a griffin is old enough, he discovers his power. Mine is the power to change my shape; push either way to be fully human or fully griffin." He smiled, blissfully. "I could fly at last. Had to learn first, though."

"An' then yeh came here?"

"When I felt ready," said Kullervo. "And then I met you. I didn't know what to do at first, but when I met you, I wanted to help you."

Silence.

"It's not easy being a half-breed," Kullervo said quietly. "Is it?"

"Harder for you than me," said Laela.

"But when I came here, I saw at least one of us had done well." He reached across the table, and awkwardly tried to take her hand. "The world will never be kind to people like us, Laela. We can never belong. Not unless we fight for it. But the way I see it is that it's always easier when you're not alone. Isn't it?"

She looked into his odd, sad face, and felt a lump in her throat. "Yeah," she said huskily.

Kullervo withdrew his hand. "You and me, Laela," he said. "We can show them what us half-breeds can do."

"You bet we will," Laela said. "That was an amazin' story, Kullervo. An' a sad one. I wish . . . I wish things could've been better for yeh. I really do."

"The past is the past," he said. "The future will be better. That's what I've always believed. For example, the future will include my eating *this*. And that'll be much better than just looking at it was."

Laela laughed as he stuffed the piece of cheese in his mouth. "I love it!" She picked up her cup. "Here's to the future. Bigger an' better than anythin' else the past had to offer!"

Kullervo grinned and downed his drink. "Exactly."

"Now then," Laela said later on, when the food was gone.

"When yeh got here, yeh said somethin' about lookin' for a woman called Skade."

"Oh." Kullervo looked away. "Yes, I did."

"Can I ask why yeh were lookin' for her?"

"I was curious about her," said Kullervo. "I heard she was born in Withypool. People talked about her yellow eyes, like mine. I suppose I always felt close to her. I knew she had gone to Malvern, and I thought if I said I was looking for her, it would stop people thinking I was a spy."

"Shame she's dead," said Laela. "I would've liked to meet her. Sounds like she was as mean as I am."

"Yes . . ." Kullervo muttered. "They called her the wild woman of Withypool."

"I can show yeh her tomb," Laela said.

"Really?"

"Yeah, I know where it is. I'll take yeh down now if yeh like."

"I *would* like that," Kullervo said.

"C'mon, then."

Laela knew the way well enough; she'd visited the crypt once or twice since her father had first showed it to her. She escorted Kullervo down there and told him a bit about it along the way.

"I remember when I first saw it. It was when I was stayin' in the Eyrie with my father . . . didn't know he was my father then, though. One night he came to see me. He was drunk." She cringed at the memory. "Poor bastard drank every night. Couldn't sleep, see? Couldn't forget what he'd done. Couldn't forget her. So he takes me down here, says he's got somethin' to show me. For a while I thought he was gonna kill me. But instead he showed me—this." She opened the door and took a lantern in.

Kullervo followed her to the stone tomb, with the statue of the woman lying on it. "Is this . . . her?"

"Yeah." Laela ran her fingers over the cold grey face. "Skade. I still remember my father standin' here, touchin' her face like it was real. He said he couldn't bear that she was gone, he still loved her an' he wanted her back more than anythin'. But he never could have her back, an' it destroyed him."

Kullervo lingered over the face. "She looks . . . fierce. But beautiful."

Laela didn't think there was any beauty in it at all, only unkindness. "The only one the Dark Lord loved," she said, half to herself. "Or so they say."

Kullervo barely glanced up; he seemed entranced by the statue. "Can I stay here for a while?"

Laela cocked an eyebrow. "All right, if yeh want. I'll leave the lamp."

Alone with the likeness of the dead woman, Kullervo heaved a sigh. "So this is where he came," he said aloud. "To mourn, when so many others had lost everything because of him."

He touched the face, his talons tracing the sharp features and cruel eyes. Eyes that were too big, too slanted.

He lifted the lantern, hooking it with his talons, and moved it further down, searching. There were the hands, folded over the stomach. He examined them and hissed to himself.

Each long finger was tipped by a small claw, perfectly rendered in the stone.

Breathing hard, Kullervo took a step back. He almost left but stopped himself.

"I have to know," he whispered.

He put the lantern down and felt around the edges of the tomb. There was a join, sure enough. He worked his talons into the gap and lifted hard. It shifted ever so slightly, but instantly settled back into place.

Kullervo crouched at the base of the tomb, took a moment to brace himself, and put all his strength into it. Muscles bulged in his back and arms. He breathed in deeply and shoved even harder, not giving an inch.

At last, the lid moved. He continued to work at it, teeth gritted. On his back, the wings flared upward, pointing toward the ceiling.

The tomb opened with a grinding of stone and a gasp from Kullervo. He shoved the lid aside, leaving it half-on, and finally let himself rest. A blast of cold air escaped from the dark space inside, and he shuddered when the smell of old bones hit his nostrils.

He snatched up the lamp and shined it into the tomb.

The hollow skull of a griffin stared back.

Kullervo breathed in sharply. He almost started to laugh again. “It’s true. Gryphus help me, it’s true. *You*.”

He reached into the tomb and lifted the skull out. It came easily, dry skin and feathers still clinging in places. In the flickering light, the empty sockets seemed to wink at him.

Kullervo stared at it for a time, then hugged it to his chest. He slid down the side of the tomb and onto the floor, holding the skull close, and let out a sob. “Oh, gods . . . it’s all true. It *was* you.”

Only the silence answered him. The silence that had been there all his life.

Kullervo’s grip tightened on the skull.

“This is my place,” he said. “I should have come here years ago. Then I might not have been too late. But what could I have told him? What would *he* have done? Welcomed me?” he spat. “As if he would have been proud. Of *me*.”

Silence.

Tears dripped onto the skull.

Kullervo lifted it, so he could look at it face-to-face. “You abandoned me, Mother. But I won’t abandon her. Because I—” he sobbed, and lost his voice for a moment—“I still have a life, and so does she. You left me to die, but I didn’t. I never will. Life is mine, Mother. The life *you* lost. And I’ll keep it, no matter what.” He stood up abruptly and put the skull back into the tomb. “The past is dead. Long live the future. Long live the half-breed Queen.”

This time, moving the lid felt like nothing. Kullervo took a moment to wipe the tears away and breathed deeply to calm himself. Now he knew the truth, and that was enough. He had a place now, and a home—a *real* home, and a real friend who could help him.

But still . . .

The question followed him out of the crypt and back up into the tower. *Should I tell her I’m her brother?*

9

Leaving

That night, Kullervo paced back and forth in the disused room that had been given to him, and talked to himself—a habit he'd had for most of his life.

"Should I stay, or go? I want to stay. It's home. It should be. Could be. She doesn't trust me yet. Not enough. That griffin hates me. Won't trust me no matter what I say. Got to do it some other way. Be useful, Kullervo. Prove yourself. Danger's here, anyway. Deal with danger, get trust. Simple."

He sighed and sat down. His skin itched all over his legs and back. That was always a bad sign. He rolled up the leg of his trousers, and saw the tiny strands of fur prickling through the skin. His body, at least, had made up its mind. Time to go, then.

Kullervo left the room without another pause and went to work.

Small spikes had thrust out all over his chest and stomach. Soon, they would split open into new feathers. His entire head and face ached dully. He checked his exposed skin and hastily pulled out a feather-spike that had appeared on his neck. Time was short.

There was only one thing left to do, and that was find the High Priestess' quarters. He stopped the first person he met and asked for directions.

"Why should I tell ye?" the person asked said, suspiciously. "Who are ye, anyway?"

Kullervo opened his mouth to begin a polite response.

What came out instead was a low, venomous griffin hiss. *"Tell me."*

The unlucky servant turned the colour of milk pudding. "Council Tower. Close to the top. There's a moon on the door."

Kullervo let him go and set out as fast as he could. Walking was becoming difficult. He could feel the bones in his feet shifting. Fortunately, he knew where the Council Tower was, and he was already in one of the upper levels of the tower he was in at the moment. He had always had a good sense of direction, and he found the nearest of the covered bridges that linked the towers and used it to enter the Council Tower. Inside, he went upward, inspecting door after door until he found the one with the silver-inlaid moon carved on it. He rasped to himself and turned the handle—not easy, with the talons in the way.

Locked.

Kullervo hissed. Yet again he could feel the rage building up inside him, sending signals to the gland that controlled his magic. It put more power into his system, and he groaned as dozens of new feathers spiked out all over his body. Hidden inside a trouser-leg, his tail twitched and darkened with fur.

Fighting against the transformation now taking him over, he slammed into the door shoulder first. It shifted slightly. Snarling, he threw himself against it, using the effort to make the feeling go away—that terrible, animal ferocity that wanted to twist him into its own shape.

The lock broke, and the door swung open. Panting, Kullervo went inside.

As soon as he entered, the smell hit him. It was just like the opening of the tomb. But this was an alive smell—stale, but alive. Other scents mingled with it, but he picked up the strongest one, the territorial one, and isolated it. He limped over to the bed and lifted the covers, taking in the odour. Human, female, elderly. *Not good for food,* said the griffish side of him.

He smiled to himself and moved on into the nest. There he picked up a stray feather from the straw, and ran it back and forth over his nostrils. Male, this griffin. Male, and powerfully magical. Kullervo put the feather into his tunic, and returned to the bedroom. A torn piece of sheet soon joined the feather. He paused to help himself to a dagger and a belt, and left.

There was no time to return to his quarters, so he ran off helter-skelter through the tower, searching desperately for a quiet place, any place. Every room was occupied. Panicking now, he sprinted into the first linking bridge he found, and into another tower. He didn't know this one, but it was almost deserted. Every room he looked into was full of crates and boxes.

A storage place. Perfect.

He chose a room at random and shut himself in. A heavy box ensured that no-one would open the door, and he stumbled into a corner and lay down, gasping for breath. Safe.

Kullervo could feel the skin on his hands and arms thickening. Soon, it would begin breaking apart to make scales. His spine hurt hideously.

Fumbling with the cloth, he pulled his clothes off. Underneath, his skin was mottled with patches of grey fur and feather. Freed, his wings stood out proudly. Long spines had begun to appear, ready to form the flight feathers.

Kullervo's hands felt wrong. The bones were lengthening and shifting position under the skin, making a pair of griffin paws. Moving fast, he wrapped the dagger in his clothes, and used the belt to tie it up.

And not a moment too soon. He had scarcely finished, when agonising pain rippled down from his head to the end of his tail. He went rigid with it, teeth clamped together. Tears streamed down his face, stinging the wounds Oeka had left on his cheek. With a clumsy, jerking motion, he thrust the bundle out of the way and fell onto his side. For a while, he lay still, then he began to twitch as the transformation really began.

His spine cracked, twisting into a new shape that sent a jolt straight through his tail. He moaned, able to hear the grinding of bones as his feet extended, stretching out into paws. On his back, muscles bulged out, connecting to the bones and joints in his wings, strengthening them for flight.

That wasn't the worst.

An almighty crack split the air, so loud it sounded like the breaking of a tree. Kullervo let out an unearthly scream, and his lower back appeared to fold inward and downward as his pelvis broke and re-formed into something narrower, made for four-legged walking.

His scream continued, and rose as the very worst part

came. The bones in his skull separated, plate by plate, flexing unnaturally until they showed through the skin. They thrust forward, distorting his face and shifting his eyes to either side of his head. His teeth melted together and pushed out of his mouth, fusing into a beak that swallowed up his nose, leaving two fleshy holes at the base.

After that, Kullervo fainted, but his magic continued to work, busily reshaping his body. His skin put forth thick fur, and feathers. His ears sank into his head, leaving only the very tips, which sprouted long plumes that pointed back toward his wings. His arms became scaled from the elbow downward, while his feet had become padded like a cat's.

The whole transformation took most of the night, and when it was over, it left Kullervo the grey griffin huddled on the floor like a dead thing.

It was past noon the next day when Kullervo woke up, and when he did, pain greeted him. His entire body ached and throbbed like one big wound.

He opened his eyes a crack and waited until the world came back into focus. Things looked different through griffish eyes. Colours were warped. Objects far away were easy to see; objects up close were incredibly detailed. Any sort of motion caught his attention immediately.

His body was too weak to move yet, so he lay completely still and occupied himself by taking in everything in view. His brain still felt muddled, so he exercised it by searching through his memory. He remembered the scents of Saeddryn and Aenae, and he used them to build a picture in his head. Human and griffin. One would be far more dangerous than the other. But finding them would be good. He could see so much of Tara on his search. This was the land his father had ruled, and where he had died. Now he, Kullervo, would make it his home. Homes were things that had to be understood in order to be homes. Yes. Important.

Kullervo closed his eyes again and slept.

When he woke up the next time, he felt much better but ravenously hungry. Nothing left for it, then. He flexed his new limbs, hearing the cracks as the bones settled into place.

Everything seemed to work. He got up laboriously and shook himself. That felt good.

Griffish instincts told him to groom, so he did. When his feathers were in order, he folded his wings and walked slowly around the room, testing his legs. They worked fine, but he still felt weak. Food was the only thing that could help.

He made for the door, his head full of images of fresh, bleeding meat.

A large, heavy box blocked his way.

While he was shoving it aside, he remembered the bundle and darted back to pick it up. With the belt dangling from his beak, he put his chest against the box and pushed again. It slid aside, and he shoved the door open and went out into the passageway.

The scent of food led him to another room, far below the bottom level in an underground chamber where it was cool. Dried sides of meat hung from the roof.

Kullervo's mind blanked out. When he came to, he found himself in the middle of the floor, gulping down enormous chunks of meat. He had broken the ribs underneath, and shards of bone were going down, too. It hurt, but he hadn't seemed to notice.

The more human part of Kullervo's mind idled, not needing to do anything while the animal gorged itself. It would have been too hard to do anything anyway; the animal part of his mind overwhelmed the human part with waves of such intense pleasure that thinking too much about it seemed like blasphemy.

Eventually, the feast ended, and Kullervo lay down—stomach visibly bulging—and rested. He could feel the food already being digested inside him, feeding new energy into his system. Eventually, it would replenish his magic. Until then, becoming human again was impossible. Not that he wanted to do it. He had already decided to stay in griffin form as long as he could. It made him feel so much stronger. And being able to fly . . .

He huffed happily to himself. *Soon, very soon.*

Laela was up on top of the Council Tower, enjoying the view, when Kullervo arrived. He shot up over the tower with a loud and joyful shriek, so fast she almost missed him.

She backed away, looking upward, and saw him loop and dive in the air high above. The sun hit her eyes, and she narrowed them and looked away.

Kullervo finally came down to land—clumsily. He hit the ground unevenly and tottered sideways before recovering himself, but unlike an ordinary griffin, he didn't try to act as though nothing had happened, or groom himself to get back some dignity. Instead, he turned to face her, breathing hard but full of energy. If he'd been human, he would have been grinning. "Flying!" he said. "I love it!"

Laela couldn't help but laugh at him. "Ain't really tried it myself, but it looks like fun."

"Being able to fly makes me much happier to be what I am," Kullervo said solemnly.

"That's good," said Laela. Beside her, Oeka snorted and walked away with a flick of her tail.

"Now," said Kullervo. "It's time. I'm ready to leave. I came here to say goodbye and see if you had anything else to tell me."

Laela rubbed her chin. "We ain't got much idea where she mighta gone, but my gut says she's hidin' in the mountains."

"Which mountains?"

"Er . . . come to that, I dunno if they got a name. But there's a gorge an' a stone circle, called Taranis' Throne. Here, I got a map for yeh."

She unrolled it for him and held it up.

"I see," he said eventually. "There's Malvern, and I can see the mountains I flew over to come here. So the other mountains are up North, then?"

"Yeah." Laela examined the map. "Hey, there's a name on this thing. "The . . . First . . . Mountains. What, that's what they're called? Huh. Odd name. Anyway, that's the ones yeh wanna go have a look at. The gorge oughta be easy to find; it's right near the flat part where the stones are. Can yeh read maps all right?"

"I can. May I take it with me?"

"Sure, but I dunno where yer gonna put it," said Laela.

Kullervo lifted the bundle he had brought with him. "Tuck it into the belt."

"Good idea." Laela loosened the belt slightly and stuffed the map underneath. "Lucky it's made outta leather. There yeh go."

"Thank you." Kullervo put his head on one side. "I'll find this traitor for you, Laela. I swear. All I want in return is to be your friend."

Without even meaning to, Laela smiled wistfully. "I can always use another friend."

"So could I."

She couldn't stop herself from coming over and hugging him around the neck. "I do know how yeh feel," she whispered in his ear. "I really do."

Kullervo lifted a foreleg and clumsily held her to him. "I need you, Laela. I've been alone in the world far too long. Please, just don't leave me. Please."

She pulled away, suddenly embarrassed. "Come back soon, Kullervo. Don't make me worry about yeh."

"Don't worry about me," he said. "I'm stronger than I look. Good luck!" With that, he scooped up his precious bundle and flew away.

"Good luck to you, too!" Laela called after him. "I—" She stopped and turned sharply, as something moved past her.

It was Oeka. The small griffin stood in an awkward half-crouching stance, with her eyes fixed on the retreating Kullervo. She was hissing.

"What's up with you?" Laela asked irritably. By now she was heartily sick of her partner's constant sour behaviour.

Oeka looked back at her, narrow-eyed. "I am done with this," she said. "Keep your guards close, and hope that they are enough. I have wasted far too much time standing over you like a nesting mother."

"What are yeh talkin' about—?" Laela began.

Oeka drew her talons over the stonework, leaving four long, pale lines. "You ignore me, you argue with me, you say you do not need me. Clearly, I am no use to you. If that is true, then so be it. You may rule your territory—without me."

Laela took a step toward her. "No, wait—stop! Don't leave—!"

Oeka looked back coolly, through her dark green eyes. "Try not to die," she said, and leapt into the sky.

10

Bones, Spirits, and Caves

Kullervo didn't hear Laela's half-screamed yell of dismay. His ears were full of wind, and he was far too excited to be paying much attention anyway. He soared up and over Malvern, loving the feel of the wind in his feathers. The lands of Tara spread out ahead, inviting him to explore. He forgot all about his promise to Laela and set out.

Beyond the city were green fields, split by a winding brown snake of road. Other griffins flew here and there, straying beyond the city walls, but Kullervo ignored them. He could see the distant shapes of forests far in the distance, and he struck out toward them.

So this was the land his father had ruled. From the stories he had heard during his childhood, he'd always thought they would be snowbound and freezing. But though the air was cold, the landscape itself didn't look much different than the many others he had seen in his life. Above, the sky was grey, threatening rain, but he thought it made everything look silvery. Timeless.

Beautiful.

With a griffin's shape came a griffin's senses and instincts. They included a strong sense of direction. Kullervo knew how to find North—any child could do it. But as a griffin it was different. The four directions were so important in his mind that he sensed them rather than sought them out and found himself keeping to a northward course without even thinking about it. He had been able to change his shape for some years now, but this was only the second time he had flown any great distance. Despite that, he found himself obeying other instincts—noting landmarks below him, constantly checking both sky and land for any threat. And for prey.

As time passed, he saw villages, and cities built around the river. Mentally, he ticked off the places he recognised from the map. Wolf's Town, not far from the place where the river forked. Warwick, dark and walled. Fruitsheart, off in the distance by a huge lake.

It took him most of the day to reach Warwick, and though he was tempted to land there and scout things out, he was still determined to see the First Mountains before he did anything else. Besides, he was tired out and going into a potentially dangerous city now was a bad idea.

He landed in a nearby forest instead. He was hungry, but there was no food about, so he drank from a pool and slept, safely, in the branches of a tree.

Next morning, he awoke, desperate for food. Fortunately, Laela had told him that Warwick's lands were full of sheep, and he had taken that into account while planning his journey. Keeping a safe distance from the city itself, he visited one of the farming villages in the hills around it and filched a sheep from an unattended flock.

The griffish side of him was more than happy to eat it raw. In this shape, the hot, bleeding meat tasted wonderful, and Kullervo savoured every piece.

Re-energised, he flew on before the sheep could be missed, moving straight on toward the mountains, which were already looming large on the horizon.

He reached them just after midday. But when he arrived, it was to find something unexpected.

At the foot of the mountains, there was a tower. No city—not even a village—just a solitary tower, tall and solid, thrusting into the sky like a pointing finger.

Kullervo flew straight to it and circled around, examining it with fascination. It looked like a griffiner tower, but there were no doors at its base, and only one opening, right at the top. The whole thing was made from dark grey stone, flecked with silver mica, and as far as he could see there were no other signs of civilisation for miles around.

Once he was certain it was safe, he landed on the tower's flat top and rested. The stones were flat and well joined, warm from the sun even though a cold wind was blowing down from the mountains. He found a hole in the centre, with a ramp leading down. It was huge, obviously made for griffins, and he cautiously went through it.

It led to an enormous, round room, one so big that it obviously filled the entire top level of the tower. The solitary opening he had seen earlier led into it, but there was no way down to a lower level—just the ramp leading to the roof and the one arched exit meant for a griffin.

The room had no furniture but was instead meant to be a gigantic griffin nest, with straw and dry grass piled everywhere. There was an oversized, rounded water trough, fed by a pipe from the roof. It gleamed in the light from the opening.

Kullervo went closer and clicked his beak in astonishment. "Gold! It's gold!"

He tapped the shining trough, and, sure enough, the yellow surface dented slightly under his beak-tip. Not just gold but pure gold.

Fascinated, Kullervo explored further. There were no fresh scents here—no sign that anything had lived here recently other than the odd bird. He found bones scattered among the nesting material, most of them cracked into pieces. At one time, at least, a griffin had lived here.

But what griffin would be great enough to have a roost like this?

The afternoon sun, drifting downward to shine through the opening, gave Kullervo his answer eventually.

Shadows appeared on the wall opposite the opening, cast there by the light. Kullervo looked upward, and saw the words cut into the stone. They had even been inlaid with silver.

SKANDAR'S TOWER.

Kullervo chirped to himself, in amazement. "The Mighty Skandar! This was his place! So . . ." He turned, looking again at the golden trough, the mouldering nest and the shattered bones. "So this was . . ."

He lay on his belly, and made a wheezing noise.

"So the great King Arenadd made this place for his partner. Another home, by the mountains. They must have been his favourite place. How many times did he come here? Did they come together, to be away from Malvern? Were they . . . happy here?"

A hiss escaped from Kullervo's chest. He stood up, his tail swishing from side to side. With a loud scream, he smashed his head against the water trough. The gold dented and cracked, and he struck again, and again, until a piece of it broke away.

Not seeming to notice the blood welling in his eye, Kullervo bounded toward the wall and reared up, setting his talons into the words that stood out there.

He snarled, and pulled downward with all his might. His talons curved and snagged on the stone, leaving rows of ugly scratches that tore the silver out of the carving.

Kullervo turned and stalked out, up the ramp, and out of the tower.

The cool air calmed him down. He scored his talons through his chest-feathers, and impulsively took to the air. Flying would make him feel better.

He circled for a time, until his heartbeat had slowed. But the joy and excitement of his journey was gone now, and he set out toward the mountains without ceremony, wanting to finish what he had set out to do and be done with it.

On a wide plateau, not far into the mountains, he found Taranis' Throne. Thirteen dark stones jutted out of the snow like jagged teeth, forming a circle around another stone. This one lay on its side, flat-topped like a table. Kullervo landed on it and peered around at the stones, taking in the elaborate spiral carvings cut into them.

The stones were weathered, pitted and smoothed by the wind. To Kullervo, they looked as if they had stood there since the beginning of time itself. They were sacred, these stones, and his griffish senses picked up the feeling of magic in them and the earth they ringed.

Soon, Kullervo began to feel uneasy. The silence in the circle became oppressive and threatening, and the stones seemed to rise higher, making bars of shadow on the snow around the altar where he perched.

His fur stood on end.

Kullervo flew up and out of the circle as quickly as he could. He went in search of Taranis Gorge instead, but it proved a little harder to find. The plateau dropped away on three sides, and there were plenty of valleys around it. Which one was the gorge he was meant to find?

Confused, he landed on a mountainside ledge and put his bundle of possessions down in front of himself. The map was still there, tucked securely under the belt. He gripped the bundle in his talons and tugged at the map with his beak. The leather kept slipping free when he pulled on it. After several tries, he pierced it with the tip of his beak and yanked it free, pinning it down before it could blow away.

Fumbling with his talons, he unfolded the map and held it open, peering at the lines and text on it. The griffish side of him found the map perplexing and couldn't grasp the concept of reading the place-names on it. No griffin could read, or had the ability to learn how.

Using human-like abilities now was hard, but Kullervo had practised. He concentrated hard, ignoring the griffin's insistence that the marks meant nothing, and wrestled the meaning out of them. There was the circle—*Taranis' Throne,* he repeated mentally. *Circle means stones. Throne.* And there, to one side of it, a dark mark and a label. *Gorge. Mark there . . . means Gorge. To . . . West. Sunward.*

Kullervo turned to face west, and let himself relax. The map had told him what he needed to know.

He did his best to put the map back, but it quickly proved to be impossible. Griffin talons were simply far too clumsy to manage it. Irritated, he lifted the bundle in his beak and took the map in his talons. One forepaw would now be hampered, and he hoped he wouldn't run into any danger. If he did, the map was lost.

The gorge, at least, was easy to find now. He flew low over it, watching the ground for any sign of movement. If Saeddryn and Aenae were indeed here, then Aenae would attack him the moment he got too close. The big griffin's territorial instinct would be the first thing he acted on when he saw an intruder, regardless of what he and his human had planned.

Kullervo flew back and forth several times, braced for an assault.

None came. He flew even lower, until his back paws brushed against the treetops. Still nothing—

A cry split the silence. Panic-stricken, Kullervo turned clumsily on one wing and wheeled away from the source. He recovered and turned in the air, looking quickly for the sight of another griffin coming at him.

He saw nothing, but, moments later, the cry came again. It was the harsh, piercing scream of an adult male griffin—not the customary territorial call but the much more frightening screech of a griffin challenging another to a fight.

Wisely, Kullervo didn't return the cry and accept the challenge. He flew higher, ready to flee, but didn't leave. He searched desperately for any sign of another griffin, knowing that unless he saw Aenae with his own eyes, there would be no proof that he had found what he was looking for.

The cry came a third time, and even though the aggressive griffin didn't come flying up to the attack, Kullervo finally spotted him. There, in the side of a mountain, was a cave. The griffin was standing in the entrance with his wings spread, screaming violence at the hovering Kullervo.

It was not Aenae.

Kullervo hovered uncertainly, torn between fleeing and staying to look closer. But his fear gradually receded when he realised that, despite his screaming threats, the other griffin hadn't moved. Even from here, Kullervo could see that it wasn't Aenae. He knew what Aenae looked like—he had memorised the description of him. This was a griffin of monstrous size, dark and silvery, with a jet-black beak and an enormous wing-span.

Skandar.

Kullervo faltered as the obvious conclusion arrived. This had to be Skandar. What other griffin had this coat, this massive frame? What other griffin would be hiding here, in a place the Mighty Skandar had lived before, with his human?

Kullervo circled around over the cave. Below, Skandar continued his abuse. Now there were words in among the screechings and snarlings.

"You go! Go or die! Mighty Skandar kill! Kill you!"

Kullervo knew all too well what Skandar was capable of, and what he could and would do to anyone who made him angry or disobeyed him. But he stayed where he was, kept there by the knowledge of what finding Skandar meant. Skandar must know the answers to questions Laela had avoided. Answers that could change everything. Of all the people in Tara, only Laela and Skandar had been present when King Arenadd had supposedly died. Laela refused to talk about what had happened.

But perhaps Skandar would be different.

Kullervo could taste it now—the sense of something that had defined the world for him all his life. His father. The giant griffin down there, threatening to kill him, could lead Kullervo to the man he had missed since childhood. To him, it meant more than the Kingdom or Laela, or his quest, or anything else. Even the extreme danger he was about to put himself in didn't matter.

And that was why Kullervo tilted himself downward, and flew straight toward the cave. "Mighty Skandar!" he called. "I am your servant—"

That was as far as he got. Skandar shot out of his cave like a boulder out of a catapult. He came straight at Kullervo's chest and throat, and his intention was plainly not to hurt, or drive away, but to kill.

In the end, only Kullervo's small size saved him. Instinctively, he struck the air with his wings and shot straight upward and over Skandar's head. The wind from the giant griffin's wings filled Kullervo's, and he used the momentum to fly away as fast as he could. Skandar chased him, but though he was terrifyingly fast for his bulk, Kullervo was faster and more agile, and he just barely managed to flick his tail out of Skandar's reaching beak.

Skandar might still have caught him, but before they had gone too far, he abruptly broke off the chase and flew away. When Kullervo risked turning back to investigate, he saw that Skandar had gone back to his cave.

He landed in the branches of a pine tree and gasped for breath. His mouth tasted of blood.

Fortunately, he'd managed to keep hold of his precious bundle, and he deposited it in a fork of the tree before settling down to rest. When he was calmer, he started to think.

Something didn't make sense here. Why was Skandar so reluctant to leave the cave? Even if he had chosen this as his new territory, no griffin would turn back like that if there was another male about.

There had to be something important in the cave, and Kullervo resolved to find out what.

But how?

Briefly, he considered changing back into a man. Maybe Skandar would see his resemblance to his own human and be prepared to listen.

Kullervo rejected that idea very quickly. In human form, he would be even more defenceless, and would have no easy way to escape. And the transformation would leave him too weak to change again without plenty of food and rest. In these mountains, the chances of finding a good meal were beyond tiny.

It had to be the griffin shape, then. But what could he do?

Eventually, hunger stirring in his stomach gave the answer. Skandar would have to leave his cave sooner or later if he wanted to eat. All Kullervo had to do was wait.

But first things first. He tucked the map away with the rest of his belongings and flew away from the tree to hunt.

Kullervo had never been a very good hunter, but patience and several failures finally won him a feral goat. He carried it back to his tree and ate it before he went to begin his vigil.

He found a vantage-point on the side of a mountain not far from Skandar's cave, and there he settled down, his eyes fixed on the cave-mouth.

There was no sign of Skandar. He must be inside.

Kullervo waited.

He waited through the night and into the next morning. During that time Skandar only left his cave once, very briefly, to drink from a small pool at the base of the mountain. He was within sight of the cave the entire time and returned to it instantly. After that, he did not emerge again.

Kullervo didn't give up. He stayed where he was, not even leaving to drink. The pool was too close to Skandar's cave for comfort, and he didn't want to be seen.

But Skandar did not come out.

Kullervo groomed himself to occupy his time. When he eventually started to get hungry again, he fought it down, reminding himself that Skandar must be hungrier. The only question was who had the most endurance.

Nearly two entire days passed before Skandar finally left his cave. The dozing Kullervo woke up with a jolt to the sound of massive wing-beats, and nearly died of fright when the shadow fell over him. He scrambled to his paws, but the shadow passed over and was gone, and as he looked upward, he saw Skandar flying away over the mountains.

Kullervo hissed his triumph and opened his wings. He beat them a few times to work out the stiffness and flew toward the cave without a moment's delay.

The moment he landed at the lip of the cave, a foul stench punched him in the gullet.

Nostrils burning, he took a few hesitant steps inside.

The space was comparatively small—it was hard to imagine how Skandar had managed to fit inside. It was also far less impressive than he had imagined; all jagged rock and cold wind. And that smell . . .

At the far end of the cave, he could see something lying on the floor. He moved toward it, and the smell grew and thickened until he could almost taste it. He had already guessed what he was going to find.

It was a rotting human corpse.

Kullervo nosed at it, examining it as closely as he dared. The body wore a mouldering pair of leggings that had turned a sickly brownish colour, and boots whose leather had cracked and peeled open in the damp. Everything else was exposed.

He could see the pale flesh, bloated and split, the limbs bent and twisted in ways that showed the broken bones through decaying muscle. There wasn't much left of the face at all. The eyes had disappeared into their sockets, and the skin had worn away to show the skull beneath. The lips had drawn back over the teeth in a twisted snarl.

But there was enough left for Kullervo to see. Enough black bristles still clinging to the chin, enough long, curly strands of hair left to stir in the wind.

Kullervo looked at the dead, sneering face whose empty sockets seemed to stare back, and felt sick and afraid.

All his life he had tried to imagine how his father would look at him when they finally met, and now he knew. King Arenadd had greeted his son with a smile.

* * *

Kullervo rested by his father's body for a while, fighting back the human tears that the griffin's mind rejected.

Despite his hesitation, he knew what he had to do. The King's remains must be taken back to Malvern. They were the proof Laela needed that he was indeed dead. And they should be properly buried as well. Whatever Arenadd had been, he deserved a proper resting-place.

Kullervo pushed away the emotions threatening to force his body to change shape and stood up. He wrapped his talons around the body and began to drag it toward the entrance.

Something snagged on an outcrop, and the corpse tore open with a sick, wet noise. Instantly, the smell burst out, a thousand times more powerful than before.

Kullervo let go of the disintegrating body and stumbled away. He vomited, and the stench of acid joined the miasma.

The shape-shifter couldn't take it any more. He turned away toward the entrance, and there was the Mighty Skandar, blocking his way.

The monstrous, dark griffin didn't move. Here, in this confined space, he looked twice as big as before. His slab-like shoulders brushed the ceiling, higher than the heavy, streamlined head and pitted black beak.

Kullervo flattened himself against the ground, openly cringing under Skandar's gaze. "No, please don't . . ."

Skandar took in Arenadd's stinking remains and the small griffin cowering in front of him. His chest and flanks seemed to inflate, and a slow hiss filled the cave.

"Mine."

Kullervo backed away. "Please, Mighty Skandar, I am your servant. I meant no—"

"MINE!" Skandar screamed. "My human, mine!"

There was no room for a leap. Skandar made a horribly fast, scrabbling charge, straight at Kullervo.

The shape-shifter's mind shut down, man and griffin. He tried to back away, but there was nowhere to go. Slipping in the rotting flesh under his paws, he pressed himself against the cave wall.

A shocking blow to his face smashed his head against rock. He ducked to avoid the next one, and stupidly ran straight at

Skandar. One talon caught in a crack, and he felt it snap clean off as he shoved between the raging monster's forelegs and crawled under his belly. With no room to manoeuvre, Skandar wriggled backward to try to catch him, but he was too slow. Kullervo burst out and into the open air.

But Skandar would not be escaped again. He freed himself from the cave and whirled around, rearing onto his hind legs.

One massive talon hooked into Kullervo's haunches. Chunks of fur and hide came away and the smaller griffin was hurled onto the lip of the cave. Something inside him cracked, but there was no time to tell what. Before the pain had even registered Skandar was on him. One hind leg twisted and screamed agony at him, and an enormous crushing grip closed around the base of his wing.

Kullervo screeched and flailed helplessly, unable to pull free. He kicked backward with his good hind leg, catching the giant griffin in the chest, but he might as well have kicked a boulder. Skandar shook him mercilessly, like a dog with a rat, and hurled him down the mountainside.

Kullervo never knew how he managed not to fall to his death. He tumbled head over tail, bashing into rocks, too confused to know what to do, and in the end it was pure griffinish instinct that saved him. He rolled over a rock and into space, and his wings opened out of pure reflex, and beat hard.

Some inner voice screamed that his wing was broken, he couldn't fly, his body had been torn apart, he couldn't fly, shouldn't fly . . .

But he flew. Blindly, maddened by fear, he flew.

Maybe Skandar chased him. Maybe he let him go. But there were no more attacks. He had escaped.

11

Oeka's Choice

Oeka *had* heard Laela's cry, but she ignored it. She turned her back on Malvern and flew southward as fast as she could. To Laela, it must have looked like she was fleeing, and in a sense she was. For a griffin, every journey was a flight anyway.

Oeka had never really flown any great distance before. She had spent her early life entirely in Malvern's Hatchery with the other unpartnered griffins and had never had any reason to leave—at least until she had chosen Laela.

Life in the Hatchery was competitive and often rough. Unpartnered griffins were given all their basic needs, but nothing else, and the only special privileges were got by being able to dominate the others. Normally, a youngster like Oeka would be at the bottom of the pecking order, but she was different.

Other griffins became able to use their magic when they reached maturity, or sometimes even older than that.

Not Oeka. Her powers had begun to emerge when she was scarcely a year old. They had been weak back then, but they were more than enough to win her respect and allow her to dominate the other hatchlings. As she grew, so did her gifts. Her talents were rare and special, and she knew it.

She had always believed that she would have a human one day—and only the best would be enough. None of the ones she saw were enough, no matter how much potential they had or how much importance they had already earned. Oeka had ignored them all, and eventually her real ambition had emerged. The only human she would choose would be nothing less than the heir to Malvern's throne. She had intended to choose one of Saeddryn's two children, but both were claimed before Oeka's chance came.

And then Laela had come. On that day, even though Oeka hadn't known the King's secret plans, something had happened. The moment she saw her—this one, this half-breed companion to the King—the small griffin had sensed something. Some voice, some part of her magic that had been hidden until then, showed itself.

Uncertain, Oeka had attacked the human to test her. Laela had impressed her by fighting back and so, almost on impulse, Oeka chose her.

Now, she knew the inner voice had been right. She had waited a long time in the hopes that it would come again and bring new abilities with it, but it never had. And Laela was weakening.

That was something Oeka would not accept.

She flew on, pushing herself as hard as she dared. Ahead, the Northgate Mountains were easily visible. She had never seen them, but all griffins knew where they were. For a riderless griffin, they were less than two days' flight away. And she had to reach them quickly.

Every griffin in Malvern had heard the rumours about what was hidden just beyond them. The Mighty Skandar, who Oeka liked to think was her father, was said to have found something special on his way from the South. A cave. A magical cave, whose entrance was said to only reveal itself at certain times. The Spirit Cave.

Oeka reached the Northgates and landed on a handy ledge to rest. Not far away, she could see Guard's Post, the fortress built into a pass that humans used to travel into the North. Now-a-days, Guard's Post was there mainly to keep watch for invaders from the South. The King had made a law that made it absolutely forbidden for anyone who wasn't a Northerner to be allowed through Guard's Post. Laela had only been admitted because she was a half-breed. And because she had bribed the guards.

Griffins, though, were free to come and go as they liked. No human could stop them anyway.

With that thought, Oeka made a side trip to Guard's Post. She had always wanted to see it. She landed on one of its two towers and was immediately intercepted by another griffin. This one was male, and big—probably one of Skandar's many husky sons.

"Speak, youngster."

Oeka held her head up proudly, showing off the rings on her forelegs. "I am the Mighty Oeka, master of this territory, who chose the Queen of Malvern."

The other griffin moved away at once, lowering his head to her and saying nothing.

"Go and bring your human," Oeka demanded. "He must bring me food."

The griffiner in question came running, and in no time at all Oeka had been supplied with a haunch of fresh mutton. She ate it while paying no attention to the griffiner's polite questions, or the other griffin's plea to be allowed to mate with her. He was far too inferior to be a potential mate, and she was too young for it besides.

Her stomach full, Oeka had a nap on the griffiner's bed, then left the tower without having said another word to anyone in it.

She flew away from Guard's Post, keeping the pass below her, and, a few wing-beats later, she entered Southern territory.

After that, it was just a question of finding the Spirit Cave.

Griffins said that after the Mighty Skandar had visited it with his human, nobody had ever found the cave again. Oeka knew that the chances of seeing it from the sky were very poor.

But she had a way of looking that no-one else did. She kept on flying, searching the area just beyond the mountains until she found the place the stories mentioned—a human place with a singing hill. That was easy. "Singing hill" was just a griffish term for a Sun Temple. Oeka had seen the ruins of one in Warwick, and she knew what to look for.

The nearest human habitation to the mountains was quite close to them, built by a river as they generally were. Oeka saw the dome of the Temple without having to fly too close. Satisfied, she turned back toward the mountains, found a tree, and came in to land.

Safely perched, she closed her eyes and let herself relax, breathing slowly and steadily until her heartbeat slowed too. She concentrated on shutting down all her senses—sight, hearing, scent, and touch. They were unimportant now. Not needed.

When she was ready, she unleashed her other sense.

Her beak opened. Every griffin worked magic by disgorging it from its throat, but while other powers were raw and savage, Oeka's was different. What came out of her beak looked like a thin, swirling mist the colour of new grass. It spread out from her and faded out of sight without a sound, as though nothing had happened at all.

But it had.

Oeka felt it moving away over the land, drifting off in every direction. It spilled into hollows and holes, covering everything it came across, and all the while it sent back information about what it found. Minds. Everywhere, minds. Animal minds, almost like her own but so much simpler. Her magic soon found the human place she had seen, and a myriad of vague emotions wavered back toward her. She shut them out and pushed harder, feeding more energy into her search.

Until, at last, she found what she was looking for. Faint signals began to reach her—faint, but insistent. Immediately she focused on them, pulling all her energy together and directing it toward what she had sensed. The signals became more powerful. Minds, she thought. But no minds she could identify.

Slowly, a tingling began to build in her magic gland. In her mind, voices whispered so softly she could only just hear them. *Come . . . come . . . come to me . . . Oekaaaaa . . .*

Oeka's eyes snapped open. Without stopping to rouse herself or even to think, she took off and began to fly back toward the mountains. Toward the voices that pulled her on. She already knew that she had found the Spirit Cave.

The cave was by the mountains, in a heap of tumbled rocks. It wasn't much to look at; in fact it was disappointingly simple. No grand entrance, no yawning darkness, just a gap among the stones only big enough for a human. A full-grown griffin would never fit.

Oeka landed on the dirt just in front of it and sat on her haunches to look speculatively at the hole. It might have looked unimpressive, but as a griffin, she could feel the immense power lurking just beyond.

All magic came from the earth. Humans couldn't sense it, couldn't use it. They knew almost nothing about it. Of all the creatures in the world, only griffins had the ability to absorb it and use it for their own purposes. That was why they had become so much more intelligent than other animals. A big brain was needed to control and understand magic.

But even though griffins could use magic, they were only a part of it. Magic would always belong to nature. Some places seemed to attract it and store it. And there were a few places—just a few—where it was even stronger. Magic had saturated those places, sometimes so much so that even humans had a vague sense of it. Sometimes it could even affect the physical world in unnatural ways. When that happened, places like the Spirit Cave came into being.

Oeka only knew of one other place where magic was this powerful, and that was at the place known as Taranis' Throne. But that was different magic—dark magic that no griffin could use.

The Spirit Cave wasn't like that.

Oeka stood up and breathed in deeply, savouring the air. The magic was so thick here that she could scent it, without the use of any of her powers. It tasted of earth and stone, and blood, and ice.

If a griffin came to a place like this, and knew what to do, then even something as unpredictable as the Spirit Cave was nothing more than power. Pure power, ready to be harnessed.

She could still hear the voices, calling her name. Echoes of the dead, called out of the earth by magic. There were many different intelligences here. Old intelligences. Many of them tasted of anger.

For the first time, Oeka was afraid.

Oeeekaaaa . . . the voices whispered.

Oeka hissed. *They are powerful,* she told herself. *But so am I.*

She raised her wings and went forward, into freezing mist.

* * *

Oeka couldn't tell when she had passed through the cave entrance. Pure whiteness swallowed everything, blanking out the entire world around her as if she had gone blind. The entrance was invisible—if it even still existed. She had been expecting this. She pressed on, following the sound of the voices. At first they were indistinct, seeming to drift around somewhere ahead of her. But as she got closer, they became clearer and louder, until they had merged into one voice softly calling her name. Oeka kept on toward it, but no matter how far she went, it was always just ahead of her. Distant. Tantalising.

She stopped and sat down. "Do not play with me, fool," she said. "I am not a butterfly to be batted about. Show yourself to me."

Silence.

"If you will not show yourself, then I shall force you," Oeka warned. "Stop hiding."

I am not hiding, Oeka, the voice whispered, and as it spoke the whiteness faded away and was gone.

Oeka looked around. She was standing in a perfectly ordinary sandy-floored cave, and there in front of her was another griffin. Female, much older than herself, and the deep green eyes called up memories that she had kept buried for nearly all her life.

Oeka, my daughter, the other griffin said, in a voice like a sighing wind.

Oeka stared. She stood up without thinking, and took a step toward her mother—but she stopped herself. She dipped her head, very coolly. "Greetings, spirits. I am the Mighty Oeka, ruler of Malvern. And you are an illusion, meant to confuse the weak-minded."

Clever Oeka, the illusion said. *I knew that you would be powerful from the moment you came out of your egg.*

"All of Malvern knows of my power, spirits," Oeka said.

Coldness began to needle at her. *But you are not content even with that, are you, daughter?*

Oeka felt her mind begin to numb and shook off the power trying to break in. "Do not waste my time with tricks. My mother has been dead since I was a hatchling."

The illusion came closer. It was warm. The fur smelt sharp and spicy with life. Real. *I am your mother, Oeka,* the voice insisted. *The magic here calls back the spirits of the dead. In this place, I can speak with you again. Trust me.*

Oeka moved, subtly repositioning her back paws. "Very well. What do you want with me, Mother?"

To comfort you, and to advise you. You are troubled.

Oeka could feel the presence beginning to press in around her, smothering and cold. The illusion . . . her mother . . . seemed to be growing larger, the eyes filling her vision, the voice whispering insistently.

"Lies!" she screamed, and leapt straight forward.

Her outstretched talons hit her mother in the chest and throat. The impact was shocking. She fell backward with a thud and scrabbled upright to see the illusion dissolve into wisps of white.

A huge, rumbling shook the cave. Oeka staggered as the floor began to move. Dirt fell from the ceiling, and cracks split the walls. Alarmed, the small griffin darted toward the nearest corner. Too late. The floor shook more violently, and she lost her footing and fell hard onto her belly. She clawed at the dirt, trying to get up, and an almighty crack split the air. A chunk broke out of the ceiling and fell straight toward her.

There was no time to dodge. Oeka pressed herself to the ground and braced herself.

The chunk hit her and disintegrated.

Oeka dared to open her eyes. She wasn't hurt. Amazed, she got up again. The whiteness had seeped back. Around her, the cave broke apart, each piece crumbling and changing back into the white wispy substance that had made it. In moments, she was surrounded by the spirits again, and this time they were not whispering.

The mist flashed red and began to turn hot. *Arrogant little chick. Power-hungry. You will destroy, destroy, destroy . . .*

Oeka faltered under the hatred that surrounded her. But as the voices grew louder and angrier, she reared up and screamed. *"Enough!"*

The spirits closed in to attack, but she was ready. Despite her exhaustion, despite the danger, she unleashed her magic. Using a gift she had only just begun to discover, she hardened her mind, pushing away anything else that touched it. Her senses shut down. Deaf and blind, free of the accusing voices and confusing visions, she ran.

The protection would only last so long. As soon as her magic faltered, the spirits would have her—and then she might never escape.

The only sense left to her now was touch. She ran in circles that grew wider and wider, keeping her head low to the floor she could not see. The spirits had made it invisible to her before, but she was still in a physical place. The cave still existed around her, and somewhere in it was the thing she had come to find.

Her mind began to falter. Her magic, already weakened by the search for the cave, ran low. Out there, the spirits were still trying to break in, and their own supplies of power were infinite. Soon, they would have her. Very soon.

Where is it? WHERE?

Her beak clinked on something. She stopped and turned clumsily, scrabbling around in the dirt for it. The object slipped out of her talons, but she trapped it against a wall and delicately scooped it up in her beak.

The thing sat on her tongue. It was heavy and smooth, odd-shaped. A rock, maybe, or a bone?

It didn't matter.

Oeka relaxed her magic, and her senses came back. Immediately, she cringed. Everywhere, what had been pale and still was swirling and rushing all around, dark like storm clouds. What had been soft and whispering was shrieking and howling. *No, no, no, no! Fool, no!*

But no matter how loudly they screamed their protests, the spirits were powerless.

With the object in her beak, Oeka couldn't speak. But she spoke in her mind. One word, full of triumph. *Mine.*

She threw her head back and swallowed the object.

In that moment, the Spirit Cave was destroyed. The mist, the cold, the howling voices, everything was pulled away and inward. Out of the land, and into Oeka. For one long, agonising moment her mind was a confused mass of a thousand voices all screaming at once; and then they were silenced.

When Oeka came to, she found herself standing under a

tree, near the spot where the Spirit Cave's entrance had been. But now there was nothing there but a heap of tumbled stones. The luring voices, and the white mist, were gone forever. The massive power she had sensed before had gone with them. But that didn't matter. She had done what she had come to do.

Now, the power of the Spirit Cave was hers.

12

Gwernyfed

Kullervo never did remember what happened after his escape from Skandar. He flew out of the mountains with a speed he had never imagined was possible, but even after they were well behind him, he didn't stop. He flew on, his mind lost in a haze of pain that grew worse. His rational, human mind was swallowed up by the griffin's maddened instincts. The griffin took control and dragged him on, unthinking, focused on nothing but escape.

Eventually, a small part of his human mind managed to come through, and he could think a little. He was badly hurt, and he knew it. He needed a healer urgently, but where should he go? He didn't know if any of the cities could shelter him. If he landed at one, he could be taken prisoner or even killed. He had never lived properly as a griffin and knew nothing about how these things happened. Especially in the North, when there was war in the air.

But he had to have a healer. Without one, he would die.

His mind began to fog up. With one last effort, he thrust the idea into the griffin mind. *Find a city. Fly to a city. Human nest. Fly . . . human nest . . . help . . .*

The man-griffin flew on.

Luck wasn't on Kullervo's side that day. He flew in what he thought was a southward direction, but it had begun to rain. His wounds hurt savagely; he was losing blood. His mind grew hazy and confused. Not knowing where he was going, he was buffeted about by the wind and eventually forced to land. Thinking vaguely that sleep would help, he crawled under what he thought was a rocky ledge and curled up, shivering in the wet.

He woke up in the morning and found himself soaked through. Too tired to move, he lay with his head lolling on his talons and watched a swarm of little black specks prickle at the edge of the gaping wound in his leg.

They were ants, feeding on his blood.

Eventually, thirst made him move. He dragged himself out of his shelter, and thrust his beak into a handy puddle. Gulping down water made him feel stronger, and his mind began to work again. Had to fly on. Had to find help. He tested his wings—they were painful, but uninjured at least. They would do.

He lurched into the air and flew on.

That was how the next few days passed. Hopelessly lost, unable to hunt, unable to find humans who could help him, he wandered through Tara with little idea even of direction. His wounds reopened, and festered, until he was too weak to go any further.

On that last, half-remembered morning, he came across a tiny village in the middle of nowhere. There, he landed by a building and promptly collapsed. His last thought was that whoever lived here might help him. If he were human . . .

Magic tore at him, and he blacked out.

He woke up in unbelievable pain. Immobilised, too overcome to even scream, he lay on his side and gasped convulsively. Hands touched his head; he heard voices somewhere but couldn't understand them. His foreleg jerked forward and moved around, and he eventually realised that someone was wrapping it up. Help, then? Someone helping him?

Something he thought was water poured into his mouth. He swallowed it and tried to relax. Some of the pain receded.

Voices, rising and falling. He couldn't see anything.

He slept, woke, and slept again.

Food came, when he was awake. He didn't know or care

what it was, and only swallowed it as it was put into his mouth. He swallowed liquids, too—maybe water, maybe medicine. Either one was good.

The pain began to go away, and he felt himself getting better. As proper consciousness came back, he struggled to make sense of his surroundings, wanting to know where he was. He found himself lying on his back. That wasn't right. His wings were trapped underneath him, and he could feel his tail trailing between his back legs. His head felt wrong. Too light. Something kept brushing at his cheeks.

He fought to make himself wake up. His whole body felt very warm—there was a blanket over him. He blinked and looked upward. There was a ceiling above him. He was glad to see it, but confusion quickly took over. Why was he in a bed? Why . . . ?

He tried to move and found himself lifting a pair of human arms. Human. He was human? He couldn't remember changing. Had it happened while he was unconscious? It had happened before. His talons were gone, and his fingers were tipped with misshapen fingernails. Those usually took a while to grow.

He felt his face. No beak. Everything seemed normal. His arm was bandaged. He could feel something trapped under the pillow. Fumbling with the covers, he slid a hand underneath to investigate. Wings! Just his wings. But they were still coated with feathers.

Kullervo inspected his bare chest. It was also covered in feathers.

Something went wrong, he thought muzzily.

His carers must know what he was now. What were they going to do? He consoled himself that at least they had helped him so far. They might not be enemies. But he would have to be careful.

He lay back and waited for someone to come and check on him.

After a while, a door opened somewhere, and a woman appeared. She was young, with brown hair and . . . blue eyes?

Kullervo's brow furrowed.

The woman gave him a nervous smile. "Hello. You're awake." She spoke Cymrian, without the harsh accent of a Northerner.

Kullervo coughed. "Yes. Don't know . . . what—happened."

"It's all right." She came closer and gave him some water. "You've been ill. Do you feel better now?"

He took the water gratefully. "Yes. Thank you. Name's Kullervo."

"I'm Ellan," said the woman. She was looking at him cautiously, almost with . . . awe?

Kullervo was too exhausted to think about it. "Am I going to be all right?"

"I don't know. But I think you will. You're strong."

"I'm a freak," Kullervo mumbled. "You weren't meant to see me like this."

"Oh, no, it's all right," Ellan said, too quickly. "We're honoured . . . I mean . . . we thought that you . . ."

"What?" Kullervo squinted. "Feel sick. Need more water."

"Oh, yes, of course. Sorry." She provided it. "Is that better?"

He closed his eyes for a long moment and nearly fell asleep. But the need for answers was too important, and he forced himself awake. "What's this place? Where?"

Ellan glanced over her shoulder. "This is Gwernyfed."

A Northern place-name, Kullervo thought. For a little while, he'd thought he had somehow ended up back in the South.

"You," he said. "You're Southern. Why are you here?"

Ellan winced and bowed hastily. "Gwernyfed's our secret," she said. "We live here. The last survivors."

Kullervo just stared at her.

"We were living in the North when the war started," Ellan said. "We were all born in this country. After the Dark Lord took over, we refused to leave. The North is our home. So we came here to Gwernyfed. We had friends—Northerner friends, who helped us. This is our place now, and no-one knows we're here. We hoped nobody would find us."

"But I did," said Kullervo.

"Yes." Ellan was watching him carefully. "We weren't sure . . . you look like a Northerner, a little. But the wings, the eyes . . ."

Finally, Kullervo realised. "You think I'm—"

"We hoped."

He turned his head away. "Gryphus' Messenger."

"A man with a griffin's wings and golden eyes," Ellan said. "A man who flew down from the sky to us. We believed Gryphus sent you to help us."

Silently, Kullervo thanked the gods—whichever of them might be listening. He was saved. "You're right," he said. "I was sent. I am a messenger. You helped me, so I should help you."

Ellan's face lit up. She looked as if she were going to laugh out loud. "It's true! I *knew* it. Some of the others doubted it, but I knew."

Kullervo smiled at her. "How can I help?"

"Oh." Ellan looked taken aback. "With blessings, if you can, holy one."

"Of course." Kullervo let the smile grow warmer. "Is there anything else?"

"Protection from the Dark Lord," Ellan said with real fear.

Kullervo pulled up short at that. An image of Arenadd's rotting remains flashed behind his eyes, and he shuddered.

"I'm sorry," Ellan said. "I should never have said that name in front of you, holy one."

"It's all right." Kullervo shifted under his covers. "I need to rest. When I'm awake again, anyone else who wants to visit me can. I'll help them any way I'm able."

Ellan bowed. "Thank you, holy one. I understand."

Now that he knew he was safe, Kullervo could afford to take some time to recover. He spent most of his days in bed and let his hosts keep him clean and fed. Plenty of people came to visit him once word got out that he was awake and talking, and many of them brought food and medicines. Kullervo was used to this sort of treatment by now. At least, he was used to people coming to stare at him. He accepted the attention placidly, thankful that nobody was throwing anything at him or trying to pull on his wings or feathers. These people were afraid of him, but they honestly believed in him as well, and he quickly saw that this was different from how it had been before. His transformation back into human form had gone wrong, but not in a bad way. He had kept most of his fur and feathers, and his tail was still furred and had the feathery fan on the end. His feet were clawed and padded, and his legs were improperly shaped and no good for walking. But despite that, his face was properly human, and his hands and arms. He looked bizarre, but not hideous, and that made all the difference.

Maybe Gryphus was smiling on him after all.

He soon had a good idea of how many people were here in Gwernyfed and what they were like. At least twenty different people came to see him, and of those, most were Southerners of varying ages. From the way some of them spoke and carried themselves, he suspected they were griffiners—or had been once.

There were some Northerners among them, too, most of them acting as if they were more interested in him for his oddity rather than convinced that he was divine.

The third type of human that he saw was far more astonishing.

Half-breeds.

Several children came to stare at him one day. One or two of them were pure Southerner or Northerner, but most of them weren't. Black hair, with brown eyes. Brown hair with black eyes. Pale skin, and a stocky build.

Kullervo could hardly believe it. He beckoned and smiled to the children, and as they timidly came closer, their mixed features leapt out at him. Half-breeds!

"Are you from Gryphus?" one small boy asked.

"Yes, that's right," said Kullervo. "What's your name?"

"Gath," said the boy.

Kullervo listened to them ask their questions and did his best to answer, but his mind was elsewhere. He had never imagined anything like this in his life. A place, just this one place, where the two races lived side by side as equals. They were even intermarrying. This place had been founded by people who had every reason to hate each other, but somehow they had found a way to co-operate and survive. And in twenty years, Malvern had never suspected that they even existed.

Privately, Kullervo swore to himself that he would never, ever tell anyone that Gwernyfed existed. And, if he had to, he would kill to protect it.

The next day, when Ellan brought him breakfast, he asked her who led the settlement.

"All of us, really," she said. "We make most of the decisions together, anyway. Lord Rufus was the one who started it, though. And the griffin always gets her say."

Kullervo started. "Griffins? There are griffins here?"

"Just one," said Ellan. "She can't come here to see you, of course, but she's very curious."

"I'll have to go out and meet her," said Kullervo. "But what about Lord Rufus? Who's he?"

"He used to live at Malvern," said Ellan. "He was a griffiner, but he was disgraced and his griffin left him when they found out he was in love with his servant. She was a Northerner. When the Dark Lord and the monster griffin attacked Malvern, Lord Rufus nearly died, but his lover helped him escape. They joined with a group of others who were running away, and Lord Rufus took charge. They ran from place to place, trying to find a place to hide, and a lot of them died. Lord Rufus' lover was one of the ones who was killed. Lord Rufus kept the others going until they found Gwernyfed. It was in ruins, and most of the people there had been killed by other Northerners for refusing to join the rebels. The people who were left let Lord Rufus stay because they thought a griffiner would rebuild their village and show them what to do. He did." Ellan smiled. "My mother was one of the people Rufus brought here. I was still in her womb then."

"And so Lord Rufus rules Gwernyfed now?"

"Sort of. He's a guide, though, not really a ruler. He's got old. But we all believe in him." There was genuine affection in Ellan's voice. "When other people came here, he took them in no matter what race they were. He believes we should all live together in harmony, like the clouds in the sky."

"I wish we could," said Kullervo, with a bitterness that surprised him.

"We've managed it well enough," said Ellan.

Kullervo pulled himself together. "I'd like to meet Lord Rufus. I think I know some things he might be interested in. Will he come?"

"I'm not sure. I think so. If he hears you were asking him to. I think he's been keeping away on purpose." Ellan looked troubled.

"Ask him to come, then," said Kullervo. "And tell him I said not to worry—I won't bite."

"I'll tell him," she promised.

Kullervo waited eagerly to meet the famous Lord Rufus. But nearly three whole days passed before he finally came. By then, Kullervo was well enough to get out of bed and try to walk again—not easy, with his misshapen legs, but he managed to hobble around with the help of a stick. He liked to sit by the fire-place and watch the flames, and think about all the things he had seen and heard.

One evening, there was a knock at the door, and Ellan opened it and ushered in yet another visitor. Kullervo turned to look and saw someone he didn't recognise. An old man, with a pure white beard. His nose had obviously been broken at some point, and an old scar gave him a permanent frown.

"Lord Rufus," Ellan said.

The old man nodded to her, but his eyes were on Kullervo. Slowly, he walked toward the fascinated shape-shifter, saying nothing but watching him intently.

"Lord Rufus." Kullervo inclined his head. "It's an honour to meet you."

Lord Rufus squinted slightly. He folded his hands together in front of his chest and lowered his own head toward them. "Holy one," he said at last.

"Call me Kullervo, my lord."

"Kullervo, then." Rufus' voice was rough, and his face was weather-beaten, but there was something direct and honest about the way he looked at Kullervo. "The honour is mine."

"It shouldn't be, my lord," said Kullervo. "I've been told about everything you've done. I wish I could have been half as brave, but I never have."

Rufus gave a slow, hesitant smile. "You mean you . . . you think what I've done was good, holy one?"

"Of course I do," said Kullervo. "Why shouldn't I? You saved lives, you protected people, you made a home for them better than anything I could ever imagine. A place where Northerners and Southerners live together in peace—this place is amazing. I never would have thought that it could be possible."

At that, Rufus lost his air of uncertainty and smiled properly. "Is that the truth, holy one? You approve of all this? I thought . . ."

"I approve very much," Kullervo said firmly. "I don't know why you'd expect me not to."

"It's just that—I loved a Northerner, and—" Rufus bowed his head. "I believed I was damned for it. Cut off from Gryphus forever. But I loved her too much to stop myself. I thought that you were here to . . . to . . . that you would be angry with me."

"Never!" Kullervo said it more loudly than he had expected. "Never. Gryphus never condemns love, never. What you did was a good thing, Rufus. Believe me."

"I do." The old man looked more joyful and relieved than anyone Kullervo had ever seen.

"I want to thank you, too," Kullervo added. "You've taken care of me for I don't know how long, given me shelter. Saved my life."

"Of course we took you in," said Rufus. "We never turn anyone away. And turning away an agent of Gryphus—! Are you feeling well?"

"I am," said Kullervo. "I'll be better before long. And I can start to repay you however I can. Tell me, Rufus—what is it that you want?"

Rufus shook his head. "Nothing really. We have everything we need here. All we need is good rain, and . . ."

"And?" Kullervo prompted.

"And to be safe," said Rufus. "Every day I pray to Gryphus to protect us, to keep the Dark Lord and his minions away. It's worked for this long, but one day . . ."

"One day you'll be found," said Kullervo. "I understand."

"Yes." Rufus' voice was full of bitterness. "The Dark Lord finds everyone he thinks is an enemy. No-one escapes him for long. We might not know much here, but we do know what happened to the others. Other survivors, others who hid. The Dark Lord's followers hunted them all down. None of them were spared. Only a few escaped and found us here, and we have nowhere to go. One day, I know we'll be found. But I pray to Gryphus that I won't live to see that day."

"That won't happen," said Kullervo. "I swear it won't. I

will do everything in my power to keep Gwernyfed safe; you have my word for it."

"I believe you. But Gryphus didn't protect Malvern. He didn't protect any of the others. The Dark Lord found them."

"But he won't find you," said Kullervo. "He's dead, Rufus."

Rufus stared. "What? The Dark Lord Arenadd—dead?"

"Yes. He died a few months ago. I've seen his body. He's dead. Rotted. He's not coming back. Not this time."

"But how . . . ?"

"Nobody really knows," said Kullervo. "Some say he was assassinated. Some say he left Cymria forever. And some say the Night God came for him and took him into the void to be with her. But I don't believe any of that," he added coldly. "He died like an ordinary man, and like an ordinary man, he rotted away. The Mighty Skandar went with him, and he won't ever come back. I can promise you, Rufus, neither of them will ever come for you."

Rufus found a chair and sat down heavily. He looked speechless. "All those years living in terror of him, and now he's gone. I can't . . ." He looked up sharply. "Who rules in Malvern now? Did the griffiners come back—?"

"His daughter took the throne," said Kullervo. "Queen Laela."

"He had a daughter?"

"Yes." Kullervo thought of Laela, and wondered if she was worried about him. By now, she must be. He couldn't bear the thought of going back to her to tell her he'd failed.

Rufus sagged. "Then we're still lost. A Dark Lady to follow a Dark Lord. This . . . Laela will be the one to find us."

"Oh no!" Kullervo actually laughed out loud. "No, Laela's not that sort at all! She's nothing like her father. She looks like him, they say, but she's no Dark Lady. I think if she found you, she'd want to protect you, not kill you."

"Why?" said Rufus.

"Because she was raised in the South," said Kullervo. "And because she's a good-hearted person. She listens to people. And she's a half-breed."

Rufus looked completely bewildered. He choked on a laugh. "What? The Dark Lord—with one of *us*?"

Kullervo smiled to himself. "He wasn't that choosy about

who he went to bed with. Trust me. Yes, he bedded a Southern woman, apparently. I don't know her name, but I heard she was a noble."

"Wait. Wait." Rufus' brow furrowed. "A Southern lady . . . surely . . . Gryphus' talons."

"What is it?" said Kullervo.

"There was a griffiner living in Malvern," said Rufus. "She came there just before the war began. She was married to some common thug—a city guard, I believe, who'd somehow been chosen. They had a baby girl, but there were rumours . . . people saying the child's head was always covered, but underneath there was black hair. People muttered that it was a half-breed."

"It must have been Laela," Kullervo decided. "She was born in Malvern, so I've been told. Her mother died when the Eyrie was overrun."

"Hah." Rufus laughed again. "I shouldn't laugh, but . . . the Dark Lord, loving a Southerner? Madness."

"Love is madness," Kullervo said sharply. "Often."

Rufus quietened. "Yes, I know. So this Laela is a better person than her father, you say?"

"She doesn't kill people," said Kullervo. "All she wants is to make the North stronger and keep its people safe. In fact," he added thoughtfully, "having her on the throne could help you, eventually. I think that when the time comes, she could well decide to try to negotiate with the South. Maybe open trade routes with them. Even let them come here to live again."

Rufus looked wistful. "The North, reborn! I've tried to imagine it. I think we all have."

"And so have I," said Kullervo, who had only begun to a while after arriving at Gwernyfed. As he watched Rufus sitting there, trying to take in everything he had just discovered, Kullervo decided there and then just what he would do when he returned to Malvern.

He would tell Laela that he had found Gwernyfed.

He would tell her that it was a ruin, with not one single inhabitant. He would tell her to have it struck off the maps. Maybe, one day, he would tell her the truth. But for now, it would be his secret. He promised himself that.

"Thank you, holy one." Rufus' solemn tones broke in.

"You don't know how happy all this has made me. There'll be celebrations in Gwernyfed when the others have heard the news. But with your permission, I'll wait until you're well enough before I tell them."

"That would be wonderful," said Kullervo. "Actually, I've . . . I've never been to a party before," he said shyly.

"Never?" Rufus chuckled. "Then we'll have to make sure this one is worth coming to, won't we?"

"I can't wait!" said Kullervo, privately deciding to get better as fast as he could.

13

Ghosts

Seven long, awful days after her sudden departure, Oeka returned to Malvern. She landed unceremoniously at the top of the Council Tower, and the pair of large males who intercepted her fled in terror before she had said a word or done a thing. She went down into the audience chamber, where she settled down on her marble plinth and rested on her belly with her eyes closed.

Laela arrived a short time later, puffing a little from having run up several flights of stairs. She went straight to Oeka, red-faced. "Nice of yeh to show yer beak again."

"Hello, Laela," said Oeka, without opening her eyes. She spoke very slowly and deliberately, with an odd reverb to her voice.

"Oh, wonderful," Laela growled. "Yeh just piss off for a week without sayin' a word about where yer goin', an' that's all yeh've got to say for yerself. I'm still alive an' technically in charge, in case yeh give a damn."

"I knew you would survive," Oeka said in the same slow, flat voice.

"No thanks to you. Where've yeh been, anyway?"

Silence.

"This ain't been a good week for me at all." Laela sighed. She found a chair and dragged it over before sitting on it. "Managed t'keep it secret yeh were gone for a bit, but people figured it out soon enough. Couple of councillors decided it was a good time to have themselves a little coup. I got wind of it. Had 'em both executed and replaced by their apprentices. One of them turned out to have been in on it, so I booted him off. Didn't have much left without yeh around, though. Went to the Hatchery in the end, hopin' to get chosen again. Didn't happen. One of 'em chose Inva instead. Gave her a nasty shock. She's taking to it well, though."

"You should not have gone to the Hatchery," said Oeka.

"Well, what was I supposed to do?" Laela said hotly. "Yeh ran off on me! I was gettin' close to just givin' up an' handing the throne over to bloody Saeddryn!"

"You are a fool," said Oeka, "if you thought that I would not return."

"I had no bloody way of knowin', an' you know it, Oeka."

"You do not understand our ways," Oeka said with flat contempt. "I would not leave you unless you were disgraced, or crippled, or had lost your power completely. To leave you would be to abandon the supremacy we had won together, and I would sooner die than do that."

"Oh, right?" Laela sneered. "An' yeh decided to fly off like that why exactly?"

"I had something I needed to do," said Oeka. "It was necessary."

"An' what was that, then? Somethin' so important yeh couldn't even tell me about it?"

Oeka finally showed a hint of anger. "Where I went and what I did were secret things, not for a human to know. But be assured that I have succeeded. That is all you need to know. I have succeeded, and now I shall not need to leave again."

"What, that's it? It's a secret? So yeh ain't gonna tell me a thing?"

At last, Oeka opened her eyes. They were glowing, just a little. Laela started at the sight of them.

"I have increased my powers," the small griffin intoned. "The magic within me is a thousand times stronger than it was before, a thousand times stronger than that of the Mighty Skandar, or ancient Kraal. Be assured, little human—no enemy shall ever be a match for me. Together, we shall crush all resistance."

Laela pulled away, leaning back in her chair. "Made yerself stronger . . . ?"

"Yes. Over time, I shall unravel the energies in me and use them to unlock new powers—powers beyond imagining."

"We can use 'em t'fight?" Laela sounded scared, but excited.

"Not to fight," said Oeka. "But to destroy. There will be no fight against my might. Only defeat."

Laela said nothing.

"Do not be afraid," Oeka said. "I will never hurt my human." She put her head on one side, just how Laela remembered, and suddenly looked like the griffin she had been before. "Shall you forgive your partner, and trust her again, Laela?"

Laela smiled gratefully. "I s'pose I could see my way clear since yeh asked nicely. Want some food?"

"Yeeeesss . . ." Oeka's eyes closed again. "Bring food, if you can. I must rest now and begin to weave my magic together."

Laela left, a little too fast. Once outside, she allowed herself a deep breath.

She had been happy and relieved to see Oeka, as much as she'd been angry. The situation had been far more desperate during her absence than she had admitted, and having Oeka back meant she could finally breathe easy again. But what she had sensed in the audience chamber had been more than unsettling—it was terrifying. As a human, she couldn't see anything, if it was there, but there had been a sense there all the same—a feeling of immense pressure in the air, like a thunderstorm about to break. It made her skin prickle.

"Oeka, what have yeh done to yerself?" she muttered out loud.

After Lord Rufus' visit, many more new people came to see Kullervo—people who must have stayed away beforehand. Many of the newcomers were Northerners. Noticing this, Kullervo decided that, like Rufus, they had probably been afraid that "Gryphus' Messenger" was there to wreak some kind of punishment. Now Kullervo had reassured Rufus, he must have told them it was safe. The newcomers were friendly, and all his visitors were much more talkative than before. They treated him like a friend—someone to be respected, but welcomed.

Nobody had ever treated him this way before.

To his embarrassment, many of them brought babies or small children for him to "bless." He did his best, laying his hands on tiny foreheads and saying whatever words felt best. It seemed to be what they expected.

As promised, Rufus hadn't passed on the news of the King's death, but the villagers did seem to know about the planned celebrations—in honour of Kullervo's arrival, or so they said. Everybody who mentioned it talked about it excitedly.

Kullervo was desperate to get up out of his bed and to finally see the village for himself, and he insisted on spending as much time as possible moving around the room. With Ellan's help, he began to test his legs and eventually taught himself to walk with the help of a crutch. It felt awkward, like trying to walk on two legs while in griffin form, and in fact his legs were still more or less stuck in that state. The bones in his feet and ankles hadn't adjusted themselves, and he had to walk on clawed and padded toes with his elongated heels raised off the ground. The crutch stopped him from falling forward, but he moved with a peculiar, hunched, hobbling motion that made him feel stupid.

It would have to do.

As soon as he felt strong enough, he asked Ellan to escort him out of the house.

Outside, it was raining. Blinking in the light, Kullervo moved forward, his paws sinking into the mud. His tail moved from side to side, and his wings shifted feebly on his back—they might have stayed feathered, but the powerful muscles that moved them were gone, and they were too weak to even fold properly, let alone manage a flap. Kullervo draped them over himself for warmth—they were fine for that, at least.

And now—Gwernyfed.

The village was smaller than he had expected. He counted about twenty houses, all of them small, rough things made from wood. There wasn't much difference between each one in size though he did spot a few barns. An open patch of dirt served as a village square, and there were chickens and ducks wandering around near a stone well.

Kullervo smiled. "A place doesn't have to be an Eyrie to be home," he said to himself.

"What was that?" Ellan said.

"Hm? Oh, nothing. So, this is Gwernyfed."

"Yeah. What do you . . . uh . . . how do you like it, holy one?"

"I like it." Kullervo looked around—people were already coming over to see him. He pulled his wings around himself more tightly, suddenly embarrassed. Clothes wouldn't fit on his deformed body, and since his genitals were tucked away under his tail, griffin style, he had come out naked. It hadn't occurred to him to feel self-conscious until just now.

The people who hurried over to him didn't look bothered. They exclaimed over his griffin-like fur and paws, and came closer to touch his wings. He let them, of course, though his mind was elsewhere.

"I've been told there's a griffin living here," he said. "I want to meet her if I can."

"Of course ye can, sir," a Northern man said. "An' she's interested to meet ye, too."

Kullervo couldn't see anything nearby that looked like a good home for a griffin. "Where is she?"

"She lives in a barn just over that-a-way," said the man. "We always hoped more griffins would come, but there were only the one."

Kullervo wasn't sure what to expect from this griffin, but he wanted to find out. "Can I go to meet her?"

"She's not here just now, holy one," a woman said. "I don't think she is, anyway. She flies away in the daytime, looking for food. But she'll be here for the celebration."

"Oh, good. Have you decided when it'll be?"

"Whenever you choose, holy one." The woman curtsied and blushed.

Kullervo coughed. "Well then . . . I declare that the celebrations shall happen . . . tomorrow night!"

The children who were there cheered.

"I'll go tell Lord Rufus," said the Northern man. He nodded politely and hurried off.

"Perfect." Kullervo looked at Ellan. "I'd like to see more, if you don't mind."

"There's not really much to see, holy one," she said apologetically.

"Show me that, then," said Kullervo, and despite his aching back, he hobbled through the entire village, listening as the inhabitants told him about all the different landmarks. It wasn't exactly riveting stuff, but he listened happily anyway. Around him, many of his followers were already planning for the celebration, and from the way they talked about it, Kullervo had the feeling that parties of any sort were a rare treat in Gwernyfed.

Caught up in the general joy, he had almost completely forgotten about Laela.

If anyone had been afraid that rain would spoil the festivities, they were proven wrong. A bright and sunny day followed a grey one, and the preparations went ahead. All those who were available left their work for the day, and, together, the inhabitants of Gwernyfed put up decorations on every building. A group of men dug a fire pit in the middle of the square, and children helped gather wood to pile inside. Others put the food together—choosing a pig to slaughter and cook on a spit over the fire pit, baking bread and little cakes sweetened with honey, boiling eggs, putting apples on sticks ready to roast.

Kullervo watched it all, and helped with the lighter tasks. He wished he could do more, but in his current condition, it just wasn't possible.

The fire pit was lit at sundown, and by the time a clear, starry night had fallen, the celebrations were in full swing. The pig steamed as it roasted on its spit, and children were holding apples on sticks over the flames until they blackened and hissed. Several of the villagers had brought instruments and launched into a piece of music Kullervo guessed was a jig. Every single one of the musicians was terrible, but nobody minded.

Once the festivities were well underway, Lord Rufus appeared. To Kullervo's amazement, he was wearing an outfit of the sort griffiners wore at important ceremonies—a velvet tunic covered in hundreds of cunningly sewn griffin feathers over the chest. Below that was a patch of fox fur that extended into a hanging tab that was decorated with a fan of feathers in imitation of a griffin's tail. At the back, long flight feathers formed a kind of cape. The outfit was moth-eaten, and many of the feathers had fallen off, but it gave Rufus a kind of majesty as he stepped up onto a crate by the fire pit.

The musicians stopped playing. The revellers around the pit quietened down and turned to their leader, waiting for him to speak.

Rufus scanned the crowd until he saw Kullervo. He beckoned.

People helped Kullervo to reach him. "There you are, Rufus. I was missing you!"

Lord Rufus smiled at him. "Welcome, holy one." He straightened up as he spoke, addressing the others more than Kullervo himself. "All of us are gathered here to celebrate the arrival of this man. The winged messenger of Gryphus himself, sent to us."

People cheered.

"Many of us were afraid, when he first came, that he was here to punish us," Rufus continued. "To judge us. I was one of those people. But we were wrong. Kullervo came here not to hurt us but to help us. He has promised to do whatever he can for Gwernyfed, and for us."

"All hail the sacred messenger!" many people shouted.

Kullervo accepted it with a slight bow.

"But," Rufus resumed, "what none of you know yet is that Kullervo came here for another reason. He came to bring us a blessing, a gift that only I have heard. Tonight, I will pass on what he gave to me."

A hush fell.

Rufus bowed his head for a moment. Then he looked up. "The Dark Lord Arenadd," he said, very softly. "The Dark Lord Arenadd, the destroyer, the Shadow That Walks, the Man Without a Heart—the Dark Lord Arenadd . . . is dead!"

Utter silence followed.

"Dead?" someone repeated.

"Dead!" Rufus repeated.

Others were looking at Kullervo. "He's really dead?"

With a mighty effort, Kullervo spread his wings wide. "It's true!" he said as loudly as he could. "Rufus is telling the truth. The King of the North is dead. I saw his body with my own eyes. Dead. Rotted."

"What is this?" a voice interrupted.

It came from the other side of the fire pit. Everyone there turned hastily, as something approached.

"Tell me the truth at once, twisted monster," the voice said. It was loud, harsh, and not human.

People moved out of the way as the griffin approached.

She was brown, long-bodied, and slim. Behind a grey beak, eyes the colour of the sky glared straight at Kullervo.

The shape-shifter shook off his surprise and came toward her. "Hello," he said. "So you're the griffin who lives here. I was hoping to meet you."

The brown griffin's tail was lashing aggressively. "I take no pleasure in meeting a deformed thing like you. Answer my question. What is this? You say that *Kraeai kran ae* is dead?"

Kullervo let the abuse slide off him. "Yes. He disappeared months ago, along with the Mighty Skandar. I went to look for them and found the Mighty Skandar hiding in the mountains, guarding the King's remains. It doesn't look like Skandar will ever leave the mountains, and his human is dead."

"Dead," the brown griffin repeated. "How was he killed?"

"I don't know," said Kullervo.

"But if he is dead, then who rules the Eyrie at Malvern?"

"His daughter, Laela. She's a half-breed."

"Half-breed!" the griffin huffed. "Then the human pup at Malvern truly was *his* offspring. I had my doubts. She will not last long either way." She looked at Kullervo. "You have not answered my question. Who rules at Malvern?"

"I told you, Laela—"

"No!" The brown griffin snapped her beak shut an inch away from his face. "I do not care what tiny human sits on a wooden nest. Who rules in Malvern?"

Kullervo finally caught on. "Oh. Oeka does."

"I do not know that name. What griffin is that?"

"She's only young," said Kullervo. "But very powerful in magic."

The brown griffin gave a contemptuous hiss. "Every young griffin thinks she is powerful in magic. A hatchling and a half-breed believe they have this territory of the North? Madness and stupidity. They will both be dead by the next full moon."

"Maybe," said Kullervo. "Can I ask your name? How did you get here?"

"That is for me to know," said the griffin.

"Fine. But can I at least know your name? I'm Kullervo."

"You are a misshapen insult to nature," the brown griffin said coldly. "What magic made you? Were you a griffin who overreached himself? Or a human who got in the way?"

"Neither." Kullervo finally began to get angry. "I was born this way. And what about you? Were you born this obnoxious, or did you *overreach* yourself?"

The brown griffin drew back slightly. "I see." She was silent for a moment. "I am glad to hear your news," she said at last, rather stiffly. "In return you may have my name. I am Senneck."

She turned and walked away through the village. The last Kullervo saw of her was her tail, swishing gently from side to side.

The square had gone quiet. The people around the fire pit looked shocked and nervous, and conversation resumed in bits and pieces. Kullervo stayed just where he was and stared at his hands.

Lord Rufus put a hand on his shoulder. "Are you all right, holy one?"

Kullervo looked up. "What? Yes, I'm fine."

"I know what she said to you." The old man frowned sadly. "Don't be too hard on her. You don't know what she's suffered in her life."

"She lost her human," Kullervo guessed.

"She lost more than that." Rufus gestured at him to come and sit by the fire. They chose a spot that was nice and warm and settled down side by side.

Kullervo watched the flames. "Tell me about her. Why is she here?"

Rufus followed his gaze. "You know all about the war, yes? Everyone does in the North. When the Dark Lord came, no-one knew what he was capable of at first. We in Malvern assumed he was just another rogue—albeit one with a griffin. But we did know what he had done, or part of it. He came from a city far in the South, a place called Eagleholm. He committed a murder there . . . more than a murder. Eagleholm was . . ."

"What?" said Kullervo. "What did he do?"

"Eagleholm was destroyed," said Rufus. "Utterly destroyed. It was the Dark Lord's first genocide. Afterward, he and the monster griffin, Skandar, came to the North. Some say it was to find their mistress, the Night God. Either way, when they came here, so did Senneck."

"She was with them?"

"No. She came from Eagleholm. That's where she was hatched. After it was destroyed, she flew to Malvern with her human. I met him once. His name was Erian Rannagonson. Nobody thought much of him; he was just a boy. A bastard, raised on a farm. But we underestimated him, and Senneck."

"Erian," Kullervo repeated. "I know that name . . ."

"You should." The old man smiled ruefully. "He was Queen Laela's uncle. Whether she knows it or not."

"Holy Gryphus! Are you sure?"

Rufus shrugged. "Lady Flell was his half-sister. Anyway, Senneck and Erian had come in search of the Dark Lord. And eventually, they found him. They took him prisoner, brought him back to Malvern. He was tried for his crimes and finally executed."

"I know about that," said Kullervo. "They hanged him . . ."

"I know," Rufus said grimly. "I was there, Kullervo. I was there that day. I saw him hang with my own eyes. But he didn't stay dead. He came back, and . . . well. You know the rest."

"What about Erian?" said Kullervo. "And Senneck?"

"The Mighty Kraal lived in Malvern then. He was so old, nobody knew where he came from originally. There was no-one more wise, and *he* saw what this bastard boy Erian was. He believed that he was the only one who could kill the Dark Lord, and so he sent him and Senneck to an island to find a special weapon. They were gone a long time, and while they were gone . . . terrible things happened. Our beautiful cities fell one by one. Everywhere, the Northerners rose up and turned on us. The unpartnered griffins turned traitor and joined the enemy. We were so confused . . . frightened . . . nothing we did was enough to stop them."

"But Erian came back," said Kullervo.

"Yes. He and Senneck flew back to Malvern, just when everything looked lost. They were our last hope. When the Dark Lord finally invaded Malvern, Erian met him there in the Sun Temple. He was killed, and Malvern fell." Rufus' eyes were bright with grief. "My whole life died that day. So did Senneck's. She lost her human . . . and both of her offspring. Her home. Everything."

Kullervo looked away from him, toward the stars and the cold moon. He thought of Senneck's blazing blue eyes and tried to imagine her as she might have been. He thought of himself, too, nursing a pain inside of him that could have mirrored hers.

"What would be worse?" he murmured to himself. "To lose everything . . . or to never have it at all?"

"What's that, holy one?" Rufus asked.

Kullervo didn't look at him. Then, without even thinking, he started to talk. "I never knew my parents. I never had a real home. I don't know if anyone ever loved me. Every day, the world was nothing but . . . confusion . . . noise . . . so many things I couldn't understand. I used to wonder if I had a place in the world, or if nothing really did have meaning, if I were as alone as I felt."

Rufus looked concerned, and he patted Kullervo on the shoulder. "Don't despair. Nothing is done, as long as we're alive. You have a purpose in this world, Kullervo. You were sent here to bring us hope."

I wasn't, Kullervo thought miserably. *No I wasn't. I'm a liar and a fake. Not even my own body knows what shape it is.*

"But I still have the sky," he said aloud. "And I know I have a family. That's all that matters now."

Silence.

"I started without a family or a home," Kullervo said eventually. "So I can't imagine what it would be like to lose those things. Poor Senneck."

"She's angry," said Rufus. "At the world, and at the Dark Lord. I believe she would have gone after him herself if she hadn't seen sense. It must have been a big shock to her to hear that he's dead."

"I can understand that," said Kullervo. "It was a shock to everyone."

"Now," said Rufus. "I think it's time we got back to celebrating! Let's go and get something to eat, shall we?"

"I'm right behind you," Kullervo said, in his usual cheerful voice.

14

Beer and Punches

Three days after Oeka's return, Laela rebelled.

Everyone was gone. Oeka had vanished again, Iorwerth was away, and she was alone. Alone with nothing but other griffiners, who mostly despised her.

Laela didn't feel like a griffiner, and with Oeka gone again, it was easy to sustain that feeling. She was a commoner at heart and always would be.

One evening, she sat in the room that had once been her father's and thought of that. So much had changed, and it was overwhelming. Had it really taken her that long to realise it?

She looked around the room. It was a simple one, especially considering that it had once belonged to a King, with plain walls and a thick, woven carpet on the floor. The only furniture in it was a bed, a writing desk, the wardrobe, and a chair by the fire. Laela sat in it now, feeling the warmth soak into her. She had to admit that even though it could have been far grander, this room was still finer than anything she had seen in her old life. She had been brought up in a house with only two rooms, and carpets had been out of the question.

But now she found herself wondering if she had been happier in that house than she had ever been here. She and her foster father Bran might have been poor, but what did that matter? There she'd only had him for company because the rest of the village didn't want to know her, but she hadn't been alone. Bran had loved her, and she'd loved him. Power and privilege couldn't make up for that.

And more than that, she was tired of lying, tired of manipulating. Tired of being a ruler. She missed being among commoners, and people who spoke plainly like she did. She missed being treated like an equal, or even an inferior.

But those days were over now, weren't they?

Laela thought of that, then, slowly, the idea came to her.

She pushed it away at first. It was ridiculous. Dangerous. Stupid. *Forbidden.*

But the moment the word "forbidden" occurred to her, the idea started to look better and better. She was tired of behaving herself. And, anyway, she was Queen, wasn't she? If she decided to, she could do whatever she damn well pleased, couldn't she?

On an impulse, Laela made her mind up there and then.

She stood up sharply and went to the wardrobe. She'd taken to storing some of her own clothes in it, and now she sorted through them, muttering impatiently until she found the outfit she wanted. She hauled it out and threw it down on the bed, and pulled off the fancy gown she'd been wearing. She tossed that aside and picked up the new outfit. It was a plain dress made from blue wool—the same dress she'd been given the first day she lived in the Eyrie, when Arenadd had found her and decided—for mysterious reasons of his own—to take care of her.

The dress felt unfamiliar now, and itchy. Surely, it hadn't been like this before? She'd grown up wearing things like this, hadn't she?

She stubbornly smoothed it down and hauled out the pair of mud-caked boots she'd worn on her journey from the South. They, at least, were still comfortable.

She thought of putting on a cape, or some kind of hood, but decided against it. She didn't need to hide her black hair here, and there was no way of hiding her eyes unless she wore a mask or something. But she knew from experience that most people wouldn't notice them anyway.

She stuffed a knife into her belt, and picked up a small money bag from the desk, and tied it on as well before going to open the little door at the back of the room. It was the same door she had come through when Arenadd had brought her into the Eyrie the night he'd found her, and the passage beyond it went down an endless staircase to the bottom of the tower.

Laela trudged patiently down it, remembering how she'd come up it that night. Had it really been such a short time ago? By now, the whole thing felt like a dream, or something that had happened to her ten years ago, in another life. But she supposed she was a different person now, wasn't she?

She smiled to herself. Last time she went into the city alone, she hadn't known how to handle herself at all. She'd been alone, and confused, and not known a damn thing about anything. She'd been bailed up by a pair of thugs, and it was only pure luck that Arenadd had come by and rescued her.

That was why the passage was there, or why he'd used it. Like her, her father had got tired of life in the Eyrie, and he liked to go out into the city sometimes to be alone and mingle with his subjects. And if he'd done that, why couldn't she?

Laela admitted to herself that she wasn't immortal like him, but that didn't scare her. She could handle herself now, couldn't she? She'd been taught how to fight by Arenadd himself. But more important than that, she'd learnt that she wasn't just some stupid girl who could barely read. She was Laela Taranisäii now, and she'd done great things. A few ordinary people out in the city couldn't bother her much.

But she wasn't going looking for a fight. All she wanted tonight was some company.

Laela opened the door at the bottom of the tower and emerged into the moonlight. She remembered the way from there easily enough and dashed across the open ground to the little gate in the wall around the Eyrie. It wasn't guarded, and she unlatched it and slipped through and out into the city.

Malvern opened its streets to her, and she stopped there and breathed in deeply, savouring the moment and feeling a freedom she hadn't expected to feel.

But the thrilling thought occurred to her then that she *was* free. If she wanted to, she could walk straight out of the city right now and go wherever she wanted. There was nobody watching her, and nobody here cared what she did. She could say and do what she liked.

At last.

Laela grinned to herself and started walking. She knew exactly where she wanted to go.

Malvern was gloomy at this time of night, but it wasn't quiet, and it wasn't completely dark. Lights burned in many of the windows, and out in the street, the city guard had lit the lamps on each corner. The guards on night patrol were about, many of them stationed under the lamps to keep an ear and eye out for trouble—and to make sure nobody stole the lamps, which would probably happen otherwise. Laela knew what people were like; they'd steal anything that wasn't nailed down even if they had no use for it.

Once that thought might have annoyed her but now, ridiculously, it made her smile. You knew where you stood with commoners.

She walked on, thrilling at how people went straight past her without a second glance. One man bumped into her and never even looked at her, let alone apologised. Laela strolled along, one hand on her money bag in case someone decided to filch it, and smiled dreamily. Being ignored . . . what a blessing it was.

She knew where she was going now and quickly kept on toward it until she saw it up ahead, the faded sign swinging gently in the cold wind that had started to blow. She could read just enough to make out some of the letters on the sign, but she didn't need to read it; she could make out the picture without any trouble. A raised carving of the moon, painted with flaking blue paint.

The Sign of the Blue Moon.

Laela paused under the sign and smiled sadly to herself. This was the same tavern where Arenadd had brought her after he'd found her, thc same one where she had gone searching for him later when he'd disappeared. By now, its owners must be used to odd people showing up, but that wasn't why she'd chosen it.

She suddenly realised that she was nervous, just a bit. But she fought the feeling down, took a deep breath, and went inside.

She stepped into a babble of voices and clinking mugs. The tavern's single ground-floor room was full of tables, and most of them were occupied. Nobody paid Laela any attention, and that was how she liked it.

She went straight to the bar and waited for the bartender to notice her. But she wasn't the only one there, and she quickly started to get impatient as everyone else got their drinks, and the bartender didn't so much as glance at her.

"Oi!" she finally shouted. "Get over here an' give me some damn service!"

The bartender came over. "Knock that off," he snapped. "Ye ain't the only one here wantin' a drink, girl." And he went on past her to serve a man further down, who'd arrived well after her.

"What the—?" Laela fumed. Who did this man think he was? She . . .

Her anger subsided, and she frowned to herself. Right. Of course. She wasn't Queen here, was she?

But she still wanted her drink.

She took a gold oblong out of her money bag, and tapped it on the counter, just as she'd done that day when she bribed the bartender here for information. Not the same bartender as this, luckily, though he was giving her so little attention that he probably wouldn't have recognised her anyway.

That did the trick. The bartender, a scrawny middle-aged Northerner, came back. "Now what can I get ye, girl?" he asked.

"Gimme a beer," said Laela. "No, make that two."

"Righto." The bartender poured them out from a jug, and took her oblong. Laela held out her hand for her change, but there wasn't any. "Hey!" she said.

"What?" the bartender said impatiently.

"I gave yeh a whole gold piece," said Laela.

"So?"

"So where's me change?"

"There isn't any," said the bartender. "The Queen put a new tax on beer."

"I nev—" Laela began. "That's an outrage!" she finished hastily.

"Too right it is, but there ye go." The bartender shrugged and moved on.

Laela took her beers and went to find a table. She didn't remember making any new taxes, but probably the Master of Taxation had done it. Now-a-days, people tended to come to her with suggestions like that, and half the time she said yes because she trusted their judgment. Maybe she'd agreed to this one when she wasn't really listening.

She found a table in the corner and sat down to drink, listening closely to the talk all around her.

It seemed she wasn't the only one who objected to the new tax.

"—half-breed bitch!" one man growled. "Who's she think she is, taxin' our beer?"

"Yeah!" Laela agreed without thinking. "Beer shouldn't be this pricey; it's a scandal!"

The man glanced at her, then nodded. "Yeah! Bitch oughta be strung up!"

Laela grinned. "No, the Master of Taxation should be strung up. The Queen just needs her ears cleaned out. She wouldn't've said yes to it if she was payin' attention."

"Nah, it's the Queen," the man insisted. "Stupid girl thinks she can rule us, it's shameful. Before her, we had a *real* ruler, one we could be proud of . . ."

Laela scowled. "Shut up, she's doin' her best."

"Oh yeah?" the man came over to her table. "Doin' her best, is she, girl?"

Laela finished off her first beer. "Yeah!" she said. "She didn't ask to be Queen anyhow, did she?"

The man set his jaw. Behind him, his friends started to nod among themselves—but probably not because they agreed with her.

Laela knew she was making trouble, but she didn't care. Nobody in the Eyrie talked back to her like this, and people didn't say what they were really thinking. This, she thought, was exactly what she'd been missing all this time.

She put her boots up on the table and started on the second beer. "The Queen ain't so different from you," she said. "She grew up a commoner, remember?"

"Yeah, well, if she's like us, I ain't seen it," said one of the man's friends. "What's she doin' for the common people?"

"Yeh reckon that Saeddryn cares about yeh, then?" said Laela.

"She ran the Temple," said another of the man's friends. "Anyone could go to the ceremonies, an' she'd do them herself, an' bless any man what asked for it. Saeddryn was always the one out here lookin' out for us; even great King Arenadd never did that much."

"But he was busy," the third friend added hastily. "Had lots to worry about."

"An' so does the Queen," said Laela.

"My arse," the first man shot back.

"Oh yeah?" Laela drained the mug, and stood up. "You wanna make somethin' of it?"

The first man laughed. "Don't be daft. I don't hit girls."

Laela grinned. "That's all right, 'cause a girl's gonna hit you."

She punched him in the face as hard as she could.

The man took a step back in surprise, but then lurched forward and hit her back, hard enough to knock her over.

Laela stumbled backward over a chair and hit the ground painfully, but she got up quickly enough and launched herself at him.

Around her, the tavern erupted in shouting.

"He hit a girl!"

"He insulted the Queen; get him!"

"Get 'em out of here!"

Laela didn't care. She didn't bother to pull out her dagger either. This was a fist-fight. She punched the man again, in the jaw, ignoring the pain in her knuckles. He tried to punch her again, but she only grabbed him by the tunic and kneed him hard in the groin.

Around her, other people had started to join in, some to stop her and others to attack the man who'd punched her.

Laela, though, started to laugh. She lashed out at anyone who came at her, almost indiscriminately, using every trick she'd learnt from Bran and anything else that sprang to mind. Another woman tried to take her by the shoulder, and Laela head-butted her in the face. She kicked someone else in the kneecap with the heel of her boot and jabbed the man who'd punched her in the eyes.

It was chaos.

In the end, a pair of city guards barged in and put a stop to the fight, sometimes pulling people apart by force. The fighting died down quickly enough, and people slumped down to nurse their bruises or stood and glared defiantly at each other.

The two guards quickly took charge of the situation.

"All right, who started this?" one demanded.

The man Laela had punched spoke up. "It was her!" he

yelled, pointing at Laela with one hand while clutching his swollen eye with the other. "She hit me first!"

"No she didn't; ye hit a girl, ye great coward!" another man butted in.

But others spoke up, yelling in support of the man with the swollen eye. Laela didn't try to defend herself, but only grinned wickedly through a heavy nosebleed.

"All right, get her out of here," one of the guards snapped at his colleague.

Laela didn't object, but let them throw her out of the tavern.

"An' don't come back!" one of them called after her.

Laela scurried off and stopped to rest, leaning against a wall. She ached in several places, and her nose was still bleeding, but she'd never felt so alive.

She dabbed at the blood on her face and whooped to herself. "Whoo! What a night!"

Once she felt a little calmer, she set off for home, limping slightly but feeling better than she had in ages. She even started to sing to herself—an old peasant ditty she'd learnt when she was little.

"I danced around the tree when yeh came to look for me, round an' round the tree we went, round an' back again . . ." She couldn't remember the rest of the words, and occupied herself with trying to remember them for the rest of the walk to the Eyrie.

Climbing back up the stairs was much worse than climbing down them, especially with a badly bruised leg, but she stomped up there without complaint.

Up in her room, she poured some water into a bowl and cleaned her face before changing out of her dress into something more respectable. It was past midnight by now, but she felt too alive to sleep.

Once she was dressed, she barged out of the room and on through the Eyrie's richly decorated corridors until she found the door to the room where the Master of Taxation slept and banged on it until it opened.

The Master of Taxation looked irritable until she saw who it was, and quickly pulled herself up and tried to look dignified despite being in her nightgown. "What can I do for you, my lady—" She broke off. "My gods, what happened to your face?"

Laela ignored the question. “I got a job for yeh,” she said.

“Yes, my lady?”

“I want yeh to go to yer office right now and write up an order to get rid of the beer tax. Yes, all of it. I want all beer to be tax-free from now on. An’ yeh can tell everyone *that’s* what Queen Laela’s doin’ for the common people.”

15

Homecoming

Kullervo's time in Gwernyfed was one of the most joyful of his life.

After the celebrations were done, he spent the next few days walking around the village or helping with the work. He ate as much as he could and made sure he got plenty of sleep, building up his strength.

He didn't see Senneck again in those days, and he wondered where she had gone.

Nearly a week after their first meeting, he had decided to go for a walk after dinner. He went alone, leaning on his crutch. The truth was that he was hoping to find Senneck since she was supposed to return to the village at night. There was no sign of her among the buildings—he'd never seen her there anyway. He wandered out of the village and into the orchard not far from Rufus' home.

Hobbling around a blackberry thicket, he found Senneck crouching alone among the trees.

Heart beating faster, he moved toward her.

She stirred and rasped very softly. "So the freak has returned. Speak or be gone."

Kullervo kept on coming until he had gone around her and reached her head. He kept at a safe distance. "Hello, Senneck."

She regarded him. "Were you looking for me?"

"Yes," said Kullervo. "I heard about Erian, and . . ." He trailed off.

She grunted. "So you know who I am."

"I do," said Kullervo. "And I'm sorry."

The blue-eyed griffin raised and refolded a wing. "Hopes come, and hopes die. I lost my Erian because of my own stupidity, and I have paid the price."

"It wasn't your fault what—what *he* did," said Kullervo.

"I did not listen to the Mighty Kraal. I did not believe him. If I had, I would never have allowed my human to face *Kraeai kran ae* alone. Instead, I believed that *Kraeai kran ae* was a mere human. Mad and savage, but still human. His death at Erian's hands would win us everything that I longed for. And so I let my human go to his death."

Kullervo listened to her speak and gradually realised what he was hearing. She was confessing. Confessing to guilt, admitting to weakness. Showing him her shame. Exposing the most secret side of herself.

"Why tell me this?" he asked, unable to stop himself.

She shifted her position, talons extending. "Why not? I have no reputation to uphold, no power to keep. I have nothing but myself and my memories, and you understand me and are here. Who would you tell that would care? The moon, perhaps."

Kullervo wondered if that was a joke. "I won't tell anyone. You can trust me, Senneck."

"You remind me of Erian," she muttered. "Alone in the world and as foolish as a chick. But perhaps not so ignorant." She looked at him, unblinking. "You are no messenger of a god that does not exist. You are something else that I do not recognise."

Kullervo was tired of lying. "I'm a hybrid," he said. "My father was human. My mother was a griffin who was transformed."

"Kyaaa!" she hissed. "Truly?"

"Yes."

Senneck kneaded the ground with her talons. "I have never imagined such a thing. What mad ruin of a griffin would mate with a human?"

"My mother did," said Kullervo. "That's all I can tell you."

"I see. So you were born this way."

"I can change," said Kullervo. "I have magic. I can be a man or a griffin."

Senneck cocked her head. "But now I see neither man nor griffin."

"Just now, I'm halfway," said Kullervo. "It was an accident."

"Youngsters often have troubles with their magic," said Senneck. "I had those troubles myself."

Carefully, Kullervo lowered himself into a sitting position. "What's your power, Senneck? Can I ask?"

"You may." Senneck arched her neck proudly. "My power is stone. I can change whatever I please into solid rock. Even living things."

"That's amazing," Kullervo said with genuine admiration. "Did you turn many things into stone?"

"A dog, once," she said. "And once the very surface of the ocean."

"And people?"

"Never a human," said Senneck. "Every day I wish I had done so to *Kraeai kran ae*."

"It might not have worked," said Kullervo.

"Still, I should have tried. But that is a burden I must bear." Senneck clicked her beak. "I was crueller to you that night than I should have been. To hear that *Kraeai kran ae* was dead caused me pain."

"I understand," said Kullervo.

"You spoke about this half-breed human as if you knew her," Senneck commented. "I think that you do."

"I . . . yes. I do know her. We only met once."

"But you were friendly to each other?"

"Yes."

"Then you came here to find us at her command," Senneck said at once.

"No! No. No, I didn't. The Queen doesn't know this place exists. And I'm not going to tell her. No, she sent me to look for something else, and I stumbled on Gwernyfed by accident."

Her eyes narrowed. "Then what were you seeking?"

"A human," said Kullervo. "A traitor. I think you might know her, Senneck."

"What human is this?"

"The Dark Lord's cousin," said Kullervo. "Saeddryn Taranisäii."

"The one-eyed one," Senneck hissed. "The female who fought beside him. I know her."

"She betrayed the Queen," said Kullervo. "And now she's probably plotting to take over. We know she tried to betray the King himself before he died."

"I see."

Senneck lifted a hind leg and scratched herself behind the ear. Absurdly, as he watched her, Kullervo felt his body responding to her presence. Something stirred inside him, and he shivered uneasily.

"I think you will go back to the other half-breed soon," Senneck interrupted. "This place is not your home."

"Yes, I suppose I should go back," Kullervo mumbled. "Laela must be wondering where I am. And she needs to know about what I found."

"Very well," said Senneck. "I understand." She stood up. "When you are ready to go, come and see me."

"Why?" said Kullervo.

"Because I am coming with you," said Senneck.

Kullervo and Senneck left Gwernyfed only a day or so after making their agreement. Kullervo didn't feel strong enough to make the change again before they left, but Senneck agreed to carry him for the sake of speed.

They said goodbye to Rufus and the others early in the morning. Kullervo had tied his wings in place to stop their catching the air and had wrapped himself in a thick, woollen cloak. That and the wings kept him surprisingly warm.

Rufus said his goodbyes with genuine sadness. "It's been wonderful to have you here, Kullervo," he said. "You don't know how much happiness you brought us all."

"I can guess." Kullervo smiled. "I'll never forget what you did for me."

"I hope you do remember us." Rufus paused. "You're not going to come back, are you?"

"I'll try," said Kullervo.

"Then I'll keep watch for you." Rufus gave him a bundle of food and turned to the waiting Senneck. "And you, Senneck.

I have to say the place will seem very different without you. You were one of our oldest friends."

Senneck flicked her tail. "This place has never been a true nest for me. But it has been a shelter. Now I am ready to leave. The story of Senneck is not done yet. Soon they will know my name again."

"They will." Rufus bowed to her. "You're a mighty griffin, Senneck, and a hero in your own right. See to it that they know that."

"I shall. Come, Kullervo. It is time for us to leave."

To Kullervo's surprise and embarrassment, Rufus gave him a hug. "Goodbye, holy one, and good luck. Go with Gryphus."

"I will."

Senneck crouched low, and Kullervo climbed—clumsily—onto her shoulders. He settled down between her wings and neck, as he had seen griffiners do, and put his arms around her neck as far as they would go with the bundle of food tucked in front of him.

Senneck had already straightened up. "You are safe?"

"I think so . . ."

"Do not fall," she advised. "I have not carried a rider in many years."

"I'll, uh, do my best. Try not to—"

She broke into the shambling preflight run before he could finish. He shivered and sat as still as he could, trying hard not to be jolted out of his seat when her wings unfurled and began to thrash.

Senneck took off.

Kullervo could feel the wind pulling insistently at his wings, trying to peel them away from his back. He pulled them back as well as he could, thanking Gryphus that he'd thought to tie them together. His tail was less lucky; it flapped about between Senneck's wings like a flag on a string, completely useless. Still, he did manage to stay in place more or less, and he had an advantage because he knew the rhythms and the movements of flight so well himself. He had never flown on griffinback before in his life, but *being* the griffin meant so much more.

Once they had levelled out and settled into a steady pace, he revelled in the wind and the feeling of weightlessness once again. The sensation of joy in flight was so great that he felt his bones creak, wanting to make the change. Not now, he told it. *Not now.*

This time, pure will-power was enough.

Senneck didn't seem bothered by her burden. She was a little unsteady at first, but she soon found her balance and turned to fly south as if she knew exactly where to go. Perhaps she had never forgotten the direction that had brought her to Gwernyfed in the first place.

In flight, there wasn't much for Kullervo to do but balance. But he had to stay alert for safety's sake, and he occupied himself with thinking and watching the view.

He wondered about Senneck. What was she planning to do when they reached Malvern? Kullervo wasn't sure, but he trusted her. She had no reason to hate Laela and every reason to hate Saeddryn.

Kullervo believed that Laela would help her. Take her in, as she had done for him. Help her. Give her a home again. Surely Laela would do that for the griffin who had once been partnered to her own uncle. He smiled to himself, imagining how they would greet each other. Laela's surprise and excitement. In a way, Senneck was a part of the family she had never had. Like Kullervo.

They could be together now, surely they could. Him and Laela and Senneck, a human and a griffin and a man who was halfway between the two. Three of them who had been lonely but would never have to be again. They could make a family.

He clung to that idea, believing it with all his might. Maybe he hadn't found Saeddryn, but he had found Senneck. And Skandar, him, too. Poor Skandar.

What he had found was still a good thing, surely, good for Laela.

He thought of Laela and wondered if she was all right. But she must be, with Oeka there to keep her safe. She was tough.

"Wait for me a little longer," Kullervo said aloud. "I'm coming, sister. I'm coming home."

Laela sat alone in the dining hall and massaged the bruise on her forehead while trying not to start yelling incoherently. There had been enough of that for one day.

The dining hall had been serving as her audience chamber ever since Oeka had returned, and the old one had become too . . . unpredictable. It was Oeka's lair now, and Laela hadn't even set foot in there in several days. She hadn't spoken to Oeka either. And Oeka hadn't come out. Not once.

Since she had returned, the small griffin had stayed in the audience chamber, crouched in silence on her marble platform with her eyes closed. Nobody wanted to go in. Even the servants had stopped cleaning it. Because, even though Oeka was the only one who went in there, she wasn't alone.

Strange things had begun to happen in the audience chamber. People reported hearing voices, and seeing light flash through the windows and the entrance. Sometimes, there would be odd smells, too, often an unsettling, cold kind of smell with a metallic edge to it, like ice or steel.

As time passed, the signs became more extreme—and frightening.

Laela herself heard crackings and breakings, unearthly howls and faint screams. White mist poured out into the corridor outside, and escaped through the windows into the sky around the tower. Even people down in the city had begun to notice the light that sometimes shot through the openings at night.

It was worse than that. People who ventured too close to the chamber complained of mysterious headaches. A few unlucky servants suffered temporary blindness or loss of hearing, and a guard who decided to investigate lost all his memories and couldn't even remember his own name for two days. All the victims recovered eventually, but the audience chamber and its occupant were feared by almost everyone in the Eyrie.

Eventually, Laela herself had decided to try to put a stop to whatever Oeka was doing. Even all these weeks later, she still couldn't remember what had happened after that. All she remembered was a vague vision of the archway that led to the chamber, shadowed and dusty, and a pain so intense it blinded her. She had woken up the next day in the infirmary, and was told that she had been unconscious for the best part of a day. Nobody would come out and say it, but she had heard rumours that she had been raving in her coma.

After that, she didn't dare to visit even the ramp that led to the chamber, and declared the entire level off-limits to everyone. A guard had been posted to stop people's trying, but he wasn't really necessary. No-one was stupid enough to disobey.

With all that, and with Oeka gone from her side, the last few weeks had been some of the worst in Laela's entire life. All she was thankful for was that there had been no word from Saeddryn. It seemed the former High Priestess was biding her time. The people of Malvern seemed quiet enough. And the Moon Temple's rebuilding was well underway. The new High Priestess was doing her job well.

Not for the first time, Laela wondered what had happened to Kullervo. There hadn't been any news of him; it was as if he had vanished off the face of the earth the moment he left Malvern. She hoped he was safe. He was the only person she knew aside from Oeka who would still tell her the truth.

Lunch arrived to interrupt her brooding. She ate it unenthusiastically and washed it down with some herb-flavoured water. Wine didn't hold any attraction for her any more.

She was picking through the bowl of strayberries provided for dessert when Inva came in. Beside her was her new partner, Skarok. He was white mixed with mottled grey, only half-grown, with the gawky, scrawny look griffin youngsters often had. Despite that he, and Inva went oddly well together, and Inva had that new air she had had ever since becoming a griffiner—that proud, dignified way she carried herself.

Seeing them together gave Laela a stab of pain in her heart. "How's it going?" she asked tonelessly.

Inva came to the table and made a quick bow. "My lady, a griffin has landed and wants to speak with you."

"What griffin?" said Laela, instantly suspicious.

"She will not give a name. But she has brought a rider—"

"A freak," Skarok interrupted harshly. He tossed his head. "I would have killed it, but the female would not let me."

"Freak?" said Laela. "What sort of freak's this, then? Human?"

Inva's look was guarded. "It is . . . a winged man."

"Wait, what? *Wings?* Like griffin wings?"

"Yes. And the tail and fur of one as well. He seemed eager to see you."

There was only one man in the world who fitted that description. "Kullervo! He's back!" And Laela jumped out of her seat and was through the door before Inva or Skarok could react.

She ran up the corridors and the ramps until she reached the entrance where the guard was still posted to keep people away from the audience chamber. Luckily, there was another way to the tower-top, though—a trapdoor meant for emergencies. Laela had had a ladder installed, and she climbed it now, ignoring it when she trod on the hem of her expensive velvet gown. The trapdoor was closed but she all but head-butted it open before pulling herself up and into the open air.

It was freezing on the flat tower-top, but Laela didn't notice. She saw the nameless griffin, resting just by the other entrance, and close by its side there was—

"Kullervo!"

He turned at the sound of her voice and ran toward her. Or, at least, tried to run. He made a clumsy, shambling rush toward her, stumbled, and fell flat on his face.

"Gryphus' talons, what are yeh trying to do?" Laela exclaimed as she pulled him to his feet. "Kullervo! It really is you!"

His face was covered in tiny feathers, but the grin hadn't changed. "Laela. I'm so glad to see you!"

"I'd say the same, but yeh kinda look . . . nothing like how yeh did before. What in blazes happened?"

"Oh, don't worry about it," he said. "The change went wrong. I can fix it when I want to; there just wasn't any time."

"Fair enough. Where have yeh *been*?"

"Dangerous places," said Kullervo. He gestured with an arm that had a raw red scar down its length.

"Holy gods, what did that?" asked Laela.

"I'll tell you later. Come on, you have to meet my new friend! Where's Oeka?"

"She's . . . uh . . . busy." Laela looked at the griffin, who had been waiting patiently. "Who's this?"

Kullervo leaned on her as they moved closer. "Laela, you won't believe who this is."

The griffin stood up. She was brown and looked as if she were getting on in age; her haunches were bony, and her beak was chipped. But she carried herself with immense dignity. "So this is the half-breed Queen?" she interrupted, bringing her head down to peer at Laela's face. "Yes . . . I see it. The mixed colours are obvious."

Laela glared. "Who are yeh, an' why should I care?"

"I am Senneck, and your griffish is pathetic."

"Thanks. I love makin' new friends, it's great fun. Have yeh got anythin' useful to say, or should I come back later?"

Kullervo, as always, had to play the peacekeeper. "Laela, this is *Senneck*. She was Erian's griffin."

Laela's sneer disappeared. "What?"

"My human was brother to your mother," Senneck said. "I remember you when you were a squealing pup in her arms."

Laela swore. "*Senneck!* Erian's—really?"

"She is," said Kullervo. "She was here when our—when Malvern was taken."

"I thought yeh were dead," Laela said with an edge to her voice.

"So did every human and griffin in the North," said Senneck. "But almost no-one knew that you even existed." She brought her face close to Laela—so close that her breath ruffled the Queen's hair. "Spawn of *Kraeai kran ae*. I remember the day when your mother showed you to us. Erian told her to smother you."

"Senneck—!" Kullervo exclaimed.

She lifted her head away. "Your mother would not listen. Erian could not understand why she would keep the child of her father's murderer. She should not have brought you to the North, and she paid for it with her life."

Laela's stare had become very steady. "Ole Uncle Erian was a twit. An' from what I hear, he paid for that with *his* life. A life *you* didn't save. That sound right?"

Senneck drew back, hissing. "How dare you speak to me that way! You have no right—"

"*Stop it!*" Kullervo's yell broke into the argument, and he pushed forward and actually put himself between them. "Stop it!" he shouted again. "Don't *be* like this!"

To her shock, Laela saw there were tears in his eyes. "Kullervo—!"

"Stop it." Kullervo gave each of them a fierce, distraught look. "You're not meant to do this. You should be friends."

"Why?" Senneck rasped mockery.

"Because—because you're *family*." Kullervo almost wailed the word. "You knew her uncle, Senneck. You knew her mother. You said you knew her grandfather, too. You're one of us."

"Griffins do not care for family," Senneck said at once. "And no human is family of mine. Nor a friend."

"Well, you should!" Kullervo roared. "Unless you want to be all alone forever."

Laela grabbed him by the arm. "Kullervo, for gods' sakes calm down! Yer goin' hysterical!"

He took several deep breaths. "We *should* be friends," he insisted. "All three of us together."

"Yeah, right," Laela sneered.

Kullervo looked away from them both, toward the Northern horizon. "We have a common enemy," he said. "Don't we?"

"The shape-changer is right," Senneck said abruptly. "I have not returned to spit insults at you, half-breed. Once, I wished for nothing but to kill *Kraeai kran ae*, but now I know he is dead. But his cousin is alive, the one who helped him to destroy my home. If I cannot have revenge on him, then I shall take it from her."

Laela cracked her knuckles. "*Now* I like what I'm hearin'. So yeh wanna help us fight the one-eyed hag, eh?"

"No," said Senneck. "I am going to kill her."

"Even better." Laela drew herself up and adjusted the circlet on her head. "But I gotta say I'm surprised you'd fight for me, what with me bein' Arenadd's daughter. You fought him, an' all us Northerners once, right?"

"I did, but that is in the past," said Senneck, unmoved. "I am a griffin, and I do not serve ideals. The cause I fought for once was lost long ago. Now, I will fight for revenge. And if I must fight beside half-breeds and Northerners, so be it."

"All right then," said Laela. "My way is to take help when

it's offered, an' yours'd be damned useful. So I'm gonna make yeh a deal. I'll give yeh somewhere to live an' food to eat. While yeh rest up, I'll have a good think an' talk to some people an' when I'm ready I'll tell yeh an' we'll make some plans."

"I will not wait," said Senneck.

Laela shrugged. "Fine, but yeh might wanna stay. If yeh do what I asked, then when I'm ready I'll tell yeh exactly where she is an' what t'expect when yeh get there."

"You know where she is?" said Kullervo.

"Kaanee did a good job," said Laela.

"Very well then." Senneck made a rattling noise in her throat. "I shall wait. But be warned: I shall not wait long."

"Yeh won't have to," said Laela. "Don't worry."

Senneck inclined her head briefly and began to move away. "I shall find a place to sleep and come to find you later."

Laela nodded and waited until she had flown away.

When they were alone, she turned to Kullervo. "Now what was *that* all about?"

His eyes had gone red. "She shouldn't have talked to you like that."

"That's just how griffins are, Kullervo. Don't be such a baby."

He jerked as if she had just slapped him. "I didn't want it to be like that," he mumbled. "I thought . . ."

"Thought what?"

"I thought you'd be happy to see her. That she'd be happy to see *you*. You must look like her human did, and I thought . . ."

"Griffins don't think like that. Don't yeh know?"

"Not really. I don't know." Kullervo sagged. "I like her. I thought she would be kinder to you."

"Fat chance." Laela gave him a lopsided look. "Yeh really are innocent, ain't yeh?"

"Am I?"

"Anyone what thinks a griffin could be *kind* has gotta be innocent. Where did yeh find her?"

"Hiding in the mountains," Kullervo lied. "But that was after I found someone else."

"Who? I know it wasn't Saeddryn."

"It was your father," said Kullervo.

Laela went rigid. "What? He ain't—?"

"I found his body."

"But—but what was it doin' there?"

"Skandar must have taken it with him," said Kullervo. "He was there, guarding it. I'm sorry, Laela. I tried to bring it back here, but Skandar wouldn't let me. He almost killed me." He held up his arm, displaying the scar.

Laela winced. "I wouldn't've asked yeh to do that if I'd been there. But look—my father's . . . the King's body . . . what was it . . . like?"

"Rotted," Kullervo grimaced. "Falling apart."

"Oh." Laela's expression was unreadable. "An' Skandar?"

"I don't think he's going to come back," said Kullervo. "He barely even leaves that corpse alone to hunt."

"Didn't think he'd come back." Laela looked relieved. "Just as well. Havin' him here'd be another complication. He's unpredictable, he is. An' bloody dangerous, but I'm sure yeh know that."

"I do," Kullervo said dryly. "I just wish I could have brought the body back. That way you'd have proof."

"Doesn't matter." Laela offered him her arm and led him away toward the trapdoor. "I lost the chance to make myself stronger with that. Looks like I'm gonna have to win this the old-fashioned way now: with a big ole heap of violence."

"Oh no. What's been happening here?"

"Bad things," said Laela. She helped him through the trapdoor and followed him inside. "I got a bad situation, Kullervo. Real bad."

"How bad? What's Saeddryn doing, do you know?"

She took him down the ramps, back toward the dining hall. "Kaanee an' the rest did their work. Saeddryn's at Warwick. A lot of the old guard joined up with her. Her son Caedmon's at Fruitsheart, an' her daughter Arddryn's holed up at Skenfrith. We don't know exactly what they're doin', but the picture's bein' drawn better all the time. Warwick's got some big arrow shooters built up on the walls. Skenfrith's been having some loud gatherin's in the taverns. Fruitsheart looks like it's bidin' its time so far, but they've been askin' some tough questions whenever a griffiner comes to visit."

"They're going to declare war," Kullervo said at once.

"Probably. Only question is, what're we gonna do about it?"

"What does Oeka think?"

Laela's mouth became a thin, hard line. "Yeah, I got a few more things to tell yeh . . ."

16

Seeing

Before going to talk with Laela again, Kullervo did something he had been meaning to do for some time. He locked himself in his quarters, barricaded the door, and began the transformation. It took more concentration and energy than it ever had before, but his body responded eventually, shifting back toward human. Fur and feathers shed onto the floor, and bones grated and shifted. His legs and hips had to change the most, but they managed it eventually.

This time, he didn't black out, and once the pain had cleared, he felt rather proud of himself. He slept for a while, and woke to find the sun going down outside his window. He tested his legs—they ached, but they worked, and, after a few false starts, he got up, pulled some clothes on, and walked stiffly out of the room.

A servant showed him to Laela's own quarters, and she answered the door. "Oh, Kullervo, there yeh are," she said. "Come in."

He entered, shutting the door behind him. "Sorry I took a while. I didn't think it was a good idea for anyone to see me like that."

"Doesn't matter," said Laela. She looked tired, Kullervo thought. In fact, she looked exhausted. There were dark smudges under her eyes, and her hair was greasy and tangled. She looked as if she hadn't rested or eaten properly in days.

Her room at least was warm and well lit. Two chairs had

been set up in front of the fire-place, and Kullervo sat down in one, wincing as he bent his knees.

Laela took the other. "It's good to see yeh again, Kullervo," she said. "It really is. I missed yeh. Worried about yeh."

"I missed you, too," said Kullervo. "And worried about you. I'm so sorry I didn't come back sooner, but I was hurt—"

"Never mind." Laela waved his apologies away. "I'm just glad yer all right."

Kullervo glanced around the room, but there was no sign of anyone else in it. "So where *is* Oeka?" he asked. "It's odd seeing you without her."

"She's . . . in the audience chamber," said Laela.

"Oh. What's she doing in there?"

"Ain't got a clue," said Laela. "She hasn't come out. Nobody's goin' in either."

"Why not? Is she sick?"

"Maybe." Laela looked miserable. "I dunno what's wrong with her. It's nothin' I can understand; I'm human."

"I don't get it," said Kullervo. "What are you saying?"

"It's magic is what it is," said Laela. "She's doin' somethin' with magic. Whatever it is, it's made that whole level impossible to go into."

"How?"

"There's"—Laela waved a hand vaguely—"lights. Noises. An' somethin' else. It gets into yer head, does bad things. I don't reckon Oeka's controllin' it either because it got to me, too, when I tried goin' in there."

Kullervo looked bewildered. "It must be magic, but I don't know what. To be honest, I don't know that much about magic. Griffins learn it from each other, but none of them would teach me, you see. I had to work it out myself."

"Nobody knows what it is," said Laela. "I only know what she told me. She went off, see. Flew away the same day you did. Went south. Came back a few days later, but wouldn't say where she'd been. All she said is she'd done somethin' to make herself stronger. Said she had to 'unravel' somethin', so she could get new powers."

"I suppose that must be what she's doing, then," said Kullervo. "But we'll have to hope it doesn't go wrong somehow."

"Yeah, I bloody well hope so," said Laela. "'Cause if it

does, I'm as good as dead. Now look, it's time I told yeh more about what's goin' on."

"I'm surprised you'd trust me that much," Kullervo said mildly. "You hardly know me."

Laela smiled uncertainly. "Maybe. Truth is, I got no-one else much. Inva hardly speaks, I don't trust nobody in the Eyrie, an' Oeka's . . . not around. There's only Iorwerth. I'm makin' plans with him already, in case it comes to a fight. But that ain't why I trust yeh."

"Why, then?"

"Yer an outsider," said Laela. "Not from here. Yeh don't care about the Night God, or Saeddryn, or any of that, an' nobody else's got a stake in this except me."

"I could be working for the Southerners," Kullervo pointed out.

"Yeah right!" Laela laughed roughly. "The same Southerners what kept yeh in a cage an' called yeh a freak? I know what that lot are like, an' they don't take kindly to our sort." She softened. "Yeh ain't given me no reason to think yer two-faced as well as two-shaped. Yeh said we were the same type, an' I believe yeh. That's why I trust yeh."

Kullervo smiled. "All right, then. What do you want me to do?"

"We know where Saeddryn is now," said Laela. "That's where I'm sendin' yeh."

Kullervo lost his smile. "Why? I'm not going to kill her for you."

"Relax. I'm sendin' yeh with a message, that's all. But it's gotta go straight into her hands, understand? No-one else's."

"What message?" Kullervo clasped his hands together. "Are you really going to declare war on her? Is that the message?"

"We don't want war," said Laela. "Not yet. The message is this: I'm givin' Saeddryn a chance to surrender along with Caedmon an' Arddryn. If they come here an' lay their weapons down, they'll be safe. I'll make Caedmon my heir, an' Arddryn and Saeddryn can go live in Maijan. They'll be left alone as long as they stay there, an' Caedmon'll be kept safe."

"And if she says no?"

"That's the next part of the message." Laela's eyes narrowed.

"She says no, an' they all die. Starting with Torc. She says no, an' he'll be executed. Painfully. In public."

"He hasn't done anything wrong!" Kullervo said. "You can't do that to him, Laela."

"Don't worry, I ain't gonna do it. She won't let me do it. She'll surrender. No way she'll let her own husband die. Even if she tries to hold out, her kids won't let her do it. They'll want their dad safe."

Kullervo relaxed. "So all I have to do is deliver this message?"

"That's right. I'll have it all writ down. Carry it over in griffin shape an' deliver it that way. When yeh get there, just tell 'em yeh got a message from the Queen—but keep it hidden. Don't let nobody take it from yeh. Don't let anyone else read it before she does."

"I can do that."

"Good. An' . . . be careful, all right? I ain't gonna lose yeh now when I've just got yeh back."

"Don't worry." Kullervo winked. "I'm a survivor."

"We half-breeds gotta be, ain't we?" said Laela.

". . . I'm a survivor . . . gotta be . . . gotta be . . . survivor . . . I'm a survivor . . ."

High up in her lair, Oeka's beak opened and her tongue moved silently as the words echoed in her head. She hadn't opened her eyes or used her normal hearing in some time now—at first the senses had been too much of a distraction, and by now they were gone altogether. As she sat there, still as stone, taking each howling spirit apart and using its energy to build into her own mind, she felt the structure of her brain physically changing. With no room to grow inside her skull, the part that controlled her powers found other ways to expand.

She hadn't eaten once since her visit to the Spirit Cave. Normal griffins absorbed new energy from the food they ate, but the solid lump of pure magic lodged in her stomach made all that unnecessary. She could feel it feeding her body, replacing every scrap of energy she used and adding even more on top of that. Once, manipulating this much magic for this long would have killed her ten times over, but not any more. No, not any more . . .

Oeka gulped slightly—the only movement she had made all day. Around her, the spirits screamed in protest as they were unravelled and ruthlessly absorbed. It was becoming faster and easier all the time—so much so that by now she could begin to experiment with some of her new gifts. She reached out effortlessly with her mind and tasted the thoughts of Kullervo and Laela. Laela was easy. *Sad. Angry. Desperate.*

Kullervo, much harder. *Secrets,* Oeka scented. *Hidden things. Something hiding. Fear, yes, fear. And . . . anger?* She grasped at the vague feelings as they slid out of her grasp, frustrating and elusive. This mind was impossible!

She angrily shut them away and turned her full attention back to her work. More power, more energy needed to unlock this mind. She *had* to know.

Gradually, though, other thoughts seeped through. Laela's emotions were worrying. She had been watching them over the last few days, and now that she began to think about them, she wondered what they could mean. How much time had passed? What could be happening out there while she was locked away?

A hiss snaked through the glowing air. Power would be no use if Laela failed while she was gone. Everything could be lost in a single stroke, then all she had put herself through would be useless.

Slowly, Oeka began to let herself relax. It took a huge effort to stop the process, and, for a few moments, she began to think she was stuck and would not be able to stop until the last of the spirits had been used. But the magic rushing around her finally slowed and drew inward at her command. She took a deep breath—deeper than should have been possible—and pulled it all inside her, back to the source in her stomach. The source absorbed it, and she could feel the icy burn in the spot where it waited. The feeling was far less powerful than it had been before, however, and she knew she must have used a good chunk of what she had collected at the Spirit Cave.

When everything felt normal again, she opened her eyes.

She was blind.

Panicking, she lurched up off the platform and toppled off

the edge. She hit the floor with a thump and a jerk of pain—those senses, at least, were still there. But her eyes—her eyes were useless. She called out, but heard nothing. Was she deaf, or mute? Or both?

Oeka lay still for a time, paralysed with fear. What had she done to herself?

Little by little the enormity of it crept up on her. She had spent so long in that cloud of magic, using it to alter herself, and she had had no idea of how much it had changed—how much it had corroded away her mind. She had gained so many new powers, but she had crippled herself as well.

But that did not mean she was helpless now, surely . . . ?

Cautiously, she reached out with her mind. Tendrils of thought—her extra senses—extended to touch the room. Focusing now was far too easy, and she pushed harder, flexing new abilities that had gone unused until this moment.

It worked. Using forms of vision so sophisticated they went beyond mere sight, she built an image of the world around her. Its colours and details were wonderfully vivid and sharp, giving up information that normal eyes could never see. She saw the walls and knew where the marble had been mined and shaped, and how it had been cut and polished. The tapestries gave off odours of the hands that had woven them. Dead insects, caught in the spider-webs on the ceiling, sighed faint whispers of their lives.

Oeka concentrated on shutting out the unnecessary details and got up off the floor. Moving stiffly, seeing without eyes, she walked toward the door. Her body worked the same way it had before, at least. She wondered if she could still fly.

As she left the audience chamber, she selected a single sense and let it spread out through the Eyrie tower—searching for Laela's mind. She found it. It tasted of frustration and the tang of fear.

Oeka went to find its owner.

Laela was in one of the unoccupied griffin nests, arguing with Senneck.

"I will not stay here," the blue-eyed griffin warned. "The traitor shall die at my talons."

"Not now," Laela said.

"You promised me that you would not make me wait."

"I said I wouldn't make yeh wait *long*. Listen. We're still negotiatin', right? I ain't lettin' this turn into war unless I have to. I'm gonna try an' get her to settle this peaceful-like, before I go doin' anythin' else."

"She will not *negotiate*," Senneck said. "She is like her cursed cousin. Dominance is all she wants. Tell me where she is, and I shall kill her for you. That is my only wish."

"If it comes to war, then so be it," said Laela. "All I need is a day or so. Just long enough for Kullervo to carry his message an' come back."

"So you are sending the shape-changer?"

"Yeah."

"I shall go with him."

"Oh yeah, why?" Laela gave her a narrow look. "So yeh can go behind my back? Don't think yer gonna fool me that easy, Senneck."

"The half-shape is weak and a fool," Senneck said evenly. "He will need my help, or he will not survive."

"I see. An' why do yeh care, exactly?"

"He brought me out of my exile and told me that my human's murderer was dead. I will repay him this way."

Laela looked puzzled—gratitude, from a griffin? "That's sweet of yeh, but I want yeh to stay here."

"You cannot make me obey you, human," Senneck hissed. "You do not even have a griffin!"

"I do, an' considerin' yeh were on the other side in the war I shoulda had yeh put down the moment I caught sight of yeh. So if I were in yer place I'd stop bein' so uppity."

The threat didn't have the effect Laela had been hoping for. Senneck rose, rasping angrily, and took an aggressive step toward her. Laela held her ground, but prepared to back away fast if anything happened—

—and then the feeling swept over them.

Senneck felt it first. She halted and crouched slightly, her tail flicking uncertainly. She huffed and shook her head, hard, as if trying to dislodge something from her feathers.

Opposite her, Laela groaned and put her hands over her ears. "What *is* that?"

I come.

The voice echoed in Laela's head. "What—?"

Faint whispers filled the air, and the room grew suddenly colder as Oeka came in. She moved slowly, a little clumsily. Her eyes were open, but unfocused, glowing faintly.

"Gryphus' talons!" Laela exclaimed, using the Southern curse without meaning to. "Oeka! What in the gods' names—?"

Oeka's beak opened slightly, but no sound came out. *I have returned,* the voice said in Laela's head—Oeka's voice, she realised suddenly. Only now it was slow and rich, not a griffin's voice but . . . something else.

"Oeka!" Laela said again. "I thought—are yeh all right? What have yeh been doin' all this time?"

The eyes stared blindly, straight ahead. *I am transformed. You cannot comprehend the powers I carry.*

Senneck had stayed in a defensive hunch since the smaller griffin had appeared, but now she uncoiled and came closer, sniffing. "You are Oeka?" she looked sharply at Laela. "Is this the griffin who chose you, half-breed?"

"Yeah." Laela mumbled, not looking at Senneck.

Senneck had transferred her gaze back to Oeka. "I sensed the magic under my talons when I arrived. Now I know it was you, little one. What have you done?"

Oeka didn't answer. Light and shadows shifted on her face, making it look as if she were leering.

"She went to some place," Laela said. "Wouldn't say where, but she said she got more magic somehow."

Senneck's hackles rose. "Fool!" she screeched at Oeka. "What have you done? You have tried to expand your magic! You sought out a place of power, I know it. Did your mother never tell you what would happen to you?"

I have taken what was there for my use, Oeka answered coolly. *If you are too weak to do the same, then so be it.*

"You are not strong enough for this," said Senneck. "I can sense the energies you are trying to contain. You will not contain them for long. They will destroy you."

No. Oeka's head rose sharply. *I have contained them. They are mine now. I have absorbed them into my mind. You cannot hide a single thought from me, Senneck. I know your past, and*

I know your intentions. She stretched her neck, and her beak jerked up and down in a parody of scenting. *I see a day when the sky turned dark and a ring of fire burned above you. I see a white griffin fall from the sky. I see you on the ground, spreading your wings over a dead human as you say his name and know your end. I see years of despair, and a twisted creature that is neither man nor griffin. This one is large in your mind . . .*

If Senneck was affected by this, she didn't show it. "You think you are a mighty magic-user, but you are nothing but an overgrown chick. Your foolery will be the end of you, one way or the other. It does not matter if you believe me or not; this old griffin shall live to see your death."

Oeka's head turned blindly toward Laela. *The old one will not betray you. She will go with Kullervo and do what she can to help him. She is full of hatred, but she is more patient than she seems.*

Laela rubbed her face with both hands. When she uncovered it again, it had assumed a patient, stolid expression. "Fine. Whatever. I got it. Senneck, yeh can go with Kullervo if he says yes."

The shape-shifter will do as you have asked him, was all Oeka said. *He loves you.*

Laela reddened. "So yeh can sense all that now? What'm I thinkin' now, then?"

You are uncomfortable, but you accept what you see, said Oeka. *You think that this is beyond you and that you can do nothing but believe what you are told.*

"Yeah, well, what would a human know?" said Laela. "Are yeh gonna stay with me now, then?"

Yes. I am done with my work. For now.

"Good. Well . . . let's go get some rest, then."

"I will go and speak with Kullervo," said Senneck. She stalked out of the room, very dignified. As she passed Oeka, she hissed to her. "Beware. You have already blinded yourself. What part of yourself will you lose next?"

Oeka ignored her. *Laela. I am sorry that I have been away for so long. Now I am back, and I can be at your side again.*

Laela drew back, trying not to look at the glassy eyes and sagging jaw. "I don't like this, Oeka. Yeh don't look right. An' what if yeh kill yerself, like Senneck said?"

Oeka's feathers fluffed out angrily. *The old hen knows*

nothing. I am more powerful now than she can possibly imagine.

"Yeh said," Laela growled. "Fine then. I ain't gonna pretend I understand any of it. But yeh ain't gonna do that again, understand? No flyin' off, an' no lockin' yerself away. From now on, yeh tell me everythin'. Not a day later, not twenty years later, *now*. When yeh know it, yeh tell me. No more doin' whatever yeh feel like without a word to me. I ain't gonna stand for it, got that? I'm the Queen here, an' it's about time I got some soddin' respect."

Oeka's eyes didn't turn to look at her, but her head jerked in Laela's direction. *I understand. I will not keep important things from you again. There will be no need.*

"There better not be. Now"—Laela softened—"do yeh need some food?"

I do not eat any more. Oeka put her head on one side. *But perhaps I will try.*

"I'll take that as a yes."

Laela had some meat brought up. Oeka gulped it down, awkwardly, as if she had forgotten how. She gagged a little after it had gone down.

"Are yeh all right?" Laela asked.

The small griffin lifted a talon and rubbed it down the side of her beak. *The meat had no flavour . . .*

"Bad cut, maybe?"

No. Oeka's beak opened wider, tongue arching. *I cannot taste.*

Laela swore. "Oeka, this ain't right. Blinded, not able to taste—can yeh hear any more, or are yeh just hearing my mind?"

It does not matter. Those senses were crude things, useless compared to all I feel now. The world is open to me. There was ecstasy in Oeka's mental voice. *At last, I can truly see.*

"If yeh say so," said Laela.

17

Messengers

Kullervo had been provided with quarters intended for visiting griffiners. They were only modestly furnished by griffiner standards, but to him they looked wonderfully luxurious. Solid spice-wood furniture, a big feather bed, and a rug made from the hides of the same Northern-bred sheep whose long black wool had once been used to make the hated slave robes. In this form, it was thick and soft and had been placed in front of the fire-place, where there was a good fire going. Kullervo ignored the wine that had been laid out for him—he had never tried drink—and stretched out on the rug.

Delicious warmth covered him like a blanket, and he yawned and stretched. Instinctively he rolled over onto his side, curling up like a sun-bathing griffin. His bald wings twitched away from the hearth, and he yawned again and curled his tail around himself. It was an ugly thing, without fur or feathers, all pink like a rat's. The tip flicked from side to side, catlike, tapping against his side.

Kullervo dozed and had a half-formed dream of gentle hands holding him up.

He woke up feeling happy and drowsy. Something was touching his leg. He opened his eyes a crack and saw something dark in front of his face. It was rough and pitted, curving away from him, and he looked at it for a while before he realised it was a talon.

I've split in half at last, he thought dopily. *My griffin shape is lying next to me.*

The thing touching his leg moved, and he opened his eyes properly and realised that there really was a griffin lying beside him.

Senneck.

From here, her flank was a sandy-feathered mountain looming above him.

Kullervo smiled sleepily. "Good morning."

"It is not morning," came her reply.

Kullervo said nothing. He yawned and rolled his head back so that his neck cracked pleasantly. Senneck was lying on her belly, partly rolled onto one side, with her legs curled in and her wings draped lazily over her flanks. Her head was raised, watching him.

Kullervo remembered that he was naked, but he didn't feel embarrassed. Griffins didn't care about that sort of thing, and why should they?

"How long have you been here?" he asked, not getting up.

"I came to see you but found you asleep," she said. "I rested while I waited for you to wake. It was not so long."

Kullervo rolled onto his front. "You've never seen me in this shape before, have you? Well . . . here I am, I suppose. This is as human as I get."

She blinked slowly. "You have not lost your wings."

"Not my tail either. I can't grow new bones. If I lost a wing, it would never come back."

"Then how do you change?"

"My bones . . . change inside me. Make new shapes. I don't really know how it works, but I can feel them doing it. It's very painful," Kullervo added matter-of-factly.

Senneck cocked her head. "Interesting. The half-breed says that she has given you another task."

"Yes, just to carry a message."

"I already know what the message will be and who it will go to," said Senneck. "I have decided to go with you."

Kullervo blinked. "Really? Why?"

"It will be better than staying here to rot. And I wish to see my enemy again and remember her scent."

"I'd like you to come," said Kullervo. "It'll be better than travelling alone. And if there's trouble, two of us would be better than just me."

"You are right. We must leave soon."

"Agreed. I just need some time—I have to become the griffin again so I can fly there."

Senneck tilted her head forward. "When shall you do that?"

"Er . . . now, maybe. I feel strong enough."

"I do not understand how you can use magic in that form," said Senneck. "Does your magic gland stay with your wings and tail?"

"I think so. I can't use it the way I do when I'm a griffin, though." Kullervo sat up, cross-legged. "When I'm human, it's much harder to control. I can't just concentrate and make it happen."

"Then how do you activate your magic?"

"Sometimes, I do it by accident," said Kullervo. "If I feel threatened or very angry. When I *want* it to happen, I think of something that makes me upset. My body reacts, to try to protect me by making itself stronger. Growing talons and claws, that sort of thing."

"*Shaaaaeeee* . . ." Senneck hissed, but without aggression. "So you shall do this now?"

"Yes, I think I will. Might as well."

There was an awkward silence. Senneck stayed where she was and watched Kullervo. He sat and looked back uncomfortably.

"It's not a nice thing to see," he said eventually. "I always do it in secret."

"Do it now." Senneck got up, sitting on her haunches. "I will watch."

"It's really not nice," said Kullervo. "Nobody's ever seen me change. Well . . . some people did see me once, when it happened by accident. They were terrified."

"I am not so easily frightened," said Senneck. "Make the change. I am curious."

Her lack of trepidation made Kullervo feel unexpectedly pleased. He was almost flattered. "All right, then. Just—don't touch me. And don't let anyone else come in, no matter what happens."

"Very well." Senneck moved back a way and settled down attentively.

Kullervo looked away from her, toward the ground, and closed his eyes. Memories bubbled to the surface, and he focused on them, letting old voices fill his ears.

Faces staring, staring, always staring. Some afraid, some openly revolted. The worst were the ones who showed pity. It was always guarded pity, tainted with contempt.

What is that? That thing, what is that thing, what is it? Gryphus' talons, it's so hideous! What is that thing? Don't touch it— That thing, thing, thing, thing . . .

Pain and misery hardened in Kullervo's stomach. His fists clenched, remembering times when they had beat against things—walls, faces, himself, tearing at the twisted wings that thrust out of his back. *Freak! Freak!*

Anger coursed through his system, hot and vital. Somewhere deep inside him, it touched some hidden switch. Instantly, pain spiked over his skin as the feathers began to sprout.

The change took hold.

A little way away, Senneck started slightly. She had seen Kullervo go still, apparently concentrating, and had noted it when he began to breathe harder, his face twitching the way human faces did when they were distressed in some way. Still, nothing seemed to be happening.

Then he went rigid, in a way that looked very familiar to Senneck. His mouth opened, and she braced herself, expecting to see the magic come forth. But none did. He only gasped, and hunched slightly. For a moment, it looked as if nothing else were going to happen, until she saw the little spines appearing all over his skin. They thickened, and grew longer, and opened out into feathers. Fur sprouted, too. Kullervo didn't react much at all, and Senneck began to think that he had been lying when he had said the process was painful.

At least, she thought that until she heard the first crack, then the ominous creaking and sinewy tearing noises that came from somewhere inside him. She looked on, revolted, as his form began to pull itself out of shape, and the vile noises grew louder. Kullervo threw his head back and let out an unearthly howl.

Senneck made no move to help him. Nor did she look away. She stayed just where she was through the entire process and did not look away until the last vicious breaking sound had died away.

Kullervo lay unconscious in his griffin form. Senneck did move closer then, to sniff at his wing. He had the rough, musky scent of a mature male griffin. She huffed her surprise. He was small, and odd-looking, but he was still a griffin—a real one. Not an illusion or a false shape, but a true griffin.

"Then you do have the blood of a griffin in you," she said aloud. "You are a true hybrid as you claimed . . . how can this be?"

She wondered how much of his story he had really told her and how much he had kept back. But she determined to find out. There would be time on the journey, and she would see how much of a true griffin he was.

Kullervo took a day to recover from the change, and, when he was ready, he went to see Laela. He caught up to her in the council chamber, with Oeka back at her side.

Kullervo faltered at the sight of the small griffin. Her eyes were glassy, and the eyelids drooped, making her look tired and ill. But there was nothing sluggish about the way she moved when she came down off the platform and swaggered up to him. *You taste of disgust,* an unearthly voice said.

Kullervo took a step backward. "Oeka? What's wrong with you?"

I have taken what is rightfully mine. Her beak lowered, putting her forehead closer to him, and she tensed.

Kullervo felt something push at him, inside. His head ached, and he shook it dazedly. "Stop that!"

Oeka gave an unformed, ugly hiss. *You cannot hide from me forever, freak. I will find what lurks in your mind and tear it free, one way or the other!*

"That's enough, Oeka." Laela's voice interrupted. "Leave him alone unless yeh want to carry this thing yerself."

Kullervo moved away from the blind griffin and looked at Laela. "What is this? What happened to her eyes?"

"Don't ask," Laela said shortly. "Now, are yeh ready to go? Is that why yer here?"

"Yes. Senneck and I are going together."

"Thought so. Here it is, then." Laela held up a wooden tube whose ends were covered in wax. Long leather straps dangled from it. "This is a message-holder. Got the scroll inside, see? I'll tie it on yer back, between yer wings, where it'll be safe. Pull it off when yeh get to Saeddryn an' put it in her hands. No-one else should be able to get at it."

"Clever. Should I crouch so you can put it on me?"

"Don't worry about it; yer too short to worry about that." Laela came over and attached the message-holder, buckling the straps around his wings and under his belly. "How's that feel?"

Kullervo tested his wings. "The straps chafe a bit."

"Got it." Laela loosened them. "That better?"

"Yes, thank you."

"Great." Laela nodded in satisfaction. "Got the idea from the Amorani messenger dragons an' had it made special. It's a good fit."

"I need a map now," said Kullervo.

Laela produced one and held it up for him. "This trip oughta be simple. Here's Malvern, right here. See the river? That's the River Nive. Follow it south till yeh find the spot where the two rivers meet. The other river's called the River Snow. Follow that one north an' keep goin'. I ain't sure how far it is, but Warwick's right by the river. Here, I got a picture of it."

The picture was surprisingly vivid, painted on a piece of fine sheepskin. It showed a city, as seen at a distance from the air. The walls around it were tall and forbidding, made from dark stone, and, at the centre, the griffiner tower looked like the limbless trunk of a burned tree.

"Good, ain't it?" said Laela. "It was done by some griffiner. Don't know his name, but they called him the Master of Art for a joke."

"He was very talented," said Kullervo. "So this is Warwick?"

"Yeah. I ain't seen it myself, but I showed it to Iorwerth an' he says the Master of Art got it right. Kaanee agrees."

Kullervo studied the painting, doing his best to memorise the details. "I think I can remember this."

"Shouldn't be hard," said Laela. "Now, the map. I was thinkin' maybe I'd put it under the strap on yer back. Senneck can pull it out for yeh if yeh need it."

"That could work."

After several attempts, Laela managed to secure the rolled-up map. Oeka stood by in silence. It was hard to say if she was aware of what was going on—those dead eyes couldn't watch anything, but maybe she was using some other sense to see what her human was doing. Laela and Kullervo both kept a careful distance from her and pretended there was nothing unusual in the room.

"There, all ready!" Laela said eventually. "Where's Senneck?"

"Waiting for me at the top of the tower. She said to tell you, 'Do not worry, your pet shape-changer is safe with me.' "

"She's such a charmer, ain't she?" Laela rolled her eyes.

"It's just her way. I don't mind."

Laela put her head on one side. "Yeh really do trust her, don't yeh?"

"I do."

"Why? Yeh know what she is."

"It's because I know what she is," said Kullervo. "A sad, lonely griffin who only just found a reason to live again."

"Don't be fooled, Kullervo," Laela said. "If she still had her human an' all the power she had before, she'd have killed the both of us by now."

"I don't believe that, Laela."

"Believe what yeh like, then. But watch yer back." Laela hugged him. "Be careful. Don't get yerself lost again, all right? Come back quick, for my sake."

Kullervo rubbed his head against her. "I will. I promise."

She let go of him. "Get going, then. Do me proud."

Kullervo kept his eyes on her, saying nothing. When the atmosphere became uncomfortable, he quickly transferred his gaze to the floor.

"What is it?" Laela asked.

Kullervo looked up again. "Laela, I should tell you something."

"What?"

He scratched at the floor, neck arched and bristling defensively. "I should have told you before, but I was afraid."

"Tell me now, then," said Laela. She had tensed.

"I—" Kullervo began, and stopped.

Oeka pushed in. *Tell her now or be gone, you deformed freak of nature.*

At that, Kullervo did something nobody would have expected. He reared up, opening his wings wide, and hissed.

Oeka lashed out mentally.

It didn't work.

Kullervo struck. His talons caught her in the shoulder, throwing her to the floor. Laela rushed in to stop him from attacking again, but he only turned around and stalked out without another word.

Oeka got up clumsily. She was bleeding. *I am hurt.*

"Serves yer right," Laela snapped, and ran out after Kullervo.

She caught up with him in a corridor part-way up the tower. He was moving fast, but slowed when she called out to him.

Laela caught up with him. "Kullervo, are yeh okay?"

"I'm not hurt," he said shortly.

"That ain't what I meant."

"I shouldn't have hit her," Kullervo said, without looking at her or slowing down any further.

Laela kept pace with him. "She was asking for it, talkin' to yeh like that. I dunno what's got into her. Don't want to know, either."

"She can't see into my mind," said Kullervo. "It makes her furious."

"She ain't never been content with not havin' somethin' she wants. Look, what were yeh gonna tell me?"

"It's not important."

Laela knew he was lying the instant the words were out of his beak, but she didn't say so. "All right, then. Have a good journey."

"I will." Kullervo paused to nudge her gently with his beak, then turned toward a handy opening in the tower wall. It was there to serve as a door for griffins, and he launched himself easily through it and flew away. Off to find Senneck and begin his flight to Warwick.

Laela went to the opening to watch him go. She felt sadder than she had expected, and lonely as well. She had come to like Kullervo more and more every time she met him, and with Oeka in this state, having him there to confide in meant even more.

She hoped he would be safe.

18

Fate

Warwick was a large city—one of the largest in Tara. It wasn't the richest—that honour went to Fruitsheart—but it had some of the strongest fortifications of any Northern settlement. Saeddryn had spearheaded the small group of rebels that had conquered it all those years ago and, for her, it was an obvious place to go. She had also lived there for a time after Arenadd's crowning, before official duties called her back to Malvern.

Warwick only had one griffiner tower at its centre, as opposed to Malvern's five, but it was a large one and even had its own council chamber, of sorts.

That was where Saeddryn gathered, with Aenae and her group of friends. There were Penllyn and Seerae, who had come here well ahead of her to be ready for her arrival. Nerthach and his partner, the oddly named Yissh. Lady Morvudd and Reakee. And lastly there was Nerth. Old Nerth, who had fought in the rebellion and been left with a lame leg that had stopped any griffin from choosing him. He had the place of honour on Saeddryn's right-hand side, and he listened in grim silence while she spoke.

"More word has come from Malvern," she said. "The half-breed seems to be preparing. Griffin-killing spear launchers are goin' up on the walls. The royal army is buildin' its numbers. They've left us be so far, obviously, but they're more than ready for a fight."

"Then let's go!" Morvudd said. "Attack!"

"I told ye no," said Saeddryn. "We're not going to Malvern."

"Why do we not go?" Yissh demanded. She was already extending her talons in anticipation.

"Listen," said Saeddryn. "We're the right side in this fight. An' if we're going to win, we have to stay that way. We've done nothing wrong, only the half-breed has. So we're going to wait. *She* has to attack *us*. An' when she does, Caedmon an' Arddryn will be ready on either side. The traitors will be wiped out, an' when they're gone, *that's* when we march on Malvern. With the Kingdom cleaned up, the throne will be ours, an' no-one in Tara will want it any other way."

"Come on!" said Nerthach. "Why wait? The longer we do, the more the half-breed bitch digs her claws into our land. Who knows what damage she could do—what she's doing already! And she's got Lord Torc in her clutches—for all we know, he's being tortured right this moment."

Saeddryn suppressed a shudder. "Torc knew the risks. We'll do what we can for him, but there's only so much we can do."

"Lady Saeddryn is right," Nerth interrupted, speaking up for the first time in the entire meeting. "We could attack Malvern now, but imagine how much damage we'd do. That city is ours by rights, an' we want it in one piece—and there's one more thing. Think of who lives in Malvern."

"Griffiners?" Morvudd suggested. "What does that matter?"

"Griffins," Aenae rasped. He glared at the woman. "Unpartnered griffins. The same griffins that helped to conquer the city in the first place. If you had been alive then, you would know how much destruction they caused."

"Aenae's right," said Saeddryn. "Attack Malvern, and the unpartnered will come out. We'd be torn to pieces. They won't come out here themselves; no-one commands them any more. But Malvern is their territory."

"Yes," said Nerth. "It's not worth the risk—all the lives we'd lose. We attack them on our own terms, away from any cities." He gave Morvudd a filmy-eyed but stern look. "Ye don't want street fighting, missy. Take that from someone who's tried it."

"And it's more than that!" said Saeddryn, trying to take control of the conversation. "The half-breed is already a usurper. The moment she attacks us—tries to kill the rightful heirs to King Arenadd's throne—she shows everyone her true colours."

"Everyone likes a good villain," Nerth said wisely. "This half-breed's ours. Just stay patient."

Saeddryn smiled slightly. "If ye want to put it that way. Now then, has anyone else got news for us?"

"One of our griffiners snuck out of the city early this morning," said Morvudd. "He got away before anyone could stop him."

Saeddryn swore. "Where was he going? Not t'join the Queen, surely?"

"No chance," said Morvudd. "Don't worry."

"Why are ye so certain? Who was he, anyway?"

Morvudd smiled. "My son, Gethen. I can trust him, and he left a note besides. He's gone to look for the King."

"Another one!" Penllyn exclaimed.

"He knew you wouldn't let him go, holy one," Morvudd said. "That's why he never asked permission. I'm sorry."

Saeddryn slid a finger under her eyepatch and rubbed the scar beneath. "A hundred people must've set out to look, an' not one has found him. Gethen won't have any better luck than them. The King doesn't *want* to be found. An' we need all the griffiners we can find."

"I'm sure he'll come back soon," said Morvudd.

Nerth was frowning. "I can't help but wonder if the King returned . . . whose side would he choose?"

"The side he always chose," said Penllyn. "His own."

"If the King were here, this wouldn't be happening," Saeddryn said sharply. "Now, if we've done talking, we should get going. There's work t'be done."

"I wish to fly over the city again, to watch for danger," Aenae said. "Come, Saeddryn."

He left without waiting for her. Saeddryn nodded to the others, dismissing them, and went out through another door. She hadn't gone far when she heard someone coming up behind her, and glanced over her shoulder to see Nerth limping up to join her.

She slowed to walk beside him. "How are ye, Nerth?"

"Getting old," he said. "Getting tired. It's what I do. They should call me the Master of Old an' Tired."

Saeddryn chuckled. "Ask Arddryn or Caedmon when he's on the throne, I'm sure they'll be willin' to give ye any title ye choose."

"Hm." Nerth pulled his fur-lined cape over his shoulders, covering his arms. "If I live that long."

They reached the old man's own quarters and went inside to sit by the fire. Saeddryn kept watching the flames. The lines on her face had deepened and turned darker with shadow, and the patch on her eye looked like a blank hole.

"I watched ye grow up, Saeddryn," Nerth said gently. "Other people might see the mighty warrior, or the High Priestess, the royal Taranisäii, but I remember the tiny girl who only wanted her mother to hold her, an' love her."

Saeddryn said nothing, but her mouth tightened.

"She never did, though, did she?" Nerth went on. "She stayed in them mountains all those years, an' never saw how beautiful her little daughter was. I know that's why ye fight, Saeddryn. I know that's why ye never give an inch. It was all for her, wasn't it?"

Saeddryn rubbed her upper arm with her hand, as if trying to warm it. "I just want t'be there for my children. They deserve the best I can give. The North is theirs by rights."

"I think most of us reckon ye plan on making a Queen out of yerself," said Nerth. "It's what I thought."

"No. I'm too old, Nerth. I wanted the throne, but not for myself. Not any more. I know I won't live to see this through."

"Come on now, Saeth," said Nerth. "Yer half my age an' I'm still goin' strong."

"No." Saeddryn was holding both her arms now, wrapping them around herself and hunching closer to the fire. "I'm going to die. I can feel it. The cold is in me, an' I can't make it leave me. I thought maybe I was sick, but now I know. It's my death. The Night God is waiting for me."

Nerth touched her shoulder. "Don't talk like that. Yer Saeddryn! Saeddryn the holy woman, the great hero! They sing songs about all the brave things ye did. Tara loves ye. Believes in ye. An' so do I."

She smiled and reached out to touch him affectionately. "The Night God won't come for me yet. Not yet. Not until I've done what I have to. She has one more task for her Saeddryn."

"Aye, so she does," said Nerth. "An' I'll be here with ye t'see it through. I've been with ye this long, an' this will be *my* last task."

Saeddryn still looked sad. "I just wish Arddryn were here, an' Caedmon. I miss them."

"They'll be here soon."

Neither of them mentioned Torc even though they were both thinking of him. Saeddryn rubbed her dead eye again, and a shudder of guilt went through her. But there was nothing she could do.

Kullervo and Senneck flew, following the river north. Kullervo went slightly ahead, proudly refusing to ride Senneck's slipstream, and she kept politely behind him even though she was the more powerful flier.

She watched him, with his slender grey wings rocking slightly as they adjusted themselves to correct him in the air. In griffin form, he was much smaller than she had expected, but she supposed that it made sense. Changing shape would take enough energy as it was, without making him grow larger as well. In fact, she had estimated that, ignoring the wings, he was the same size now that he had been as a human. Most likely he would never get any bigger. He would be stuck looking like a half-grown youngster for the rest of his life. How humiliating.

Not that Kullervo seemed to care. From all she had seen of him so far, he was immune to feelings of embarrassment. There was something to be said for that.

Abruptly, Kullervo slowed his flight. A moment later, he tilted himself and dove for the ground. Startled, Senneck overtook him, wheeled around, and followed. She couldn't see any signs of danger, but she decided to trust him.

The land below them was forested, not densely thanks to the village close by, but there was plenty of cover. Kullervo landed with a crash in the branches of a willow tree. Senneck saw him clinging to his bouncing perch as she touched down on grass.

Kullervo hopped down from his tree and went to the river to drink. From his calm behaviour, Senneck guessed that he hadn't decided to land because of any danger.

She relaxed and went closer. "What is wrong? It is too early in the day to stop."

Kullervo threw his head back to swallow. Beak dripping, he turned to look at her. "I know, but I think we should wait until tomorrow before we go on."

"Why? Are you tired?"

"I've seen Warwick," said Kullervo. "It's not far ahead. We could get there before dark, but I think we should wait here and make sure we're well rested before we go in."

Senneck sat on her haunches. "That is a sensible plan. Do you think there is food here?"

"Maybe. Try the riverbank; there could be frogs."

They had both eaten plenty before they left Malvern, and the meat in their guts had been enough to sustain them this far. Despite that, they both set out to forage for a few bites to keep them going. Kullervo tried the riverbank, and did indeed manage to catch a frog or two, along with a crayfish, which he scooped out of the water with his talons. Senneck disliked getting her paws muddy, so she went further inland and tried the trees.

Her sense of smell led her to the burrow of a ground-bear. Normally, digging one up was too tedious to bother with, but she was in the mood for some sport. She ripped the ground up with her talons, biting through the roots of the tree that grew above the burrow. When she was far enough into the earth, she thrust her head down into the remains of the hole and dragged the bear out. It fought back, kicking at her face with its own formidable claws, but she broke its spine with a few quick blows.

Excited by the hunt, she threw the corpse around and batted at it with her forepaws, and even tossed it into the air to catch it in her beak. She played like this until she heard herself and realised she was making little squeaks and chirps like a chick.

Embarrassed, she ripped the bear's belly open and pulled out the innards.

Kullervo found her while she was in the midst of her meal, but he wisely kept his distance until she had finished eating.

Senneck rolled onto her side and lay there contentedly, tail flicking. "We will move away from here to sleep," she said, as if nothing had happened. "It is not good to sleep where there is a smell of blood."

"I agree," said Kullervo. "It gives me bad dreams."

"I meant that the smell would draw other griffins," said Senneck.

"Oh yes. Of course." Seeing that she was showing no signs of wanting to move just yet, Kullervo stood up on his hind legs and began to sharpen his talons on a handy tree.

"So," said Senneck. "Tomorrow, we shall find the traitors."

"If everything goes to plan. Listen, Senneck—you don't have to come with me."

"But I shall."

"You can; it's just that I want you to be s—I mean, if I don't get out, then you can go back and tell Laela."

"I shall come with you," Senneck repeated. "And we shall *both* tell Laela."

He gave in, hastily bowing his head to show her superiority to him. "I trust you to keep me safe. Just please don't attack anyone. Even Saeddryn."

"I am not a fool," she hissed. "To attack her there would be death."

"Of course. I said I trust you, and I do."

"Then you trust far too easily."

Kullervo said nothing to that.

Later on, toward nightfall, they moved away from the bear's remains and found a hollow between two trees. They settled down there, lying side by side for warmth. Normally, two griffins would never sleep this way unless they were mates or family, but Kullervo knew very little about griffish customs, and Senneck seemed to think of him as human anyway.

They groomed and drank before retiring, and lay together in silence the way griffins usually did.

Kullervo watched the stars come out. "Senneck?"

She moved her head to show she was listening.

"There's something I want to tell you. I might not have, but . . . in case something goes wrong tomorrow, and I don't survive, I thought I should tell you."

"Yes?"

"It's important," Kullervo said. "I've never told anyone else, not even Laela. But I feel that . . . that you . . . that I can tell you."

"Speak, then," Senneck said, typically brusque.

"I'm . . ." Kullervo curled his talons together, and braced himself. "I'm Arenadd's son."

Senneck went quiet.

"I'm sure of it," Kullervo said, words rushing out of him now. "I never knew him, but I'm sure of it. I was born in the South. A woman came to a place near Withypool. She had yellow eyes, like mine, and claws instead of fingernails. She was pregnant. But when she gave birth, she gave birth to an egg. My egg. That woman—my mother, wasn't human. She was a griffin. A griffin who took a human lover. My father. Her name was Skade. The one they called the wild woman of Withypool. And Skade only had one lover. Arenadd."

There was a rustling, as Senneck stood up. She put her beak toward Kullervo, thrusting it into his feathers and huffing angrily. "Your scent. I knew that I knew your scent! And your eyes. You have your mother's look."

"You knew her?"

"Yes. I was there when she was a prisoner at Malvern. I went with Erian when he took her away, to be released. *Kraeai kran ae* offered himself up in her place. We captured him, and let the female go free. We knew nothing of who she was. But when the rebels rose up and began to kill, she was there by *Kraeai kran ae*'s side. The only one on their side who was not the same race as the rest. The mate of *Kraeai kran ae*."

"The only one he loved," said Kullervo. "He never knew that she had his son. She abandoned me and never told anyone I existed."

"She did not want a deformed hatchling," Senneck said.

"No."

The sandy griffin shifted around, apparently thinking. "You did not tell the half-breed Queen that you are her brother?"

"No. I haven't told anyone."

"But you have told me," said Senneck.

"Yes. And I want you to keep it a secret, too. Please, can you do that?"

Senneck said nothing.

"But if I die," said Kullervo, "then tell her. Tell Laela. Please."

Unseen in the dark, Senneck's eyes narrowed. "I will tell no-one," she said at last. "Unless you die. You have my word."

She came and lay down by Kullervo again, her flank pressing against his. "And I will stay with you. No human or griffin shall ever hurt you while I am alive. That is my promise."

"Thank you, Senneck. I knew I could trust you."

"And so you can," she said softly. "Always."

When morning came, Kullervo and Senneck set out for Warwick. They made the short journey in silence, keeping close together, and when the walls were about to pass beneath them, Senneck went ahead and circled upward to fly just above Kullervo, ready to defend him.

When they passed over Warwick's walls, both of them saw the huge spear-launchers, some half-built, that had been set up all along the ramparts. The completed ones were manned and loaded, and one or two of them swivelled on their bases to follow the intruders. Senneck, using some trick that Kullervo had never seen done before, angled herself downward to shield his back with her body. But none of the spear-launchers fired.

Kullervo didn't relax. Ahead, he could see griffins, circling over the tower. Already, they were reacting to his presence. Some flew down to land on the tower, ready to defend it. Dozens more came straight at him, screeching challenges. Wisely, Kullervo didn't screech back. He flew slowly and carefully, keeping his talons curled in.

The other griffins were already on them. Saying nothing, they swarmed around, wings pressing in on Senneck and Kullervo. They didn't attack, but when Senneck opened her beak threateningly, one smacked her in the head with his talons. Two others came in even closer, forcing her downward.

"Land!" one called at last. "Land now!"

They had no choice. The Warwick griffins kept on, herding them toward the tower.

Kullervo's heart was pattering against his rib cage. Fear made him clumsy; he nearly fell when he landed, looking around frantically for Senneck before he had recovered. She landed, too, more gracefully, and took a step toward him.

Something huge and heavy smashed Kullervo's head into the ground. He cried out, but talons wrapped around his neck, pinning it down. Griffin beaks snapped shut around his wings, breaking the feathers.

"Hold still, or we will break your wings," a voice rasped.

One of Kullervo's eyes was being crushed into the stone beneath him. The other swivelled desperately, catching a glimpse of Senneck fighting as she, too, was captured.

"Intruders," the voice said. "Are you here to fight?"

"No!" Kullervo's beak couldn't open properly. "Message," he garbled. "From the Queen!"

The talons loosened on his neck. "You come from the runt and her half-breed?"

"Yes," said Kullervo. "They sent us. A message. For Saeddryn."

Something tugged at the message-holder. "What is this?"

"The message. Leave it alone. It's for Saeddryn."

"Let us go!" Senneck's voice rose out of the hubbub. "We are not here to fight, you fools."

"Let go of his wings," Kullervo's captor ordered. The other griffins obeyed, and the talons let go of his neck.

Kullervo dragged himself upright, and found himself looking at a huge male griffin, whose pale eyes were fixed on him. Instinctively, he bowed his head. "I am Kullervo. I am not a fighter."

"I see that," the big griffin mocked. "Weakling. But your companion—who is she?"

"Only an old one, Aenae," another griffin said.

Senneck shook off the talons holding her. "I am Raak," she lied. "I came with Kullervo to protect him. And you—" she huffed at Aenae. "You seem familiar."

"I am the son of the Mighty Skandar," Aenae said arrogantly. "And I am the rightful master of this land. Speak more respectfully to me, old one."

Senneck regarded him. Then, to Kullervo's astonishment, she lowered her head. "I am humbled to meet you, Mighty Aenae."

"Better," said Aenae. "Now, messenger. You will give me this message, and I will take it to my human."

Kullervo screwed up his courage. "Take me to your human, and I'll give it to her."

"You are not here to tell me what I must do," Aenae threatened. "This is my territory, and you will do as I say."

"This message is only for Saeddryn," said Kullervo. "And besides, only human hands can remove it."

Aenae reached down and tried to snatch the little cylinder, but the straps held firm.

"Only Saeddryn can remove it," said Kullervo.

Aenae regarded him for a moment, unblinking. "Very well, then," he said at last. "Come with me. And I promise you—if you do one thing that I do not tell you to, I shall kill you."

"Raak should come with me," said Kullervo.

Aenae barely glanced at Senneck. "The old one will stay here."

"Don't hurt her," said Kullervo. "Please. She's no danger to any of you."

"Go," Senneck called. "I will wait here for you."

Kullervo allowed himself to be led away, but he kept his eyes on her until she was out of sight. He hoped she would be safe.

Aenae went through an opening in the tower roof, forcing Kullervo to go ahead. He passed rows of other griffins, who snapped at the shape-shifter and chirped amusement when he jerked away from them in fright. Two of them followed Aenae down into the passage.

Inside the tower, away from the hissing griffins, Kullervo felt even less safe. The walls seemed to press in on him; he felt like he was in a prison whose door had been locked behind him. Down here, he wouldn't be able to fly away, or to help Senneck. He tried not to think of what they might be doing to her. And ahead was Saeddryn—and he could only guess what she might do when she read Laela's message.

Kullervo walked slowly, head low, and tried his best to be brave.

"Turn here," Aenae rumbled behind him.

Kullervo obeyed, entering a large, round room. The two griffins who had come with Aenae used the extra space to close in on him, keeping close and ready to strike if he moved. Aenae glared a warning at them and left.

Kullervo sat on his haunches and waited. He didn't even dare groom himself. The two griffins reeked of aggression.

"Deformed weakling," one sneered.

"What pathetic creatures they send to us," the other said to his companion. "An ugly runt and a dried-up old hen. Humanless outcasts must have no other use."

"Perhaps that hatchling at Malvern hoped we would dispose of them for her," the first griffin suggested.

Or perhaps we'll *be the ones to dispose of* you, Kullervo thought to make himself feel braver.

Aenae returned. With him was a woman. She was past middle age, lined and greying, and one of her eyes was covered by a round leather patch. Even though Kullervo had never seen her before, he recognised her.

"Saeddryn."

The old woman regarded him, from her griffin's side. "Who are ye?"

"Kullervo."

"Speak respectfully to my human," Aenae snapped.

"I'm Kullervo," said Kullervo, ignoring him. He stood up. "Queen Laela and Oeka sent me. I have a message for you."

Saeddryn looked sharply at him. "Aenae says ye won't let anyone but me see it."

"That's right. I was given detailed instructions. Only you can read the message. It's here, on my back, if you can remove it."

"That so?" said Saeddryn, instantly suspicious.

"Do not worry," Aenae interrupted. "I will help." He came forward, and shoved Kullervo onto his belly. One of the two griffin guards held his hindquarters, and the other stood on one of his wings while Aenae held his head. Kullervo didn't resist. He lay as passively as he could and waited.

Saeddryn came, and, after some fumbling, she cut the straps and took the message-holder. Aenae let Kullervo up once she was at a safe distance, and all four griffins watched her open the tube and unroll the scroll.

She read it, expressionless.

"What does the hatchling's human say?" Aenae asked.

Saeddryn rolled the scroll up. "Surrender."

"Ksha!" Aenae tossed his head. "They think we would do that! They will die for their idiocy."

Without even thinking about it, Kullervo made a move

forward. Aenae blocked him at once, but he looked past him, to Saeddryn. "Please," he said. "Consider it. Your family will be safe. Everyone will be safe. No-one would have to die. Laela keeps her word. She's a good person."

Saeddryn's eye narrowed. "What griffin talks like that? Who are ye?"

"I was raised by humans," said Kullervo, which at least was true. "Listen to me, please. Laela doesn't want war. She doesn't want to kill anyone. She only wants peace for Tara and for her family. Please, see reason. You fought to make this Kingdom. Why let it be torn apart again?"

Saeddryn's face was stone. "This Kingdom was made by Taranisäiis, and it's our duty and our right to rule it."

"Yes, exactly," said Kullervo.

"So ye see my point," said Saeddryn. "The half-breed is not a Taranisäii." She tore the scroll into pieces and threw the remains onto the floor. "Aenae—I think this one can go back to Malvern with our reply."

"A good idea," the big griffin said. He looked at Kullervo. "Perhaps his companion can help to carry him. I do not think the hatchling and her half-breed will need to see all of him to know our answer. Send back his ugly head."

Saeddryn hesitated—then nodded. "They've seen too much. Kill them both."

Kullervo flattened himself to the floor as Aenae and the two griffins closed in on him. "No! Please, don't! I haven't done anything wrong!"

Aenae's talons came for him, but Kullervo's small size saved him again. He ducked under the bigger griffin and ran, bolting blindly for the door. Too slow. The two griffins came up behind him, tearing at his hindquarters. He leapt, and fell hard onto his belly, rolling over to thrust his talons at his attackers.

The two griffins had backed off slightly to avoid his flailing tail, and he took advantage of it and used his momentum to roll forward, straight at them. His talons hooked into a flesh, making deep gashes. He pulled himself forward, dragging at the screeching griffin's skin, and aimed his beak for the throat.

He had forgotten Aenae. The huge griffin darted in, and a kick sent Kullervo tumbling into a wall.

Pain juddered in his bones. But he was not done yet. He reared up, rising onto his hind legs. Wings open wide for balance, he screamed. *"Then damn you! Damn you all!"*

The three griffins ran at him. This time, Kullervo didn't try to fight back. He turned toward them, holding out his forelegs to embrace his end.

Something cracked inside him. *No,* he thought. *Not now. Not now!*

Aenae and his two friends stopped in bewilderment, as Kullervo's feathers fell like autumn leaves. Sickening noises came from inside him, and his eyes rolled back into his head.

Saeddryn, sheltering behind a row of benches, pulled a horrified face. "What the—?"

Aenae had backed off, tail swishing. "Do not touch him! This is not natural!"

The other two griffins didn't need any warnings. They moved away, hissing, as Kullervo dropped onto his side and began to convulse.

Kullervo was unaware of them, or anything else. The pain had closed its jaws around him again, and there was nothing he could do. This time, he didn't struggle to make himself stay awake.

19

Death Comes

Outside, the wind had grown icy and taken on a tang of ice. Winter wasn't over yet, and Senneck guessed that snow was on its way.

She might have put on a passive performance while Kullervo was being led away, but she had no intention of staying where she was, especially if it might snow and make flying more difficult, if not impossible.

So she waited. She waited until the griffins around her grew bored and began to drift away, sensing the excitement was over. She lay on her belly and did nothing, knowing how easily griffins lost interest in something that didn't move. Sure enough, more of them left, taking off to resume their endless circling or returning to their nests. A few still stayed on the tower-top, some dozing in the sun, but others walked around her, keeping watch.

Soon, they, too, grew bored. But they began to look for ways to amuse themselves.

"Why have you not chosen a human?" one asked. "A magnificent young female like you would have only the finest, surely. A dung-scrubber, perhaps, or a cripple?"

Senneck ignored the insults.

"Mate with me!" one of the males said. "I must have you! You are so sleek and beautiful, I am hot in my loins!"

"You shall not have her!" another male mock-hissed. "She is mine!"

"Oh, so you shall fight me for her?" the first one said. "Then so be it!"

The two males reared up and batted at each other, dancing about like kittens.

Senneck yawned widely and looked away. Young fools, hardly more than chicks. They thought they were invincible because they still had their strength. Probably they both had humans as well, or thought they were above choosing them.

One of them hopped closer to her. "Come!" he said. "I have fought for you and won! Let us mate!"

Senneck stood up. "I do not mate with chicks," she said.

He lost his playfulness at once. "I am no chick! I am fifteen summers old!"

"And I am too old to listen to your stupidity," she said, and smashed her talons into his face. He fell, and while the others reacted angrily Senneck took off. She flew hard, thrusting herself straight upward, and before they could reach her, she rolled, turned, and flew away as fast as she could.

More than a dozen griffins chased her. But even in her old age, Senneck was fast, and she had a head start. She flew out of Warwick, dodging the spears that were launched at her, and didn't stop until her pursuers gave up and went back. When she felt safe enough she came in to land by the riverbank, not far from where she and Kullervo had camped the previous night. She waited there a while before she crept back toward Warwick.

She found a spot not too far from the walls and hid herself behind a heap of rubbish that had been dumped outside. From here, she had a good view of anyone coming or going.

She lay down to rest.

There had been very little point in staying in Warwick. Clearly, Kullervo would only leave if the traitors allowed him to. Under such close watch, Senneck would have had no chance of doing anything. Freed, she would be far more useful. All she had to do was wait, and when she saw him flying out of Warwick, she could rejoin him. Or, if need be, cover his escape.

If he ever did escape.

* * *

Kullervo came out of his stupor and found himself surrounded by bright light. The ground beneath him felt cold and rough, and there was no fur to shield him from it. His wings flopped nakedly at his sides.

Human.

He struggled to get up and found his vestigial talons scraping on stone. His palms were filthy. Pain wrapped around his wrists, weighing his arms down, and he heard a clinking when he moved.

Kullervo realised that he was in chains. Feeling weirdly calm, he kept his eyes open until they focused and took in the solid walls around him. There were iron lamps up near the ceiling, plenty of them, casting harsh yellow light on his bare body.

"Awake?"

Kullervo looked up to see a face looking through the bars. Human, female. He said nothing.

"There's a blanket for you," the voice said. "Wrap yerself up. I'll have some clothes brought."

Kullervo spotted it and dragged his chains toward it. Pulling himself into a sitting position with the blanket over his shoulders, he looked at the woman. "Who are you? Why am I here?"

The woman blinked. "By the Night God, you *do* know how to speak."

"Your name," Kullervo repeated.

"I'm Lady Morvudd. They tell me your name is Kullervo, yes?"

"Yes." Kullervo tugged pointlessly at the shackles on his wrists. "Why am I here? Why have you chained me?"

"What are you?" Morvudd asked.

"Take these chains off me," said Kullervo.

"Answer me," she said sharply. "What are you? Man, or griffin?"

"Both. Let me go!"

"You're going nowhere, whatever you are," Morvudd said. "Whether you're man or griffin, you're on the half-breed's side, and that makes you an enemy. We might have killed you already, but after what you did, Lady Saeddryn decided to keep you a while. See what you had to say. As for me, I came to see you out of interest. I've never seen anything like you in all my life."

"I'm not telling you anything," said Kullervo. Anger began to bubble inside him, and he wrenched the chains. They were looped through a metal ring in the wall and wouldn't budge. "Let me go! I came here on a peaceful mission, just to carry a message. I'm not a fighter, I—"

"But the half-breed trusted you enough to send you here," said Morvudd. "And from what I hear, you talked about her like you knew her well. We're interested to hear more."

Kullervo tried to relax. "Like what?"

"Like what she's planning. Like how many griffiners are helping her. Like whether the unpartnered are on her side or ours. Like whether she's going to come here to attack, or if she'll lead the army somewhere else."

"I don't know!" Kullervo yelled. "I don't know anything, I'm just a messenger!"

"Makes no difference to me." Morvudd shrugged. "It's not my business to find out. I just want to know about you. Where'd you come from? Are you a griffin that changes shape or something else?"

Kullervo opened his mouth wide and hissed at her.

She took a step back from the door. "All right, then." She rubbed her forehead, evidently embarrassed. "I'll leave you. Most likely they'll find out those answers anyway." She turned away, throwing one last remark over her shoulder. "My advice is to give in quickly. Save yourself some pain."

Left alone, Kullervo pulled at the chains again. The walls around him seemed to press inward, closing like the jaws of a trap. He felt about to suffocate.

Panic thickened the air. Shedding the blanket, he lunged forward toward the door. The chains pulled him up short. Scrabbling at the floor, digging his talons in until they broke, he screamed. *"Let me out! Let me out! Don't leave me here, please, please let me out, I have to get out! Please!"*

Nobody came, and the chains would not give. But Kullervo fought them anyway.

Fought them until his wrists bled.

* * *

Another day in Malvern. Four days since Kullervo and Senneck's departure, and another day of sick uncertainty and loneliness for Laela.

Not that she was truly alone. Oeka was still there. Only now she was . . . different.

The small griffin's condition, if it could be called that, had only grown worse. Her eyes had gone from merely glassy to physically deteriorating; little by little, their surfaces lost their smoothness, becoming nubbly and lustreless. Soon afterward, the colour faded as well, and what had been deep green and jet-black whitened and turned cloudy. Oeka didn't eat any more, or sleep, or speak. Laela was certain that she had lost her sense of hearing, too, but it wasn't easy to tell. The small griffin seemed able to sense more or less everything around her, one way or another. If she didn't hear you speak she would reach into your mind and sense what you were saying. If she couldn't speak, she would pass her words to you through her own mind. As for the lack of food and sleep, neither one seemed to have much effect on her.

Laela didn't want to talk to her partner any more. There was no point. Oeka knew what she was thinking, often before she herself knew. There was nothing you could say to her that she didn't already know. She must already have known that Laela couldn't bear the sight of her any more, but she never said anything. Maybe she had changed almost beyond recognition, but she still had no interest or care for her partner's feelings.

The only people Laela had now were Iorwerth and Inva. Iorwerth had his own duties to worry about, but at least with Inva, there was an excuse to talk to her.

Now that she had been chosen, Laela's attendant had been forced to start learning things even she hadn't known. In the end, Laela had decided to teach her.

Today, they were practising with weapons.

Laela had a wooden sickle in her hand, and she darted around Inva with it, fending her off. The secret with sickle fighting was to use the curving blade to hook your opponent's own sickle out of her grip, but it was much harder than it looked. Inva was faster than she looked.

Laela dodged her arm and aimed a blow for Inva's armpit.

Done properly, in a real fight, it could slice through an enemy's tendon and cripple her arm. Inva turned fast, bringing her own sickle around in an arc, and hit Laela in the back of the head with the blunted point.

"Ow!"

Immediately, Inva dropped her sickle and folded her hands together. "My apologies, my lady."

Rubbing her head, Laela pushed the sickle toward her with her boot. "Knock it off and pick that up. We ain't playin' masters and slaves today."

Inva obeyed. "My apologies—"

"Shut up an' hit me." Laela meant to perform a quick blocking manoeuvre immediately after saying this, but Inva took her at her word and made a powerful, slashing blow across her throat.

"Damn!" By now thoroughly aggravated, Laela shoved forward. Not for the first time, she forgot her father's lessons and remembered what she had been taught by another father long ago. *Someone tries t'start somethin', don't take it. Thump the bastard.*

Laela grabbed Inva by the elbow, pulling the sickle away, and head-butted her full in the face.

Inva yelped and fell onto her backside. She clutched at her nose as it started to bleed.

"Shit!" Laela hurried to help her up. "Gods damn it, I'm sorry. Didn't mean to do that."

Inva got up and dusted herself down, very dignified. "Do not apologise, my lady. You defeated me."

"Yeah, by cheatin'."

"There is no cheating in a fight," said Inva. "It is not a contest. You win, or you die."

Laela grinned for the first time in days. "That's what ole Bran always said."

"He did?"

"Actually, he said, 'Get the bastards before they get you,' but it was the same thing."

And he was right, Oeka's icy whisper broke in. *All is fair in war.*

"Unfair, yeh mean," said Laela, losing her grin.

Laela, I have sensed Senneck returning. She is not far.

"An' Kullervo?"

I cannot sense him.

"Doesn't mean he ain't there. Where's Senneck?"

Flying into the city. I will instruct her to come to you when she is close enough.

Inva had felt Oeka's mental speech. She had an odd, rigid look on her face. "I will go to find Skarok," she said, referring to her own partner. Skarok normally kept close to his partner's side, but if Oeka was about, he would disappear. Not one griffin in the Eyrie was prepared to go near her any more.

Laela let Inva go and waited alone in the practice yard for Senneck. She marvelled that Oeka could sense her so far away.

I can scent another mind further and further away every day.

"Great. What's next?"

I cannot see the future.

"That ain't what I meant."

But soon, Oeka went on, ignoring her, *I will learn to see the past.*

"What's that mean, then?"

I will see what has been here before us. Shadows of humans and griffins that were once here.

Laela gave up and decided not to ask just what help that would be. Now-a-days, Oeka didn't seem to care about anything except finding new ways to be deeply, deeply unsettling.

Laela turned her attention to the sky instead. Sure enough, a few moments later, she saw Senneck coming. Alone. She had already begun to expect the worst before the blue-eyed griffin even landed, and when she saw her up close, that was enough to confirm it.

Senneck looked exhausted. Her fur and feathers were dirty and bedraggled, darkened in a few places by blood.

She wasted no time with pleasantries. "Kullervo has been captured. I do not know if he is alive."

Laela felt the news like a blow to her chest. "Saeddryn took him?"

"Yes. They had me as well, but I escaped. I waited two days, but he never emerged from Warwick."

Laela swore. "Where did they take him? Did yeh see?"

"Yes. We were escorted to the tower and taken prisoner.

Kullervo told them why he had come, and Aenae agreed to take him to Saeddryn. Kullervo asked if I could come, but they refused. I waited a while on the tower top, under threat by other griffins, until I decided it would be better to leave."

"Why didn't yeh stay there?" said Laela. "Waited until he came out?"

"Because I realised that even if he did come, Saeddryn could come with him. I remembered that she had seen me and could recognise me. And I would have been no use surrounded by enemies who would not let me take off."

"Then yeh don't know what they said to our message."

"If they have taken Kullervo, it can be for only two reasons," said Senneck. "Either they will torture him to make him speak, or they will kill him. Perhaps both. With one or the other, it is clear that they have no intention to surrender. You have a war ahead of you, little half-breed, and I hope that you are ready for it."

Senneck is right, said Oeka. *They have refused our offer. It is time to declare war. And first of all, you must kill Lord Torc.*

Laela's face had gone blank. "But I can't . . . he's family. I thought Saeddryn would . . ."

But she has not, said Oeka. *She desires our throne so much that she has sacrificed her own mate for it. If you are to fight her, you must prove that you are as powerful as you claim. Powerful enough to do what you have promised to do.*

"A leader keeps her promises," said Senneck. "This human called Torc must die."

Laela thought of her father. "I always swore I'd never be as cruel as Arenadd was."

"And you are not," said Senneck. "Do you kill for pleasure?"

"No, but—"

"Then you are not him. Kill Torc. Begin the war. As for me, I will return to Warwick at once. I will find Kullervo. And I will kill Saeddryn. That is my own promise, and I shall keep it."

There are no lies in Senneck's mind, said Oeka. *She has told the truth. We have no choice now. Do not be a soft-hearted youngster now, Laela. Be a Queen.*

Laela set her jaw. "Fine. If it's war Saeddryn wants, then it's war she'll get. Senneck, take some time to rest an' we'll meet again to talk. I'm off to see Iorwerth. We got plans to make. An' then I'm gonna go see Lord Torc an' tell him his wife just killed him."

Torc had been expecting Laela to come back. Since he had been imprisoned and she had come to see him that first time, he had waited for her to return.

As a noble, he hadn't been treated too badly. They had moved him to one of the finer cells, where there was good furniture and even a rug on the floor. The food was good, too, and he had clean clothes and access to books if he wanted them. The door was still thick and kept locked and guarded at all times, but nobody seemed to think he would try to escape.

He never did. As the former Master of Law, he knew these dungeons very well—had even interrogated prisoners himself in this very cell. He knew it well enough to know that there was no way to escape. Once he had thought of appealing to those of the guards who knew him or who might be sympathetic, but these were new guards hired by the Queen and her new captain of the guard. Torc's old friend Garnoc was gone—demoted or worse.

There was no way out for Torc. Not any more. And even if there were, he knew there was no place for him to go.

He sat in a chair by the brazier and warmed himself. The firelight moved shadows over the back of his hand, where an old scar still stood out. Once, it had been swollen and red, flaring pain whenever he touched it. Now it was faded, but nothing would ever make it disappear. Not it, or the ring of little marks around his neck. Nothing ever erased the scars of a slave.

It was funny, really. He had been born in captivity, and most of his life had been spent in cages of one sort or another. And even now, when he was a free man—a Taranisäii, married to the rightful heir to Tara's throne, one of the highest nobles in the land—here he was in the very same place he had begun.

He had had far too much time to think about that.

He thought about Saeddryn, too. Saeddryn, whom he still loved even though he knew he would never see her again. Saeddryn, who had given him his children. He knew he would never see them again, either.

And he thought about death, and how all other things came to an end.

All while he waited, for Laela.

When she did come at last, he didn't have to look up. He heard the door open and the thud of boots on the rug, and caught a faint whiff of underarms. He snorted to himself. What a Queen this was, who wore boots under her gown and never used scent or bathed properly. What a pathetic world this was, where a girl like her could rule the great Arenadd's Kingdom.

"I waited for you," he said, without moving.

The boots stopped. "I wouldn't've thought there was much else to do in here."

Torc looked up and felt the hatred swell in him. "You've come to kill me."

Laela wore Arenadd's crown, and her face was gaunt. "Not me. We just had a message from yer wife."

"You found her, then. Where is she?"

"Warwick, but I bet yeh already knew that." Laela breathed hard, through her nose. "I told her if she wanted to get yeh free an' see her whole family protected, all she had to do was get back here an' end this. No-one would've been hurt, not even her."

"You told her to surrender, or you'd kill me," Torc said flatly.

"I told her to choose," said Laela. "She chose to let you die. Sorry, Torc. But this ain't my fault. It's hers."

"Kill me, then, half-breed. But you will never win the North. Soon, the true rulers of Tara will come back; and then you'll pay."

"We'll see about that." Laela beckoned to the guards. "Get him outta here."

Torc allowed himself to be led out of his cell, the guards walking on either side. Going to his death at last.

20

No Turning Back

In the city, just outside the gate that led to the Eyrie's outer courtyard, the execution platform waited. It was the same one that had been there two decades ago, rebuilt after the war. Taranisäii bodies had hung from it before.

Today, though, there was no noose set up. A block had been laid out, and an axe, with a burly man to wield it. Now-a-days, a Taranisäii could have a more dignified execution, as if that made any difference.

A crowd had gathered to watch, and it was much louder than those Torc had seen at past executions. Louder . . . or angrier? It was hard to say.

Standing up on the platform, he looked at them, then at the block that stood ready for his neck, and felt his soul fall away inside him. So many years, and so much life, all leading to nothing but this. An axe and a jeering crowd. All for nothing.

He felt like vomiting. Looking away from them, he saw Laela there, watching him through those hard blue eyes. In that moment, no matter how much he tried to deny it to himself, she looked so much like her father. The wind stirred at her curly hair and tugged at the black gown she wore, and her face had something of that cold, set look that Torc remembered so well. It was a look that had no pity or hesitation.

"I'm sorry, Torc," she said, very softly. "It'll be quick. I promise."

Torc only stared at her.

Beside Laela was Oeka. She sat hunched, like a small brown gargoyle, and her eyes were whitened and vile. She didn't move or react at all when Laela turned to address the crowd.

"People of Malvern! My people! Listen to yer Queen!"

They quietened.

"This man is Lord Torc Taranisäii," Laela said. "Husband to the traitor, Saeddryn Taranisäii. He helped her to escape from Malvern before she could be arrested for her treason against my father, King Arenadd Taranisäii. That makes him a traitor against me, against Tara, an' against its people. Today I formally announce that Saeddryn Taranisäii, along with her son Caedmon an' her daughter Arddryn, an' the griffins Aenae, Rakek, an' Shar, are outlaws. All of them will die, an' anyone who helps them shares their sentence. Saeddryn, Caedmon, an' Arddryn are banished from my father's family, an' can no longer call themselves Taranisäii. Any of their children are illegitimate an' will have no inheritance from me or my father. As for Torc, his own sentence will be carried out immediately."

The crowd howled in response, shouting who knew what. Torc had no idea. Were they condemning Laela or himself? Or both?

Madness gripped him. "You'll never win, half-breed!" he screamed at Laela. "They'll tear you to pieces! The Night God will strike you down, you hear me?"

Laela bared her teeth. "When yeh see the one-eyed bitch, tell her I sent yeh."

Torc's guards pulled him toward the block, and now he fought back, struggling with all his might, trying to get at the half-breed and kill her. "Curse you! *Curse you!*"

But it was no use. They took him to the block and made him kneel. The crowd below surged forward, a mass of open, yelling mouths and staring eyes. The guards around the platform lowered their spears, ready to hold them off—

—and silence fell.

It rippled out over the crowd like wind passing through the branches of a wood, stirring the leaves in layers. One by one, all those there, from the guards to the crowd to Torc himself, lost all their will-power and their voices.

Every single one of them felt the power take hold of his or her mind. Everyone heard the voice.

Be still.

Oeka had uncurled herself. Her wings opened, spreading like a canopy. The head turned, blind eyes staring at everything.

My human rules this land now, and my human alone. No living creature, human or griffin, shall stand in her way and live. I am the Mighty Oeka, most powerful of all griffins, the greatest wielder of magic there has ever been. I rule this land, beside my human, and it is my power that you should fear.

People in the crowd began to groan, as the presence in their heads closed in tighter and tighter until it hurt. Nobody there seemed able to do anything, not even Laela, though she didn't look as if she were in pain like the others.

Then Oeka let go. *You are no traitors,* she said. *You shall not be hurt. But see, now, what I shall make of liars and betrayers.*

Torc screamed.

Oeka's power released the crowd and the guards, and closed around him instead. As they recovered, wincing and clutching their heads, they saw what happened to Torc.

He put his hands over his face, pressing down on it as if trying to squeeze the agony out of his head. A moment later, he screamed again, a scream that rose higher and thinner, until pain roughened it into a howl.

To Torc, it was as if every moment of suffering in his entire life had come back, all at once, all together. His vision went, fading into bloody darkness, and he felt the suffering squeeze his entire body harder and harder, paralysing him. As he screamed on, it doubled, then doubled again, burning away every nerve in every part of him.

At last, mercifully, his mind broke. He laughed, then cried, and began to tear at himself, ripping his own skin until his fingernails broke.

Oeka had finished with him. Without having moved a muscle, she silently reached into the ruins of his mind and gave it one last push.

Torc went rigid. For a moment, he almost smiled. Blood dripped from his nose, and his eyes wept red.

Then he toppled forward onto the platform, and did not move again.

In the awful silence that followed, Laela managed to find her voice. "Take him away," she croaked. "Now!"

Oeka had already stood up. *Obey,* her mental voice warned. *Or suffer the same fate.*

"Has he talked yet?"

"Not that I've heard, my lady."

Despite herself, Saeddryn was impressed. "Not at all?"

"No. I asked everyone down there, and they said all he does is whimper and say the half-breed's name over and over. He won't say anything. Not where he's from, what he is, or anything about what the usurper's planning."

"Hm." Saeddryn rubbed her forehead. "Maybe he really doesn't have anythin' to say. No sense in letting him go, though."

Lady Morvudd, who had brought her the news, gave her a cautious look. "What else can we do with him, then?"

"If Penllyn's convinced that they've tried everything, then . . ."

"Yes?" Morvudd perked up.

"Then go ahead. Ye have permission from me. Do whatever ye like with him."

"Anything, my lady?"

"Try not to kill him. If ye can."

"Oh no," said Morvudd. "I'd never do that." Her forehead creased. "We should never have let him be tortured like that. He's one of a kind, Saeddryn. There's never been anything like him before, and maybe there never will be again."

Saeddryn frowned at her. "We didn't ask him to side with the usurper. Now get going. I've got more important things to worry about."

Morvudd left with a bow, leaving Saeddryn to walk over to the window and look out. The window was open, and a cold breeze touched her face and made her missing eye tingle.

She hadn't meant to be so snappish with Morvudd, but the truth was that she didn't feel well today. A sense of unease had been with her ever since Kullervo's coming.

By now, the half-breed must have missed him. The old

griffin who had come with him must have returned to Malvern after her escape, and no doubt the half-breed would have guessed what Kullervo's capture meant. Saeddryn had sent no reply, but she didn't have to. Nor did she want to. She had never intended to go along with Aenae's decision to send the shape-shifter's head back to Malvern. Let the half-breed be the aggressor. That had been her plan before, and it still was now.

By now, though, the half-breed would know her offer had been rejected, and Saeddryn knew her well enough to be certain that she would do as she had promised.

By now, Torc must be dead.

Saeddryn couldn't put it out of her mind. Nobody had said anything, but they must all know, too. Poor Torc. His only crime had been his marriage to her—a marriage she had never wanted. Since her teenage years, Saeddryn had been resigned to the fact that she would never marry for love. But Torc had loved her. And, for a time, she had been able to love him back.

She shuddered and closed her single eye. "Forgive me."

"Saeddryn!"

She turned sharply, tensing until she saw the massive shape blocking the doorway. "Aenae. What is it?"

The big griffin's feathers were fluffed out, ragged-looking. "Rakek has come, and your daughter."

"What? What's Arddryn doing—? Where are they?"

"Up on the tower-top. I would not let them enter our territory until you had come."

Swearing, Saeddryn ran out. Her missing eye made it much harder to move about in confined spaces, especially at speed, and she banged into several things along the way. She emerged into the open air bruised and even angrier than before, and when she saw her daughter quietly waiting, her temper boiled over.

"What are ye doing here?" she roared, ignoring the cringing Rakek altogether.

Arddryn ran toward her mother and threw herself into her arms.

Astonished, Saeddryn tried to pull away. "What is this?"

Arddryn only held on more tightly. She was sobbing. "He's dead. He's dead! They *killed* him!"

Saeddryn held her daughter back. "Who—?"

"Mother, it's Dad. The half-breed killed him. She executed

him, in public! Right in f-front of everyone . . . !" Arddryn sobbed harder.

Saeddryn felt the coldness eat away at her heart. "Oh Night God help us . . ."

Arddryn let go. "They didn't even give him a trial!" she screamed, red-eyed. "They just dragged him out and killed him, like some common criminal! And I heard—I heard—"

"Calm down. Heard what?"

Arddryn rubbed her face hard. "They're saying he was killed with magic. By the usurper's griffin."

"Ye mean that little brown thing—Oeka? I didn't think . . . how could she be that powerful?"

"My human speaks the truth," Rakek interrupted. "We have heard the story, from a griffin who flew to us from Malvern. The small one has done something to increase her power. Her magic has grown by a hundred times. It is said that no-one, human or griffin, can hide a secret from her, that she can control others and crush the mind of a human like a bone in her beak. It is said that this is what she has done to your mate, Saeddryn."

Arddryn shuddered and sobbed again.

"But how?" said Saeddryn. "How did she make herself stronger?"

Rakek and Aena looked at each other.

"How?" said Saeddryn.

"There are ways," said Aenae. "Secret ways. Griffish ways. We do not talk about them to humans."

"Yer both certain this is true, then?" said Saeddryn, to Arddryn and Rakek.

"Yes. A griffiner came all the way from Malvern to tell us."

"Then why didn't ye send them here to us?" said Saeddryn. "I told ye to stay where ye were, Arddryn."

Arddryn looked bewildered. "Mother, it's *Dad*. How could I just—I had to see you! I needed—"

"Needed t'come cry on mama's shoulder instead of doing yer duty?" Saeddryn said harshly. "Yer a griffiner, not a little girl, an' I expected better of ye than that."

Arddryn went pale. "How *could* you? How could you say that? They killed him—don't you even care?"

"Of course I care!" Saeddryn shouted back. "He was my

husband. But this is more important than him, or me, or any of us. This is about Tara."

"And that's all you care about!" Arddryn screamed. "That's all you've ever cared about! You care more about having that cursed throne than you care about your own family!"

Saeddryn slapped her. "Don't ye dare say that to me, girl. We're Taranisäiis. We were born to love this land, an' protect it, an' to die for it if we have to. Yer father understood that, an' so did yer grandmother. King Arenadd knew it, too. All of them laid their lives down for Tara, an' one day soon, so will I. When that happens, it'll be yer own turn, Arddryn. Ye and Caedmon will be the last true Taranisäiis, an' when I'm gone, it'll be up to ye to fight for our land. Would ye see all our lives lost for nothing? So much struggle wasted?"

Arddryn looked away. "No," she muttered.

"Good. Then be a Taranisäii now. Go back to Skenfrith, an' be ready. The war begins now, an' we will show this half-breed murderer who the Night God really chose."

If Arddryn had intended to throw her own anger in her mother's face, she never got the chance. Rakek, probably sensing that this could go nowhere good, stepped in.

"Your human is right," he said, to Aenae. "My human and I shall stay here tonight, with your permission, and tomorrow I shall take her back to Skenfrith."

Aenae jerked his head briefly. "You may stay, and the humans will give you meat. Do not let your human stray again, Rakek."

"I understand and will obey. Come, Arddryn."

Red-faced, Arddryn let herself be herded away inside.

Standing by to watch, Saeddryn felt a deep and terrible shame burn in her stomach. But she said nothing and only made a mental note to invite Arddryn to dinner. The poor girl was trying her hardest. And besides, this could be the last time they ever met.

Grim-faced, Saeddryn went inside with Aenae.

Despite the awful news Arddryn had brought, Saeddryn found herself slipping back into old habits. As she went down the tower to call her council back together, she thought over the other information that Rakek had provided, about the half-breed's partner. This one who had killed Torc with some new power. This *Oeka*.

If Oeka had become as all-powerful as Rakek had suggested, then the implications could change everything. Unless it was just hearsay . . . but griffins weren't given to exaggeration. Especially not when it came to another griffin's being stronger than themselves.

Saeddryn sped up. And broke into a run.

21

Senneck's Return

Even though Senneck was in Malvern now, and enjoying the comforts of the Eyrie, she had been doing the very opposite of what she would have done under normal circumstances. Although she was desperate to know absolutely everything happening in the Eyrie, she stayed away. Away from the half-breed Queen and, more importantly, away from the repulsive thing that Oeka had become. The little creature revolted her but frightened her as well. She understood by now just how deeply Oeka could see into the minds of other creatures, and she would not let that happen to herself. Not again.

Senneck didn't know just how far Oeka's power could reach. Five wing-beats? Ten? Fifty? There was no way to tell.

A crippling paranoia had taken hold of her. She had seen the execution of the human, watching from a perch well out of sight. She knew full well that if Oeka looked into her mind and found disloyal thoughts there, then she would do the same to her. It could happen in an eye-blink.

Senneck hid away in her nest and brooded obsessively. Did the twisted little monster already know? Had she already sensed what she, Senneck was thinking, and decided to bide her time? How long would it be until that fatal blow came?

Still, Senneck didn't lose her courage. She ate and slept as much as she could, determined to build her strength, and when she was awake, she kept her thoughts as vague as possible, focusing on irrelevant things and using them as walls to hide what Oeka should not see.

Mostly, she thought about Kullervo and the coming fight. She was desperate to leave for Warwick, but she couldn't. Not yet, not on her own. She had to wait until the half-breed fool had made her plans and assembled whatever fighters she would send.

Someone would come and tell Senneck when the time came to leave. Or so she hoped.

After two days of rest, she noticed things beginning to happen in and around the Eyrie, and gladly went to investigate.

She already knew the location of the Hatchery, home to the unpartnered. Unlike the one where she had grown up, this Hatchery occupied one of the Eyrie's towers. Today, there was something going on around it. Griffins flew here and there, going in and out via the openings in the walls, and from her vantage-point, Senneck could hear the racket they were making. Odder than that, when she looked closer, she noticed that many of the unpartnered now circling over the tower sported red marks of some kind on their bodies. Blood? No, the patterns were too similar.

Puzzled, she took off from her perch and flew toward the Hatchery. Unwilling to go inside, she landed on a ledge jutting from the adjacent tower and watched more closely. Picking out an unpartnered from the flock, she watched him until he perched nearby. She saw that the red marks were stains on his feathers. They ringed his neck and spread onto patches on his back and belly. Odd, but there was something familiar about them, too.

Unable to decide what they could mean, she flitted over to another ledge, this one on the wall of the Hatchery. From there she called out.

"You!"

The male looked up sharply. "Did you speak to me?"

He was bigger than her, but she refused to duck her head to acknowledge his greater strength. "Why do you have red stains on your coat, youngster?"

She was being rude, but the younger griffin obviously thought she was too old and pathetic to bother with. "They are war plumage, old hen. The unpartnered are going to war!"

Senneck was surprised. "What griffin will lead you?"

The other griffin cocked his head scornfully. "The great Kaanee, of course."

Senneck remembered *that* particular traitor. "The one who chose a dark human as his own? What mighty leaders you unpartnered have."

The youngster took offence at that. "Watch what you say, old one. It is said that a griffin much more powerful than you mocked him for his choice long ago. He severed the fool's head and crushed it with his talons for all to see."

Senneck snorted in disgust and flew away. She had never seen griffins as arrogantly contemptible as these. With luck, they would all die on Warwick's walls.

Still, at least if they were going to be there, the city would be certain to fall. Senneck decided to go and find this Kaanee at once.

The confusion made it easy to slip into the Hatchery. There were no floors inside; instead, the tower was lined with nests and perches set into the walls that left plenty of room for flight. Unpartnered were everywhere, arguing and mock-fighting with each other, anticipating the bloodshed to come.

Finding Kaanee was easy enough—down at the bottom of the tower, a knot of unpartnered had gathered around a griffin that Senneck recognised easily enough—if not for his appearance than for his age and the confident way he stood. His human was beside him, with a few others, using rags dipped in red water to stain the feathers of the griffins who pushed in to demand it. Kaanee only stood there and watched. Very regal.

Senneck's thin frame helped her now. She squeezed past the bulky bodies of the jostling unpartnered, nipping rumps and shoulders where she had to, until she reached the clear space around Kaanee.

"What do you want?" he said immediately.

Senneck paused a moment, looking him over. He was brown, tawny, and darker than herself, and his eyes were yellow. Younger than her, but not by very much, he looked like a griffin in the prime of life. The power he wielded made him seem even more solid than his stocky frame suggested. Briefly, Senneck wished she were younger. This one would have made an excellent mate.

She bowed her head to him. "I have heard that you are preparing to attack the traitors at Warwick. I wish to go with you."

"Are you one of the unpartnered?" he asked.

"I am," said Senneck, sadly reflecting that this was more or less the truth now.

"Go to my human, then, and be marked. We will fly out soon."

"I do not understand why they must be marked this way," said Senneck. "I have never seen a thing like this before."

"This is the first time we have done this," said Kaanee. "The traitors will have griffins with them, and we must know each other or we will attack our friends."

Senneck chirped to herself. "A wise idea. I will be marked, then."

Kaanee's human, overhearing her, came over and wiped the cloth on her feathers without asking permission. Senneck nearly attacked him out of sheer reflex, but stopped herself and lowered her head to let him do it. The red water felt cold when it trickled through her feathers.

Once the human had finished, she left the Hatchery and returned to her nest. Someone had left food, so she ate it and settled down to rest, facing the exit. When the unpartnered flew out, she would be ready to follow.

She found herself looking forward to the assault on Warwick. It had been a long time since she had last had to fight. Too long.

As she lay there on her nest of straw, sunlight warming her face, she thought of Erian.

He had never been a human much interested in thought and planning. He had always been meant for action—usually hasty, foolish action, but action all the same. *His* great love had always been fighting. He had been good at it, too, with the long metal talon he called a sword. If he were here now, he would be as excited as she was, or even more so.

Senneck imagined him there with her, pacing back and forth with his sword in his hand. She could almost hear his complaining voice. *I want to leave now! Can't we just go ahead? Why do we have to wait for that lot?*

"Because we cannot always charge in, little human," Senneck said aloud. "Not the way you did through your whole life."

She heaved a sigh, and the ghostly image of the yellow-haired boy pouted and disappeared.

Senneck closed her eyes. It did no good to dwell on the past. She had spent too many years thinking of it, and it was time to move on.

She thought of Kullervo instead. Another human, more or less, not much older than her Erian had been. And, though they were so different, she thought that in a way they were very much the same.

How odd that she would find herself looking out for the son of her human's killer. But, then, Kullervo was nothing like his father. Gentle where Arenadd had been vicious. Stoic when Arenadd had been self-pitying. He was as humble as Arenadd had been power-hungry, and as messy as he had been vain. No wonder the world saw fit to trample him into the mud at every opportunity.

Senneck's tail twitched. "I will find you, Kullervo. I will take you out of that cruel place and make you safe again. I failed to save my Erian, but I shall not fail you. I promise it."

Pain shuddered in Kullervo's back and limbs as they tied him down. He didn't struggle, not now. Fighting back only made them hurt him more. He had come to understand that a long time ago, or so it seemed.

There was no way to tell how many days had passed. In all that time there had been beatings, and starvation, and questions, questions, always questions. When he would not answer those questions, more beatings came, and worse. He had tried to make the change more than once, despite how weak he had become, but he couldn't do it. Something blocked him, inside, and the change refused to happen. Once, feathers sprouted on his back and wings. They ripped those out, one by one.

Now, though . . . what now? They never told him what they were going to do.

They had taken him into a big room with plenty of light, where there was a table. Then they had taken his clothes off and made him lie face-down, tying him in place. Lying with his face pressed into the wood, he wondered what else they could possibly do to him. Rape, now? Was it going to be rape?

He closed his eyes and tried not to think of that.

The thud of a door, and a guard's voice. "He's ready, milady."

"Good. You can go now. Yes, all of you."

The door opened and shut again, then there was silence. Kullervo heard footsteps, coming to his side, and the woman's voice again.

"Kullervo. Can you hear me?"

He said nothing.

The woman moved closer, and he heard her hiss shock between her teeth. She fiddled with something by his shoulder, and the rope holding his head down loosened. He lifted his head and looked dully at her.

She was finely dressed and looked very pale. "Kullervo," she said again. "Do you remember me? Please just say something."

Kullervo coughed and dropped his head onto the table. "Griffiner," he mumbled. "From before."

"Yes, that's right. My name is Lady Morvudd." She touched him and pulled away when he flinched. "It's all right; I'm not going to hurt you. Sweet Night God, what did they do?"

"Hurt," Kullervo spat the word out clumsily. "I can get better. Not going to die."

"You didn't talk, did you?"

His eyes closed. "Don't know anything. Just an ugly monster from an egg, that's all."

"You're not ugly," Morvudd said softly. "You're very special, Kullervo."

He sneered at her. *"Freak!"*

She recoiled. "Your teeth—"

The sneer faded from Kullervo's swollen face, and he stopped speaking.

"They're not going to hurt you any more," Morvudd said. "You're here now because I'm going to examine you. I want to try to learn more about you. Just lie still."

Kullervo said nothing. He lay there and thought of Laela, and Senneck, and let her do whatever it was she wanted. She was lying, anyway. *She* was the one here to hurt him now.

Morvudd moved around the table, muttering to herself. She touched his wings, lifting and flexing them, massaging the flesh to feel the shapes of the bones and joints. Every so often,

Kullervo heard a faint scratching as she wrote things down. She felt his spine, too, and the muscles on his upper back, before she moved on to his tail. It hadn't been tied down, maybe because it was damaged. A guard had stomped on it, and now it had gone stiff.

Morvudd felt her way along it, from the base toward the tip. When she reached the swelling halfway along, Kullervo cried out. The tail wrenched out of her hand and smacked her hard in the face. Kullervo heard her yelp, and hissed to himself.

"I'm sorry," she said a moment later. "I didn't mean to hurt you. I won't touch it again."

She inspected his legs, instead, showing particular interest in the bones and how they moved. She didn't say anything until she reached his feet, and happened to flex one of his toes.

"Holy night!" she let go immediately. "Claws. *Retractable* claws! I didn't know you had . . ." There was a frantic scratching from her pen. "Do you still have talons as well? Let me see your hands . . ." His left hand curled into a fist when she tried to examine it. "Please could you relax? I need to see—"

The fist clenched harder. "Leave me alone," Kullervo growled, slurring through broken teeth. "Don't touch."

"I'm not hurting you, am I? I'm trying to be careful—"

"Leave—me—alone," his voice rose. "Let me up. Let me get dressed."

"I'm not finished yet," said Morvudd.

"I want my clothes. I want to get up."

"Look," she said, in kindly tones. "This is important. You're a creature unlike any other, Kullervo. Every scholar in Tara would want to read about you. All I want to do is *learn*."

He began to pull at the ropes holding him down. *"I—am—not—a creature!"*

"I didn't mean it that way," Morvudd soothed. "You're special, Kullervo, very special. Neither man nor griffin, but both, and your ability to change shape is—"

But Kullervo was beyond listening now. Muscles bulged and rippled weirdly along his back and shoulders, and he began to fight against the ropes, twisting and bucking. A snarl burst out of his chest, and his hands contorted. Morvudd backed away, opening her mouth to call for the guards, but her eyes went straight to Kullervo's hand, and widened.

His fingers spread wide and rigid, and something moved under the skin. Something cracked, and Kullervo bellowed.

Long, sharp spikes curved out of his fingertips, right before Morvudd's eyes. They thickened, and darkened, spreading upward to cover the last joint of each finger.

Morvudd gaped and grinned disbelievingly. Forgetting the guards, she moved away from the door and snatched up her notepad again. Keeping a safe distance from the table and the contorted shape on it, she began to sketch frantically.

As the talons grew, the skin on Kullervo's hands thickened and cracked, turning into scales. On his back, feathers sprouted from his wings, and his tail and backside darkened with fur.

That was all. Morvudd frowned, waiting for more to happen, but it didn't.

Transformation was only partial, she scribbled down. *Perhaps his distress or weakened state interrupted it in some way. Fur sprouted on—*

Caught up in her recording, she had taken her attention away from Kullervo.

He panted and groaned. The changing had made him grit the remains of his teeth, and now his mouth tasted of fresh blood. But—

His fingers flexed, and he felt the stiffness at their ends. Felt the scrape on the wood. *Talons!*

Kullervo hissed. He brought his arm up, drawing it through the rope until he could grip it. His talons caught in the fibre, and he began to work them back and forth, faster and faster. He didn't even check to see if Morvudd was looking.

She noticed eventually. "Stop that! Guards! G—"

The rope snapped. Stupidly, Morvudd started forward to try to stop him. Kullervo twisted, turned, and wrapped his talons around her neck.

"Help! *Help me!*"

The door burst open, and guards came running.

"Drop her!" one roared.

Kullervo snarled, blood turning his mouth into a dripping wound. "No. Take the ropes off, or she dies."

The guards hesitated, and his grip tightened on Morvudd's throat.

"Do it!" she gasped. "Do it now!"

Kullervo felt the ropes fall away, and he sighed, very softly. "Good." Still holding Morvudd, he sat up.

Her eyes met his; they had begun to go red. "Please, let me go. You don't want to hurt me, Kullervo. You're not a monster."

Kullervo rasped a laugh. "You said I was a creature. I wanted to be a man, but if I can't, then I must be a beast." He dragged her toward the door, using her to shield himself from the guards. When one came too close, he lashed out and tore the man's face with his talons.

In the corridor outside, more guards were coming. Too many. Kullervo pressed himself against a wall, holding Morvudd in front of him.

"Give up," she said. "Give up now, or they'll kill you."

They were closing in, blocking the way to his left. That only left the right.

With a quick, brutal blow, Kullervo slashed Morvudd's throat wide open. He hurled her body at the guards, turned right, and ran.

22

Over the Walls of Warwick

Senneck stayed at the back of the flock, as the unpartnered flew toward Warwick. It was humiliating. She had imagined herself at the front, flying proudly with all the lesser griffins patiently behind her. She had imagined her return to Warwick as *her* journey, not theirs. *Her* fight. Not theirs.

But the unpartnered were many, and nearly all of them were younger and faster fliers than her. Senneck fumed. Outstripped and left behind, forced to fly at the back by these hatchlings who knew nothing! Hadn't it been her who had lived through the war? Her who flew over the sea to the Island of the Sun, pregnant and carrying a human on her back? How many of *these* youngsters had ever seen real fighting?

Senneck found herself hating them, and she promised herself that when she reached Warwick, she would kill any of them who got in her way when she went to find Saeddryn. That, at least, would be something reserved for her alone.

Snow had started to drift down now, and despite her resentment, flying at the back of the flock almost certainly saved Senneck's life. The unpartnered split up when they reached Warwick, flying in over the walls from all directions at once. Even so, the defenders spotted them well before they arrived, and they were ready. The giant bows on the walls were completed and ready, and they did their work.

Senneck saw the unpartnered ahead of her rush over the city walls, and she saw them begin to fall. Dozens of griffins, impaled by spears, spiralling down among the snowflakes onto the roofs of the city. Some of them, injured, fluttered and screamed before they joined their fellows. The outcome was always the same.

The survivors flew higher, trying to stay out of range, but, in the end, it was mostly their sheer numbers that saved them. The humans using the giant bows turned them this way and that, aiming for any griffins foolish enough to be flying close together.

Senneck hung back, truly frightened now. She had never seen a weapon that could bring down a griffin like this, so fast and so easily. The unpartnered were being decimated.

Some, though, had more sense. Kaanee had made it past the walls, but he went no further. He circled back, drawing himself in as if to call.

Instead, what came out of his beak was magic. A thin beam of silvery light hit the wall-top, slicing clean through the stones. When it touched one of the horrible weapons, it fell apart with a crack and a scream from the guards loading it. Kaanee, showing astonishing control, directed his magic toward others, destroying them one by one. Eventually, his magic faltered, and he flew away to lead the assault on the tower, but he had cleared a good portion of the wall. Senneck flew over the gap and joined the battle.

The griffins of Warwick had risen out of the tower. Riderless, they rushed to attack the invaders.

Senneck had gone barely any distance when a griffin flew straight at her, screaming a challenge.

She didn't screech back, or change her direction, but flew on as if nothing had happened. The other griffin, apparently thinking it would be an easy fight, curled his body inward, ready to latch onto her the moment they met.

But Senneck hadn't survived as long as she had for nothing. At the very last instant, she flicked a wing and rolled out of the griffin's path. He shot past her, flailing clumsily as he tried to turn back. Senneck had been ready for that. She angled her wings and executed a spectacular back-flip. More by luck than judgment, she hit her attacker square in the head with her hind paws. She felt her claws catch on something, and kicked away from him as hard as she could.

Fighting in midair was extremely dangerous, so rather than

try to engage him again, she flew away and upward, struggling for more height. In situations like these, height was almost always the advantage.

She didn't have to look back to know the male was chasing her.

There were other fights going on, all around her—she caught a few brief glimpses as she ascended. All around, griffins wheeling and tearing at each other, filling the air with screams and screeches. Below, the roofs of Warwick were already littered with broken corpses among the gathering snow.

Senneck turned when she was high enough and saw the male griffin rising to meet her. One side of his face streamed blood, but if anything, he looked even more savage for it. *"You will die!"*

Senneck didn't waste her energy on threats. She hovered, fluttering rapidly to stay in one place, and extended her talons.

The male came on. Stupidly, he chose to attack her from underneath. His beak hooked into her belly, right where she was most vulnerable, and he slackened his wings and let himself fall, putting all his weight into tearing her bowels open.

An instant before he dropped Senneck's talons sank into his neck, just behind his jaw. She twisted sideways, hard. His beak lifted out of her skin, then he was thrashing, beating his wings in her face, lashing out blindly with his talons.

His own struggles killed him. Dragged upward by his weight, Senneck's talons pulled through his flesh, into the soft spot just under his beak. When they hit the underside of his lower jaw, she pulled them free.

The male fought to stay in the air, but not for long. Senneck flew out of his reach and saw him weaken and falter. Then he fell, trailing red droplets that followed him to the earth like rain.

Senneck didn't stay to watch him hit the ground. She flew in a wide circle, trying to get her bearings. Her wound smarted horribly.

Over the city, it was chaos. Griffins were everywhere, both unpartnered and Warwickan. Below, she could see more fighting in the streets. Unpartnered they might have been, but her comrades had brought humans with them. A handful of griffiners had come along, and some of the unpartnered had agreed to carry human soldiers with them. Humans could go places a griffin couldn't, and they were good for healing injuries.

Senneck huffed satisfaction. Ignoring the enemies in the sky, she made straight for the tower. Those petty fights could wait.

Evading a half-grown female who tried to intercept her, she landed on the tower-top and took shelter in the opening leading inside. From there she scanned the sky quickly, watching for a griffin who could be Aenae. There wasn't much chance of that; there were far too many others flying all over the place to pick out a single one.

She would have to take a risk, then. Surely, Aenae would be there fighting to protect his territory. If not, then he would be with his human, protecting her. He couldn't do both. Ultimately, it came down to whatever he chose: the honour of fighting or simple good sense.

Senneck would take her chances.

She turned and went into the tower. Inside, it was unnaturally quiet; every griffin that lived there must have gone to fight.

But not every human.

Senneck reached the bottom of the ramp, turned a corner, and nearly walked into something blocking the corridor. Bloody feathers thrust into her face, a dead eye stared. She backed away, hissing, and something hit her in the side.

A human appeared from an entrance in the wall, spear thrusting into her. Two more came out from behind the dead griffin, two more spears came for her head.

Senneck lurched backward, rearing up instinctively. The spear fell away from her flank, and she lashed out with a forepaw, crushing that human against the wall. The others stayed where they were, using the dead griffin for cover. One threw his spear. It was aimed at her chest, but her paw came in the way, and the point sank into it.

Senneck screamed. Falling back with a wing shielding her head, she bit at the wooden shaft. The point came free, but blood and skin came with it. Maddened, she charged at them. She hit the dead griffin, knocking it forward. It rolled over, throwing the two humans off balance. Senneck leapt over the corpse and killed one with a blow of her beak. The other one fled, but she chased him and cut him down from behind.

The silence that followed felt crushing.

Senneck's sides heaved. She stood for a moment with her

injured paw raised, and felt sweat and blood trickle down her flank. Her tongue burned with the taste of killing.

"Kraaaaa . . ."

She felt her heart pound, and shook herself. Only four kills, three of them humans, and she was already tired. But oh how alive she felt at last!

Where a human would have laughed, Senneck snapped her beak hard and bounded away. Searching for revenge.

Arddryn had been the one to warn her mother about the unpartnered.

She and Rakek had stayed the night, and left at dawn the next day, without a goodbye from Saeddryn. But the sun was barely up before they returned, running to the rebel council with a terrified story of seeing a massive flock of griffins coming from the south. Rakek said that they had odd red marks on their feathers, and that he had seen a strong-looking male at their head, with a human on his back.

Saeddryn had known instantly that it had to be Kaanee. Kaanee, and the unpartnered. Her guess had been right. Oeka's newfound power had been enough to bring them back into action, and Warwick was in dire trouble. Their only luck was that they had plenty of warning now, and time to prepare everything. Saeddryn had called her council together—all except for Morvudd, who had vanished somewhere—and gave her orders.

Arddryn hovered nearby, her face twisted with anxiety.

"—an' everythin' else we worked out before," Saeddryn finished. "Hurry up. And for shadow's sake, someone find Morvudd!" As always in moments of stress, her old, rough accent leaked out in her voice.

"I should go," Arddryn said when the councillors had left. "Leave Warwick." But she cast a questioning look at her mother.

Saeddryn hesitated. "No. Stay. There's probably no time; ye don't want t'be caught out in the open all on yer own. We need all the help we can get, too. 'Sides, it's time ye learnt by doin'. Stay close by me, don't leave Aenae or me, *ever.* Keep Rakek close." She jabbed a finger at Arddryn. "I mean it. *Keep him close.* This lot comin' aren't here t'take prisoners, understand?"

"I know that!" Arddryn snapped, fear making her angrier than she should have been.

"I said *do ye understand?*" said Saeddryn. "This ain't going to be play-fightin', it's going t'be real. In a fight, a griffiner who leaves her griffin is dead."

Rakek came closer, standing over his human so that she was standing between his forelegs, just under his chest. "Do not be afraid. I shall not let you be hurt."

"I trust you," said Arddryn. "You, too, Mother."

Saeddryn softened. "Good. Have ye got yer sickle?"

"Yes. I think I can do this . . ."

"Ye can. Arddryn, ye can. Yer a Taranisäii."

"I know," Arddryn said rather gloomily.

"Oh . . ." Saeddryn gave her a hug. "I've been hard on ye, girl, too hard. I'm sorry for that. All I wanted is t'see ye be all ye were meant to be. I believe that's what ye have become, an' I'm proud of ye, Arddryn. Prouder than I can say."

Arddryn hugged her back. "I know. I do my best."

"Good!" Saeddryn let go. "Now all we have to do is stick together an' see this day through as best we can! An' knowin' who we are, our best will be great."

"I'm sure it will be." Arddryn offered up a weak smile.

It was fine bravado, but bravado was all it was. Both of them knew just how dangerous this day was going to be.

Arddryn stayed with her mother as she supervised the defences, issuing orders left and right. This was the first time she had seen her do something like this. It was almost bewildering.

In all Arddryn's life, her mother had been many things—a griffiner, a priestess—a mother, of course—but now she admitted to herself that, at bottom, she had always thought of Saeddryn as mostly just an old woman.

In her more bitter moments, she had sometimes wondered just how much her mother had done to win the war. Someone so cranky and dried-up couldn't possibly be a *real* warrior. People probably just respected her because she was the King's cousin, and *he* was just a creepy drunk. It was all nonsense.

Now, though . . .

"Block all the ways in an' out of the tower. Yes, all of them. I want men with spears at every door, an' make sure they know how t'use them. Nerth—where's Nerth? Get him over here *right now*. Aenae, can ye go talk to the griffins? Just make sure they all know the plan."

Nerth appeared. He was even older than Saeddryn and had an ugly, wrinkled face. "What's the plan for me, Saeth?"

"There ye are." Saeddryn put a hand on his shoulder. "Arddryn an' me are gonna be in the council chamber for this. I want ye with us."

"Oh, that's it, is it?" Nerth thumped his stick on the floor. "Yer gonna make me sit this one out, eh? Think old Nerth can't take a fight no more, eh?"

Saeddryn laughed. "Don't be daft. I need ye with me, Nerth. My best warrior has t'be there to guard me an' my daughter."

"Right." He cackled. "Don't worry, I won't let ye down."

"I know ye won't. Get some men together; we need the doors barricaded." Saeddryn sighed. "It's a cruel thing, but me an' Arddryn have to live through this."

"I want to fight," Arddryn put in suddenly.

The two elders ignored her.

"The Taranisäiis must survive," Nerth said solemnly. "I'd die to make certain of it."

"Do not argue with them," Rakek said aside to Arddryn. "I, too, would choose to fight, but we must please them for now. Our time will come."

Grumbling, Arddryn let herself be led into the council chamber. Frightened servants brought in food and blankets, while others carried in heavy objects and stacked them up on the inside of the doors, leaving just one still open. Saeddryn helped, dragging benches over to the one remaining door, where they would be ready to put in place when the time came.

Rakek wandered around restlessly, looking for a place to settle down. Aenae hadn't returned.

"Now." Saeddryn turned to Arddryn. "I don't know how long we've got, but wait here. Once I'm through that door, block it up with the benches an' don't lift them away for anything."

"But aren't you going to stay with us?" said Arddryn.

Saeddryn smiled, a soft smile that made her look much younger. "There's still work I have to do. I'll come back an' join ye when I'm ready. No need to worry; they're not here yet. Nerth, are ye ready?"

He nodded sternly. "Got my sickle, an' that's all I need."

"I trust ye." Saeddryn came to him and hugged him. She whispered something in his ear and kissed his cheek before she let him go.

Arddryn started toward her. "Mother—"

Saeddryn ruffled her hair. "I'll see ye soon. Be brave, an' don't ever give up." She went to the door, and through it, pulling it shut behind her. As it closed she looked back through the gap. "Block it properly. Don't open it for anything, not for *anything*, understand?"

The door closed.

Waiting.

For Arddryn, that was all the battle for Warwick was. She stayed in the chamber with Nerth and Rakek, not knowing whether the enemy had come yet or how close the fighting might be. Saeddryn and Aenae didn't come back.

Arddryn hadn't wanted to talk to Nerth, but after a long, long silence she couldn't bear it any more.

"What's going on out there? Where's Mother?" She asked the question without looking at him or Rakek, appealing to the empty seats around her.

"Don't know," said Nerth. "Can't hear a thing. Can ye?"

"No, nothing. We're too deep in the tower. I just wish I *knew*!"

"We'll know eventually," said Nerth.

"That's not the point!" Arddryn sat down, head in her hands. "I wish I was out there. I should be fighting with everyone else."

"I always thought ye didn't much like fighting," said Nerth with a grin.

"I don't, but this is different. This isn't *playing*, this is real. I don't want to die, or let Mother die. She's always telling me to be a real Taranisäii, and now she won't let me!"

"Ah, well, if I were yer dad, I'd let ye fight. But with Lady Saeddryn, it's different," Nerth said sagely.

"Different how?" Arddryn looked sulky. "She just doesn't trust me. She treats me like a little kid."

Nerth cackled. "I tell ye, Arddryn, ye may be a Taranisäii, but yer as silly as every other girl I ever did meet."

"What's that supposed to mean?" she snapped.

"Listen to her!" said Nerth, apparently to the ceiling. "Her mother puts her in charge of leadin' a whole city, an' she thinks she's not getting any respect out of her!"

"That's not what I meant," said Arddryn. "She talks to me like I'm *stupid*."

"Maybe that's 'cause that's how ye act sometimes," said Nerth.

"Wh—how *dare* you speak to me like that?"

"I speak to people the way I reckon they deserve to be spoken to. I'm too old to do it any other way." Nerth pulled out his sickle and flicked it back and forth, with surprising grace and skill. "Ye do yer mother a disservice, Arddryn. She's tough, aye, an' hard sometimes. Hard lives make people hard. An' though I don't agree with it, she put ye here for what she thought was a good reason."

"What reason?" said Arddryn.

"T'keep ye safe," he said simply. "Because she can't bear the thought of losin' ye the way she lost her mother."

"She didn't care that much about Dad, did she?" Arddryn's pain twisted into a sneer.

"Damn right she did. Maybe she didn't always get on with Lord Torc, but she loved him right till the end."

"She betrayed him."

For the first time, Nerth looked uncertain—even ashamed. "It was somethin' she never stopped regretting. Torc understood that."

Arddryn shuddered. "I wish I'd never known about it. How could she—and with *him*? He was horrible. Just being near him made me feel sick inside."

"He did that t'some people," Nerth muttered. "I dunno if—"

Something hit the other side of the door, hard. Arddryn screamed and nearly fell over her chair to get away.

Rakek was at her side in an instant. "It could be nothing—"

Another thump, and another, and the muffled sound of scrabbling hands. *"Help!"* a voice screamed from outside. *"Hel . . ."*

The door shuddered in its frame, rattling the benches piled against it. The voice had gone silent.

Arddryn breathed deeply. "Oh, gods."

"I think it's gone," said Nerth.

Thump. The door shook under the impact. As if that was a signal, two other doors began to jerk against their hinges as something massive beat against them. Arddryn heard the scraping of talons and frustrated snorts and hissings.

She pulled closer to Rakek. "Night God help us."

"Do not be afraid," he said. "They cannot get in. If they do, I shall kill them."

One of the enemy griffins left after only a few attempts, and the other gave up a short time later. But the other one, the first to come, stayed. The scratchings grew louder, and soon Arddryn could hear splintering wood. One of the benches near the top came loose and fell down off the pile.

Rakek ran to the door, wings raised, and stood hunched in front of it, already spoiling for a fight. "Come through here, and die!" he called.

There was a brief pause in the thumpings and scratchings before they resumed, harder than ever. A deafening crack split the air, and a hole appeared, the tip of a beak thrusting through the wood.

Arddryn backed away toward Nerth, groping for her sickle. "What do we do? Nerth, do something; just tell me what to do!"

He took her arm. "It's all right, it hasn't got through yet—"

The attacking griffin kept up its attack, focusing now on the hole. Its beak hooked in and out, ripping pieces of wood away until the hole was almost big enough for its head to fit. It stopped for a moment to look, and Arddryn glimpsed a blue eye glaring through at them.

"I am coming for you," a voice called mockingly. "You, little chick, you will die first."

Incensed, Rakek flung himself at the hole, scrambling over the stacked benches. They fell away under his talons, and he tumbled backward. A bench landed on top of him, but he got up, thrusting it away and scrambling for the door.

Nerth started forward, horror-struck. "Stop, idiot!" he yelled. "Get away from there!"

Rakek wasn't listening. He pushed the benches away and attacked the door, trying to get at the other griffin.

Nerth gave Arddryn a shove. "Get over there! Stop him!"

She pulled herself together, and ran. "Rakek, don't!"

Outside, the enemy griffin threw her whole weight against the door, and broke it apart.

With a scream, she charged over the pieces and leapt straight at Rakek.

Nerth appeared at Arddryn's side, pulling her away. "Get back! Girl, move! Tip that table over an' hide behind it, *now*!"

She obeyed, ducking behind the wooden barrier. Nerth stood in front with his stick in one hand and his sickle in the other. He was breathing hard. "Don't worry, girl, Rakek can do this. He's strong."

Arddryn looked over the edge of the table and felt sicker than she had ever done.

The griffin fighting Rakek was female, long-bodied, and long-legged, her bony form bloodied in several places. She was bigger than Rakek, and fast.

Rakek attacked her recklessly, his red-brown form darting this way and that to avoid her talons. He called out taunts and threats, trying to provoke her, but she fought silently, unmoved and ruthless. She aimed a blow for his head, with her beak. Rakek avoided it and bit for her throat. She was too tall for him, and he missed but left a gouge in her chest.

The female pulled back and reared up onto her hind legs, talons spread wide. Rakek took his opportunity and sprang, straight for her unprotected belly.

She dropped the instant he moved, and her talons came down. They hit him square in the back. He pulled backward, but her talons had hooked into him and would not let him go. She took her opportunity and smashed the back of his skull with her beak. Rakek's whole body shook under the blow, and he made an awful, howling noise.

The female unhooked her talons and drove her beak into the back of his neck, shaking it violently.

Arddryn heard a dull snapping sound, and saw her partner go limp.

That was when she screamed.

Nerth took a step back, and bumped into the table. *"Shit!"*

The enemy griffin stepped over Rakek's body. She didn't run, or hurry at all. She only walked, slowly and deliberately, body low to the ground. Stalking.

Arddryn could only see Nerth's back. He was shaking. "Nerth, don't—"

Nerth said nothing. He squared his shoulders, lifted his head high, and bellowed. The bellow carried him on, straight at the murderous griffin, his sickle pointed for her eyes.

The griffin raised a paw and knocked him away. The blow looked slight, even gentle, but it sent the old man tumbling across the room. He hit the floor and rolled several times before coming to rest. He didn't get up.

Arddryn had stood up without even meaning to. She didn't know where her sickle was. Everything felt very far away now. The room seemed to fade, and she couldn't see Rakek's body, or Nerth's. The thought crossed her mind, the mad thought, that she couldn't be hurt now. Not now, when she felt so frozen.

As if in a dream, she stepped out from behind the table and raised her hands to the griffin. "You don't have to kill me."

The griffin said nothing.

"I have no weapon," said Arddryn. "I won't attack. Take me prisoner instead. My name is Arddryn Taranisäii, and there's a reward for whoever brings me to Malvern."

The griffin stopped.

Hope swelled in Arddryn. "Keep me here and wait until your leader comes. You can hand me over to him and tell them I'm your prisoner. I won't—"

"You are not the one," the griffin said abruptly. "You are only a youngster. Where is the elder one? Where is Saeddryn Taranisäii?"

"My mother isn't here," said Arddryn. "I don't know where she is. She and Aenae went out to help with the defences and never came back."

"You do not know where they have gone?"

"No."

The griffin lifted a paw and shoved her onto the floor. Arddryn's head hit the floorboards hard, and she groaned. "I told you, I don't know—"

The griffin's talons wrapped around her chest and began to squeeze. "Tell me where she is."

"I don't know!"

The talons squeezed harder. "Tell me where she is."

"I said I don't know!"

Harder, and harder, until the tips began to draw blood. "Tell me where she is."

"I don't know!"

The talons closed, until Arddryn felt her bones crack. She screamed out something that made no sense, breath gurgling in her chest.

"Tell me!" the griffin screamed. "I will find Saeddryn, and she will die at my talons, now tell me where she is! *Tell me!*"

Arddryn said nothing. Her eyes bulged, and her fingers scrabbled uselessly at the floor.

Senneck tightened her grip even further. "Tell me!"

Arddryn opened her mouth and coughed up blood.

Senneck let her go, but it was already too late. The girl flopped out of her grip, eyes glazed in an empty stare.

"Shhhhhyaaaa!" Senneck rasped out a griffish curse, and turned away. Her guess had been wrong. The traitor could be anywhere.

She ate some of the dead griffin to give herself some energy, gagging at the foul taste. When she had had her fill, she lay down to rest and lick her wounds. She had gathered a few, but she wasn't badly hurt. She had it in her for one more fight.

But how to find Saeddryn and Aenae? It was chaos outside; how could she ever hope to get to them? And Aenae . . . how could she fight him? Any son of the dark griffin would be massive and powerful. To fight him in the air would be suicide.

Her only hope of winning against Aenae would be to fight him at close quarters, somewhere his size would hamper him. But where? How?

Senneck glanced back at Arddryn's body, and her eyes narrowed as something occurred to her. It would be a risk, but it could well work.

Finding Saeddryn herself would be difficult and dangerous, but perhaps there was a way to make Saeddryn come to her. If she used the proper bait.

23

Revenge

Luck and sheer rage had freed Kullervo, but they only lasted him so long. He evaded the guards as long as possible, but there was no hope of escaping that way. There were locked doors everywhere, and he was exhausted and in pain. Before long, he had begun to stumble, his hurt legs refusing to bend the way they should. Breath burned in his lungs.

Helpless fury filled him. He had thought he was free, but there was no way out of this place. He was lost, guards were closing in, and, any moment now, they would have him. The only thing he was certain about was that he would never go back to that cell. He would fight back until they killed him. He would take death rather than spend one more day in that place. It was his choice to make.

Not much of a comforting thought.

He turned a corner and spotted a door that was open. There was no-one on the other side, so he ducked inside and shut the door behind him, hoping to hide until the guards had gone. The door didn't have a lock, so he wedged a chair under the handle and turned to look around. Cupboards lined the walls. A storeroom?

Kullervo began wrenching the cupboards open, pawing through the contents. Food! He stuffed bread into his mouth, nearly choking on it in his haste to swallow. In other cupboards, he found spare blankets and tied a couple around himself in place of clothes. Outside, he heard footsteps coming closer. He froze and dove behind a cupboard, but the footsteps went past without pausing.

Kullervo growled to himself and finished his food while he went through the last of the cupboards. He needed a weapon.

There weren't any, of course. Nobody would be stupid enough to keep weapons in a prison and not lock them up.

The gods hate me, Kullervo thought.

He broke a leg off a handy chair instead, and went to the door to listen. No sound of anyone around. Should he stay here longer or make a run for it? The guards would be back the moment they realised he must be hiding.

Kullervo sighed and took the chair away from the door. He couldn't stay. Not unless he wanted to be cornered. He turned the handle and peeked out into the corridor. Everything looked quiet.

He slipped out and went back the way he had come, moving as silently as he could.

Ahead, he caught the sound of leather brushing against stone. He tensed and prowled forward, raising the chair-leg. The sound seemed to be coming from around a corner. Closer . . . closer . . .

Kullervo flattened himself against the wall by the corner, and not a moment too soon. A guard stepped into view, and Kullervo hit him with the chair-leg as hard as he could.

"Hey—!" Taken by surprise, the man staggered back, grabbing for his sword.

That buried griffish instinct rose up in Kullervo, and he leapt, talons swiping for the man's throat.

The man screamed and punched him hard in the face. Kullervo fell backward, hitting the wall. When he landed, pain exploded in his back. He tried frantically to get up, but his legs wouldn't move properly, and every movement made the pain worse. That was it. The guard had him now. He curled up pathetically, trying to protect his head, and waited for the end.

Nothing happened.

He risked a look up and saw the guard lying a little way away, unmoving.

The pain in Kullervo's back subsided after a while, and he dragged himself to his feet, staring fearfully at the guard on the floor. The guard was breathing, just barely, but his throat was leaking blood all over his tunic. His sword had landed near the wall.

Kullervo picked it up and limped away.

Saeddryn and Aenae fought side by side, down in the streets. Aenae had wanted to attack the invaders in the air, but he couldn't do it with Saeddryn on his back, and there was no question of leaving her alone. There was fighting enough on the ground.

Saeddryn killed an enemy soldier with a blow from her sickle and ran along in Aenae's wake as he charged down Warwick's main street, scattering the human fighters in his path. The big griffin killed almost anyone who came too close to him and his human, and Saeddryn had been fairly safe for most of the time. Most of the unpartnered avoided Aenae altogether.

"We have t'get back to the tower!" Saeddryn yelled, rather half-heartedly. Aenae either didn't hear her, or wasn't listening at all, because he ran on without pausing. He was leaving her behind.

Ahead, a griffin burst through a window and launched itself at Aenae. He rose to defend himself, and the other griffin recklessly attacked.

Saeddryn caught up, stopping at a safe distance. An enemy soldier, running past, saw her and stopped. He peered at her and grinned. "High Priestess Saeddryn?"

Saeddryn bared her teeth at him and beckoned with her sickle. "I'm the one who knows the way to the Night God. Come closer, an' I'll show ye."

The soldier already had his sword in his hand. "Thanks kindly, old woman. My wife keeps sayin' how she wants a new house. Yer head should be enough to get us one." He ran at her.

Saeddryn sidestepped his first blow, and aimed a blow at his outstretched arm. Her sickle bounced off his padded leather armour, and she hissed a curse and bounded backward when he swung his sword for her chest. Still grinning, the soldier brought his sword down on her arm. She pulled away at the last moment, but the blade bit into her flesh. She gritted her teeth as blood wet her arm. "Damn ye!"

The soldier closed in. "C'mon, hag, can't ye put up a better fight?"

Saeddryn struck, straight at his grin, and blood splattered over the ground.

"Argh!" The soldier staggered back. The grin was gone, and so was the end of his nose. His hand went to the wound, and he stared dully at Saeddryn.

She darted forward and killed him with a ruthless upswing.

Aenae appeared behind her as if by magic, bloodstained and panting. "Come. Our nest is in danger."

"What do ye mean—?" Saeddryn looked up, and panic tightened in her throat. Smoke had begun to billow from the sides of the tower. "Oh no."

"Quickly, get onto my back," said Aenae.

Saeddryn almost vaulted over his neck and onto his shoulders. He was still wearing his harness, and she held on tightly as he took off.

Aenae spiralled upward around the tower, avoiding the unpartnered. From his back, Saeddryn could see the smoke coming from several different openings in the building. In one or two places, flames were visible. It took her a few moments to notice something odd: that all the fires seemed to be coming from only one level. She thought quickly, trying to guess which one it could be, and her heart wrenched. The council chamber!

Aenae chose an opening in a level below the smoke, and landed just inside.

Saeddryn almost fell off his back. "The council chamber is alight—quick, we have t'get Arddryn out of there!"

Aenae snorted briefly and ran off up the corridor. Saeddryn followed, and all her exhaustion seemed to fall away in an instant—the instant she thought of Arddryn—and fear began to eat at her. She hadn't thought . . . the council chamber had seemed safe enough, and Arddryn . . .

Oh, Night God, what have I done?

They returned to the door, that last door that they had left by not so long ago, and Saeddryn groaned aloud. "No."

Aenae went in first, just a little way. He stopped and turned back to look at her. "They are dead."

Saeddryn followed. "What—?"

A thump came from behind her, very soft. She stopped.

Aenae looked past her. "Saeddryn, come to me, now!"

She ran to him immediately, slowing and turning when she reached his side. Her grip tightened on her sickle.

A griffin had dropped into the doorway, blocking it. Female, earthy brown, and strangely . . . familiar?

The griffin's blue eyes fixed directly on Saeddryn's face. "You remember me."

Saeddryn had seen the red dye on the creature's body, and that was all she needed to know. "Where is my daughter?"

The brown griffin's stare didn't waver. There was a gleam in her eyes. "You remember me, Saeddryn Taranisäii. Remember me, from all those years ago."

The fear bit at Saeddryn again, black and all-consuming. "I think . . ."

The brown griffin began to hiss. "I am Senneck. Senneck, hatched at Eagleholm, partner to Lord Erian Rannagonson, who was killed by *Kraeai kran ae* at Malvern. I am Senneck, and I remember you, who stood by the cursed one's side and helped him to destroy my home."

Saeddryn bared her teeth. "*Senneck!* I remember ye now. Why are ye here? Why are ye even alive?"

Senneck yawned and stretched, mocking the both of them. "I have come to kill you, scum of the North, and you, son of the dark griffin, you as well. See, I have begun by killing your daughter, Saeddryn."

"*No!*" Forgetting the danger, Saeddryn looked frantically around the room. Her eye found the grisly tableaux left there for her to see.

Rakek's remains, partly stripped, lay by an overturned table not far from where Nerth had fallen. Arddryn's body rested against her partner's, the head slumped backward.

Saeddryn took a step toward the huddled bodies, stopped, and retched. She turned away, back to look at Senneck. Her mouth moved, but she said nothing. Her eye stared at the brown griffin, and there was nothing there in her face but bewilderment.

Senneck kneaded at the floor with her talons. "As my chicks were taken from me, so yours will be taken from you. When I am finished here, I shall go to Fruitsheart and kill your son. A son for my son, a daughter for my daughter. But no death shall please me as much as yours, Saeddryn."

Aenae opened his wings. "Move away, Saeddryn. We have heard enough of the old hen's ravings." He charged.

Senneck took a step backward and braced herself.

Aenae crossed the room with terrifying speed, all his strength aimed straight at the older griffin. For a heartbeat, as Senneck watched him come, she thought she saw another griffin there—not Aenae, but the Mighty Skandar himself, bearing down on her in all his fury. Panic swelled in her chest, but it was too late to move. Too late to do anything other than what she had planned to do.

She opened her beak and unleashed her magic.

A light filled the chamber, pulsating, green as grass. It enveloped Aenae, stopping him mid-charge. Saeddryn yelled something, some incoherent thing that might have been her partner's name.

The light faded slightly, and a cracking, grinding sound echoed off the ceiling. It died, too, with the light, and there was Aenae . . . or what Senneck had made of him.

A stone statue stood in the chamber, grey dust falling from its sides. Aenae, son of Skandar, frozen in an attitude of rage and fear.

Beyond him, Senneck faltered and nearly collapsed. She coughed, the sound dry and thin.

Few people could have had Saeddryn's presence of mind in that moment. *She's weakened herself!*

Forgetting everything and all danger, she ran past the stone griffin and hurled herself at Senneck with all her might. Nothing mattered then, not grief, not fear. Revenge was the only thing left.

The sickle hit Senneck on the head and neck, opening ugly gashes everywhere it reached. Senneck rasped and ducked her head, protecting the vulnerable underside. With a scream of frustration, Saeddryn took her by the beak and pulled, wrenching at her head to make her expose her throat.

Senneck finally recovered and jerked her head upward, butting Saeddryn away.

Saeddryn stumbled, but she didn't fall. *"Curse ye!"* she bellowed, and lashed out one final time.

The sickle hit Senneck's beak, so hard that it left a long groove behind. The blade broke.

Senneck made an awful, hacking sound, almost like a laugh. "Fool," she said. "To think that you could have a hope against me."

Saeddryn hurled the remains of the sickle at her. "I curse ye, Senneck, I curse ye in the Night God's name! I curse ye to die and fall into the void forever. *Kill me!*"

Senneck said nothing more. She brought her talons down, and tore Saeddryn Taranisäii apart.

24

Victory

The fight for Warwick had lasted a long time. Half a day of fighting, in the streets and in the air, and in the tower itself. As the sun sank, a massive silence pressed down from the sky and filled the snow-covered city. The battle was over.

Above the buildings, a few griffins circled—very few. Most of the survivors were down in the city, wounded or too worn-out to fly. Every so often, a cry would break the silence, a death scream or a victory screech, but there were very few signs of celebration. Even the soldiers now picking through the city for any last resistance looked more tired than excited.

Up on the tower-top, Kaanee and Iorwerth stood together and watched. Both were wounded, and Kaanee's eyes were glazed with exhaustion.

"We've won," Iorwerth murmured. "But ye know, Kaanee, I don't *feel* triumphant. Just tired and . . . tired."

Kaanee said nothing.

"Why should I feel good about this, though?" Iorwerth said. "Those old battles were for a great cause. This was just a cruel joke." He laughed humourlessly. "We fought for the right to rule ourselves, and now we're fighting each other. And for what? I tell ye, Kaanee, the Taranisäiis were a gift once, but now they're starting to feel like a curse."

Kaanee blinked and shivered. "We are warriors, Iorwerth. We live to fight. You said that it was your way as a darkman to fight."

"Yes, but against my own kind—!"

"Humans are your own kind," Kaanee huffed. "Do not be like a female with chicks; you are male and must protect your territory."

Iorwerth struggled briefly with the griffin's clumsy metaphor. "I suppose you're right." He rubbed his wrist and sighed. "We should go and search the tower. If Saeddryn's still alive, then she'll be hiding there somewhere."

"I saw Aenae in the city," said Kaanee. "And I would have fought him if I had not been too far away."

"Let's just hope they didn't get out of the city. I haven't had any reports, but it'd be hard to be sure . . ." Iorwerth limped down the opening and into the tower, where he had to climb over a dead griffin and three dead men. He muttered to himself as he pushed the bodies aside. What an ugly business war was.

He and Kaanee moved down the tower, hampered by corpses and other debris along the way. There were soldiers everywhere, ostensibly searching for survivors although most of them seemed to think they might find them in cupboards and jewellery boxes.

Iorwerth yelled at them to get back to work, rather half-heartedly. They'd go straight back to what they'd been doing the moment he was out of sight.

About halfway down the tower, a man came running to meet him. "Milord! Iorwerth!"

"What is it?"

The man was panting. "In the council chamber—ye should come see this, hurry."

Iorwerth glanced at Kaanee and followed the man at a run.

His knees were trembling by the time they arrived. The soldier stopped at a broken doorway and gestured at him to go in.

Iorwerth entered, and pulled up short. "What the—?"

A life-sized stone griffin glowered down at him.

"Who put *that* there?" Iorwerth exclaimed. "I don't remember . . ." He trailed off.

Kaanee inspected the statue. "Human magic, to make a griffin from stone. I smell blood here, Iorwerth."

Iorwerth said nothing and only walked away toward the bodies. Some of his followers were already there and had laid one of them out on a handy table. The other two were on the floor.

Iorwerth knew them both. "Arddryn. Rakek. What were they . . . ? Oh sweet shadows. I—"

"Sir?"

Iorwerth saw the soldier beckoning to him. "What?" he snapped. And then, *"No."*

Nerth lay on the table. His legs were bent at unnatural angles, and his head lay on its side.

Iorwerth touched the old man's hand. "Nerth. Not ye, too. What were ye doing here? Why didn't ye—?" He covered his eyes and groaned.

"Sir? Sir? *Sir!*"

Iorwerth finally realised that someone had been trying to get his attention. "What do ye want?"

The soldier who had called him over wrung her hands. "Sir, we want t'know what ye think we should do with him. I mean, he can't stay here . . . he needs a healer."

Iorwerth stared. "What? He's—"

"His legs are broken, an' maybe his back, too," the soldier said. "Takin' him outta here'd be a bad idea if ye ask me, sir. I dunno if there's a healer about."

Alive! Iorwerth touched Nerth's neck, feeling for a pulse. It was there. "Don't move him, leave him here," he rapped out. "Go find Lord Aeron, he's our healer. He should be in the tower somewhere. *Go!*"

They ran out.

Iorwerth knelt by Nerth's side and gave his hand a squeeze. "Don't worry, Nerth, we'll save ye. Yer going to make it."

Nerth's lips moved, and he coughed and cried out.

Iorwerth put a hand on his forehead. "Lie still. It's going to be all right."

"So ye say, Iorwerth," Nerth croaked, without opening his eyes.

Iorwerth felt relieved. "Where does it hurt, can ye tell me?"

"Everywhere. They've done for me, boy, I'm all broke in pieces."

"A healer's coming, don't be afraid."

"I ain't scared, boy!" Nerth wheezed. "No need t'be scared. I was a faithful darkman all my life. It'll be the silver fields for me, with all my family what the Southerners killed."

"I don't want to see ye go there yet, Nerth," said Iorwerth.

"Ye won't, boy, ye won't. Sure I'll see ye there one day, though. When I'm gone, don't bury me here, understand?"

"Where do ye want to be?" Iorwerth asked.

"The Throne, Iorwerth, the Throne. It's where every darkman comes home, among those stones."

"I know. I've always wanted to see them."

"Now's yer chance." Nerth gave a hacking laugh, and went quiet again.

Iorwerth glanced over his shoulder. "Where's Aeron, for gods' sakes?"

The soldiers still there looked uncomfortable. Kaanee had left.

Iorwerth looked at Nerth again and hated himself for what he had to do next. "I need to ask ye this, Nerth, and please just tell me. Where's Saeddryn? Did ye see her?"

Nerth's breath rattled in his chest. Very slowly and painfully, he said, "Ye won't find her here, Iorwerth. She's gone."

"Gone where?"

"Gone where the Bastard's griffin sent her. Same place it's sendin' me." Nerth winced. "I didn't know . . . no-one knew . . . still alive out there, waiting . . . came back, she did, that griffin. Came back for us. Killed me first, then Saeddryn's little girl. Then Aenae, then Saeddryn."

The old man was rambling. "Listen," said Iorwerth. "Can ye tell me where Saeddryn's body is? I'll take it back to Malvern and see it treated properly, I swear."

Nerth's hand twitched, maybe trying to point. "Here. Door. Not far."

Iorwerth left him and went to that spot. But there was no body. Only a huge bloodstain, splashed over the floor and onto that statue that stared at the open door and the trail that led through it.

Senneck walked through the passageways under the tower, head up to scent the air. It was just as well that the space down here was so narrow for her; her wounded forepaw had stiffened, and if she hadn't had the walls to support her, she might have fallen. Her talons were caked with Saeddryn's blood, but she looked completely unflustered.

For her there was no sadness or regret, or dismay in the aftermath of the battle. Nor was there any particular sense of triumph. Saeddryn and Aenae were dead, and that goal was behind her. After the killing, she had taken Saeddryn's mutilated remains out of the tower and hidden them outside the city. No-one would steal her victory from her; the body would go back to Malvern with her. But first, she had one more thing to do in Warwick.

Find Kullervo.

If he was still alive, then he must be down here somewhere.

The prisons were very quiet—almost deserted. Senneck came across one or two humans, but they all ran from her. She found bodies, too, but nobody tried to stop her. She moved on without much caution; it was far too close down here for there to be another griffin about, and that was the only sort of opponent she was truly frightened of.

In the end, though, it wasn't a griffin or a human that defeated her. She kept on for as far as she could, until she reached a door. It hung partly open, but the frame around it made the passage narrower—just narrow enough that she couldn't fit through. She struggled mightily to get past it, but her wings caught and one wedged itself into a gap and wouldn't come out.

She backed up, scrabbling at the floor, and screeched when her trapped wing caught. For a few awful moments, she thought she wouldn't be able to free it, but when she flexed the joint it just managed to fit.

Senneck lay down, trembling slightly. No way through, no way around. In this place, even turning around would be a struggle. But she would not leave without Kullervo.

She began to call his name as loudly as she could. It echoed off the stone walls and off into the gloomy corridors, and she called again, hoping that perhaps it might reach Kullervo wherever he was.

She kept calling for what felt like a long time, stopping occasionally to rest.

During one of those rests, she heard something coming from beyond the doorway. A voice?

"Kullervo!" she called again.

The sound again. Not a voice. She heard a dragging noise, something slapping faintly on stone.

"Kullervo?" she stood up quietly, readying herself for a fight.

". . . Senneck?" Kullervo's voice.

"Yes," Senneck said. "It is Senneck. Come to me, quickly. I must take you out of here."

The dragging sound again, and there he was, staggering toward her in his human form. He was thin and hurt, wearing clothes that didn't fit, but when he saw Senneck, he showed his old grin. Most of his teeth were broken or missing.

"Come!" Senneck said again. "Warwick has fallen, and the traitor is dead. Now you and I must return to Malvern and claim our reward."

Kullervo didn't seem to hear her. He came straight to her, dropping the sword he had, and put his arms around her neck. "Senneck," he said, mumbling a little through his shattered teeth. "I'm so happy you're here." He pressed his face into her feathers.

Senneck didn't move. "They have hurt you."

After a long pause, Kullervo lifted his head away from her. "I'll get better in a while. Just look at me, Senneck, they found a way to make me even uglier. Eheheheh." He cackled pathetically.

Senneck rubbed her head against his swollen cheek. "I do not care how you look, Kullervo. I am only glad that you are alive. Come, now. Follow me, and we will leave this dead place and rest a while before we go back to our home."

"Home," Kullervo murmured. "That's Malvern, isn't it?"

"Yes. Come now."

Senneck backed away along the corridor until it widened into a room, and she managed to turn around. Kullervo followed close behind. He moved clumsily, as if he had hurt his back or legs, but something in him held up, and he kept going without complaint.

Senneck kept on, looking back every so often to check on him. When they were out of the underground, and there was room, she stopped and lay down.

Kullervo joined her, blinking in the light. "You're hurt! Your paw—are you going to be all right?"

"I have been fighting, but I am well," said Senneck. "You are much weaker. Climb on my back, and I shall carry you."

Moving slowly and hesitantly, Kullervo sat on her shoulders, just between her neck and wings, the way he had seen griffiners do. She didn't have a harness on, of course, so he held on to her neck the best he could.

Senneck stood up with a lurch, and moved on.

Riding on her back while she walked was uncomfortable. With every step her shoulder-blades jabbed upward into his legs, and the motion made him rock alarmingly from side to side. Her limping made it worse. But Kullervo hardly cared. She was warm beneath him, and her feathers were soft, and the familiar scent and sight of her filled him with relief and a sense of joy that surprised him. All he wanted to do was talk to her, to try to express just how glad he was to be with her again, but he said nothing. It wouldn't mean anything to her. He held on to his happiness all the same, nursing it like a child with a doll.

Senneck didn't walk very far. She kept on until she reached the first level of the griffiner quarters, then stopped at the nearest opening in the wall. "I am going to fly now," she told her passenger. "Hold on and do not panic."

"I'm not afraid of flying." Kullervo laughed. "Go!"

Senneck launched herself into the air with ease, and soared up over Warwick. On her back, Kullervo let go of her neck and held his arms out like wings, and let out a call.

"Kulleeeervooooo!" It sounded more like a whoop than the challenge it should have been, but it excited Senneck, too. Without thinking, she flew in a wide circle and did something she hadn't done in far too many long years.

"Senneck! Senneck!"

Kullervo laughed wildly and called his own name again, until it rose and mingled with hers. For him, it was a declaration of freedom. For her, it was something much more. After such a long time, she was back at last, and all the North should know it. She had had her revenge at last. She put all of that into her call, and gloried in it.

Kullervo jerked alarmingly on her back, and quickly took hold of her neck again. She stopped calling when she felt his talons dig into her and flew away out of Warwick.

A little way away, outside the walls, she landed in a snowy clearing. Her wounded forepaw bent sideways, and she staggered to a halt against a tree, hissing.

Kullervo fell off her back, crying out when he hit the ground. "Are you all right?" he asked, rising to his knees.

Senneck flopped onto her belly, and nibbled tenderly at her paw. "This will take time to heal." She thrust it into the snow and sighed as the cold soothed the pain.

Kullervo peered around at the clearing. "Free at last," he muttered. "And never again . . ." He broke off and scooped up a double handful of snow, rubbing it over his face and eating lumps of it to quench his thirst.

"Yes," said Senneck. "I am glad to see you safe again. Erian would not have approved."

Kullervo looked at her. "You never talk about him."

"What is there to speak of? He was my human, and now he is gone."

"I don't really know much about him," said Kullervo. "Just that he tried to stop my father, and my father killed him." He wheezed a laugh, through his broken teeth. "I can't imagine he would like it if he knew you carried me. The Dark Lord's son!"

"Erian did not like half-breeds," Senneck said matter-of-factly. "He saw Laela when she was small, and told her mother that she should smother the child before other humans knew."

Kullervo grimaced and ate some more snow.

Senneck sniffed the air and checked the sky before getting up and moving to the shelter of a wattle tree. "It is good that you escaped and came to meet me. I would not have been able to free you myself."

Kullervo held up a warped hand, displaying the talons. "These freed me."

"You fought them to escape," Senneck said approvingly.

Kullervo looked away. "Yes. I didn't think I would get away ever. If I could have changed . . ."

"Why did you not change?"

"I don't know. I think . . . I mean, I think it was being in such a small space, with all those chains, it just—I'm just too much of a coward."

"I do not understand," said Senneck.

"Small spaces," Kullervo blurted out. "Bars. Chains. They scare me. Scare me half to death. They don't have to do anything to me; just being locked up is enough. I can't change when I'm like that. My mind just freezes up." His bruised face had turned pale. Even talking about it seemed to bother him, and he crawled in under the tree and curled up against Senneck's flank, hugging his knees. "Coward," he mumbled, apparently to himself.

Senneck raised a wing, brushing him with the feathers. "They hurt you. To make you tell them things."

"They hit me," said Kullervo. "Pulled my feathers out. Didn't give me food. Broke my teeth." He said all this quite calmly. "I never talked. Pain doesn't bother me much. You learn how to live through it."

"Then you told them nothing?"

"Nothing."

"How did you escape?"

"Today," said Kullervo. "Today, they took me out into a different room. They took all my clothes off, tied me face-down, and I thought . . . thought they were going to . . ." He shuddered violently and didn't stop for a long time.

"What did they do?" Senneck asked, almost gently.

"Someone wanted to *study* me," said Kullervo, and for the first and only time there was real hatred in his voice. "Wanted to look at my wings and my tail, and take notes and draw diagrams. They had me tied up there naked, a *specimen* for a scholar." His lips drew back over his teeth, and he hissed—a griffin's hiss that didn't belong with that ugly, human face.

Now Senneck looked angry. "*Eeyakka-ree!* How dare they do such a thing? To hurt is one thing, but no creature should be humiliated that way. You are not an object to be prodded."

"The woman said I was a creature," said Kullervo.

"We are all creatures," said Senneck. "You should have killed her."

"I did." Kullervo looked miserable.

"Then I am proud of you," said Senneck. "Was it a good kill?"

"I tore her throat out with my talons."

"Excellent."

"I killed five people today," Kullervo said in a flat, hollow tone. "I never killed anyone before in my life, but today I killed five. I couldn't help it, I was just so angry, and afraid . . ."

"Silence!" Senneck rasped. "I will not hear you apologise

for what you have done. You freed yourself and saved your own life and punished those who deserved it."

Kullervo didn't seem to hear her. "I never wanted to hurt anyone. Why can't people live together, and be happy? Why do they have to fight and kill each other?" he spread his hands, baring the talons. "I know what I look like and what I am, but I don't want to be just that, I want to be more."

Senneck said nothing.

Kullervo bowed his head. "All I wanted was a family. All I wanted was a friend."

"You have family," said Senneck. "You have your sister."

He looked up. "I thought she was going to come and help me. Why didn't she come?"

"Oeka would not allow her to leave Malvern," said Senneck.

Kullervo looked bewildered. "Oeka . . ."

"You have not seen her since you were captured," said Senneck. "She has become . . . twisted by magic." She rubbed her beak on Kullervo's head. "You are not a monster. I tell you, Kullervo, if you wish to see a monster, then look at Oeka. *That* is what a true monster is."

"She hates me," said Kullervo.

"And fears you," said Senneck. "But we will speak of her later. For now, we must rest."

"Can I lie against you? It's cold out here."

"Yes. We should share our warmth." Kullervo snuggled down against her, and she covered him with her wing. It was indeed cold in the clearing, but both of them were exhausted.

Senneck stayed awake longer than Kullervo did, watching out for danger. When he woke up, she would talk to him again. There were many things to tell him. He would understand. And when that was done, and they had talked over what they were going to do, it would be time to go home.

25

Dreamings

While Senneck and Kullervo slept together, night came. The moon rose over Warwick, shining white light on its streets. It shone on the tower, where a sleepless Iorwerth looked up to see Lord Aeron come in. He already knew what he was about to hear.

"He died."

"I'm sorry, sir. There was nothing I could do. A younger man, maybe, but . . ."

"What have ye done with the body?"

"Nothing, just covered it up."

"Good. Have it put in the vaults. Tomorrow, Kaanee and I will take it up to Taranis' Throne."

"Yes, sir."

When the healer had left, Iorwerth looked out the window, and the moonlight shone into his eyes. "Night God," he said. "I'm sorry."

The moon seemed to stare back. He knew it was the Night God's eye up there, cold and accusing. He couldn't bear to meet it any more, and he looked away. All he could think of was Nerth, looking up at him and accepting death—the death that was Iorwerth's fault.

What have I done?

The moon shone on Senneck and Kullervo, too, where they slept, Kullervo hidden under Senneck's wing like a guilty secret.

It shone on the snow-covered mound not far away, where something had been buried.

It shone in the void and guided Saeddryn Taranisäii forward.

She stood alone in the blackness and knew who she was seeing in front of her.

She knelt and bowed her head. "Master."

Rise.

Saeddryn did. "Master. I know ye, Master."

Of course you do, said the Night God. *You have served me all your life, and have earned a place beside me.*

Saeddryn did not smile. Her hand went to her throat. "I remember . . ."

Yes. Your death will be your final memory. Saeddryn, I have a task for you.

Saeddryn could hear something, some distant pounding that thudded in her ears. Her vision began to flash red, and she groaned. "That griffin killed me . . ."

Yes, the Night God said dispassionately. *You died because you fought the half-breed, the Risen Sun, the one the griffins call* Aeaei ran kae. *My people thought that it was the bastard that Arenadd killed, but they were wrong. It was the child. I warned Arenadd that she was a danger to him, but he would not listen. He was disobedient, and I took his powers and dragged him into the void.*

Saeddryn snarled. "I knew that half-breed brat wasn't t'be trusted."

And you were right. The Night God smiled. *But I expected no less. You were faithful and loyal all your life. Your cousin was a lost soul, full of doubt. For half his life he denied me, hated me, shut me away. When life crushed him, he turned to me at last in hatred, and I made him my greatest servant.*

"He was weak," said Saeddryn.

Yes. At his core, he was weak. Too many years alone, too much of a life lived in lies. But you, Saeddryn, you are strong. The Night God reached up to her face, and took the full moon out of the hole where her eye had been. It hovered just above the palm of her hand, throwing light on both their faces. *My avatar has been destroyed, but now I must have him back.*

Arenadd will not do; he will not kill his own daughter. That is why I have chosen you, Saeddryn.

"Me?"

Go back. Go back and become Kraeaina kran ae, *the Shadow That Walks, the heartless warrior, the Mistress of Death. Go back and do my will one last time.*

In a flash, Saeddryn remembered Arenadd. She thought of a gaunt, lonely man who had lost all his joy in the world, a man who had cried out to his dead beloved without knowing the woman he embraced was his own cousin. She thought of those twenty cold years when she had grown old while he remained young . . . but ancient inside, and dead.

"No! Please no. Don't make me like that, I beg ye, Master. Don't make me live like that."

I will not. The Night God's brow furrowed. *I promised Arenadd power and wealth for his loyalty, and he accepted, and was given it. But you, Saeddryn, you shall have whatever you wish for the moment you have done all I ask.*

"Let me die, then," said Saeddryn. "I want a promise. I'm an old woman, an' my time's done. When I finish this, I want t'be allowed to rest. That's all."

You have my promise, said the Night God. *When your task is done, you shall die as every mortal does and will go to be with your husband and your daughter.*

Saeddryn smiled. "I'd like that. I only wish I were stronger. My knee's gone bad, an' I've only got one eye."

That has never troubled me, the Night God said. *When an eye is gone, all you must do is find a another.* She took the full moon in her hand, and pressed it into Saeddryn's face. For a moment her eye-socket felt freezing cold.

Go now, said the Night God. *And remember your task.*

Saeddryn stood up. "What do ye want me to do?"

Kill the half-breeds, the Night God commanded. *Kill them both and place a true Taranisäii on the throne of Tara. When you have done it, you may rest.*

Saeddryn's eye narrowed. "*Two* half-breeds?"

You know them both. The usurper, and the freak who calls himself a man-griffin.

"Man-griffin? Ye mean that thing I had locked up?"

His name is Kullervo. Kill him.

"I will."

Good. Now go back, Saeddryn.

She turned but saw nothing except blackness. "How? I don't know the way."

Do not worry. You shall have a guide.

"It's this way," a voice said, from beside her.

Saeddryn turned. *"Arenadd?"*

Arenadd curled his lip at her. "I saw you die. Who would have thought the Bastard's griffin was still alive? She certainly taught *you* a nasty lesson." He snickered.

"I knew I was going t'die," Saeddryn said. "Ye put yer curse on me, cousin, like ye did with all those poor girls."

"Maybe, but why should I care?" said Arenadd. "*You* were the one who got *me* drunk and pulled me into bed." He shuddered.

Arenadd, do as I have commanded, the Night God said.

He cast a look of pure hatred at her. "As you wish, Master. Saeddryn, take my hand."

It felt like ice. "Now where—?"

Arenadd tugged, and the darkness rushed away around them. The Night God disappeared. Saeddryn felt herself being pulled forward, faster and faster, until the memory of her body distorted and streamed out behind her like water. She could still feel Arenadd's hand holding hers, and she gripped it tightly.

To her surprise, Arenadd squeezed back, almost . . . reassuring?

The darkness bloomed into white, and the feeling of his hand went away. As Saeddryn's journey ended, she thought she heard a voice calling, distant and forlorn. *"Don't make my children suffer, Saeddryn. Please . . ."*

Cold, freezing cold. It was all Saeddryn found to greet her when she woke up. Instinctively, she clawed upward, struggling to escape. The cold fell away, and blinding light hit her eye. She cried out, falling forward onto something wet and icy.

Blood filled her mind, blood and bodies. Arddryn. Nerth. Aenae. Torc. Even Arenadd. Their bodies all crushed and torn into this wet, slick stuff that buried her, pulling her down into the red depths. They were all dead, all of them, and her, too; she was one of them, drowning in them . . .

Saeddryn thrashed about, gagging, feeling the pain of the wounds that had nearly torn her in half. The wet stuff churned up around her, covering her head and arms, and she slumped, mouth wide open like a landed fish.

The pain faded gradually, and she let her breathing slow. No blood. This wasn't blood.

Don't panic, she told herself. *Think.*

Her eye peeled open and saw nothing but whiteness. Was she blind?

Snow. It's snow.

Only snow.

She sat up, and almost immediately she felt different. Her pain had gone, and she felt strong. There was no ache in her joints, no faint hum in her ears. She felt more alert than she had done in years, and much clearer in her mind. All her old doubts and fears had faded away. Even her grief for Arddryn felt distant. And her sight—her sight was perfect. In both eyes . . .

Eyes?

Her hand went to her face, feeling for the familiar eye-patch. It was gone. The dead eye underneath felt the same—just a twisted eyelid, collapsed inward where the eyeball had been punctured and taken out. But she could see! As perfectly as if she had two eyes, or perhaps even better.

She chuckled softly. "Thankye, Master. I won't waste this gift, I promise."

Saeddryn stood up in the snow, moving with a new grace and power. Her clothes hung off her in bloody rags, but she didn't care. She didn't care about anything any more.

She looked around, testing her new sight, and stopped suddenly when she realised she wasn't alone.

A little way away among the trees, a massive, dark griffin stood watching. His eyes gleamed silver as he turned his head, regal and silent.

"Skandar," Saeddryn blurted.

He regarded her a little longer, and she saw his talons fretting at the snow. "White griffin come," he said tersely. "Say fly here and use magic one time more."

"Ye brought me back," said Saeddryn. "The way ye did before . . ."

"Use magic," Skandar repeated. "White griffin say carry you, make you my human."

Saeddryn smiled evilly. "Come on then, Skandar. Let's go and destroy those half-breed scum."

Skandar snorted. "Not come. Not carry *you*. Mighty Skandar have only one human. Not you. You enemy to human, make him leave nest."

"But yer the dark griffin," Saeddryn argued. "The shadow griffin. I was chosen by the Night God—ye have t'be my partner now."

"Human go fight alone," said Skandar. "Mighty Skandar not care."

"Wait—" Saeddryn began, but too late.

Skandar turned away, and leapt. In midair, he vanished.

As if that was a catalyst, all of Saeddryn's emotions began to return. She sat down in the snow, not feeling the cold, and groaned aloud.

Arddryn was dead. Torc was dead. Aenae was dead. And she was . . . ?

Suddenly afraid, Saeddryn put a hand to the side of her neck, just under her jaw.

There was no pulse there. She tried her wrists, and her chest as well, but found nothing. No heartbeat.

Oh, Night God, it's true. I'm dead. I'm like him *now. Why did I say those things? Why did I say yes?*

But how could anyone look her god in the face and say no?

Saeddryn wrapped her arms around herself, trying pointlessly to warm her cold flesh. In her mind, she thought she saw the face of the Night God again, frightening but somehow beautiful as well. The direct gaze and commanding voice reminded her of her mother.

Don't be a coward, Saeddryn, said the voice from her memory. *Don't be weak. Be a Taranisäii.*

Saeddryn set her jaw and sat up a little straighter. This was how it should be. She had been ready to die, and the Night God had given her a great gift. New strength and powerful gifts and, most of all, the chance to finish what she had started. Kill the half-breeds and put Caedmon on the throne. Her son was the true heir and the only surviving family she had. Realising that made her own pain irrelevant. Caedmon was all that mattered now, and she had to protect him.

She stood up and brushed herself down. With astonishing self-control, she pushed all her distress away into the back of her mind and made a plan. There was nothing for her in Warwick now; the city must have been overrun. She would return quietly for clothes, weapons, and food, then leave for Fruitsheart. Without Aenae, she would have to walk, but the prospect didn't bother her.

"I'm comin', Caedmon," she said aloud. "Mother's comin'. Don't ye be afraid."

Kraeaina kran ae, the Dark Lady, set out.

26

The Shadow in the Snow

Kullervo slept for the rest of the evening and into the night, not seeming to notice the snow or the cold. Senneck woke several times, but never for long. She was just as exhausted as he was—but pain made her sleep shallow and disturbed, full of dreams.

She rarely dreamed, even these days when she had so many memories tucked away, but that night she dreamed of Erian. He flickered in and out of her sleep, his face and his scent making up a memory. Old ambitions stirred in her, and old anger as well.

Unconsciously, she moved closer to Kullervo, covering him more completely with her wing.

Eventually, the ache of her wounds faded as they scabbed over, and she slipped away into a deep, peaceful sleep.

She opened her eyes, and pale sunlight hit them. Blinking irritably, she lifted her head and shook away the snow that had settled on it. The sun was well up, and the world around her had turned pure white.

She stood up, hissing softly when her limbs refused to move properly. Her wounds had swelled, and every joint felt as stiff as wood. Gingerly, she lifted a foreleg, flexing it until it loosened. She did the same for the others, and, feeling a little better, she opened her wings. They, at least, weren't so bad.

Something stirred, by her back paw. She turned clumsily, but it was only Kullervo. He sat up in the snow, clutching his head. "Oooh . . . I don't feel very well."

"Eat some snow," she advised. "We shall go back to Malvern soon."

Kullervo didn't seem to hear her. "It's so cold . . ."

"Stand, then, and walk," she said. "It will warm you."

He obeyed, wobbling slightly on his legs, and stumbled around the clearing. "Gryphus help me, I'm soaking wet. Did we sleep in the snow all night?"

"Yes. Come now, walk with me. We must do one more thing before we return to Malvern."

"What's that?" said Kullervo.

"Find the traitor's body," said Senneck. "I left a mark on a tree; it is not far from here."

Kullervo walked beside her and had no trouble keeping up—her limp had become even worse overnight.

Senneck had told the truth: she pushed through a stand of pine trees and stopped at another, larger tree just beyond them. Sure enough, there were talon marks on its bark. Snow had been piled up over its roots, and after some casting about, the brown griffin scooped it away with her talons. After a few moments she huffed to herself and moved a few steps to the right where she dug again. She tried several different spots, turning over every hump and mound.

"Where is it?" she hissed.

Kullervo stood by the tree, rubbing himself to try to keep warm. "Are you sure this is the right place?"

Senneck's head jerked irritably. "I know the marks of my own talons! Where has it gone? I did not bury it deeply."

"Maybe a wolf took it, or a dog," said Kullervo.

"No animal would be strong enough to carry it away. They would leave carrion for us to find."

"Another griffin, then?"

Senneck made a horrible grating noise. "*No!* My revenge shall not be taken from me!"

"How could that happen?" said Kullervo. "You already killed her."

"But without the carcass, there will be no proof!" Senneck almost screamed. "The world must know— *Where is it?*"

Infuriated, she churned up the snow with her talons, spraying it everywhere.

"Maybe I can help." Kullervo stepped away from the tree and came closer, peering at the snow. Senneck watched him briefly and wandered off to search the clearing.

Kullervo crouched low to the ground, looking for marks. He was trembling gently all over from the cold, but he controlled his senses and sniffed the air. It smelt of ice and pine needles and freezing spice-tree leaves, and . . . something else?

He focused on the ground. After a few moments, moving in an awkward sideways shuffle, he began to walk around the clearing.

"Senneck," he called eventually. "I've found tracks."

She appeared beside him almost instantly. *"Show me."*

He jabbed at the marks with his talons. "See, here? And more, over there. Looks like they started . . ." He began to work his way along the path and stopped not far from the tree, where Senneck's digging had destroyed the rest. He stayed there for a moment, staring at the footprints. "Senneck . . . are you . . . *sure* you killed her?"

She began to hiss. "Her body was nearly torn in two."

"Well, someone walked away from here," said Kullervo. "Someone human."

"Then *they* have stolen it."

The shape-shifter was too cold to want to waste any more time. Sighing, he walked away through the clearing, following the tracks. Senneck ran ahead of him, stopping once or twice to let him catch up.

The tracks took a very direct route, through the trees—whoever made them didn't seem worried about being followed. They had gone straight back toward the city. Fortunately, no more snow had fallen during the night, so the tracks were clear enough.

That is until they ended mid-step, right by the trunk of a tree.

Senneck reared up onto her hind legs, looking into the branches. The leaves were not dense, and the branches were widely spaced. There was no way anybody could be hiding in them.

The brown griffin ran in a wide circle, searching for the tracks, but they were gone.

"No!" she hissed.

Kullervo stood by the tree, examining the last of the tracks. "This doesn't make any sense! They can't have gone up the tree, the forest here's too dense for a griffin to have picked them up—where did they go?"

Senneck slumped and began to groom herself with quick, tense motions. "This cannot be!" she said, sounding more bewildered than angry now.

Kullervo only half-heard her. He poked at the tree with a talon, right at the spot where their prey had once been. "I don't understand this," he said to himself. "It's like they vanished into thin air . . ."

Unease prickled the back of his neck.

Senneck took a few limping steps toward him. "We must plan," she said.

Kullervo looked at her and found her watching him expectantly. "What?" he said.

"Tell me what would be best to do," she said.

Kullervo looked blank. "Why me?"

"You are human," she said impatiently. "It is your nature to think and plan, and I am tired and wounded. Tell me what we must do about this problem."

Kullervo tried to think. The cold was turning his entire body numb. His mouth hurt—talking was a nightmare. He felt close to collapse, and dark memories danced on the edge of his mind, filling him with tension. He wanted to scream at Senneck that he was in as much pain as she was, that he hadn't eaten in days, and all he wanted to do was go somewhere warm and die there.

"We have to go back to Laela," he mumbled. "And I'll tell her you killed Saeddryn. She trusts me. I'll even say I saw you do it, and that I saw the body."

"And when she asks where it is now?" Senneck pressed.

Kullervo rubbed his head. "I don't know . . . we'll say you dropped it over the river, and we couldn't find it."

"No! I did not fail, understand?"

"All right, then it was my fault somehow. I'll think of something." Kullervo's strained patience wore even thinner. "Can we go now? We need help. I just want to get out of this place. It doesn't feel right."

"Very well," said Senneck. "Come to me now. You are right; we must return before our wounds fester."

Kullervo moved gratefully toward her. She moved, too, lowering herself to the ground so he could reach her back. An instant later, without any warning, she reeled away from him with a cry.

Kullervo stopped, raising his talons instinctively. "Senneck—!"

Senneck didn't seem to hear him. She darted about on the snow, turning this way and that, lifting her wings and lashing out at nothing with her beak.

"What . . . ?" Kullervo stayed where he was, not knowing what to make of this.

Senneck reared up, flailing at the air with her talons. But she couldn't sustain the posture for long; she dropped back again a moment later. Her wounded forepaw hit the ground and collapsed, and she fell forward into the snow.

Kullervo moved toward her. "Senneck, are you all right—?"

She dragged herself up at once, hissing, and resumed her mad dance—fighting, Kullervo realised, against an invisible enemy.

An invisible enemy that was hurting her.

Wounds had appeared on her face and neck, dripping blood onto her feathers.

Kullervo stood there, faltering in indecision. This was madness, and what could he do? How could he help Senneck fight an enemy neither of them could see? How was this even possible?

Senneck had begun to slow and falter. She was losing. This thing, whatever it was, was too strong for her in this state.

"Kullervo," she croaked. "Help me. *Help me!*"

"How?" he asked helplessly. "What should I do? What is this?"

She bowed her head toward her chest, protecting her throat. "I do not know. Defend me! You are my human, Kullervo!"

Kullervo gaped, and stared. He squinted. "What . . . ?"

Something wavered in his line of vision, flickering in and out of existence. A shadow.

It moved about near Senneck's head, taunting her, hurting her, rippling over the snow in complete silence.

A smell found its way into Kullervo's nostrils; a smell of blood and steel and ice, a smell so vile it made his throat burn. It awoke something in him that he had never felt before.

"Don't you dare touch her!" he roared, and charged, limping, slipping and stumbling on the snow. He reached Senneck, and thrust his hands into thin air with a roar of fury. They emerged dragging something dark and ragged, and he threw it onto the snow.

Senneck got up, pulling herself away. Kullervo went to her side, backing away with her and staring at the thing he had caught.

Crouched among the whiteness, Saeddryn gave a low, cold laugh. She got up. Her dark gown was wet, and her hair had twisted into a series of sodden whips around her face, clinging to the ugly scar of her eye. Her lined face was pale as death, distorted by long, livid red slashes that disappeared under her clothes.

Her voice was low and full of ice. "This was far too easy. Less than a day after I set out, I find two of ye here—wounded and unprepared an' all ready for me."

"Saeddryn?" Kullervo faltered.

She snarled. "I know who ye are now, ye twisted little freak. All my dear cousin ever fathered were half-breeds an' vermin. The drunken pervert didn't even give ye his handsome looks, did he? No, ye look like yer ugly bitch of a mother."

Kullervo bared his broken teeth. "I would rather be her son than yours, you hag. No wonder my father never wanted you."

Saeddryn spat. "I'm killin' ye second, freak. Before ye, it's *her* turn." Her one eye turned on the wounded Senneck, and she held up her sickle. It was bloodied, and she waved it tauntingly from side to side. "Oh Night God, this is gonna taste sweet." She leapt into midair, and disappeared.

Senneck rose, trying vainly to protect herself. "No—"

Kullervo squinted until Saeddryn's wavering shape came back into view. "Senneck!" he shouted. "Get away! Fly away! *Now!*" He leapt.

Senneck needed no further encouragement. She turned and shambled off. Her wings opened and began to beat stiffly.

Kullervo saw Saeddryn go in pursuit, impossibly fast, almost flowing over the ground. With a scream, he ran after her, overtook her, and threw himself in the way. Something unseen hit him, directly in the chest, and he fell. But he twisted his body, grabbing at the shadow. His hands, vanishing again, caught Saeddryn by the ankles and dragged her back into view. She fell forward, screaming in rage as Senneck escaped into the air.

Kullervo pulled on her leg, dragging himself on top of her, and stabbed his talons into her throat. She punched him in the face, unbelievably hard. One of his remaining teeth came loose and began to bleed. He spat it away onto the snow and twisted his talons, ripping into her flesh.

"Die!" he screamed into her face. "Just die, will you?"

Saeddryn gurgled a groan and pushed him away. She struggled to her feet, upper chest oozing blood, and snatched up her sickle from the ground. "I'll make ye suffer for that, freak."

Kullervo rose to his knees. "You already made me suffer, Saeddryn. You didn't have the sense to just kill me."

"Trust me," she growled. "I've seen sense now."

With a supreme effort, Kullervo managed to get up. "Why are you here? Why aren't you dead?"

Saeddryn's eye burned. Not only with hatred, he realised—but also with terrible fear. "I *am* dead."

The sickle struck.

Instinctively, Kullervo shielded himself with his hands, hooking the sickle blade with his talons. He pushed it away from himself, feeling the edge catch and cut. With a yell of frustration, Saeddryn twisted the weapon sideways and out of his grip.

With a speed he never would have thought he could muster, Kullervo struggled to his feet and ran away. Not knowing what to do, he made for the city wall, limping and tripping in the snow. He could feel Saeddryn just behind him, and knew that if he fell, he would die. If he had been alone, that would have almost certainly been what happened. But Senneck was still there, and it was she who saved him.

As Kullervo left the shelter of the trees, she dropped out of the sky and scooped him up in her talons—lifting him up and out of Saeddryn's reach. Then, without even stopping to let him get onto her back, she turned south and flew away as fast as she could.

Left below, Saeddryn screamed at the sky. *"Damn ye!"*

They were gone.

She sat down by a tree, swearing. If only she had planned her attack better. She should have killed the man-griffin first, but the very sight of Senneck had filled her with so much rage that she had put her duty aside. Besides, she had thought the griffin would be much more dangerous and harder to kill. With her out of the way, Kullervo would be an easy target.

But he wasn't.

Teeth gritted with pure hatred, Saeddryn thought of how he had attacked her and the question rose in her mind. *How had he seen her?* How had he been able to do what he did, and pull her out of the shadows that hid her? She had discovered how to disappear the way Arenadd once had, and the ability had come easily. Nobody in the city had been able to see or hear her as she stole fresh clothes and a sickle from one of Malvern's soldiers. She had walked brazenly down the main street, and as long as she didn't touch anyone, she was invisible.

But Kullervo had seen her—he *must* have seen her. And he had reached into the dark realm that she had thought was hers and pulled her back. *How?*

Surely, he didn't have any powers of his own.

Doubt spiralled around her. She didn't know anything about what this hybrid creature could do. She had seen him change his shape. For all she knew, he had other gifts as well. Gifts that could make her vulnerable to him.

"Blasphemy!" she muttered to herself. Nobody but a pure-bred Northerner, a Taranisäii chosen by the Night God, should be able to touch the shadows! That this *thing* might be able to do the same was repulsive.

Saeddryn's determination to kill him doubled.

She stood up and put the sickle back into her belt. Kullervo wouldn't escape her for long. Now that this opportunity had passed her by, she had to go back to her original plan. Fruitsheart and Caedmon. The half-breeds weren't going to go anywhere; she could have her revenge at her leisure.

But the brown griffin, Senneck—Saeddryn vowed that she would have the most painful death of all. The other two could die quickly; they were duty. Senneck's death would be for Saeddryn alone, and she would enjoy it most of all.

27

Home Again

Senneck and Kullervo flew back to Malvern at last, together. It was a slow journey; slower than it had been before. They stayed away from civilisation, living off whatever they scrounged. Senneck was too weak to hunt, and Kullervo was too far gone to care what he ate. He did his best to treat his partner's wounds, and his own. That she was his partner wasn't something he doubted even though neither of them had discussed it. She had called him "her" human, and as if that settled it, she had begun to treat him that way.

Neither of them talked about the encounter with Saeddryn either, not for the first day or so. They flew, ate, and slept in silence, busy with their own thoughts, even though Kullervo guessed they were both thinking the same thing.

Finally, one evening, while he was retying the crude bandage on Senneck's forepaw, he spoke out. "What happened to Saeddryn?"

Senneck raised her head sharply. "Have you not guessed?"

Kullervo had, but he did his best to ignore the awful possibility. "I don't know," he said lamely. "I've never seen anything like it before."

Senneck laid her head down on the ground. "She has become like her cousin. *Kraeai kran ae!*"

Kullervo's stomach turned. "My father could do those things?"

"Yes. When *Kraeai kran ae* wanted an enemy dead,

nothing could stand in his way. Now the one-eyed one has inherited his powers, and I am the one she wants dead."

She's afraid, Kullervo realised. "And me as well. Oh, gods, what are we going to do?"

"I do not know," said Senneck.

"She'll want Laela dead, too," said Kullervo. "We have to warn her! She stopped my father somehow, maybe she knows what to do."

Senneck gave him a long, slow look. "But it would seem that you know what to do also, Kullervo."

He stared back at her. "What? No I don't."

"But you stopped her," said Senneck. "You saved my life."

She said this quite matter-of-factly, but Kullervo blushed with pleasure. "I don't know how I did it. I just kept looking until I saw her, then I tried to pull her away from you, and I did."

"You could see her?"

"Yes. Couldn't you?"

"I saw nothing," said Senneck.

Kullervo was silent for a few moments. "Senneck?"

"Yes?"

"Is . . . did you . . . you chose me, didn't you? To be your human."

"You are my human now," said Senneck. "The choice is made."

Kullervo smiled joyfully. "Was it because I saved your life?"

Senneck gave him a look. "I had made the decision well before that."

"Why, then?"

"I chose you because I believed you were worthy," she said. "I wanted you."

"Why, though?" Kullervo persisted. "Griffins only choose important people—"

Senneck chirped amusement. "Yes, we do, and I am proud of myself. My new human is a Prince."

"I—" Kullervo began, and stopped. "Oh. A Prince?"

"You are the son of a King," said Senneck. "That would make you a Prince, unless I am wrong."

"No, I suppose it does," Kullervo mumbled. "I never really thought about it."

Senneck yawned. "This land is ruled by the Taranisäii family. You are one of them."

Kullervo looked bewildered, then he began to smile. "Yeah . . . I am, aren't I? Kullervo Taranisäii. *Prince* Kullervo Taranisäii."

"I am glad to have chosen you," Senneck said solemnly. "In your own way, you are a noble, and you have proven that you can protect me from the cousin of *Kraeai kran ae*."

"Maybe, but I don't know who's going to protect *me*," said Kullervo.

"Do not worry. We shall find a way."

Kullervo's expression was grim. "If we don't, then we're all dead."

Laela finally went through her womanhood ceremony on the night of the full moon, the day after word of the victory at Warwick reached Malvern. The new Moon Temple wasn't finished yet, but the foundations of the old one had been cleaned and still featured the stone circle and the altar at the centre. Rituals had still been held there in the open air while the new walls went up around it, and Laela hadn't seen any point in delaying her own ritual any longer.

The news of Iorwerth's victory hadn't been greeted with any excitement from Malvern's population. Nobody in the Eyrie had seemed very happy about it either, least of all Laela herself. The best she could manage was some grim satisfaction at Arddryn's death and Saeddryn's probable death. Despite the fact that nobody had been able to find the former High Priestess' remains, Laela had formally declared her dead. She had even been gracious enough to give the new High Priestess permission to hold a mourning ceremony.

Hundreds of ordinary Malvernians had come to pay their respects. Laela had seen them from her vantage-point up at the top of the Council Tower. It had made her very glad that she had decided not to make an appearance.

It cheered her up to see plenty more people gathering for her womanhood ceremony. At least *some* of her subjects cared about her formal acceptance as a true Northern woman.

Gwenna, the new High Priestess, wore a wooden wolf

mask. Around her, the rest of the priestesses stood in a ring, each one with an animal face of her own.

Laela had to stand in front of the altar, wearing nothing but a fur loincloth that left her breasts exposed. She had argued with Gwenna about this, but the High Priestess had been unmoved. Everyone had to do it this way, she explained. It was traditional.

Now Laela stood as still as she could and gritted her teeth at the cold, while Gwenna recited the sacred words and prayers to the Night God. The ritual was peppered with questions directed at Laela—she had memorised them beforehand, and answered them without any trouble. At one point she stumbled briefly, but Oeka's voice whispered the words in her head. The small griffin had ignored the rule that only humans were allowed at the ceremony, and crouched just outside the circle with her blind eyes drooping, the mind behind them missing nothing.

At last, the moment came. Gwenna took the needles and the pot of blue ink, and came closer. "With these marks, the Night God blesses ye," she intoned. "Take them, and prove ye are a true Northern woman."

Laela knew all too well what that meant. She held out her right arm, and waited. When the needle plunged toward her chilled skin for the first time, she turned her head away and braced herself.

The pain was appalling. She felt the needle stab into her flesh, in and out, again and again, moving all over her arm with agonising slowness. Part of her could hardly believe it—this couldn't possibly go on, it couldn't be like this all the way through!

Do not cry out, Oeka warned. *Do not!*

Laela's teeth ground, and tears squeezed out of her eyes. Mentally, she listed every swear-word she knew and invented some more when they weren't enough. *Just end,* she prayed at last. *Please just be over!*

Another part of her, removed from the pain, quietly reflected on how stupid it all was. Here she was, taking part in a ritual to dedicate her life to the Night God—that same god that wanted her dead. And she was turning her back on Gryphus, whom she had been raised to believe in since childhood.

But he was no better than the Night God, she thought wildly. He looked different to her, and he ruled a different people, but he wanted all the same things. The gods were both as cruel and heartless as each other, and as bloodthirsty. *Damn the both of them,* she thought.

But curse you most of all, she yelled internally at the Night God. *I killed Arenadd, an' his cousin, an' now I'll rule the North an' there ain't a thing yeh can do to stop me. Yeh hear that?*

Well said, Oeka's voice intruded.

And then, it was over.

Shivering, Laela looked apprehensively at Gwenna. The High Priestess traced a spiral in the air over her head, and said, "Laela Taranisäii, I bid ye say farewell to the child, and turn to embrace the woman. May the Night God bless ye with a long life and many strong children, and may ye always be faithful to her and to the Wolf tribe."

The other priestesses raised their hands and murmured their own blessings. Several in the crowd called out. "Bless ye, Queen Laela! Bless ye in the Night God's holy name!"

Despite everything, Laela felt happy to hear them.

The priestesses filed out, with Gwenna at their head, and she was free to leave the half-built Temple. An attendant handed her a cloak, and she covered herself up, cringing when the cloth touched her bleeding arm. The council had come to witness the ceremony and formed into a procession behind her as she walked out past the crowd. Oeka came to her side, and they went back toward the Eyrie. The councillors' griffins had stayed away, and they had to walk as well. Laela doubted she would ever fly on Oeka's back, and she was secretly glad that, this time at least, she wasn't the only griffiner who had to stick to the ground.

You did well, Oeka said unexpectedly.

"Thanks," Laela muttered.

I feel your hatred for their ceremonies, the small griffin added. *You are wise.*

Laela said nothing.

There are no gods, and you are right to be contemptuous. Humans are weak creatures, without magic of their own, and they invent this foolery to make themselves feel more important than they are.

"Shut up."

Oeka gave her a sting of mental pain. *Do not speak to me that way!*

Laela winced but didn't apologise. She was sick to death of her partner's constant harping. Oeka had always been arrogant, just like any other griffin, but these new powers had made her a hundred times worse.

You think I am conceited, the relentless inner voice said at once. *You have no understanding.*

Laela resisted the urge to clutch her head.

Once they were inside the Eyrie, the councillors went their separate ways. Laela and Oeka climbed to their own quarters. They had now moved into Arenadd's and Skandar's rooms; Laela had had her father's bedroom redecorated in shades of blue—her favourite colour. Skandar's oversized nest was far too big for the half-grown Oeka, but she didn't seem to care. The gold-plated water trough probably helped to keep her happy even if she couldn't technically see it any more.

Once her partner had left her alone, Laela dropped the cloak onto the floor and examined her arm. The whole thing was a mass of bleeding puncture marks—she couldn't see the tattoos at all. If they were there, they were hidden under the swelling. She could at least make out the shape of them; spiralling patterns weaved their way over her skin, from her shoulder to the back of her hand. Bits of thread from the cloak were already sticking to it, and blood had crusted between her fingers.

She had left a bowl of water and a soft cloth ready before going to the Temple, and went to use them now. Gingerly, she lowered her arm into the bowl.

The water made her skin sting, but she kept her arm submerged until it settled down and began to throb dully. She picked up the cloth, braced herself, and very carefully patted down the tattoos. The cloth might as well have been a lump of sandstone, judging by how it felt, but she kept going doggedly until she had cleaned off the dry blood and half-formed scabs.

She had left a pot of ointment by the bowl, along with a towel. Once her arm was as clean as she could get it, she dried it and liberally applied the ointment. The stuff was smooth and cooling, and she sighed happily and daubed on several more layers. She wrapped a bandage over the top, and slumped into a chair by the fire to rest.

Someone had thoughtfully left a kettle of mead to warm by the flames, and she poured herself a large cup and tossed it back. It burned in her throat and warmed her stomach, and she sighed again. Thank gods, it was over.

I could have blocked out the pain, Oeka said from her nest.

"What?"

I could have reached into your mind and stopped you from feeling the pain.

Laela moved her arm to cover her face, and groaned when the bandages chafed. "Then *why didn't yeh*?"

Because it was a test, the griffin said blandly.

"I thought yeh didn't care about that crap."

No, but I wanted to see if you would succeed.

"Thanks for the confidence," Laela growled.

Rest now, Oeka advised. *We will have more work to do in the morning.*

"Can't wait." Laela glared into the fire. Yes, there was work to do. Saeddryn and her daughter might be dead, but there was still Caedmon, and he was an unknown quantity. She would *not* underestimate him, not even when it looked as if victory was certain. Something in her gut told her that this wasn't over yet. It couldn't be this easy.

Part of her wished she had been there at Warwick. To know her worst enemy had been killed, while she was miles away—it was childish, but it rankled. It felt as if the victory didn't belong to her.

"We oughta go to Fruitsheart," she said aloud, knowing Oeka would sense it anyway. "I want a part in this before it's all over. Show 'em I can fight my own battles."

I agree. I had planned to suggest it. I have idled in Malvern long enough, and with these new powers, I will be an unstoppable force. I will let my territory see what I can do!

"I know what yeh mean," said Laela. "I'd like to get my punches in as well. Let's wait until Iorwerth gets back an' discuss it with him."

Yes. He will help us to make plans.

"He's a good man, Iorwerth is."

After that, the conversation petered out, and Laela sat back to rest. She hoped Iorwerth would come back soon.

She thought of Kullervo, too, and wondered if he was all right and whether Iorwerth had rescued him, or whether Saeddryn had killed him. The idea that the shape-shifter might well be dead made her sad. They had only known each other a short while, but he had done everything she asked without asking for anything in return. In a way, he was the most loyal follower she had. She wished she hadn't sent him into Saeddryn's clutches.

"Poor thing," she murmured. "I hope he's all right."

And I hope he is dead, said Oeka.

Laela ignored her.

Kullervo's return to Malvern was an unceremonious affair. The unpartnered had reached it well ahead of himself and Senneck, and the excitement had long since died down by the time the ageing griffin and her ugly partner made their ragged, limping arrival.

Senneck flew directly to the Eyrie and landed in the nest she had claimed for her own. Kullervo almost fell off her back and lay on his side in the straw for a while, wheezing.

Senneck flopped onto her belly. She was too worn-out to fold her wings properly, and they draped untidily over her sides like two huge pieces of cloth.

Kullervo sat up, leaning on the wall. The journey had taken a toll on him, too; if anything he had become even more bony and awkward-looking than before. The remains of his teeth were rotting, and several of his wounds had become infected.

"Home ssshweet home," he slurred, and went to sleep.

Senneck dragged herself to the trough for a drink and settled down to rest. "Kullervo. *Kullervo!*"

He jerked awake. "Huh? What?"

Senneck lifted a forepaw, and slowly scratched her face. "I need a healer, and so do you. Go now and find help."

Kullervo stared dully at her for a while, then very slowly and shakily got up. "Of course. Wait here." He limped off through the archway. One wing had escaped from the cloth he had tied around it, and wobbled pathetically back and forth. He didn't seem to notice.

Left alone, Senneck sank into an exhausted sleep.

Kullervo had never felt so weak in his life, not even after a change. His vision had gone hazy and grey around the edges, and his body felt broken in every bone and joint. His stomach moaned with hunger. But his goal had filled his mind, and he clung to it, using it to push himself on.

Not far from Senneck's temporary quarters, he happened across a patrolling guard. The man took one look at him and drew his weapon, shouting some challenge or other in Northern.

Kullervo could feel himself swaying gently on the spot. "That way," he croaked, pointing back at the door he had come through. "There's a griffin in that room who needs a healer."

"Who are ye?" the guard demanded, breaking into Cymrian.

Kullervo put a hand to his forehead as if to support it. "Kullervo. Messenger to the Queen. Back from Warwick to see her. Important news."

"Prove it."

"Can't," said Kullervo. "Ask the Queen."

"How did ye get *in* here?"

"Flew." Kullervo's patience ran out. "My griffin needs a healer. Tell me where to find one."

"Show me where she is an' we'll see," said the guard.

"Fine." Kullervo turned and walked back the way he had come, ignoring the guard's exclamation of horror at the sight of the wing on his back.

In her nest, Senneck looked up as the two of them came in. "You see?" Kullervo said, gesturing at her. "She's hurt. *Go get a healer.*"

The guard looked uncertain. "I never saw ye before. How do I know this is yer griffin?"

Senneck stood up. "Because I chose him, fool!" she hissed. "Now do as he tells you!"

The guard backed off smartly. "Ye gods!"

"She said to go get a healer like I told you," Kullervo told him helpfully. "And get one for me, too!" he added. "And send someone to tell the Queen that Kullervo and Senneck are back."

"Right, right." The guard ran out.

Kullervo groaned and lay down beside Senneck. "I wish I was dead."

She covered him with her wing. "You will be better soon. Rest now."

He pressed himself against her and said nothing more.

After what felt like forever, a healer finally arrived—along with several more guards. They posted themselves around the entrance to the nest while the healer went on in, speaking cautiously in griffish. "I'm here to help."

Senneck peered up at him. "I was wounded at Warwick, and my human is also wounded and cannot heal me. You must help me."

"Of course," the healer soothed. "Show me the worst of yer wounds."

Senneck readily obeyed, and the healer opened his box of instruments and went to work. Kullervo pulled himself out of the way and lay in the straw, watching blearily.

The healer noticed him and jerked in surprise. "Sweet shadows, where did ye come from? What the—what's *that*?"

Kullervo covered the ugly bald wing with some straw. "Don't mind me." He closed his eyes.

"Oh, holy Night God." The healer stood up and ran to the archway, waving at the nearest guard. "Go get a doctor—*now*!"

Once the man had run out, the healer went back to work on Senneck—cleaning and bandaging and trimming away the feathers that had been scabbed into the flesh. While he worked, he tried to question Kullervo, but the shape-shifter said nothing. He had become very still.

A doctor arrived shortly before Senneck's treatment was finished. She looked harassed and confused, and went straight to the griffin healer. "What's all this about?"

The healer pointed at Kullervo. "What do ye think it's about? Do something for the poor bastard—he looks like he's about to die on us!"

The doctor went to Kullervo, swearing under her breath when she saw the condition he was in. “Who *is* he?”

“I don’t know.”

“He is my human,” Senneck told them sharply. “His name is Kullervo, and he is a noble. Do not let him die.”

“Understood,” the griffin healer told her. “Don’t worry; just relax. I’ve sent someone to bring food for ye—in the meantime, I’ll mix up a draught.”

Senneck drank it when it was ready, and rested, not taking her eyes off Kullervo.

The doctor peeled the remains of his clothes away and examined the wounds on his front—not noticing the wings for now. Finding the infected ones, she quickly punctured and drained them. Kullervo was too far gone to put up a struggle and only moaned softly.

“Shadows, someone’s treated him badly,” the doctor muttered. “Where’d he come from?”

“From Warwick,” said Senneck. “The traitor had him tortured.”

The doctor swore under her breath. “I don’t know if he’s going to live through this.”

“Make him live,” Senneck threatened.

Shaking her head, the doctor turned Kullervo over without much effort. Freed from their bindings, the wings flexed weakly in her face.

The doctor let out a piercing scream and scrambled away. “What *is* that?”

“My human is deformed,” Senneck said, very calmly.

The doctor breathed quickly. “I’ve—never seen anything like it before . . .”

Beside her, the griffin healer looked on with morbid fascination. “They almost look like . . .”

“Do not waste time!” Senneck snarled. “Heal him!”

Faced with her rage, the doctor had no choice but to continue. Returning to Kullervo’s side, she very tentatively touched the wings. Pulling a face at the feel of them, she went back to work on the injuries around them. That done, she turned him over again and covered him up with a blanket brought in by one of the guards.

“Well,” she said, wiping her hands on a piece of cloth, “I’ve done what I could. He'll need food and rest—a lot of it—and those wounds'll have to be checked every day."

Senneck's meat had arrived. She bit into it very gladly. "You have done well. Now you must go and tell Oeka and her human that we have arrived."

"I'll pass on the message," the griffin healer offered. "Who should I say is here?"

Senneck huffed at him. "Senneck and her human, Lord Kullervo."

When they were alone again, "Lord" Kullervo pulled himself back toward her—close enough that they were touching. "Thank you, Senneck," he wheezed.

"It is no more than what any griffin should do for her human," she said between bites.

The doctor and griffin healer had left, but the guards had stayed to watch over the nest. One of them came in and gave Kullervo some food someone must have fetched. He took it and ate, chewing with difficulty.

As soon as there was nobody in earshot, Senneck swallowed another chunk of meat and turned her head, laying it down close to Kullervo's. "Listen now," she said softly.

He looked blearily at her. "I'm so tired . . . what is it?"

"I have been thinking," said Senneck. "You are human, but you are also a griffin, and it is clear to me that you have not been taught what your mother would have passed on in the nest."

"Like what?"

"Your magic is unlike anything I have seen, but it is still magic, and you have never been taught to control it properly. I will teach you."

Kullervo raised himself on his elbows. "You will?"

Senneck's tail flicked. "No other griffin would do this, but now that I have chosen you, it is my duty to do whatever is necessary for your survival. Therefore, I shall pass on the ways of control and wielding that I learnt as a youngster. With my teaching, I think that you shall come to use your magic fully."

Kullervo lay back and reached out to touch her beak. "I'd like that. Thank you."

28

Family

Kullervo and Senneck rested for most of that day, still under guard. More food arrived for them, and fresh clothes for Kullervo, who put them on gratefully. He was beginning to get some colour back in his face, but he showed no interest in moving to the bed in the room next door—staying beside Senneck every moment.

Neither of them had any way of knowing whether Laela had been told they were back. For now, they were content to rest.

Senneck wasted no time. That evening, when they were both awake, and she was certain nobody was listening, she began to talk to Kullervo—telling him the secrets he needed to know in her quietest voice. Kullervo said nothing at all. He lay very still, staring at the ceiling or his own crabbed hands, taking in every word she said. He felt as if he had never listened so intently in his life, or tried so hard to remember everything down to the last detail. Some of it he already knew, or had guessed, some of it confused him, but as Senneck talked on, he began to feel a sense of revelation, of something opening in his mind like a flower. His heart beat faster with excitement.

This was knowledge no human had ever learnt, knowledge griffins had kept as their greatest secret and refused even to talk about in front of anyone but their own kind. To a human, most of it would have been completely bewildering. But Kullervo felt it reach deep into his mind, to the part of him that was griffish, and there it made complete sense.

Yes, he thought. *Yes, that's it! Of course!* And he listened all the harder.

When Senneck suddenly stopped, it was almost physically painful. "What's wrong?" he said immediately.

"We have been interrupted," she said.

Kullervo looked up, and his heart skipped a beat when he saw the horrible shape coming toward him. A griffin—only a small one—but . . . wrong. The eyes were white and blind, the beak sagging open. It moved jerkily, shambling along like a cripple, the wings flopping about uselessly at its sides.

"Oeka," Senneck hissed.

Kullervo struggled to pull himself up, propping himself against his partner's flank in a sitting position. "You," he said, tasting unexpected venom in the word.

The guards outside reacted even more poorly to the warped griffin's arrival. Forgetting their orders and training, they cringed away, then abruptly left the room, as if obeying some unheard command.

Oeka stood in the entrance to the nest, seeming to leer at Kullervo. *So the freak and the old one have returned,* her mental voice sneered.

Senneck regarded her for a moment and lurched onto her paws. Kullervo, holding on to her flank, stood as well—keeping a hand on her shoulder for balance.

But where have you returned from? Oeka continued.

Kullervo could feel Senneck trembling slightly under his hand. He moved closer to her. All of a sudden, she cringed and lowered her head, making an ugly, strangled noise in her throat. "Do not—"

Oeka didn't move. She hadn't even blinked since her arrival. But Kullervo could taste the magic reaching out from her to touch Senneck, violating her mind.

He started toward Oeka, raising his taloned hands. "Leave her alone!"

Oeka's head turned toward him, and Senneck relaxed as the small griffin's power left her alone and struck at Kullervo instead. He could feel it touch him, probing at his mind, but there was no pain. He hissed defiantly at her. "You can't do anything to me, you monster."

Oeka's mental screech made the walls vibrate. *Curse you!*

"Oeka!" The stern voice came from behind her. "Stop it right now!"

Oeka hissed and backed off, and there was Laela, looking angry and exhausted.

Kullervo's ugly face split into a smile. "Laela!"

Her own face fell. "Kullervo! What *happened* to yeh? I thought yeh must be dead!"

The smile disappeared, and he self-consciously covered his mouth with a hand. "I'll be all right. I just need to rest."

She came toward him, eyes concerned. "Oh yeh poor thing! What did they do to yeh?"

"They tried to make me talk," said Kullervo, very simply. "I never did. Senneck saved me."

I have scented the old one's mind, Oeka butted in. *I saw fighting in Warwick, with many dead.* Her blind eyes did not flicker. *I saw her kill the traitor's daughter, and an old human. I also saw her kill the Mighty Skandar's son. And then I saw her kill the one-eyed traitor.*

"Saeddryn?" Laela exclaimed. "Saeddryn's dead? Senneck, is it true?"

Senneck looked away. "I killed the young one, her daughter. Then I killed the one-eyed one, and Aenae with her."

Laela rubbed her forehead. "So Saeddryn's really dead. Thank gods. I got worried when they said they hadn't found her body, but Oeka's never wrong." She looked at Senneck, very solemnly. "I owe yeh a debt, Senneck—a big one. I'm sorry I didn't trust yeh before, but now—"

"Laela, stop." Kullervo came closer. "You don't understand."

She gave him a look. "Don't understand what?"

"It's Saeddryn. She's not— It's not— Laela, something awful's happened."

Laela stilled. "What? What is it? What's gone wrong now?"

"Saeddryn's not— She isn't—" Kullervo struggled for words.

Laela looked at Senneck. "What's this about?"

Senneck lowered her head. "The one-eyed one has been killed," she said heavily. "But she has not gone."

"She's come back," Kullervo blurted at last. "She's like *him* now."

Laela had gone pale. "What . . . ?"

Oeka had already realised the truth. *No! This cannot be! Do not lie!*

"It's true." Kullervo darted forward and grabbed Laela by the arm. "She's working for the Night God now, she's got Arenadd's powers. She tried to kill us! I saw her disappear like a shadow—she was so *strong*! And she was talking about how she was going to—Laela, she's going to come here and kill us all! There's no way of stopping her, I stuck my talons in her throat, and she didn't die!"

Laela found her voice. "Oh *shit*."

"It is true!" Senneck broke in. "I saw it with my own eyes. *Kraeai kran ae* has returned, and it is Saeddryn. She wants you dead, half-breed, and believe me—she will make sure that it happens. There is no stopping the heartless one."

Kullervo hadn't let go of Laela's arm. "What are we going to do? What are we going to do? She's after us—both of us, she said so! We're the ones she was sent to kill!"

Laela grasped at this last part, in search of something approaching sanity. "You? Why you?"

"Because—" Kullervo stopped abruptly. "Because . . ."

Do not worry, Oeka rasped. *I shall find the truth.*

Yet again, she lashed out mentally.

Time passed. Eventually, Kullervo shook his head dully, as if trying to wake himself up. "No," he said. "The truth is mine to tell, not yours." He straightened up, facing Laela and looking her in the eye for the first time. "She's after us because we're between her and the throne. We're the only heirs apart from her and her son."

Laela's eyes narrowed. "You?"

Kullervo smiled weakly. "Think about it," he said. "Who else could be depraved enough to make something like me? Didn't you ever wonder why your father's lover had yellow eyes like mine, or why her fingernails looked more like claws? Or maybe you could open her tomb, and wonder why there are griffin bones in there instead of human."

Her eyes widened. "You're—?"

"Yes." Kullervo's yellow eyes were full of fear, and something that had very rarely been there before—pride. "I am the King's son. I am Kullervo Taranisäii. I am . . ." He laughed softly. "A Prince. Next in line for Tara's throne."

No! Oeka's cry echoed in every mind there. Unable to attack mentally, she made a clumsy charge and hurled herself at Kullervo, talons spread wide.

Senneck sprang forward, putting herself in the way, and knocked the smaller griffin aside. Standing over her with her own larger talons at the ready, she said, "Touch my human, and you shall die."

Oeka was too shocked to strike back. Clumsily, she got up and edged away, back toward her own partner.

Kullervo ignored her completely. "Don't worry, I don't want your throne. Look at me—do I look like King material to you? I couldn't run a fruit stall. I told you the truth before when I said I wanted to help you. You're my sister, Laela. You're the only family I've got. And I promise I'll do everything I can to protect you from . . . from *her*."

Laela hadn't moved. "A . . . a brother? I got a brother?"

Kullervo smiled. "A half-brother. A half-*breed* half-brother. Who would have thought it?"

She shook herself, and mumbled, "I knew it. I knew there was somethin' about you. Somethin' familiar."

"I suppose I must look a bit like *him*. My father. Our father."

"Yeh do," said Laela.

Kullervo looked away. "I hoped I didn't. I couldn't ever be proud of something like that."

"Well, yeh should be," Laela said sharply. He looked at her, and she softened. "Our father wasn't all bad, Kullervo. He loved Skade very much, an' I believe he loved my mother as well. An' to tell yeh the truth . . . I miss him."

"I wish I could have met him," Kullervo confessed.

"He woulda been proud of yeh," said Laela. She smiled. "Like I am."

They embraced—tentatively at first, but soon pulling each other closer, and if Laela felt Kullervo's wings, she didn't show it, and if he felt pain from his wounds, he didn't complain.

In the bittersweet joy of that moment, neither of them noticed that Oeka had disappeared.

29

The Woman Without a Heart

Darkness in the First Mountains. Darkness among the stones of Taranis' Throne. Darkness in Iorwerth's heart, as he carried his old friend to his final resting place.

Freezing wind tugged at his clothes and ruffled his hair. He had come up to the plateau of the standing stones alone—leaving Kaanee to sleep in the valley below. Like all griffins, his partner had nothing but contempt for human rituals. Besides, he was tired. And the stones were no place for a griffin to be.

But Iorwerth wasn't alone. The urn that contained Nerth's ashes weighed him down—in more ways than one.

Ahead, the stones loomed. To him they looked like a group of hooded people looking down on him in judgment. Instinctively, he bowed his head as he walked the last few steps toward them. He had never seen them before, but all his life he had been told how holy they were. He hadn't needed it. He could feel it for himself.

He reached the level ground on top of the plateau but hesitated at the edge of the circle. Should he go inside?

Instinctively, he looked upward. The moon seemed to stare at him. He had never seen it so bright before.

Silent accusation pinned him to the spot.

"I know what ye think of me," he mumbled. "I'm not proud of what I did. But I have to go into the circle. I'm not here for myself, and I know the one I came for deserves to be there."

Clutching the urn to his chest, he stepped into the circle.

Moonlight made the snow within it glow, and the stones cast bars of shadow toward the altar at the centre. For some reason, the sight of the altar calmed Iorwerth down. It made him think of the old Moon Temple at Malvern, and he realised now what he was really looking at. The Throne itself was a temple, no different than the one at Malvern. He had prayed there countless times, and he could pray here, too. The one was a shadow of the other, and *this* was the real thing. This was where the power of the Night God really lived, and unlike the Temple, it couldn't be burned down or destroyed. It had been here since the beginning of time and would be here at the end.

Awed, and humbled, Iorwerth went straight to the altar and put the urn on it. Standing over it, he glanced uneasily at the moon again and tried to think of something to say. He didn't know any of the proper prayers or chants, but as he searched his memory, he remembered something he had learnt as a young man. Old words. Words that had never quite been forgotten, even after centuries of Southern rule.

Softly, Iorwerth began to recite them.

"Of earth born and in fire forged,

By magic blessed and by cool water soothed,

Then by a breeze in the night blown away to a land of silver and bright flowers.

May the Night God receive the soul of Nerth, born in Eitheinn,

Who was a brave warrior and true to his family and his tribe

May he be admitted to the night sky and become a bright star to shine upon us all."

That was the version had had been taught, and when he had finished, he said them again, louder and fiercer.

As he reached the end, he picked up the urn and opened it. "Ye were a great friend to me, Nerth, and a great man, and I'll never stop cursing the day I did this to ye. Forgive me."

He emptied the ashes out and watched them scatter over the snow.

All at once a terrible feeling of desolation crushed him. Dropping the empty urn, he knelt at the altar and covered his face with his hands. "Oh, Night God, forgive me. What have I done? It's all gone wrong. *I don't know what to do!*"

Wind blew among the stones. It sounded almost like mocking laughter.

Iorwerth stayed where he was for some time, mourning Nerth and cursing himself, and searching for an answer that would not come.

Gradually, as he calmed down, the sense of being watched grew stronger. The wind had stilled. Iorwerth's throat tightened. Everyone knew what made the Throne different than any other sacred place. This was where the Night God herself was said to reach down to touch the earth. More than that, Iorwerth knew that the stories were more than just stories. Years ago, Arenadd himself had told him the story of how he had come to the circle on the night of the Blood Moon. That night, at the moment of the sacrifice, the Night God had appeared.

Iorwerth looked around nervously. This was the place where Arenadd had discovered what he was. This was where he had been given his holy task to destroy the Southerners and free the North.

The sense of being watched grew even stronger.

"Night God?" Iorwerth called out, rather self-consciously. "Night God, are ye there? Are ye listening to me now?"

And a voice whispered back, *"Yes."*

Iorwerth nearly choked on his own tongue. "Shit!"

The voice laughed softly. "I'm listening, Iorwerth of Fruitsheart. So speak."

Terrified, Iorwerth knelt. "I need help, Night God."

"All of the North needs help," the voice replied. "What makes *ye* so special?"

"I—" Iorwerth's eyes narrowed. That voice . . . He stood up. "Where are ye?"

"In the circle," said the voice, and now Iorwerth's suspicion solidified.

"I know that voice—ye're not the Night God! Show yerself, *now*."

The voice did not reply. But as Iorwerth looked, he saw the figure appear among the shadows and come toward him.

He flicked his sickle out of his belt and into his hand with one practised movement. *"Saeddryn!"*

The former High Priestess wore a plain black dress, and her ceremonial circlet—silver with a crescent moon over the forehead. Her eyepatch had gone, leaving the ugly, scarred hole bare.

Iorwerth backed off a step, raising his sickle. "What are ye doing here?"

Saeddryn lifted her chin and gave him an arrogant smile. "Prayin', like any righteous Northerner should. It's been too long since I was here."

Iorwerth's mind raced. "How did ye get here?"

"Easily."

"Are ye alone?"

"The Night God is with me."

Iorwerth relaxed a little—she was alone and unarmed. "Forgive me if I sounded shocked, but ye're supposed to be dead, traitor."

"Traitor!" Saeddryn's smooth self-confidence turned to rage in an instant. "How dare ye stand here in this place an' call *me* traitor after what ye did." She spat at him.

"I'm not proud of what I did," Iorwerth snapped back. "Now, are ye going to surrender, or do I have to kill ye myself?"

Saeddryn sneered. "No need for that. The Bastard's griffin did a fine job of it already."

Iorwerth edged closer, getting ready to attack. "What are ye talking about?" he asked, mostly to distract her.

Stone-faced, Saeddryn reached up and pulled her dress open. Underneath, hideous red gashes ran down her chest and disappeared under the cloth. Scars, fresh scars—scars so deep they had left channels in the flesh like dried red rivers.

Iorwerth gave a little cry of disgust and horror. "*Oh!* Dear Night God . . ."

"Senneck's work," said Saeddryn, covering herself up again. "She killed Arddryn first, an' Nerth. An' Aenae."

Iorwerth couldn't bear to listen to another word. He lifted his head and gave a call—bellowing his own name at the sky as loudly as he could. It echoed off the mountains, travelling far away.

Saeddryn didn't flinch. "Callin' Kaanee won't help ye now, *traitor.*"

"Me, a traitor?" Iorwerth yelled back at her. "Don't play that game with me, Saeddryn. I know what ye did. Ye turned on the King himself, ye tried to kill him. It's ye who'll suffer the traitor's death when we bring ye back to Malvern, not me."

Saeddryn's remaining eyelid twitched. "Aye, I did those things. I won't lie about it. But I did what was best for Tara."

"Like trying to steal the throne from our rightful ruler?" Iorwerth snarled.

"Don't be blind," said Saeddryn. "Ye know what he was toward the end. Drunk every night, obsessed with the past, full of mad ideas. He wanted to *talk* to the Southerners! Trade with them—he even told me he was thinkin' of lettin' some of them *settle* here! An' Amoranis, too—he nearly *married* one of them, for shadows' sakes! An' then he takes in this little half-breed from off the street, uses her as his whore—he made her Master of Wisdom! Some stranger who traipsed in from the South, no-one knew who she was, an' he makes her his chief advisor! He had to be removed, Iorwerth. The country would've fallen apart otherwise."

"Queen Laela is his daughter," Iorwerth said stonily. "His rightful heir."

"So she says," said Saeddryn.

"He chose her to succeed him, and that's all that matters to me," said Iorwerth. "I trust his judgment."

"He was a madman."

"He was chosen by the Night God."

"Not any more," said Saeddryn.

A screech came from overhead, and Kaanee arrived—landing neatly by his human's side. He saw Saeddryn at once. "What is this—?"

Saeddryn backed away. "We need t'talk, Iorwerth. Sensibly."

Iorwerth glanced at Kaanee. "Make it fast."

"Never mind about the King for now," Saeddryn resumed. "What about the half-breed, an' all she's been doin'? Do ye really think she's rulin' well?"

"And ye'd do a better job?" Iorwerth said sarcastically.

"Not me," she said. "It was never going t'be me. Ye know who was the heir before the half-breed came along. I was only plannin' to rule a short time, until he was old enough."

"Caedmon," Iorwerth muttered.

Saeddryn smiled gently at the mention of her son's name. "Ye watched him grow, Iorwerth. Ye taught him how t'fight yerself. All of us in the Eyrie did what we could t'help him grow. The King himself taught him griffish an' presented him to the griffins. It was always going t'be Caedmon. Even Arenadd agreed with that."

"I remember he changed his mind," Iorwerth said coldly. "Didn't he?"

"Caedmon was just a boy. Every boy rebels. He's what we need, Iorwerth. Caedmon was meant to be King, an' he will be. What would ye have instead? The half-breed, making Northerner fight Northerner? Don't ye understand? Unless we act fast, this whole mess'll carry on until the Kingdom is nothin' but a bunch of warring factions. An' then what'll happen, Iorwerth? Do ye really think the South won't notice—that they won't come back lookin' to take back what used t'be theirs? Do ye want to see us lose everythin' we fought for, all because of that half-breed slut?"

Iorwerth looked away. "This *mess* will be sorted out once ye an' the rest of yer lot are dealt with."

Saeddryn laughed out loud. "As if ye believe that. The North doesn't forget, Iorwerth. We have more supporters than ye think. Until the half-breed's gone, an' Caedmon has his throne, this will *never* be over. An' Nerth will have died for nothin'."

Kaanee tossed his head. "I have had enough of this," he rasped, and leapt straight at Saeddryn.

She took a step sideways and disappeared.

Kaanee skidded in the snow, and crashed headlong into one of the stones. He righted himself and darted around, talons snatching at empty air. "You cannot hide!" he screeched.

Saeddryn's laugh echoed in the air. "Oh, I can."

Iorwerth turned around, searching in vain. "Where are ye? What—?"

"Here," she said, just behind him.

He turned sharply, and there she was. When he made a grab for her, she stepped into a shadow and disappeared.

"So ye see now," her voice said over the sound of Kaanee's frustrated hissing. "The truth. The Night God has chosen me. The powers of the Shadow That Walks have passed on to me, and I have been given a sacred task of my own."

Iorwerth's heart thudded. "What task . . . ?"

"Kill the half-breeds," Saeddryn hissed.

Kaanee had subsided, his sides heaving. "What is this magic? Where has the human gone?"

Saeddryn reappeared without a sound. "How can ye change what the Night God commands?" she said. "Would she have brought me back if she wanted the half-breed t'stay on Tara's throne?" She pointed straight at Iorwerth's face. "Choose, Iorwerth. Choose carefully. Choose wrong if ye don't remember what happens to the enemies of the Shadow That Walks."

With that, she vanished again and did not reappear, leaving nothing but a low laugh behind.

Saeddryn waited in the shadows until Iorwerth and Kaanee had gone. From where she stood, they were silver shadows, moving in total blackness.

She emerged back into the circle and shook herself. The shadows made her feel even stronger than she had already become, but she knew better than to abuse the ability. It was tempting to stay in darkness all the time, but she had known her predecessor too well to give in to that.

"I can't die," he had told her once. "But I only feel invincible when I'm in the shadows. But it makes me afraid as well. Afraid that if I stay too long, I won't be able to find the way back."

Saeddryn remembered that warning well. She also remembered what she had witnessed in the early days, just before the war began. Arenadd had thought he had magic of his own—had thought that his powers truly belonged to him. He had been wrong. No human had magic, dead or alive. It was impossible. Only a griffin could channel it, contain it. Arenadd had had powers, but they had come to him through Skandar.

Saeddryn guessed that she must be draining the giant griffin's energy every time she went into the shadows, and even if he was no friend to her, she didn't want to hurt him. He had done great things for Tara. And besides—if he died, what then? If Skandar died, she might lose her powers, or even die herself.

She wondered where the dark griffin was now. Had he already returned to watch over his human's remains? Or was he somewhere else? No way of knowing. She was on her own now, and the Night God would be her only friend.

Saeddryn's breath misted in the air. She touched her neck again, checking for a heartbeat. Nothing.

Yet again, she fought down the fear that hid deep in her stomach. *Oh, Night God help me, I'm dead.*

So far she had managed to keep her mind away from it. She knelt at the altar now and muttered a frantic prayer, concentrating all her thoughts on the Night God and her sacred duty. This was all that mattered.

"I won't be like Arenadd," she promised. "I'll be strong, I swear."

A strange feeling of unease began to prickle along her spine. Turning away abruptly, she walked out of the circle and down the mountainside.

The further away from the circle she went, the better she felt, and she began to think of her mission again. She had paid her respects, and now it was time to go to her work.

She leapt back into darkness and sped away over the snowbound landscape.

High up on a ledge outside his cave, the Mighty Skandar had watched the entire scene play out at the stones, standing impassive and still like a part of the mountain itself. He didn't see Saeddryn go into the shadows, but he flinched when he felt the magic flow out of him again. It came out through his skin, making it prickle and turn cold.

This was something he had felt before many times, and he didn't like it, but at least it was easier than before. He didn't have to spew it from his beak any more like a scream; he had learnt how to control it so that less of it would escape. He had never talked to Arenadd about it because his mate Hyrenna had always told him that magic was something to talk to other griffins about, and never humans. Not even his own human.

He had not felt his magic being taken in a long time, not since Arenadd had fallen and not stood up again. The one-eyed human was taking it now. Arenadd didn't like her, and Skandar . . . Skandar didn't care. She was just another human, like all the others, and only one human had ever mattered to him.

Skandar huffed out a beakful of fog and went back into his cave. The familiar stench of decay burned in his nostrils, and he went back to stand over Arenadd's body. It was damaged now, after the ugly little griffin had tried to steal it. Skandar hissed at the memory and pushed the body further into the cave with his beak, trying to make it look neater. The rotting limbs flopped about, seeming to move on their own, and Skandar stopped and peered down intently.

No more movement.

Skandar nudged the body again. "Human wake now?"

Only silence replied.

Skandar heaved a deep sigh and lay down on his belly. He had tried to use his magic again, to make Arenadd get up, but it hadn't worked. No matter what he did, the black energy, that captive scream he remembered from long ago, had refused to come. It was gone, and could not be used again. But Arenadd had to wake up, so that they could go home.

Home. The thought of it filled Skandar's simple mind with images and senses, of his comfortable nest with the golden trough full of sweet water, the finest meat brought to him whenever he commanded it. Females, all the finest and strongest in his territory, coming to him chirping and lifting their tails eagerly.

And Arenadd was there beside him every day, to brush his coat and make it glossy, to clean and polish his talons, or just to stay with him and talk when he wanted company.

Skandar whimpered softly. He missed his home so badly it hurt, but he could never go back. Not without his human, who had been beside him so long as his friend and the key to his power. Without Arenadd, Skandar was not Mighty any more.

"Wake!" he said again, almost forlornly. "Wake now! Human come back! Skandar . . ." His head sagged. "Skandar . . . need . . . human."

Lonely and bewildered, the griffin that had once been the Mighty Skandar slept.

30

Griffin Dreaming

That night Skandar dreamed the white-griffin dream.

She came to him as she had done long ago when he was young, her white feathers glowing with silvery light. Young and slender, very good to look at, until she turned her head and a black hole gaped in place of an eye.

Skandar stood up when she came closer to him, but said nothing as she rubbed herself against him. Her tail-feathers flicked under his beak, and he rasped softly with lust.

Mighty Skandar, her voice said. *You are all alone.*

Skandar stalked her, his tail swishing briskly from side to side. "Want mate."

She ignored him. *Skandar, why are you not at your human's side?*

"Am with human," Skandar snapped back. "Never leave until you come."

No. You are alone, Skandar. Alone in this cave.

"With human," said Skandar.

You are lying beside a rotting corpse.

"Human come back."

Arenadd is not the Shadow That Walks any more, said the white griffin. *You know that.*

"Human always be shadow that walk," Skandar said stoutly. "Always come back. Wait, and see."

There is a new shadow now, Skandar. You created her. Have you forgotten?

"Not care."

You must care, said the white griffin. *You have given the dark power to a new human, and now she is yours. You must go to her and be her partner. Help her to do what must be done.*

Skandar cocked his head. "What do?"

Your new human must destroy the half-breed ones and take back Tara's throne.

"Not care," Skandar said again.

Do you not understand? said the white griffin. *This is something that will be good for you.*

"Why want? Why good?"

You long to go home, said the white griffin. *You want your old power back. Join with Saeddryn, and she will give you back your home. You will not be an unpartnered griffin any more. You will be the Mighty Skandar!*

Skandar said nothing.

And you will fight again, the white griffin continued. *You were glorious in war. Now war has come again. You shall relive the greatest time of your life! Is that not what you want, Mighty Skandar?*

Her voice was purring, beguiling.

"Want home," Skandar said slowly. "Want fight."

Then you know what you must do. Go to Saeddryn. Fight beside her. She will be a good human for you.

Skandar looked at the floor for a time, and his tail twitched. At last, he looked up, and his silver eyes had grown brighter. "Mighty Skandar have only one human," he said. "Only Arenadd. Only one for Skandar. Never be another."

Arenadd is gone, the white griffin said. *He will never come back to you.*

But Skandar turned away. "Arenadd come back."

He will not come back!

"Will!" Skandar rose up angrily, spreading his wings wide, and pointed his talons straight at the white griffin. "Will come back! *Will come back!*" He screeched it out with all his might, again and again, until it seemed to echo all around him. *Come back, come back, come, come, come . . .*

Skandar woke up.

He woke up angry.

Rising to his paws, he spread his wings over Arenadd's body. "Come back!" he said again, in his sternest voice. "Human *will* come back, and Skandar will see it!"

Silence. Awful silence.

Skandar turned away abruptly and paced around the cave, his wings brushing against the jagged walls. "Skandar have human back one day," he said aloud. "Maybe not soon. But not do nothing! Am Mighty Skandar! Am greatest griffin in this land! Territory still mine, and humans not take it!" He looked back at the body, and his voice quietened. "Go now. Mighty Skandar will prove he is still Mighty. Will do it without human, to prove his might more. But will not forget. Will not leave. Arenadd is the human of Mighty Skandar, and Skandar will come back."

Determined now, swelling with power, he charged to the cave entrance and hurled himself out into the sky. Morning had come while he slept, and he set out over the mountains to hunt.

He hunted all morning, even after he had already eaten his first kill. By noon he returned to the cave, weighed down by two small deer. He carried them inside and laid them down beside Arenadd's body, tearing open the hides to expose the tenderest meat.

Still not satisfied, he flew outside again and searched out some trees. Humans ate green things as well as meat, everyone knew that.

Unable to find anything else, he ripped a large branch off a conifer and brought that back as well, laying it next to the deer. Finally, he touched Arenadd's forehead with his beak. "Human stay here. Have food now. Skandar come back. Promise."

He left the cave. Outside, to make certain that nothing would get in, he sank his talons into the cliff face above the entrance and pulled down, hard. Pieces of rock came crashing down in a shower of earth and snow. Skandar shovelled them into place with his paws, covering the cave entrance as well as he could. Arenadd could get out once he woke up; he was clever. But if any other griffins came sniffing about, they would never see the entrance or think it was important.

Certain that he had done all he needed to, the Mighty Skandar flew away. Heading into the heart of his rightful territory and toward the war that brewed there.

* * *

High up in the gallery above the council chamber, Kullervo sat beside Senneck and waited nervously for Laela to arrive. Below, the council had gathered and stood in a circle, human and griffin alike. Iorwerth and Kaanee were there, too, having returned to Malvern the day before.

Kullervo shuffled closer to Senneck. They were the only ones in the tiered seating that circled the chamber—this particular council meeting wasn't open to the public, and the guards outside had only let Kullervo and Senneck in because they had had direct orders from Laela herself.

"It has been far too long since I have been in this place," Senneck remarked. She stood up to peer down at the platform where Laela would stand, and sighed. "I have stood on that platform, back when it was golden like the sun. I saw the Mighty Kraal himself here in all his glory. *Raakkakee!* What a magnificent male he was! I would have given it all to be his mate, but only the highest and most powerful females could come to him."

Kullervo fidgeted. He had been given a fine set of clothes to wear, including an oversized velvet cloak to hide his wings, and they were uncomfortable. "You knew the Mighty Kraal? What was he like?"

"The largest griffin I have ever seen," said Senneck. "And the most powerful. I marvelled that he could even fly." She glanced sideways at Kullervo. "It is said his only match was his son, the dark griffin."

"Wait, Skandar is the Mighty Kraal's son?"

"Yes. I do not know if he knows it, but it would not have mattered to him if he did. He killed the Mighty Kraal himself, on the day the sun went dark and Malvern fell."

Kullervo shivered. "That must have been such a terrible day."

"It was," she said shortly. "Be ready now; your sister has come."

Kullervo stood, too, and hurried to the edge of the gallery to look down. Sure enough, there was Laela entering the chamber, with Oeka, silent and ungainly, by her side. Iorwerth and Kaanee stood aside to let them step up onto the silver-painted platform, and the meeting began immediately.

"Warwick's been won," Laela told them without ceremony.

"Arddryn Taranisäii an' Rakek are both dead. So is Aenae. As for Saeddryn . . . there's reason to believe she might still be out there somewhere. An' there's still Caedmon an' Fruitsheart left to deal with. Iorwerth an' I have talked it over an' made plans for how we're gonna deal with that. Obviously, if Saeddryn's alive, then she'll head for Fruitsheart. As for Fruitsheart, we can't expect help from the governor there. She's stopped sendin' us messages, an' the word is the people are armin' themselves. Last griffiner we sent there never came back. So I think we're safe sayin' they ain't about to give us Caedmon."

She paused significantly.

"I don't think I need to tell yeh what's gonna happen if Saeddryn gets there before we do. We're gonna strike hard, an' fast. The unpartnered are ready to go—desperate for it, in fact. Anyone got any objections?"

No-one did.

"Right then," Laela resumed. "Now listen. I know this looks simple, but it ain't. I want one thing from all of yeh, an' that's *caution*. Have someone taste yer food. Don't go nowhere without yer partner. If yeh haven't got a personal guard, get one. Keep a weapon on yeh all day every day."

"Why?" someone spoke up. "What's happened?"

"We're at war is what's happened," Laela snapped. "An' I have reason to think there might be assassins about. Good ones. Is that understood? Take it seriously. Protect yerselves an' each other if yeh want to stay alive."

Iorwerth coughed. "I understand, my lady. And I advise all of ye to listen. Not all of ye fought in the war, but I did, and trust me—assassinating councils is the first thing enemies think of."

Kullervo, watching and listening from above, could hear every word. The council chamber had been designed to make sounds from below carry, and it worked. "What about us?" he muttered to Senneck. "When are they going to talk about us?"

Below, Laela spoke up again. "Now that's all out in the open, there's one last thing for me to bring up before it's your turn. It's occurred to me that we don't have anyone servin' as Master of Diplomacy, an' I've decided it's time that post was filled." She gestured to the woman standing quietly on her left. "By the new Master of Wisdom, Lady Inva."

Several councillors protested.

"Why her?" one actually called out. "Why not one of us?"

"Yeh've all got positions already; yeh ain't got the time for another one."

"I meant one of *us*," the angry councillor persisted. "A real Northerner."

Laela cleared her throat. "All right then. Name a real Northerner what knows Amorani."

"What? What's that—that's not the—"

"That *is* the point," Laela snapped. "Inva's a griffiner, she knows about travellin', an' she speaks more languages than anyone in this damn Eyrie. An' she knows Amoran, an' that's where I'm sendin' her. Unless yeh'd rather it was *you* what went."

"Amoran?" another councillor said. "Why Amoran?"

"Just a courtesy visit," Laela said placidly. "They're our allies now after all. I'm sendin' Inva an' Skarok, an' a few helpers, with some gifts for the Emperor."

"Oh," said the councillor who had protested. "I see."

"No more complaints, then?" said Laela.

"No. Apologies, my lady."

"Helpers!" Kullervo repeated to himself.

Senneck nudged him. "She cannot tell them that it is our mission as much as Skarok's. They do not know us or have a reason to trust us."

"Amoran!" Kullervo smiled dreamily. "I can't wait to see it!"

"I have wondered what it is like," Senneck admitted. "I have heard that griffins are almost seen as gods there."

"And a winged man might be just what the Emperor needs to persuade him to fight for us," said Kullervo.

"Indeed." Senneck rubbed her head against his shoulder. "You and I," she purred. "You and I, Kullervo, shall do great things. I am certain of it."

Kullervo's heart fluttered. Ignoring the talk from below, he pressed his face into her feathers and inhaled the wild scent of them, loving the feel of her and her warmth. "And in Amoran, we'll be safe," he murmured. "She won't find us there."

"*Kraeaina kran ae* cannot survive in the land of the sun," said Senneck. "There will be nothing to fear."

They stayed where they were while the council meeting

carried on, sharing their excitement, though Kullervo couldn't have known exactly what Senneck was thinking in that moment that made her so happy and affectionate.

Amoran is the key. I will teach him all he must know to control his magic. But more than that, I shall make a lord out of him, a greater Lord than poor Erian ever was. There will be no more failure for Senneck of Eagleholm. In Amoran, I shall have all the time that I need, and I shall use it to its full. She spread her wing over Kullervo, pulling him closer to herself. *I shall not lose him. I shall not let him die. Not even* Kraeaina kran ae *can take him from me. I swear this on my life.*

When the meeting was over and the councillors left, Senneck got Kullervo onto her back and half-jumped down onto the floor and to the platform. Laela and Oeka were still there, the latter crouched in silent meditation as she had been for most of the meeting.

Laela looked tired and vaguely irritable. "That went down fine, I reckon. Looks like I got it all sorted out."

Kullervo gave her a quick hug. "I never saw you look so much like a Queen before."

Laela smiled with pleasure. "The crown helps. So, yeh feelin' ready for Amoran?"

"We both are," said Kullervo. He touched her shoulder solemnly. "Don't worry, Laela; we'll find an answer there. Someone there must know how to stop this."

"An' if they don't, then at least that husband of mine might send over some troops."

"You never told me you were married before," said Kullervo.

"Only in Amoran." She shrugged. "Marriage ain't valid in Tara unless it's a proper Northerner ceremony. Amoranis don't mind; if it's valid in Amoran, it's valid to them. But talk to him especially. If we're lucky, he might come back with yeh an' bring some extra manpower. See how it goes. Appeal to his sense of adventure if nothin' else works. I'm sure it won't come to that, though."

"Do not worry," said Senneck. "You can trust us to do as we have promised."

Laela grinned at her. "I'd be a fool not to trust my own brother. C'mon, Kullervo, let's go eat."

The siblings left together, but Senneck didn't follow. Oeka hadn't moved a muscle.

I sense great ambition in your mind, her voice accused.

"I have always been ambitious," said Senneck. "It is natural to our kind. I thought that you would know that, little griffin."

Your new human is not welcome in my Eyrie, Senneck. If you have sense, you will not return from Amoran.

"Kill us, then, if you cannot trust us." Senneck flicked her tail and stared defiantly.

You know I could have done this already if I had wanted. Oeka finally lifted her blind head. *I have allowed you to live because you are useful to me.*

"I am surprised," Senneck mocked. "I thought that you would have killed Kullervo out of mere frustration by now."

Oeka said nothing.

"After all," said Senneck, "you must be enraged that, of all the minds in Tara, his is the only one you cannot violate. And though you must want him dead, you cannot kill him. Have you seen that by now, you twisted fool? You cannot kill him, no matter how much you want to. Your magic cannot do it, and you have sacrificed so much of your own self that your talons cannot do it either."

Oeka's fury made Senneck's mind flash red with pain.

"You cannot!" she rasped again. "You are a cripple who cannot even hunt her own food!"

I do not need that nonsense any more! Oeka snarled. *I am the master of this land. I am the greatest and you are the lowest, you whimpering chick who could not protect her own human! Do you believe that you have the strength to challenge me, when you could not even do that?*

Senneck didn't rise to the bait. "Am I so low?" she asked. "I killed three of your greatest enemies while you lay here and did nothing. And now I have a new human, who is only one step away from owning all your own human's power. A human who is stronger than you."

The force of Oeka's mental attack drove Senneck to her knees. She convulsed, beak open in a silent scream. Her eyes rolled back in her head.

Blood began to well up over her eyelids.

Somehow, she found the strength to cry out. "Kill me!" she screamed. "Kill me, and my human shall avenge me! He will kill you, and you will be defenceless against him!"

For a moment it looked as if her threat hadn't worked. But then Oeka let her go, and she found herself on the floor, looking up at her through blurry eyes.

The small griffin stood over her, her own eyes white and decaying. *You will regret what you have said to me, old one,* her voice said. *You will regret it very much. You have only seen a fraction of the powers that will be mine. Soon, you will see.*

She left the chamber, her gait clumsy and hobbling.

Senneck watched her from her position on the floor. Her entire body throbbed in time with her head, and when she blinked, she felt blood try to glue her eyes shut. Trembling slightly with shock, she hissed contempt and triumph.

"Go then," she gasped to the empty room. "And see what becomes of a griffin that abuses magic. I will screech victory over your corpse."

Oeka returned to the audience chamber, moving with difficulty on her weak legs. She was vibrating with anger.

Laela wasn't in her room, and the small griffin's rage increased. Her human was with that vile monster that called itself her brother. The heir to the throne!

She rested a moment and went back down the tower, to the dining hall. Sure enough, there was Laela, sitting with Kullervo and eating lunch. Neither of them did more than glance up when Oeka came in.

She stood in the doorway, sensing their presence and motions in ways that went beyond mere sight and sound. No fear from them. No reverence either.

That was when she made up her mind.

Laela.

She sensed that Laela had asked what was wrong.

I am going downward, she told her. *To the dark place where the stone humans lie. It is time for me to work my magic again, in privacy this time. I will claim the last of my powers.*

No, Laela's mind said.

This must be done, Oeka said, and left.

To her astonishment, Laela tried to stop her. She felt the human's arms around her neck, pulling her back, while the mind driving them said, *No, no,* again. *Don't do it. Too dangerous. You could die.*

Oeka struggled, but her body felt stiff and awkward. All of a sudden, terrible, crushing despair came to her. She, who had once been so strong, was now unable to overpower a mere human! And all her senses, her sight, her hearing . . .

Confused and angry, she bit Laela's arm. It released her at once.

I must do this, she said. *I must be strong.*

This time, nobody tried to stop her when she left.

She walked down and down, following the ramps she knew so well, down and down to the lowest level of the tower, below the earth itself, where a door waited. It was closed, but she used her mind to summon a servant, who opened it for her.

It was utterly dark beyond, but that didn't make any difference to her now. She could sense everything around her, in the dark or the light.

She went down the steps and into the dirt-lined chamber where the dead humans lay in their stone boxes. How ridiculous, she thought, to keep a dead thing this way. When a thing was dead, it was nothing. It became an object, one with no use. Why keep the bones of a kill after they had been stripped bare?

Oeka found a place in the middle of the floor and spent some time churning up the soil to make a comfortable spot to lie—more from habit than anything else. That done, she settled down on her belly and allowed herself to relax. She could still feel the heart of the Spirit Cave lying in her stomach. There had been no food to move it out.

Fear twinged in her again. She dismissed it. She had made herself weak in the body, yes, but it had been a necessary sacrifice. Soon, she would make herself so powerful that not even her physical form would hold her back. Soon, she would have more magic than any other griffin that had ever lived.

Oeka put forth the captured spirits, and began again.

31

It Begins Again

"War."

Caedmon Taranisäii felt his fists clench, the fingers pressing inward until the knuckles turned white. Tears burned behind his eyes, but he wouldn't let them show.

"War," he said again, gritting it out from between his teeth. "This is war."

Beside him, his partner, Shar, extended her talons. "Yes. We shall make it war. There is no other way."

"Sweet Night God," Caedmon muttered to himself. "How did it come to this?"

"We live in a land built by fighting," said Shar. "And we ourselves were made for it. Accept that."

Caedmon couldn't take it any more. He moved away and began to pace around the room, shoulders hunched. "I can't believe it, I just . . . can't. It's all so much, so fast . . ."

Shar turned her head to watch him. "Yes," she admitted. "It has been a strange time, and so many bad things have happened in only a few days. But we must accept that. Our path is clear; that is what we must look toward now."

Caedmon stopped pacing. His hands opened and closed compulsively. "My father, dead. My sister. My mother. All of them gone—I just can't . . ." His voice cracked. "I can't believe they're gone."

Shar came closer, opening a wing to cover him like a shield. "But they *are* gone, Caedmon, and my own father with them. You and I are alive, and we are strong. We must ensure that we do not go to the soil as they have done, and we must fight to destroy the ones who have done this."

"Going to the soil" was a griffish term for dying. Caedmon struggled, fighting against the tears that wanted to escape. In the end, he twisted them into rage. He pressed himself against Shar, taking strength from her own lithe, red-feathered bulk. "You're right. I know we can do this. The North will know what the half-breed did. We'll unite them and see justice done."

"Revenge will be ours," said Shar. "And so will the throne of Tara."

"Yes," Caedmon said grimly. He stood taller, willing himself to be strong. "I am the last true Taranisäii, and it's my duty to protect Tara from Southerners and half-breed traitors. I'll purify this land just like my cousin Arenadd did. I swear it on my family's graves."

Shar purred, the sound vibrating softly in her flanks. "And I shall fight for our lives and our honour. You are my human, my precious human, and I shall protect you always and tear your enemies apart with my talons. That is my own duty, and my own . . . vow."

"Then it's settled," said Caedmon, keeping his voice steady. "We'll go and talk to Garnoc. Time to make plans."

Shar yawned. "Yes. Plans are human things; I trust you to make them well."

"I will." Caedmon picked up his sickle from the table by his bed, and the two of them left.

It had been only a few days since the worst had happened—a few days before the last survivor had arrived at Fruitsheart with the awful news of what had happened at Warwick.

All done, all of it, on the Queen's orders. Queen Laela, the false Taranisäii. Laela, the half-breed. Laela, who claimed to be the daughter of King Arenadd, after she had murdered him and stolen his throne. Laela, the traitor with the impure and treacherous blue eyes of a Southerner.

The mere thought of her filled Caedmon with hatred.

He walked down the stairs of Fruitsheart's Eyrie, taking them two at a time. At nineteen years old, he was tall and long-legged and had just grown his first beard—a small thing that ringed his mouth, which he was careful to keep neat at all times, like the curly hair that people said made him look like his great cousin. He had always taken pride in that fact, even after he had lost the awe he had once had for the former King. When other people pointed out the resemblance, it was always as a compliment.

Just now, he wished he could be as strong as Arenadd had been, as decisive . . . *he* had always made it look easy. But, then, nobody could ever imagine Arenadd Taranisäii's ever being uncertain, not even Caedmon, who had grown up so close to him.

Shar reached the tower's middle level ahead of him and waited, tail twitching. "Garnoc is close by; I smell him."

Caedmon managed to smile as he joined her. "You and your amazing beak. I wish I could do that."

"You do not need to," said Shar. "You have me. Come now, let us catch him."

Garnoc must have been expecting them because he emerged from the room he was in just as they arrived. Big and powerful despite his advancing years, his dark grey hair cropped close to his head, Garnoc inclined his head briefly by way of greeting. "Sir—"

"We have to talk," said Caedmon. "Now. Where's Hafwen?"

"In the healers' quarters," said Garnoc. "Sir, there's somethin'—"

"Go and fetch her, then," said Caedmon. "We should—" He finally realised that Garnoc was trying to say something, and broke off irritably. "What?"

"Sir, it's yer mother."

"I know she's dead, Garnoc," said Caedmon. "And I'm going to avenge her. That's what we're going to talk about with Hafwen, so come on! We have to make plans, and fast, before—"

"Sir—"

"There's no time to waste," Caedmon snapped.

"Sir, yer mother," said Garnoc. "She's—"

Caedmon couldn't bear to hear her mentioned. "I told you, Garnoc, I know she's dead. I don't need to know anything more than that they killed her."

"But she's not dead!" Garnoc shouted at last. "That's what I'm tryin' to tell yer!"

Caedmon froze. "What?"

Shar's tail ceased its endless twitch. "What?"

"She ain't dead," Garnoc said again. "They found her, collapsed outside the city gate. She's in with the healers right now. I just found out an' came to let yer know, sir."

Caedmon couldn't move. "That's impossible," he whispered.

"It's her," Garnoc said flatly. "I saw her."

"Is . . . is she hurt?"

"Don't think so. Just exhausted. I reckon—"

Caedmon heard no more. He ran. Away from Garnoc, away from Shar, away toward the healers' quarters as fast as he could go. Someone got in his way; he didn't even slow down or try to dodge him, or hear his complaint when a blow from his shoulder sent him sprawling. The door that lay between him and his mother reared up in front of him; he threw himself against it so hard it hurt, grabbing the handle with sweat-slicked fingers. The door opened inward, and he stumbled on and into the room, mouth opening to call. "Mother!"

"Caedmon!" Hafwen was there, turning to look. Not his mother, only old Hafwen. He looked blankly at her and went straight to the bed, and there . . . there . . .

Saeddryn Taranisäii lay among the pillows, apparently asleep. She looked tiny and fragile, her face pale. The eye-patch she had once worn was gone, and he could see the ugly, gnarled hole where her eye had been. She could have been dead, but her chest moved up and down very gently under the covers.

Caedmon's mad rush finally came to a halt when he saw her. "Mum . . . Mother . . ."

"Aye," Hafwen said softly. "The great an' holy Saeddryn Taranisäii, come back to us when we thought she was lost forever."

Caedmon reached down to touch his mother's face. It was cold, terribly. "How? How could she be here?"

"Don't know," said Hafwen, in her dry old voice. "All I know is the guards over the gate saw her walk up through the snow an' collapse. They don't know how she got so close without bein' spotted sooner."

"She wasn't with Aenae?"

"No, no sign of any griffin about."

Caedmon hadn't taken his eyes off his mother's face. "She can't have walked here . . ."

"Don't worry about it," Hafwen advised. "She'll tell ye about it when she wakes. For now, just be glad ye got her back, boy."

Caedmon never even considered taking offence at her tone; you didn't bother with ceremony around Hafwen. Instead, he forgot he was a grown man, forgot he was a griffiner, forgot he was a leader, and lifted his mother into his arms. He held her tightly, frightened by how thin she felt, and murmured, "You're safe now, Mother. You're safe. I'll protect you now, I swear."

Far away, deep in one of the five towers that made Malvern's great Eyrie, someone else stirred. Senneck opened her eyes and lifted her head from her talons. Beside her in the darkness she could feel the warm shape of Kullervo.

She moved, shifting very carefully away from him. He stirred and mumbled in his sleep, and she waited until he stilled again before sliding away and standing up. Kullervo rolled over into the hollow left by her body, snuggling into the straw, and slept on.

Senneck crooned softly over him, like a mother over her chicks, and slipped away.

Once she was well out of sight and hearing, she sped up, hurrying off through the Eyrie as quickly and quietly as she could. She had to get back before she was missed, and Kullervo would fret if he woke up and found her gone. Besides, he would ask questions, and questions about this night were something she didn't want.

The Eyrie passages were only dimly lit—most of the lamps had been snuffed out, and only a few were left in case of an emergency. There was nobody about, and Senneck was glad—and even gladder that the carpets on the floor helped to muffle the sound of her paws.

She travelled through the tower, always heading downward, down and down toward the lowest levels, moving with the grace of the predator she was.

It never really occurred to her to think about the irony of where she was now. She had once been Arenadd's sworn enemy, but now she was fighting on behalf of the Kingdom he had built, and had made his son her human. An Eyrie was an Eyrie, and humans were humans, and griffins had no concept of betrayal. Not betrayal of ideas, anyway.

This time, she vowed yet again, this time it would be different. She had already struck the first blow against the real danger that stood in her way. Soon, it would be time to make the second.

Carried along by these thoughts, Senneck finally reached the tower's ground level—a place she would normally never bother to visit and, in fact, had never seen before tonight. But a combination of scent, and a deeper sense, one only griffins could use, had led her to it. She halted here and began to scent around, searching for her goal. In the end she found it by following, not her nose, but the other sense—the sense that felt for traces of magic. It was harder than she might have expected; *finding* magic here was easy. The trouble was that there was so much of it that the source was difficult to locate. She closed her eyes and let herself relax, turning slowly until the tingle in her neck and head increased, and she stopped. When she opened her eyes, she saw a wall with a tapestry—a tapestry that was stirring ever so slightly.

Senneck went straight to it and thrust it out of the way, and, sure enough, there was a tunnel behind it, sloping downward and into a smell of earth and stone. It was only just wide enough for her to fit—she was thankful now that she had always been slim and that age and bad living had made her even slimmer. Holding her wings up over her head to keep them out of the way, trying even harder now not to make a sound, she descended into the darkness.

The further she went, the stronger the sense of magic became, until her entire body thrummed with it. In her throat, her own power stirred, wanting to break loose. She fought it down as if it were a chunk of food caught in her crop, and moved on.

Toward the end of the tunnel, she stumbled and lurched to one side when her forepaw bumped into an obstruction. She stopped to sniff at it. A human carcass, lying where it had fallen. She had a good idea of what had killed it: the very same thing that had stopped any other humans from coming to find their dead friend. The level of magic in the air right here was so huge that only a griffin could survive it. And maybe not even all of those.

Senneck could feel it beginning to affect her mind, confusing her senses with flashes of images and sounds that weren't there, scents of things that didn't exist, the touch of objects and creatures that had never been real. Shuddering, she pushed them away with all her strength and forced herself to see the wooden barrier that had finally blocked her way. She had no way of opening it, not without alerting what lurked on the other side. But she had never intended to.

With a great effort, trembling now with the strain of keeping her mind and body together in this sea of magical and mental energy, she crouched, with her head touching the door and opened her beak wide. Muscles flexed in her throat, the same ones used to expand it when she swallowed large prey. She retched a little with the effort, but, ignoring her instinctive urge to close her throat and leave this place, she pushed.

Her crop opened, exposing the strange little organ that stored her magic. It pulsated like a heart, flickering faintly green. It had never meant to be exposed this way, and it shrivelled a little, as if trying to protect itself. But Senneck held her position, allowing herself to gasp slightly as the magic in the air touched the gland and began to be absorbed by it.

She stayed there for a long time, unmoving, feeling it as she took in the raw magic that had been concentrated here in a way magic was never meant to be. The process held her rigid, just as when she wielded her own power, and it would take a great effort of will to break free.

All the same, she found room for a little glimmer of smug satisfaction. The griffin on the other side of this door had no idea of what she was doing. No idea that trying to weave this much magic into her own body would inevitably destroy her. No idea that her foolish quest for power had given her rival this opportunity. No idea that this was exactly what Senneck had wanted her to do and had deliberately provoked her toward.

Oeka thought her youth and magical strength made her

invulnerable, but Senneck knew better. She was older, but she was wiser, and she would win. By the time Oeka emerged—if she ever did—Senneck would be long gone, and Kullervo with her. Safe, and ready to bide her time until her day came again.

When she had absorbed as much magic as she felt she could contain, she broke away and backed off up the tunnel. Once she had reached the entrance again, she turned and hurried away back up the tower. Her throat felt swollen and uncomfortable, and she knew what she had done and what she was going to do would take a toll on her. But she could bear it, and she would.

All for Kullervo's sake.

All for her own sake.

32

The Dark Lady

Darkness was all Saeddryn saw in her stupor. The darkness of death, where her master waited.

The Night God stood over her, pale and graceful, primal in her nakedness, her single eye commanding. *You have done well so far, but do not allow yourself to be blinded.*

"Never," said Saeddryn. She looked up with absolute faith written all over her face. "Never, Master. Thankye so much, for givin' me back my sight . . ."

A gift, for your faith.

Saeddryn frowned. "I remember when Arenadd's fingers were broken by the enemy. They never healed properly . . . couldn't understand why, if he was . . ." She trailed off, embarrassed to have nearly questioned her master's power out loud.

They were broken because he did not listen to me, did not obey me, said the Night God. *He denied me in that prison, and I could not help him. Even then I could have given him back the use of his fingers, but he did not ask me to. He preferred to remain a cripple.*

"He didn't understand," said Saeddryn. "He was never a real believer, not even after he became yer avatar." *But I am.* She didn't say that part out loud, but she knew the Night God would sense it in her anyway.

The Night God smiled slightly. *There are more important things to do now than discuss your lost cousin. Wake now.*

And Saeddryn woke up. Her eye opened, blinking quickly

to focus. To her surprise, she found herself stifling a yawn. "Aaaahhh . . ."

"Mother!" The shout came from nearby, and before she could sit up, hands were touching her, and a face appeared in her field of vision, frowning and pale with concern.

Saeddryn smiled. "Caedmon. Thank the Night God, I came in time."

Caedmon looked wan and disbelieving, almost afraid, but he returned the smile. "I thought . . . you were dead."

I am, Saeddryn thought, but she couldn't make herself say it yet. She needed time to try to come to terms with it herself first. Reality came rushing back, and she sat up sharply. "Where are my boots?"

Caedmon opened his mouth to protest but backed off when he saw her face. "You didn't have any when you got here."

"Fine." Saeddryn got out of bed, barefoot, and suddenly realised she didn't have any clothes on, either. She gave a strangled cry of embarrassment and grabbed a blanket to cover herself up, but too late.

Caedmon had already seen what the sheets had hidden, and his eyes widened in utter horror. "Holy shadows, what—? What happened—?"

Saeddryn tried vainly to hide it, but she quickly saw it was pointless. She sighed and let the blanket slip away, bowing her head to look at the ruin that her ageing body had become.

Long, hideous scars spread from her neck to her stomach and down over her thighs. They were jagged and red, so deep in places that they had obviously exposed bone. One had cut straight through her left breast, which still had a deep channel in it where Senneck's talons had slashed through it and down onto the skin below, reaching all the way to her pelvis.

Caedmon had gone white. "What did that? What happened to you? How—?"

Anger and humiliation made Saeddryn's face burn—she turned away and snatched up the gown that lay draped over a chair, pulling it on roughly. "It doesn't matter. It's healed." *Healed when it shouldn't have,* her mind said treacherously. *Left as a reminder forever.*

Even Caedmon must have guessed that she couldn't possibly have survived what had left those scars. He opened and closed his mouth a few times before shaking his head quickly and changing the subject. "How did you get here? Did you escape from Warwick?"

Saeddryn adjusted the gown. "Yes," she said shortly.

"Were you the only one?" said Caedmon. "Were there others? Did Arddryn—?"

"No."

The room suddenly seemed very cold.

Caedmon bowed his head. "I thought . . . hoped . . ." He took a step closer to her. "But we've got you back at least," he said. "At least we've got you." He took her in a tight embrace.

Saeddryn hugged him back, just as glad in her own way to have him there. "I ran here," she said quietly. "*Ran*. I had to get here before they did, *had* to, before they got to ye, before it was too late."

"I'm all right," said Caedmon, not letting go. "They haven't attacked yet. But how did you come here so *fast*? Did Aenae—?"

Saeddryn pulled away. "Aenae's dead," she said. "Like Arddryn. Like Nerth. Like everyone at Warwick."

Caedmon shuddered. "Oh, gods . . ."

Saeddryn took his hand. "Come now," she said gently. "We're Taranisäiis. The last true Taranisäiis. It's up to us t'be strong now, t'show our people the way just as we did before. And trust me, Caedmon, the half-breed bitch is not going to win."

Caedmon's own expression hardened. "You're right. I've already vowed that."

"Good!" Saeddryn let go and made for the door. "Let's go. We've got plannin' to do, an' not much time t'do it in!"

Caedmon hurried after her. Another man might have tried to argue or suggested that she needed rest, but he knew his mother too well to bother.

Shar was waiting outside, and she almost reared up when she saw Saeddryn. "It is you!"

Saeddryn stopped and inclined her head toward the griffin. "Hello, Shar. Yes, I'm back t'help yer human."

Shar looked quickly at Caedmon. "And Aenae?"

"He's dead," said Saeddryn, in a short, flat kind of way.

Shar's look toward Caedmon didn't show the triumph she

must have felt, but he knew it was there. Without Aenae, Saeddryn wasn't a griffiner any more, and the implications of that were major.

If Saeddryn had noticed any of this, she didn't show it. "Where's the council chamber, Caedmon? Haven't been there in too long . . ."

"This way, Mother." Caedmon went to her side and guided her away toward it, casting a warning look back at Shar. The griffin ignored it.

Caedmon had expected Saeddryn to stay close to him and maybe need his help to walk, but he was wrong. She strode on ahead, apparently remembering the way now, and Caedmon, staying respectfully behind her, noticed something had changed. Saeddryn had lost the stiff gait of the old woman she was. Now she moved with a new and terrible grace, every stride full of certainty and power that felt chillingly familiar.

Caedmon's neck prickled. What was going on here? How could this be . . . ?

Saeddryn reached the council chamber and shoved the doors open. There was nobody in there, but she went to the circle of benches at the centre and sat down. "Where're the others? There's talkin' to be done."

Caedmon nodded briefly and went to stand on the governor's platform, along with Shar. "We'll summon them now."

"Yes," said Shar. "They must know what has happened and hear what she has to say." With that, she lifted her head and screeched her own name to the ceiling. The chamber, uniquely designed for it, magnified the sound and sent it out through the channels in the walls and roof, spreading it to the rest of the tower. It didn't take long for other griffins to hear it, and in a very short time Hafwen and Garnoc arrived. Both of them greeted their old friend Saeddryn with affection. Saeddryn only replied with a brief look and a muttered word. She looked almost indifferent. Hafwen and Garnoc, old campaigners who had become council members despite not being griffiners, sat down on either side of her—but kept their distance. Their looks toward her were wary.

Shar screeched again a few times, for good measure, and the rest of the council arrived in ones and twos. All of them were griffiners; younger men and women chosen by Caedmon for their talents and loyalty. Lady Kaefan, the Lords Cadan and Rees, and Lady Myfina, the youngest of the lot. All of them openly stared at Saeddryn—one or two even exclaimed their astonishment out loud. At a look from Caedmon, they quickly took their seats, with their partners remaining as looming presences behind them. To Caedmon's surprise, Saeddryn didn't stand up, and only stayed quietly where she was. Her single eye moved around the room, pausing occasionally to stare at different people, but her expression stayed impenetrable.

Caedmon had seen this look before, and it meant one of two things. Either she was very angry or very upset. Either one was very unsettling.

He cleared his throat. "Apologies for bringing you all in here so suddenly, but obviously it's important. My mother, Saeddryn Taranisäii"—he gestured at her, expecting her to get up, but she still didn't—"is alive and has come to find us. The only survivor from the outrage the half-breed committed at Warwick. I thought it was important for all of you to see her yourselves and to hear what she has to say."

He looked hopefully at Saeddryn, along with everybody else. At last, she stood up and came forward. Caedmon stepped down from the platform, along with Shar, and let her take their place.

Saeddryn stood there a moment, silently. She looked pale, but strong. Old, but ageless. Thin, but terrifying.

Once the silence had drawn out and become steadily grimmer and colder, she raised her head and looked at everyone. She didn't look angry or threatening, but there was something in her gaze that made everyone there—even the griffins—shift around uncomfortably.

"Warwick's destroyed," she said at last, in a low voice. "Nerth is dead. Morvudd is dead. Nerthach is dead. Penllyn, dead. Seerae, Yissh, and Raekae, all dead. Torc Taranisäii, my husband, is dead. My daughter Arddryn is dead. Crushed to death. Her partner Rakek died with her. Aenae, my partner—dead."

She listed out the dead in a cold, flat tone, dropping each name like a stone slab. All the humans there bowed their heads. Some even shed a few tears. Even some of the griffins huffed softly or closed their eyes sadly as they thought of their fellows.

"The fall of Warwick was a day we'll never forget," Saeddryn said softly. "I know I never will. And I confess that when I went into the Eyrie tower there an' found my daughter's dead body, left for me to find, I cursed the Night God right there an' then. Decided it was all over. We'd been abandoned. I'd been abandoned." She smiled very slightly. "But I was wrong. I've been sent here to tell ye that. Ye are not abandoned. True Northerners are never abandoned, no matter how often it looks that way. I believe it now, an' my message to ye is that ye should never give up hope."

The councillors smiled back at her, some standing straighter. Caedmon, watching, couldn't help but smile a little as well. *This* was a side of his mother that he recognised very well. Listening to her now, it was easy to imagine her back in the beautiful Moon Temple in Malvern, directing the sacred ceremonies.

But that was something she would never do again, Caedmon thought, losing his smile when he remembered what had happened to the Temple. Burned to the ground, almost certainly on the Queen's orders. When that had happened, he had known for certain that there were no depths she wouldn't sink to.

"Now then," Saeddryn went on, suddenly businesslike. "Here's what I know. Lord Iorwerth an' Kaanee, his partner, have taken the unpartnered an' gone back t'Malvern. But they've left a garrison in Warwick. Most likely once the half-breed's had a think about the situation she'll send them on here. Like it or not, Fruitsheart's the centre of all this now. That's all I know for now, but there's one other thing I'm going t'tell ye that I've learnt."

"What's that, Mother?" said Caedmon, using the familiar term without any embarrassment. "Anything you know could help us now."

Saeddryn acknowledged him with a nod. "The half-breed has someone workin' for her other than that poor fool Iorwerth an' that lot he commands. Someone just as dangerous, in a way. Maybe more so. A pair of spies. Both of them look harmless, but they aren't."

"Who are they?" Lady Myfina asked.

"One is an old griffin. Brown, with blue eyes." Saeddryn's own eye glinted as she gave Hafwen and Garnoc a meaningful look. "Her name is Senneck. Do ye know that name?"

They looked puzzled. "Can't say I do," Hafwen muttered, but hesitantly.

Saeddryn smiled without humour. "She's an old friend from the war. Once partnered to Erian the Bastard."

"Her!" Garnoc exclaimed. "I thought she died in Malvern!"

"So did everyone else, but she's back now an' working for the half-breed," said Saeddryn. "Remembers me very well, an' that's probably why."

"Who's the other one, then?" said Garnoc.

"The other one." Saeddryn's mouth twisted. "The other one is . . . odd."

"Human, or griffin?" Shar asked.

Saeddryn's mouth twisted even further. "Both." She rubbed her forehead, and ploughed on. "I don't understand it, but this is all I know. Sometimes he's a small grey griffin. Sometimes he's an ugly man with . . . wings."

"Wings?" said Lord Rees.

"An' a tail," said Saeddryn, unsmiling. "His name's Kullervo. We caught him in Warwick, kept him locked up. He wouldn't talk, but Morvudd had a look at him. He's got some sort of power—he can grow feathers an' fur, turn into a griffin. Morvudd wanted t'find out more, but he escaped on the day Warwick fell. Killed her in the process." Noticing the puzzlement and skepticism on the faces of her listeners, she growled, "Don't look like that. I don't lie. That's what I saw. That's what he is. He looks harmless, but he's dangerous. He tore Morvudd's throat out. Did the same t'four guards on his way out, too. He's with Senneck. They work together—fly around the place spyin' for the half-breed. They're as dangerous as each other."

"Are ye sure?" said Hafwen.

Saeddryn gave her a deathly look. "Senneck is the one who killed Arddryn. An' Rakek, an' Aenae as well. All in the same day. She's a survivor, an' all she cares about is revenge. That makes her deadly. Now." She glanced at Caedmon. "That's all

I know. Now ye must talk it over, an' decide what to do." With that, she stepped off the platform and returned to her seat, leaving Caedmon to take over.

He retook his place, hiding his utter astonishment, and did his best to take the initiative. "Er . . . ahem. Yes. As you've heard, things are bad. With Iorwerth on the half-breed's side, the unpartnered will also be on—"

"With *Kaanee*, the unpartnered will be against us," Shar interrupted. "They have not forgotten that it was he who led them to turn against the Mighty Kraal and so gave them great power. He has their respect, and seems likely to keep it."

"Exactly," Caedmon said smoothly. "And with the unpartnered against us, as well as Malvern's army—and whatever's left of Warwick's, if they can take control of it—that gives them an advantage. And, unfortunately, we have the weaker stronghold. Everyone knows that Warwick is the most-well-fortified city in Tara. But with the enemy occupying it—and you can bet Iorwerth will have left some unpartnered there—we just don't have the numbers to take it back. But we can't afford to stay here. Fruitsheart might have plenty of pears, but it doesn't have good walls. It'll be far too easy to overrun. And if that happened, it would be all over for us. We have to leave, and soon, and I know exactly where we should go."

"Where?" asked Myfina.

"Skenfrith."

"No," said Garnoc. "It's too close t'Malvern."

"That's the whole point," said Caedmon. "We establish ourselves in Skenfrith, and from there we can launch an assault on Malvern itself. We strike hard, and we strike fast, and we do it without any warning. If we can take Malvern and kill the half-breed, we win the war—and we win it by killing as few Northerners as possible." He gave Garnoc a look. "Remember, this isn't like the war you fought. This isn't against Southerners. It's against *our own people*. If I'm going to become King as I should, then my first duty is to my people. I refuse to go to Tara's throne by wading through Northern blood. The longer this war drags on, the more of us are killed, and I won't let that happen." Caedmon sighed. "You know, we keep some Southerner-written books in our libraries. King Arenadd insisted that we keep them, so we wouldn't forget what they were like. What *Tara* was like back then. I read some of the things they wrote about us." His expression became distant as he remembered the exact words. "'Left unattended, the Northerner quickly reverts to his natural state. An ungoverned piece of land, left in his hands, soon breaks down into anarchy . . . left to rule themselves, Northerners at once turn on each other and will fight until not one of them is left alive.'"

Several of the listeners actually growled at this.

Caedmon's face had darkened, too. "That's what they believed about us. Now we *have* been left to rule ourselves at last, just as they feared. Should we do what that sun-worshipping scum suggested, and fight until none of us are left? Or will we show the world that we can be better than that? Will we show our people and our country that we can be worthy to own Tara and all its beautiful cities?" He looked penetratingly at them all. "I, for one, intend to do everything in my power to lead and fight like a griffiner and not a barbarian. The only question is, are you with me?"

The councillors cheered. Even Hafwen looked impressed. Shar, fired up by her human's speech, crouched low and snarled, tail lashing. The other griffins there responded with snarls and hisses of their own, and aggressive calls directed at the enemy they would soon fight. Every griffin loved a fight. They were made for it.

"I agree with Caedmon," Lord Rees said once the excitement had died down.

"And I," said Cadan.

"So do I," said Lady Kaefan.

Lady Myfina gave Caedmon a smile that made him blush. "Nobody could say no to you now!"

"Go for it!" Hafwen interrupted, thumping the floor with her stick. "The boy's right. Nothin' good's gonna come of fightin' our own, so the sooner we end this the better. The half-breed's the only one we really need dead, so let's get to it!"

The councillors laughed and nodded their agreement. Even Garnoc grinned.

"Right, then!" said Caedmon, taking charge. "Time to go to work! Start preparing. Pass the news on to the city, see to it that everyone here who supports us comes along. Men, women—anyone who can use a weapon. I don't care if they're carrying chair-legs and rocks, I want them in Skenfrith with us. Empty the armoury, leave the treasury, and let that twit of a governor out of his cell and tell him he can take charge again once we've gone. No sense leaving one of our own behind to get killed. Organise supplies, pack clean underwear—you can figure out the rest!"

The council broke up in a mood of purposeful excitement, leaving Caedmon and Shar behind. Aside from them, only Saeddryn stayed.

Only Saeddryn hadn't laughed, or smiled, or said anything at all once Caedmon had begun. Nor had she left her seat.

Caedmon turned to her now, suddenly awkward. She was looking at him, and though her face was expressionless, he felt judged. "Er . . . how did I do?"

Saeddryn continued to fix him with that impenetrable stare. Then, at last, she smiled. "For a while I thought I was seein' Arenadd there in front of me. Not as he was when ye knew him, but as he was back when we were young." Her smile saddened. "I wish ye could have seen him back then. How he was. Full of fire an' passion, full of rage. A Northern warrior through an' through. All he cared about was winning Tara back in the Night God's name. That an' that woman of his. But after the war was done, he never was the same. Maybe he never could be unless he was fightin' someone. Without him . . ."

"You don't wish we had him back now, do you?"

Saeddryn shook herself. "What? No. No, not now. His time was done. This is our time now. Yer own time, Caedmon." She stood up and came toward him, reaching for his hands. "Arenadd's time is over, an' so is mine. This is your war, Caedmon. Yer own rebellion. Ye must win it, not me. Ye an'—" She nodded at Shar. "Ye an' Shar."

"You mean—?" Caedmon glanced at Shar.

Saeddryn nodded slowly. "I'm not a griffiner any more. Not without Aenae, Night God bless him. I can't lead now I've lost him, an' I don't want to, either. The throne's meant for ye, Caedmon, an' I'll do whatever I can t'guide ye there. Look on me as a useful servant, to use how ye choose. I'll let ye do the judging yerself."

Caedmon was surprised. "You'll still be on the council—"

"No." Saeddryn grimaced. "I've been on enough councils. I'll advise ye if ye want, but it's down to ye an' the offsiders ye choose. Garnoc an' Hafwen can be a great help too—make sure ye listen to them. I'm just . . . a helper. Use me however ye see fit."

Caedmon said nothing. He held her hands in his, and he could feel the coldness.

Saeddryn didn't let go. "It's been a long road," she murmured, apparently to herself. "I thought it ended long ago. But I'm glad t'have this chance, this last chance t'set things right . . ."

"You're like him, aren't you?" Caedmon said softly. "You've become like him."

Saeddryn nodded jerkily.

"You came back, like he did. That's why you've got those scars. That's how you got away. You're . . ." Caedmon reached out, and she didn't resist when he touched her neck. He let go and moved away sharply a moment later, his face turning pale. "My gods. It's true. You're—"

"Yes," said Saeddryn. She touched his face, holding it between her hands. "Ye look like yer father, ye know. I know people say ye're like Arenadd, but I see yer father in ye. Poor Torc. He was the sweetest man I ever knew. He deserved a better wife than me."

Caedmon said nothing. He could feel her hands, her cool, dead hands touching his face. It made his heart flutter.

"I'm not back," Saeddryn told him quietly. "Not really. I can't be a real part of the living world again. Before, I didn't understand why Arenadd became like he did—why he hid away, why he seemed so distant even when he was right there in front of ye. He was a dead man among the living, an' he was more alone than any living man could ever be. Ye can't imagine what that feels like, Caedmon. I couldn't either, when I was alive. Now I wish I could've understood, that I could've been kinder . . . but how could I? He was in a different world than me. Than all of us. Now I know. Now the Night God's made me see for myself."

"You don't look so different," said Caedmon, trying to smile.

"But I am, an' I know it," said Saeddryn. "Still, I won't complain. I'm grateful that the Night God gave me this chance t'be here with ye, t'see this whole thing through an' know I didn't die in vain."

"Won't you live forever, though?" said Caedmon.

"No. The Night God made me a promise. When this is over, I can go t'my rest at last. After all . . . by then I'll have nothing more t'keep me here."

Caedmon let out a sob and pulled her into his arms. "Mother—"

Saeddryn held him in return. "There, there, Caddy, no need t'be sad. This is a gift. The Night God's gift."

Caedmon almost sobbed again at the sound of his childhood nickname, but he pulled himself together and only let himself hold her a moment longer.

"I have the power now," Saeddryn murmured. "Use it. Use me. Send me after whoever ye choose, an' I'll kill them for ye. Ask me t'get somethin', I'll steal it. Whatever ye need. But ye are the one who must decide."

Shar had been listening to all this in silence. "*Kraeaina kran ae* is right," she said. "We have a powerful follower in her. Think quickly, and decide. We can have her kill whomever we choose."

Caedmon's bright-eyed look faded, and he scowled as the look of a leader returned. "I know just the one."

Saeddryn smiled savagely. "I thought so."

Kullervo woke up feeling cold. Fear gripped him briefly, and he groped around until his hand touched warm feathers. He slid back over toward Senneck and relaxed against her flank, his heartbeat slowing again.

She stirred in the gloom. "I did not mean to wake you."

He turned his head a little, her feathers tickling his face. "I thought you were gone."

"Do not be afraid," Senneck rumbled. "I am here, as I always will be."

"Yes," he sighed. "I know. Don't worry about it." The last few words were mumbled, and his breathing deepened as he slipped back into sleep.

It was a shallow sleep this time, though, and dreams came with it—half-formed dreams whose vagueness only made them more unsettling. He dreamed of bars, pressing in against his face and arms, and a room that grew smaller and smaller, until he couldn't breathe. Those were old dreams, from a past he had barely described to his new friends. But other dreams came, too.

He dreamed of flying in his griffin shape, but his feathers moulted away, and he fell, turning over and over to a ground that rushed toward him without ever getting any closer. As he struggled to save himself, it became a face—one-eyed, terrible, the mouth opening wide to swallow him whole.

He woke up shivering and sweating, and light touched his eyes. *Dawn,* he thought confusedly.

When he sat up, the real world made a welcome return. Morning had come, and Senneck was there, placidly grooming her feathers. The yellowish light touched her grey beak and tinged her sandy brown feathers with gold. Kullervo stayed still and watched her with a secret joy in his heart, noting how her sky-blue eyes half-closed when the light touched them. He could smell her feathers and fur, that warm, rich scent that every griffin's coat had but which was never so sweet except when it came from her. Her head moved in quick, sure strokes, dragging her beak over her wing feathers with a soft, rasping sound. There was something so certain about her, Kullervo thought—it was in everything she did. Even though he had only known her a few months, she had become the most solid and constant thing in his life, and he had come to accept that she always knew what to do, was always strong, always resolute. That must be why she made him feel so safe.

A smile lit up Kullervo's face, and his broken teeth made it no less sweet or gentle.

Senneck's head turned sharply toward him, making him freeze, but she only said, "You are awake. Come now, groom and make yourself ready. We leave today."

"Of course!" Kullervo stood up, still a little unsteady on his legs, and rubbed a hand through his hair. "I suppose I should make the change now, then," he said reluctantly.

"No," said Senneck. "You are much too weak to risk using magic now."

"But I have to fly to—"

"*I* shall fly," said Senneck. "Am I not your griffin now? It is expected of me to carry you with me when we have business far away."

"Oh. Yes." Kullervo fidgeted, obviously still unused to their newly made partnership.

Senneck nudged him gently with her beak. "It is no burden to me, Kullervo. Even in human shape, you have the light bones of a griffin. You are easy to carry. But I would carry you even if you were the fattest human in this Eyrie because you are *my* human."

"If I were fat, I'd lose weight." Kullervo grinned.

"I would force you to," said Senneck. "I will carry *you*, not you and every meal you have eaten!"

"But you said—"

"That is not important. Groom now and eat."

"Oh. Yes. I should get something for you to eat first—"

"No," said Senneck. "I will not eat until we arrive. I can fly further on an empty stomach. But you may eat."

"All right then," said Kullervo. "I'll try and be quick . . ."

Senneck sat placidly and watched him scurry around their chambers. He washed his face in the bowl of water provided and gave his hair a quick comb before putting on the new set of clothes that his half-sister had had made especially for him. They were thick and warm, well-made but not obviously expensive—for now, it was better that Kullervo didn't draw too much attention to himself.

The tunic had been specially tailored to give it extra room at the back for his wings. Once wearing it, he looked as if he had a hump.

The trousers had been made slightly baggy, to help hide the tail—that was easier to hide, at least.

Many humans would have given anything to have Kullervo's ability to change into a griffin at will, Senneck thought grimly. But none of them would have taken it if they knew the real cost of having that power. The cost of being a hideous deformity in either shape, the cost of living with both human emotions and griffish instincts—and the agony of the transformation itself. It was easy to underestimate Kullervo, as she had once done herself, but the truth was that it took someone exceptional to live the way he did—or even have reached adulthood at all. But he was weak in other ways, and that was why he needed her.

Kullervo ate some of the food that had been left for him, chewing with evident pain. "Ugh . . . my teeth," he mumbled through a mouthful of bread. "Useless! They'll have to feed me mush like I was a baby!"

"They will heal," said Senneck.

"My *gums* might heal, but I won't grow any new teeth." Kullervo swallowed and grimaced.

"Humans cannot grow new teeth?" said Senneck, genuinely surprised. "I have seen that their claws grow back even when they are cut, and I thought . . ."

"Not teeth," said Kullervo. "If your beak was broken off, it wouldn't grow back. Teeth are the same."

Senneck's tail twitched. "But you have the power to grow a beak. Perhaps you can learn to grow teeth as well."

"That'd be nice," said Kullervo, looking wistfully at an apple.

"We will see," said Senneck. "When you have learnt to use your magic fully, we will see."

Kullervo began to get excited. "Yes, on the ship. You'll teach me, and it's going to be wonderful! We'll see Maijan, and Amoran, and the *sea*!"

"I have seen the sea," said Senneck. "It is nothing special."

"And we'll meet this Amorani Prince—a *real* Amorani Prince!" Kullervo went on, oblivious. "And we'll find a way to stop Saeddryn, I just know it. We'll stop her, then we'll be able to live together here, with Laela." He glanced anxiously at Senneck, but his expression quickly hardened. "And then we can be happy at last."

Silence followed this little declaration. Senneck's expression did not change—because a griffin's expression never does—and Kullervo began to look embarrassed.

"Come here," Senneck said at last. When he did, she rubbed her head against his cheek and purred softly. "You truly are unbreakable, Kullervo. You, who seem so weak, are far stronger than you seem."

"I'm not," he mumbled. "I let them catch me. I let them lock me up and hurt me and break my teeth."

"But you never gave in. You did not let them break you, or destroy your innocence, and that is what makes you who you are." Senneck lifted her head. "Come," she said softly. "You have eaten now, and it is time for us to go to meet Skarok and his human."

"Time for us to go," said Kullervo.

"Yes," said Senneck, and the two of them left side by side, Kullervo holding on to her wing like a child holding its mother's hand.

Up on top of the tower, they found Laela waiting alone. It was unusual to see a griffiner, especially one as highly ranked as herself, without her griffin beside her. But Oeka had more important things on her mind than her human, or her duties. Or at least things she thought were more important.

Laela wore one of her father's robes—this one very thick, with a fur-lined hood and sleeves. Like the rest of his wardrobe, it fitted her perfectly, but then she had always been very much like him.

Kullervo embraced his half-sister warmly. "Good morning!"

She returned the hug. "Nice to see *someone's* up. Did yeh sleep all right?"

Kullervo shrugged. "Senneck and me are all ready to go."

Laela smiled slightly. "I can see that. I bin up here waitin' by myself for Inva to show up. Guess she slept in, but she'd better not keep me waitin' much longer. My arse is about to drop off, it's that bloody cold."

Kullervo chuckled. "That's not how Queens are supposed to talk!"

Laela smirked. "I ain't been Queen long, but I been it long enough to know how I can talk: however I bloody well want to."

"I see your partner has not shown her face," Senneck interrupted. "Has she returned?"

Laela's smirk disappeared. "No, she ain't. No sign of her since she went off. Just more ugly stories about things turnin' weird in the Eyrie. I know where she is, at least."

"In the underground, where the dead are taken," said

Senneck. "Be wary, Laela. Do not go too close. Oeka cannot control the power she is trying to use and will not recognise you. Nor will she be able to protect you."

Laela's mouth tightened. "I know. I just wish I could've stopped her. I wish I understood what she was doin' . . ."

"She does not understand it herself," said Senneck. "Your only hope is to wait until she emerges—there is nothing anyone can do, whether human or griffin."

"I know."

"But I'm sure she'll be all right," Kullervo said uneasily.

They stood together in awkward silence until Inva and her partner, Skarok, finally arrived. Once his human had dismounted, Skarok shook himself and sat on his haunches, staring insolently at Senneck. She stared back stonily.

Inva bowed stiffly to Laela. "I am sorry for my lateness, my Queen."

You didn't stand on ceremony with Laela, but you *always* stood on it for Inva. "Take it easy," Laela said awkwardly. "Yer entourage has gone on ahead—don't want a big flock of griffins all flyin' together in times like these. Now, are yeh ready?"

"We are," said Skarok.

"Good." Laela took a scroll out of her sleeve and handed it to Inva. "This is my message to the Prince. Keep it safe. While yer on the boat, keep an eye out—I got no doubt there'll be a message sent to yeh."

"How do you know?" Kullervo butted in.

"'Cause I already sent one of my own," said Laela. "It'll have got there a while ago."

"Who did you send?" asked Senneck.

"Nobody." Laela grinned and rubbed her hands together. "There was an Amorani diplomat, Lord Vander. He used a little messenger dragon a while back t'bring us a note. Funny little thing; never saw one like it before or after. Well, we never sent it back. I remembered we had it hangin' around, so I gave it a new note an' let it fly off. Inva says them things always get back where they came from; they're better'n pigeons. Anyway, I'm thinkin' yeh'll see the little bugger again sometime, so keep yer eye on the horizon."

Kullervo's eyes shone. "Wow! A real dragon! I thought there was no such thing! Did it breathe fire?"

"Don't be daft," said Laela. "It's just a kind of lizard what has wings for front legs. We had to keep it in a room with a big fire so it wouldn't go torpid. Anyway, that's everythin' I had to tell yeh, so yeh'd better get goin'."

Inva nodded. "I will see your orders carried out. I know Prince Akhane well, and he will not be able to resist the chance to see this woman . . . this heartless one. He will help us."

"He'd better," said Laela. She nodded curtly. "Go on, then. Get goin' an' fly fast!"

Kullervo gave her another quick hug before he got onto Senneck's back. "We won't fail you. I promise. And in the meantime, keep yourself safe! I want you to still be here when I get back."

"You got it." Laela smiled. "Good luck, Kullervo, Inva—Senneck. An' you, Skarok. I'm trustin' you to keep my best diplomat safe!"

"I will not fail you," Skarok said, with all the arrogant certainty of youth. He took off moments later, and Senneck followed. The two griffins flew in tandem, Senneck riding on Skarok's slipstream without embarrassment.

Kullervo turned his head to look back and saw Laela grow smaller and disappear into the distance. She looked very alone, and vulnerable, and he shivered with fear for her.

"Don't worry, Laela," he murmured to himself. "We'll be back. We'll do this for you. I swear we will."

33

A Window to the Past

Oeka, Tara's dominant griffin, ruler of Malvern's Eyrie, master of the unpartnered, owner of the human who was Queen, Oeka the all-powerful—Oeka who had once been green-eyed and beautiful—Oeka was lost.

She had forgotten how to judge the passing of time. Had she slept? She knew she had not eaten. Nor had she felt hungry. To begin with, when she had put herself into the trance needed to work the magic she was building into herself, it had been a struggle to shut out the physical senses that remained and would be a distraction. But as she worked on it, she became more and more effortless, until now . . . now she realised that she couldn't feel her own body any more. She didn't know if she had moved once, or whether she was even still breathing. Locked into the cloud of pure energy that surrounded her, she couldn't panic or even feel fear. Instead, the knowledge came coldly and simply, as a fact and nothing more.

She had already become blind, deaf, and mute. Now she was paralysed as well.

But none of that mattered. She had expected to pay a price, and that price had been paid. The price of her own body and the mundane senses and abilities that went with it. She had been prepared for that, and beside it, the rewards made it almost irrelevant.

What did it matter that she would never fly again, when she

could project her mind anywhere she wanted and be invisible and invulnerable? What did it matter that she would never lay eggs, when she could reach into any mind and take whatever she wanted? What did it matter that she couldn't walk, when she had the ability to crush any enemy in an instant using nothing but pure will-power? And what did it matter that she was blind? Her mind reached out, and it could see so much further, and take in so much more . . .

She reached out now, effortlessly, to touch the mind of her human. Emotions wavered there. Laela felt lonely, but she felt resolute. She was doing well. Holding on. And that arrogant, withered old hen Senneck was gone, which was good. Along with the twisted freak called Kullervo, which was even better. If Oeka had had her way, she would have crushed the pair of them. As it was, she would have to hold herself back. They could still be useful, after all.

No! What use were they, next to her? With this power she had now, she could do anything. Even *Kraeaina kran ae* would be nothing but an insect beside her sheer might. Others might not see the cursed human, but Oeka would sense her mind the moment she came close, and she would squash it in an eye-blink. It would be easy.

Oeka left Laela alone and turned her attention back to her task. She had already decided that she would not stop until she had used all the power she had taken from the Spirit Cave. It was hers—why not use it all? And when she was finished, she would be even more powerful than she was now.

Down in the crypts beneath the Eyrie, the atmosphere distorted. The air became hot and cold by turns, and disturbing noises howled around the walls. Vague images flickered here and there before disappearing. At the very centre of all this, Oeka's body lay on a stone slab, silent and unmoving. It looked dead. Worse than dead. The eyes were white and unseeing, disintegrating outright from lack of use. Feathers and fur had come loose and begun to shed onto the floor. The beak was open, tongue dry and cracking.

With her body useless now, all she had left was her mind.

But even that was starting to fall away.

She kept on going, unable to feel exhaustion, possibly even unable to stop. Piece by piece, the last of the energy was used up. Piece by piece, she felt herself disappear into the void of magic. She forgot how to sense temperature. She forgot what meat tasted like. She forgot the feeling of the wind in her wings. She forgot her mother's face and the first soft stumblings of infancy.

She even began to forget where she was and why she had begun to do this to herself.

But, just as the void gaped ahead of her, the last of the magic finally ran out.

Oeka relaxed out of her trance, and that was it. She found herself in her new form at last.

Pure thought, anchored to nothing. A mind without a body, free to go wherever it chose. A mind so powerful it had almost gone beyond mere thought altogether.

Oeka—or what she had become—drifted up through the levels of the Eyrie to find Laela.

Laela was lonely. Kullervo was gone, and Inva. Oeka was as good as gone. Even Iorwerth was away.

She had never really told anyone just how alone she often felt in the Eyrie. And now it had become even worse. Everyone around her was a potential traitor. Every corner might have an assassin lurking behind it. Once she had been Queen by popular demand. Now, only fear kept her in power. She wasn't going to lie to herself about that. She often felt afraid, and paranoid as well. The rest of the time, she just felt lonely. She had never imagined that ruling would be like this, and now she wondered if she would have taken it if she had. Either way, she knew what she was now. Laela the half-breed, the half-Southerner Queen, the bastard daughter, disliked just as much as the Southern occupiers Arenadd had driven out.

By now, only one thing was really keeping her on the throne, and that was the knowledge that, if any other ruler took over, that ruler would do what her father Arenadd had resisted doing for so long.

Declare war on the South.

Laela didn't feel any particular attachment to the place any more, but what she *did* feel attached to were common people. She wasn't much better than a commoner herself at heart—she definitely talked like one—and she knew who would pay the real price if the Northerners ever went through the mountains and into the warm Southern lands beyond.

Everybody, for a start.

So that was what Laela Taranisäii had become. She came from two different races, and she would protect them from each other come what may. Saeddryn running around with the Night God's gifts was the last thing either side needed.

Still, even Laela needed company, and now that all the people she counted as friends were gone, she resorted to summoning the only other person she remembered having been a friend in the past.

Yorath.

Her former tutor arrived in the Eyrie library, carrying his books, inks, and pens and looking nervous. To her surprise, Laela found he looked younger than she remembered. Smaller, maybe. Less impressive.

Yorath hastily put his things down and bowed to her. "Milady."

Laela looked down at him, not quite able to accept the fact that she had lost her virginity to him not that long ago. "No need for that. How are yeh gettin' on?"

Yorath looked up. "Uh . . . uh, I'm doing well, milady."

"I told yeh; there's no need for that," said Laela. "Sit down. This is our old spot, remember?"

He took a seat at a table, and she sat opposite him. "I'm sorry; I just wasn't expecting this, milady—"

Laela leant over the table. "Call me that one more time an' I'll have yer ears cut off."

Yorath gave up and grinned. "Right ye are, Laela."

"Better." Laela sat back. "Still teachin' kids, then?"

"Yes. Actually, I've been promoted. I'm a full teacher now."

"Not an assistant any more, eh?" said Laela. "Funny. I kinda got promoted too, actually. Yeh mighta heard about it."

"I did," said Yorath. "So—what's this all about?"

Laela wasn't going to admit that she'd had him brought up just so she'd have someone to talk to. "Been busy lately, but I just remembered I never finished learnin' how to read an' whatnot. So I thought it was about time we did some catchin' up."

"Oh!" Yorath looked surprised. "Well, there are better teachers than me, with a bit more experience—"

Laela waved him into silence. "Yeh were a good teacher for me, an' that's all I care about. Don't worry; I'll see yeh get paid properly."

"All right, then." Yorath started to lay out his materials. "Was there anything ye wanted to focus on right now?"

"Yeah, readin'," said Laela. "Can't risk signing somethin' when I don't know what it says. Actually, there was somethin' I wanted to show yeh."

She dumped a large book on the table between them.

Yorath inspected it without touching it. "What is it?"

"Found it," said Laela. "Hidden in my dad's old wardrobe." She couldn't resist a smirk. "Under a box of combs."

"Heh." Yorath smiled briefly. "He always did take good care of his hair. Ye could tell just by looking." He reached for the book. "Let's have a look at it, then . . ."

Laela got up and moved around the table to sit next to him, where they could both see the pages.

Yorath shifted uncomfortably and opened the book to the front page. "Er . . ." He cleared his throat, looked properly at the page, and jerked away as if it had bitten him. "Dear gods!"

Laela started. "What? What is it? What's it say?"

Yorath pulled himself together. "It's his journal. The King's journal."

Laela's eyes widened. "Really?"

"Yes." Yorath touched the page very carefully, indicating each word. " 'The Days of the Shadow That Walks'—that's crossed out, and he's replaced it with just 'Arenadd's Journal.' " He smiled hesitantly. "I suppose he thought the first one didn't sound right."

"He was right," said Laela. She rubbed her hands together excitedly. "Turn the page! Let's see what's inside!"

Yorath had already taken his hand away from it. "Laela, I'm really not sure we should read this. Not with me here, anyway. There could be anything inside; I don't have the right . . ." He trailed off, not having to add, ". . . and neither do you."

Laela hesitated briefly, then shook her head. "I can't read it without yer help. Can't see there bein' anything that amazin' in there anyway, if his life was anythin' like mine is now. Read it." When Yorath didn't obey right away, she said sharply, "Read it! That's an order."

Yorath turned the page, coughed, and began to read aloud—touching each word as he said it so she could follow along. " 'I have decided to write down what I do every day, or at least the most important parts. One day this book could be useful to historians, or future rulers, or just the curious. I have no illusions about living forever, despite what I am. Nothing can last forever, not even me, and I swear right now that if I last too long, and it gets too much for me, I will leave the North and go in search of a way to die. Not that I think I'll have to. I've changed too many things and committed too many crimes to ever be left in peace. One day, my people will turn against me, or the Night God will decide I've outlived my usefulness, or that one loose end will come back for me. That last possibility haunts me more every day.

" 'I have succeeded in building a new nation, and I have made my people as free as they will ever be, but in some ways I feel like a failure. I failed to save Skade. I failed Saeddryn. And I failed the Night God. I did not kill Flell's child the way I was supposed to. Even though my master had told me to do it, even though I knew full well that child could have the power to destroy me.

" 'Once I thought that I hesitated because Skade's death had made me stop caring, or because even I was too appalled by the idea of killing an infant in the cradle. But now I know the real reason.

" 'I did not kill the child because I knew that one day it might come back and kill me. I let it live because I wanted that to happen. With the child dead, I would be safe. With it still alive, I know there is still a chance for me.

" 'So I wait. Here in Malvern, with only my dear friend Skandar and this journal to confide in, I wait. The child will be a man in just a few years. I can wait for him to come and find me, and I know that he will come one day. He'll know what I did and what I am. He'll want revenge, just like I did. But I hope for his sake that he doesn't become what I became. I hope that, unlike me, he can keep his soul. I hope that he can give me rest. I'll still fight back, of course. It'll never be in my nature to bow down and accept the death-blow peacefully. If he wants to set me free, he'll have to fight for it. I can hardly wait.' "

Laela listened, utterly captivated. "He wanted to die . . ."

"No surprise to me," Yorath murmured. "But the child never did come. I wonder where he is now?"

Laela smiled inwardly. "Probably got no idea about any of it. This ain't no story, an' we ain't made that way really. *I* should know."

Yorath looked rather sad.

"Read more," said Laela. "Flip through toward the back. I wanna see if he wrote about me."

Reluctantly, Yorath closed the book and turned it over before opening it again. The last pages were blank, but he leafed back through them until he found more of Arenadd's neat handwriting.

"What's it say?" asked Laela.

Yorath took a deep breath, and began again. " 'Today, I vowed never to drink again. I realised that I've spent far too much time trying to hide away. I didn't care before, but when I saw the way she looked at me, I felt truly ashamed for the first time. And there I was thinking I'd lost my conscience for good! This girl is astonishing. She's changing me in ways I thought were impossible, and she doesn't even seem to realise it. But there's something about her that gets to me. The way she treats everyone she meets with the same rough and earthy good sense. She even talks to me like an equal—me! She acts as if my status and power don't matter. She treats me like a human being when no-one else does, and that makes me feel free to speak to her in the same way. I've told her things I would never tell anyone, without a moment's thought. I hope for all our sakes that she never misuses what she knows. I'm not afraid for myself, but I don't want her to be hurt.

" 'People say she looks like my daughter, but I don't feel like a father to her. I—' "

I can help.

Yorath and Laela both froze.

"What?" Laela said loudly.

I can help, Laela.

The voice seemed to come from everywhere. Felt, not

heard. The two humans looked at each other, then at the library around them.

Yorath pointed. "What's that? Can ye see that?"

Laela looked, and there was . . . was . . .

"Oeka?"

The shape flickered in the air. It was Oeka—or looked like her. A vague, wavering image hung in the air. It looked like dust motes caught in sunlight, swirling together to make a coloured sketch of a small griffin. The eyes, big and slanted, were deep green, and they were the boldest part of her.

Laela rubbed her own eyes. "Great gods on a stick, what's this? Oeka? What have yeh done now?"

The image wavered. *I have transcended my body,* whispered Oeka's ethereal voice. *I am now too powerful to be contained by flesh.*

"Oh good," Laela mumbled.

Here. The image of Oeka drifted closer. *Do not be afraid,* it said, when Laela and Yorath pulled back. *I am projecting this image. It cannot hurt you.*

"What do yeh want?" Laela asked, trying to keep herself together.

To tell you that I am well and will be beside you once again. Oeka drifted onto the table, transparent paws resting on the open book. *I wish to demonstrate my powers. Let me show you what I can do.*

"With what?" said Laela, very cautious now.

With this book. Oeka lowered her head toward the pages. *I have the power to reveal the past. This book is a piece of the past. Your father saved memories of himself inside it. Watch, and I will show them to you.*

The image of Oeka faded away, motes drifting apart, and a new voice sounded in the air. But this one was not Oeka's. It was louder, deeper—and familiar.

". . . feel like a father to her. I feel like she is my friend, and that's how I prefer it."

The voice was coming from the book.

Yorath and Laela fled from the table so fast they fell over the chairs and landed in a heap. The voice spoke on without pausing, and as the two recovered themselves and stood up to look, they saw him.

Arenadd himself, apparently sitting at the table with the open book in front of him. There was a pen in his hand and a bottle of ink at his elbow, and he wrote, tracing each word perfectly while his voice read them out. "It's been a long, long time since I had a friend other than Skandar. A human friend. I want Laela to be my friend. She's the only person I know who doesn't fear me—or hate me. She represents everything I thought I had lost—the life of a real man, a mortal man. I don't know if I had friends when I was alive, but—"

Slowly, making every effort to stay silent, Laela walked around the table to see his face. It was the face she remembered. Angular, bearded, calm. The lips didn't move in time to his voice, but she could see them move occasionally as he muttered something to himself.

Laela found her own voice at last. "What . . . *is* that?"

A memory, said Oeka, suddenly appearing by her side. *He cannot see you. This is a vision of him as he appeared when he wrote these words. Listen! He is writing a secret now.*

"—my plan," Arenadd's voice continued. "She is the key. I will make her my heir and adopt her as my daughter. Tara will be ruled by a half-breed, and not even the Night God will be able to stop it. Nothing can make me change my mind now. My master wants purity and segregation forever. No, not even that. She wants the Southerners destroyed, so that our pure race can rule forever and never mix with them again. But I won't have that. Time has changed me—I hope for the better. Once I saw a future where my people could be free to rule themselves. But now I see another future beyond that, a future I can't create. Making that future come will be up to better men than me, but I've taken the first step now. Laela is the key. Only she can see both sides. Whether she does will be up to her."

The voice went silent, and the vision of Arenadd closed an ethereal version of the journal and carried it away from the table. For a moment, he was there, walking straight toward Laela with his unseeing eyes fixed on her face; and then he was gone.

My gift, Oeka said smugly. *The past is open to me. If you wish to see it again, ask me, and I will show you.*

"It, er, it might come in handy," said Yorath unexpectedly.

He glanced at Laela, then looked at the vision of Oeka. "If . . . if . . . I was wondering . . ."

Speak. Do not speak. I can scent your intention. The vision blurred for a moment. *You are interested in history. You wish that I would show you more, so that you may write down what was said and done here long ago.*

Yorath's eyes widened.

You are right to be afraid, Oeka said, imperiously. *No mind can hide a secret from me. But you are safe. You are not a traitor. But I will not give you your wish now. I must go.*

"Go where?" said Laela.

The image of Oeka began to fade away. *To explore! There is so much to know, and I must know it! I will send my mind far away, and see all there is to see . . .*

"Saeddryn!" said Laela, pouncing on the opportunity at once. "If yeh can see that far, find out what she's doin'! Kill her the way yeh killed Torc—the war'd be over, an'—"

Oeka was now barely visible. *Wars. Humans. Irrelevant and dull. The world has so much more to offer, and I must take it . . .*

With that, she disappeared altogether.

Laela slumped into a chair. "I hate this place," she muttered.

34

Two and a Half Griffins

Kullervo's pains started within days of leaving Malvern.

He and Senneck flew together, but kept their distance from the younger Skarok and spent their nights away from him as well. He was close enough to be seen sometimes during the day when they were in the air, but he and Senneck kept away from each other, and away from civilisation as well. Laela had ordered them to travel this way since it would make them much less likely to be spotted. It meant that Kullervo and Senneck were essentially travelling alone. In the evenings, they would camp in whatever shelter they could find—usually under a tree. They didn't light a fire and lived off whatever they both caught. Even in human shape, Kullervo could digest raw meat easily. He even liked the taste.

He and Senneck travelled well together, used to each other by now, and Kullervo had never been so completely happy. He loved being with Senneck, loved it more than he could say. He loved the spicy smell of her feathers, loved her dry, rasping voice, loved lying against her warm flank to sleep. He loved it when she talked to him while they rested, teaching him what he needed to know about magic. But it was the times when they didn't talk that he loved best—the times when nothing needed to be said, and he could sit there with her in silence and know that she was there and wouldn't leave him again.

So he was happy, at least until the pains began.

They first appeared in the mornings, in his back and legs.

At first they were only a mild annoyance—just an ache in the joints. They weren't much different than the cramps he sometimes got while recovering from a change. It had been some time since his last transformation, but he had changed back and forth several times in a short period, so he supposed it must have taken a toll. And his wounds were still healing as well. So he said nothing and thought that they would go away soon enough.

But they didn't go away. And in just a few short days, they became unbearable. What had been an ache in the joints spread through every bone in his spine, legs, and shoulders, then to the muscles. He began to have headaches as well and could barely sleep at night.

Not one to complain, Kullervo kept quiet about it. But before long, he had developed a limp that got worse as the pains did. His eyes became hollow with exhaustion, and he went off his food. Senneck must have noticed, but she said nothing, and only began to watch him more closely whenever they were on the ground.

Travelling inconspicuously meant they took an indirect route to the coast, and the journey took longer than it might have done. Kullervo suffered wordlessly through it, until finally Senneck reached the harbour town called Abertawe. There was a small griffiner tower there, but she ignored it and went straight to the docks, where Skarok and Inva had already boarded the ship that would take them to Maijan.

Inva came to meet them alone, arriving just as Kullervo dismounted.

He slid clumsily off Senneck's back and toppled sideways onto the ground.

Inva, forgetting protocol, ran to help him up. "My lord!"

Grey-faced and sweating, Kullervo clasped her hand and let himself be pulled upright. "Thanks . . ."

He looked so ghastly that even Inva finally forgot her reserve. "What happened to you? You are ill . . ." She glanced quickly at the impassive Senneck.

"I'm all right," Kullervo croaked.

"You are *not* well," Inva said immediately. "You are very ill. How long have you been like this?"

"A while," said Kullervo. "I'll get better . . ." He tried to stand up properly but failed, reaching out pathetically for Senneck to support him. She was there at once, putting her head under his arm.

Inva hesitated. "You must go home," she said at last.

"He will not," Senneck interrupted. "Take us to the ship now."

Inva bowed low to her. "Sacred one, your human will not survive the journey."

"He is not ill," said Senneck. "He will recover."

"I *will*," said Kullervo, before Inva could protest. "Please take us to the ship. I need to lie down for a bit. I'll be fine."

"But—" Inva began.

Kullervo pulled himself up. "I'll get better if Senneck says I will," he said, with so much certainty that it was obvious nothing could change his mind.

Inva's lifelong training in obedience won through, and she nodded politely and led the pair of them down the pier to where a ship was moored. Three griffins waited on the deck—two females and Skarok, who came to his human at once.

"So the two weaklings have arrived at last," he sneered at Senneck and Kullervo. "And I see the human has finally sickened. Watch carefully, human, before the old one decides to be rid of you. But only if she thinks she can do better than you."

Kullervo didn't seem to notice the insults. Senneck only fixed Skarok with a long, slow stare. Skarok faced it for a few moments, but when Senneck moved closer, he hastily backed away.

Senneck huffed in a satisfied kind of way and let Inva show her belowdecks to the cargo-hold, which had been partly converted into a block of stalls where she and her fellow griffins could nest. Senneck chose one, and Kullervo went in with her. Inva began to tell him how there was a cabin higher up for him, but he curled up in the straw by Senneck's side and promptly went to sleep.

Inva quietly retreated, leaving Senneck to rearrange the nesting material before settling down close to her human. She was nearly as tired as he was and soon went to sleep as well, with her head resting on her talons close to his face.

She woke up refreshed. Looking around contentedly, she saw that Kullervo was awake. His eyes were on her face.

Griffin-coloured, but human. Now they were red-rimmed and staring.

"Senneck?" he whispered.

She moved her head closer to him. "Yes?"

"Am I dying?"

Senneck's breath ruffled his hair. "No. You are growing."

"But it hurts," Kullervo's face was full of fear. "Even changing doesn't hurt this much. Not for so long. What am I going to do?"

"I told you," said Senneck. "You are growing. You will not die. You are becoming stronger."

Kullervo relaxed a little. "I don't feel stronger . . ." He stilled. "How do you know? Do you know what this is?"

"Yes." Senneck clicked her beak. "This is my fault."

"No it isn't," Kullervo said at once. "You'd never hurt me."

"I am not," said Senneck. "The pain is necessary. I did not think this would happen, but it should not hurt you."

"What?" Kullervo lifted himself onto his elbows. "What did you do?"

"You use magic like a griffin, but you are not one," said Senneck. "As I taught you how to control your power, I soon realised from what you told me that your gland is not properly developed. It is undersized and weak, and this explains the crude way you have been using magic and why it comes so erratically. Therefore, I decided that I would feed you magic from my own gland and so encourage yours to grow."

Kullervo looked blank. "But when did you do that? And wouldn't that hurt you?"

"I absorbed some of the power the fool Oeka was using," said Senneck. "Extra energy, stored in my gland. During our journey, when you were asleep, I passed it into you." She opened her beak wide to demonstrate.

Kullervo rubbed his head. "Why didn't you tell me? I wouldn't have minded."

"It had to be done when you were asleep, without your knowledge," said Senneck. "If not, you would have resisted despite yourself. I can tell you now because the process is complete."

"Then will I get better now?"

"In time," said Senneck. "I did not know it would cause you this much pain."

"Why has it, then?" said Kullervo. "Why does my *back* hurt? My legs? You said the gland is in my throat, and that doesn't hurt at all!"

"Your gland is growing," said Senneck, in a clipped, efficient kind of way. "As I expected. But it has not contained all the energy I gave it. Your body is growing as well, to match it. It will continue to grow for a time—I do not know how long it will do this, but the hardest part is over. You will have the journey to Maijan to grow, then recover."

"You mean I'm going to get *bigger*?"

"It is all benefit," Senneck said blandly. "You will become larger and stronger, and will not need so much protection. When the pains begin to decrease, I suggest you exercise and encourage your muscles to thicken. There will never be a better time."

Kullervo gave a hesitant, broken-toothed smile. "I hope I don't get too big. I don't want to scare people."

Senneck chirped. "You have so much of a griffin about you, but you have the heart of a human."

"Sorry."

"If you did not have that, you would not be *my* human," said Senneck. She nibbled gently at his hair. "Rest now. Better times are coming for you."

Saeddryn was also on a journey. But hers was a journey alone.

The day after Caedmon and his followers arrived at Skenfrith, she had set out in secret. Nobody except she, Caedmon, and Shar knew where she was going. The half-breed couldn't know she was coming.

The move to Skenfrith had been easy enough. On their arrival, the rebels went straight to the governor's tower and crowded into the building. The governor, knowing she and her guards were outnumbered, immediately surrendered control of the city to Caedmon. With some persuasion from him and Saeddryn, she had even agreed to join their cause. Loyalty to the half-breed, it seemed, didn't take much to break.

Saeddryn had set out for Malvern on foot. She had no griffin to carry her, and horses panicked at the sight of her. Besides, she preferred it this way.

The odd thing was that she could still feel tiredness, and pain, and even hunger. She even felt the urge to sleep at night. During the tedious walking that took up the first day, she wondered about that. She was immortal now, so why did she still have mortal concerns like that?

She thought of Arenadd. When she had first known him, he had slept and eaten like an ordinary human. But over time that had changed. When she lived in the Eyrie close by him, she had seen it happen—had watched him drift further and further away from the mortal world. It was common knowledge that he ate almost nothing, and she had heard the servants whisper that his bed was never slept in. But he never seemed to weaken from it.

Was it progressive, she wondered? Had he grown that way naturally the longer he spent as an immortal?

Saeddryn tried to remember the last time she had eaten. Two days ago? Three? She wasn't sure. She felt vaguely hungry now but nowhere near as much as she should have if it had been that long.

I shouldn't need to eat, she thought. *The dark power keeps me moving now, not food.*

As an experiment, she didn't eat any of the food she had brought that day, and when she stopped at nightfall, she went without dinner.

The hunger hadn't grown any stronger.

Odd.

She didn't feel like sleeping now and decided to pray instead. It made her sad to think of the Temple she had loved and where she would have gone to pray if she could. If the half-breed hadn't destroyed it. If she were still alive and living in Malvern, and all these terrible things had never happened.

Grim-faced, Saeddryn wandered around the gully where she had stopped, picking up the largest rocks she could find. She brought them back to where she had left her bag, and when she had thirteen of them, she picked up her sickle and cleared a spot on the ground, scraping away grass and debris to expose a rough circle of earth.

She put the sickle aside and brought the stones, arranging them around the edges of the circle until she had made a ring just big enough for her to fit inside.

Picking up the sickle again, she stood at the centre of the ring and blessed each stone, touching them with the tip of the blade and murmuring the sacred words.

She imagined she could feel the Night God's grace fill the circle. An attentive silence filled the air.

Saeddryn held out a hand and pressed the sickle blade into the palm. "With this Northern blood, I nourish an' call to ye."

Red drops splashed onto the earth between the stones. Saeddryn put the sickle down and knelt, looking straight up at the moon and mouthing a prayer.

Nothing happened, and she suddenly started feeling stupid. Why was she doing this, following rituals as if she were still High Priestess, as if she hadn't spoken to the Night God face-to-face? As if she hadn't become the new sacred warrior?

She stood up, brushing her hands on her clothes without noticing the blood. "Master, I am yer servant an' will not hesitate. I'm on my way now t'start it. Just tell me if I'm doing it right. Please."

You are. The reply came at once, whispering in her ear.

Saeddryn turned quickly, but there was no sign of anyone. "Master?"

I am here. Speak.

Awe gripped her. "I did it! I didn't think—could Arenadd do this? Talk to ye any time?"

Yes. But he never did.

"Why not? Didn't he trust ye?"

No. He had no faith. He made one true prayer in his life, and that was all. He raged, he screamed, he threatened, but he did not reach out with love as you have. And so I never replied.

"One true prayer," Saeddryn repeated to herself. "I wonder when that was?"

It was on the night before his death, said the Night God. *He prayed for me to save him.*

"But ye didn't," said Saeddryn, unable to stop herself.

His time had come. Do not be afraid, Saeddryn. You are on the right path. Do you have another question to ask?

"Not really," said Saeddryn. "Just wanted reassurance, I

s'pose. Why do I still get hungry?" She added the question without really thinking.

Habit, said the Night God. *Your mind expects you to be hungry, and so you are. You may eat, or ignore it. Neither will hurt you. Rest now.*

The voice faded away.

Saeddryn stayed in the circle a while longer, meditating in silence. She didn't have anything more to ask, but being in the circle made her feel better.

And, as she sat there, she came up with a plan. It would delay the half-breed's death, but it would make the meaning of that death far more complete, and the more Saeddryn thought about it, the more satisfied she felt. After all, she reminded herself, being the Night God's avatar meant having more than just the power to kill. And this was something she had done before, many times.

Alone in the moonlight, Saeddryn began to smile. Yes, that was it. That was exactly it. She would go to Malvern, and she would make herself known in the city. She would talk to people, spread the word, pass on the Night God's message. She would win the people to Caedmon's side; and *then* she would kill the half-breed.

By the time Caedmon arrived with his followers, the city would already be weakened from within. She would tell everyone it had been his idea. It would work perfectly.

Saeddryn couldn't contain herself any longer. She stood up and lifted her bag onto her back. She left the stone circle where it was but picked up her sickle and tucked it into her belt before setting out again. Sleep could wait. She didn't need it any more anyway. And besides, this was the night, and she was strongest now.

Why make the Night God's business wait? It was the only purpose she had left.

She would not disappoint her master.

Yorath left the library with his books under his arm and his mind buzzing. In all his life, he had never seen anything as amazing as what he had seen that day, and even now he still couldn't quite grasp the reality of it.

Yorath's world was books and teaching, and he had never had much experience with griffins. To him, they were big, dangerous, and mysterious animals, not meant for ordinary people like himself to understand. He had never seen one use magic, either—not up close, anyway. But most griffins rarely did use their gifts. As far as Yorath could tell, it was a last resort for most of them.

But now the wonder of what Oeka had done and shown him had thrown Yorath's mind into disarray. So much power, all in one place. A griffin that spoke to him without even using words, a griffin that could reveal the past in the blink of an eye. Yorath had never imagined that wonders like it could exist, and now it had all been shown to him in less than a day.

As his initial fear began to die away, excitement replaced it. Oeka's judgment had been absolutely correct: he had indeed seen her power as an opportunity to uncover the past. Yorath had always been fascinated by history, and there would never be a better chance to record it than now. If only Oeka had stayed . . .

But she *had* stayed, hadn't she? Her body was still here, wasn't it? And she must still be in it somewhere. It only made sense.

Impulsively, Yorath changed his route down inside the tower. Everyone knew that Oeka had locked herself away under the Eyrie, and Yorath had guessed that meant she was in the crypt. It was supposed to be off-limits, but he had bribed his way down there once, wanting to see the carvings on the tombs. If Oeka was in there now, and he could get to her . . .

As Yorath climbed down the stairs to the ground floor of the tower, he tensed expectantly—waiting for the horrible disorientation he had felt here before to come back. But nothing happened, and when he reached the bottom without any ill-effects he started to relax. He had passed through here once before, while Oeka was working her magic, and had never forgotten the overwhelming confusion and dizziness that had struck him. It had taken almost an entire day for the headache to wear off afterward.

But he felt fine now.

Oeka really had finished, then. Thank goodness.

Feeling much safer now, he pulled aside the tapestry that

hid the door to the crypt passage. The door hung open, so he took a torch off the wall and stepped boldly down into the gloom.

"Oh dear gods!"

He scarcely even noticed the cry escape from him. For a moment he stood there, staring in horror, before the stench hit him, and he reeled away and out of the passage.

He took a few moments to recover, and when he felt brave enough, he looked again.

He retched.

There were bodies in the passageway. At least—he dared to look closer—at least three of them, lying slumped against the walls.

In the end, only the thought that one of them might be alive and needing help made him enter that passage. Gritting his teeth, he stooped to examine them, but he didn't need to check pulses to know they were beyond help. Three people, a woman and two men, huddled and pathetic in death and all of them smelling faintly of decay. Yorath saw the contorted shapes of their hands and limbs, and the memory of what he had felt before flashed across his brain. These people had been stupid enough to push through that and try to get closer, and they had died for it.

Yorath might have turned back then, but the pure stubbornness he had inherited from his father won through. The magic had gone now. It was safe here. And he had to take this opportunity in case it disappeared. History was more important. History, and preserving it.

Moving slowly, picking his way past the corpses, he moved down the corridor and stepped into the crypt. The air was clearer here, at least, and there was still no sign of danger. And there she was, right there in the middle of the floor . . .

Yorath moved closer, calling out to avoid startling her. "Hello? Oeka? It's me, Yorath. I'm friends with yer human. I've come to talk to ye . . ."

His voice faded away when he saw her. She lay on her belly with her legs spread out limply, wings draped down over her flanks like old curtains. Her head was outstretched, beak slack, blind white eyes open and horrible. Yorath had never seen something so obviously dead in his life.

But she was still breathing. He could see her sides moving in and out, ever so slowly.

"Oeka?" he said again, hesitantly. "Can ye hear me?"

The reply came very faintly, as if from over a huge distance. *Yes* . . .

Yorath started. "I just wanted to ask . . ."

Yes, the voice whispered again.

Yorath opened his mouth to say something more, but he never did remember much of what happened after that. In one instant, the sight was ripped away from his eyes. The crypt disappeared, along with his own body, and visions replaced them.

Not knowing if he was standing or falling, he saw things. Impossible things. Ancient things.

He was vaguely aware of his hands, opening a book and dipping a pen into ink. He thought he wrote something down, or drew something. But his eyes were as sightless as Oeka's, and they saw as far as hers.

He saw the North move below, flickering and warping, nothing standing still. Trees were there, but he could see a layering in them. Every tree was a tree, a stump, a sapling, and a seed still in the ground, all at the same time. Leaves fell but stayed on their twigs. Even the ground itself seemed to move, hills rising and falling, valleys widening and narrowing again. He saw cities, constantly moving between what they were and what they had been in the past. Now a city, now a village, now a mere cluster of huts. It was all confusion and change, and he couldn't grasp anything before it shifted away again.

But he did see some things clearly. As Oeka focused on details that interested her, he saw them still and become solid for just a moment. Saw Wolf's Town as one little tent by the river, smoke rising from the fire lit at its entrance. A man sat there. A griffin crouched nearby.

Then Oeka moved on, and they approached the mountains. The First Mountains, although nobody Yorath knew could tell him why they were called that.

And there, there was the plateau with the standing stones, and they were more substantial than anything else he had seen so far. They had been there a long, long time.

Oeka brought them down to the plateau, and the stones

faded into the past. He saw bare earth now, covered in spring-time grass. And people. Oeka took them to a time when there were people.

A cluster of them stood at the centre of the plateau. Northerners, clad in furs, their hair rough and ragged. The men wore beards.

They were grouped around a hole. A deep hole . . . a grave. Lowering someone into it. A man. *A burial,* Yorath thought, but something was wrong, something . . .

The man went into the grave, but he was alive, tied up and struggling. Yorath tried to reach out, wanting to help him, but it was all in the past. He saw the man in the bottom of the hole, looking up at the two who looked back. A man and a woman, side by side, and the man—the man had curly hair and a pointed beard, and a cruel gleam in his black eyes.

"This will be your tomb, Traegan," said the woman by his side. "The circle will be built over you."

"The world needs us," said the man with the pointed beard. "I will lead them."

The man in the hole laughed like a lunatic. "Lead and fight, brave Taranis! Age and die! Die and become nothing! Traegan will endure and Traegan alone. *I—am—forever!*"

He kept on laughing while they buried him, and Yorath's cry was utterly silent.

Then Oeka moved on to other visions, and Yorath was dragged with her, unable to stop himself from becoming lost in the past.

35

Heath

Caedmon had had a very long day. Since Saeddryn's departure, he had taken over the running of the city, working alongside Isolde, the woman who was still more or less the governor. Together, they had set the city's inhabitants to prepare for whatever lay ahead—a siege, or more likely an out-and-out assault from Malvern. For now, Isolde and her officials were keeping up their correspondence with the capital city, to make it look as if nothing had changed. But this was only a delaying tactic, and everyone knew it. In the meantime, anti-griffin spear-launchers were being set up on the walls, and the city guard, shored up by Caedmon's followers, were training and preparing arrows and other weapons. Shar, together with Isolde's partner, Haaek, spent time with their fellow griffins, intimidating and inspiring them to fight when the time came. There would be no doubt at all that they would fight any attacker that came to the city—Skenfrith was, after all, their own territory, and no other griffin could enter it except with great politeness. It was harder to stop them attacking perceived intruders.

Shar and Haaek visited them anyway, mocking supposed weaknesses and increasing their rage toward the anticipated invaders, as well as their determination to prove they were not weak.

"Ya-khek oo ee krak." That was a phrase Shar had taught her partner. It meant "hatched from a soft-shelled egg" and

was just about the worst insult any griffin could throw at his own kind. It implied feebleness, deformity, and cowardice, and it was the best way to make a griffin dangerously angry.

Caedmon had no intention of ever using it himself, but he watched Shar's progress with satisfaction. She did good work. They would soon be as ready as they ever would be.

He hoped Saeddryn would complete her mission quickly.

That evening, he retired to the audience chamber, which was outfitted with comfortable chairs and served as a place to relax when it wasn't in use. Myfina was there already, deep in a book.

She looked up when Caedmon came in and gave him a smile that made his heart beat faster. "Hello. You look exhausted!"

Caedmon sank into a chair beside hers. "I am."

Myfina put the book aside. "I was just in here resting, too, lest you think I was being lazy. I've been helping Garnoc. And before that I was helping Hafwen. It's been nothing but go, go, go since I got up this morning!"

"I know how you feel," Caedmon said ruefully. "But things are going well, at least. No major problems yet."

"Yes, that's because so far we *don't* have the half-breed trying to kick the gates in," Myfina pointed out.

Caedmon couldn't help but laugh at the mental image. "You know, I can actually imagine her doing that. She's got a nasty temper on her."

Myfina put her head on one side, like a griffin. "You've met her?"

"Not really. I saw her once, but I didn't introduce myself. I haven't been back to Malvern since she got here."

Myfina looked sad. "Yes . . . people wondered if you ever would come back after what happened."

Caedmon scowled, not realising that the expression made him look much younger and sulky. "I wasn't going to come back until he apologised to me himself. Obviously, he never did."

"That wasn't his way, really." Myfina coughed. "So . . . the half-breed, eh?" She shook her head. "I can't believe she expects people to believe she's *his* daughter! The whole story's insane. This girl just turns up out of nowhere, and overnight the King himself is eating out of her hand. Giving her presents, giving her official positions in the Eyrie, for shadows' sakes—I don't know what she did to him, but it worked very well."

"I don't understand it, either," Caedmon admitted. "How in the world did she win him over so quickly? I do know one thing for certain—there's no *way* she's really his daughter. For one thing . . . him, with a Southerner?" He laughed out loud at the suggestion. "And for another, she was his lover."

Myfina gaped. "*What?* His *lover*?"

"According to my mother," said Caedmon. "She said he told her so himself." He shuddered. "The idea of it . . . I want to vomit just thinking about it. Him with a half-breed! I know he had lovers over the years, but that was different. They were all from good families, all had good reputations—perfect Queen material."

"Except that they all died," Myfina said darkly.

Caedmon's mouth tightened. "Yes. Too bad the half-breed didn't join them. My gods, she's disgusting. I can't even *think* about someone so utterly repulsive sitting on our throne. First, she sleeps with him, then she claims to be his daughter!"

"But not until after he leaves the city with her and is never seen again," Myfina added.

"Yes. I don't even like to imagine what she might have done with him."

"But to *him*?" said Myfina. "She's mortal. How could she do anything to the Shadow That Walks?"

"I don't know. But I promise you right now that if I get the chance, I'll make her suffer for it." Caedmon hadn't told Myfina about Saeddryn's mission to assassinate Laela.

Myfina reached out and touched his hand. "Don't worry," she said. "You're going to win. We're all going to win. Justice is on our side."

Caedmon stared at her hand as it rested on his own and felt a blush begin. "Yes," he mumbled, hoping she wouldn't see it. "I know we will because I'm going to make it so."

Myfina smiled at him. "I believe in you, Caedmon."

The next day went off more or less like the one before it. Caedmon went back to work, with Shar and everyone else pitching in. Unfortunately, as the time dragged on, the stress started to take a toll on him, and he was feeling tired and irritable by the time he stopped for lunch with Isolde and Myfina. He wasn't in the mood for much conversation. Unfortunately, the meal didn't last as long as he was hoping it would, and he was not at all pleased when Garnoc interrupted them.

"S'cuse us, Lord, Ladies . . ."

"What is it?" Caedmon groaned.

Garnoc nodded hastily to him. "Sorry to bother yer, but something's come up an' you an' Lady Isolde here should see it."

Isolde was already getting up. "See what? We're not under attack, are we?"

"Oh, no, no, that's fine," said Garnoc. "No, it's just that you sent me t'work with the reeve here, an' he asked me to come tell yer about this man they've just arrested."

"Can't he handle it himself?" asked Caedmon.

"Normally, yeah, but it's the rule around here that with some criminals, the governor's got to be informed."

"Who is he?" Isolde asked, in a way that suggested she'd done this sort of thing before.

"Total scumbag," said Garnoc. "They've been trying to get him for months. Seems he got rich by sellin' people houses that don't exist. Swindled thousands of oblong from people all over the city. In other cities, too. He moves every time the authorities start catching on."

"Oh!" Isolde blinked. "*Him.* Yes, I've heard about him. The Master of Law personally told me to bring him his head on a spike if I ever got my hands on it."

Caedmon managed to laugh. "That doesn't sound like my father at *all.*"

"It was," said Isolde. "Lord Torc couldn't stand liars. Garnoc, tell the reeve I said to have him brought to the audience chamber immediately. I'll be there."

"Right, milady." Garnoc left.

"You don't have to come," Isolde told Caedmon. "I can deal with this myself if you'd prefer."

Caedmon, however, jumped at the chance to take a longer break. "No, I'll come, too."

"I'll join you, then," said Myfina. She grinned mischievously. "I always wanted to know what a real criminal looked like."

* * *

The moment the notorious swindler was brought into the audience chamber between two guards, Caedmon saw why so many people had fallen for his scheme.

He was tall and lanky, but carried himself with so much confidence, it made Caedmon feel instantly inferior. His clothes were so fine that they managed to draw attention away from the manacles hanging off his wrists, and he acted as if they weren't there anyway, strolling into the room with such an open, instantly likeable smile that he might as well have said, "Chains? Guards? Nah, it's just a trick. The *real* criminal's just behind us. Did I fool you?"

Caedmon very nearly smiled back at him without meaning to. He drew himself up and tried to look stern and kingly instead. Myfina, however, didn't have as much self-control and smirked to herself.

The reeve, a middle-aged man with a grey beard, coughed and finally succeeded in making people notice he was in the room as well. "My lord, my lady—Governor. This is the man Garnoc mentioned to you."

"I can see that," said Isolde, unsmiling. She turned her attention toward the still-grinning criminal. "What's his name?"

The man winked at her. "Call me Heath."

"Heath what?" Caedmon interrupted.

"Just Heath," said Heath. "Heath of no fixed abode and no fixed name, either, and isn't life so much more *exciting* that way? Don't you think?"

"I don't know, I never tried it," said Myfina, unable to stop herself.

"Then you should! But I should warn you—once you start, you'll never want to stop."

"That's enough," said Isolde, cutting across him. "Now then. Heath, if that is your name, you stand accused of fraud, theft, and multiple counts of forgery in Warwick, Fruitsheart, Malvern, Wolf's Town, and Skenfrith. What do you have to say for yourself?"

Heath looked affronted. "Theft? Fraud? I can't say I like those words much."

"What would *you* call it, then?" asked Caedmon, trying to stop himself from liking this man and failing.

"Theft," said Heath, with a nod toward him, "is taking what you haven't earned. And let me promise you, Heath earns what Heath gets."

"Is that so?" said Caedmon.

"Most definitely."

"Are you suggesting that you did, in fact, give your victims something in return for their money?" Isolde asked.

"Absolutely." Heath tried to touch his own face and failed because of the manacles. "I gave them the very best of my talents. *And* I gave them the chance to contribute to a good cause."

"What cause would this be?" said Isolde.

"A charitable one," Heath said slyly. "All the money went toward helping support a poor boy without a home or any belongings to speak of, and no family to look after him, either. Without it, he'd have starved to death in a gutter! What a waste."

"We arrested you in an expensive rented house full of velvet and silver," said the reeve. "According to your neighbours, you'd been entertaining people there all week. Loudly."

Heath shrugged. "Like I said, I needed somewhere to live. It took a lot of skill to earn enough for that house."

"And the parties?" the reeve prompted.

"I'm very generous with my wealth," said Heath. "Ask any of my new friends."

"Is that your confession, then?" said Isolde. "You cheated people out of their money and spent it on yourself and your friends, whoever they are. Did anyone help you do this?"

"No," said Heath. "All my own work." He sounded openly proud of himself. "As I told you, I'm very talented."

"I've heard enough." Isolde nodded to the reeve. "Since he confessed, there's no need for you to do anything further. Take him out of here and cut his right hand off."

Heath's eyes widened. "Come on now, milady, you can't do that! That's the hand that does all my favourite things!"

Isolde glared at him. "Tear his tongue out as well, I think. We'll see how many lies he can tell without it."

"My pleasure," the reeve growled.

Heath finally started to look afraid as his guards prompted

him to leave. "Er, now just hold on a moment here, would you? Can't I just pay a fine or something? I've got some money hidden under the mattress, if you can just let me go get it—"

One of the guards thumped him in the stomach, and he and his colleague hauled Heath toward the door.

Heath started to struggle. "Wait! No! Please, stop, I swear I'll do anything!"

Myfina glanced at Caedmon, and he could see her distress. Impulsively, he took a step forward. "Stop!"

The guards stopped, looking at the reeve for orders.

Caedmon thought fast. "I want to talk to this man," he said. "Alone."

Isolde hesitated, but she knew he overruled her. She nodded to the guards. "Let him go. Wait outside."

They let the prisoner go and left at once, followed by the reeve. Isolde went with them.

Myfina stayed where she was, looking at Caedmon. "Should I—?"

"If you don't mind," said Caedmon. "I'm sure we won't be long."

"Well . . . all right then." Myfina walked out, casting a hopeful glance back at Heath.

He grinned back. The moment the door had shut, he turned to Caedmon, all confidence again. "I *knew* you were really in charge here. The moment I came in that door, I saw you and thought, 'He's the one holding all the pieces here.' Which means *you* must be Lord Caedmon Taranisäii."

"I am," said Caedmon.

Heath nodded. "You're the image of your cousin, but I'm sure you already knew that. The very image of a King."

Caedmon didn't smile. "Don't think that just because I stopped them I'm going to let you keep your hand. Just how much money did you steal, anyway?"

"A good amount," Heath said carelessly. "I didn't keep count. That's my rule. Move often, make plenty of friends, and don't keep score. But what's *your* rule, Lord Caedmon? I know you have one of your own. Everyone does, and besides, you look like the sort of man who knows what he wants."

Caedmon actually stopped to think about this. "My rule is justice first," he said eventually.

"As handed down by *who*, I wonder?"

"The Night God."

"Of course." Heath smiled. "I thought you looked like the pious type. Justice as handed down by the Night God first, of course, but by who in the second instance?"

"Us," said Caedmon, without hesitation.

"Taranisäiis?"

"Human beings. True Northerners do what the Night God wants."

"Hm." Heath rubbed his hands together. "And how, exactly, do we know what the Night God wants? For instance, does she in fact want me to keep this nicely manicured hand of mine? Does she want this talented tongue of mine torn out and thrown away where it'll be of no use to anybody unless there's a hungry dog about?"

"What do you think?" Caedmon asked.

"You're a Taranisäii, you tell me," said Heath. "Everyone knows you're a family that's close to the Night God's heart, assuming she has one. Your mother was, at least."

Caedmon finally made up his mind. "You're a clever man, Heath."

"I know," came the reply at once.

"You're also obviously a brave man, and a resourceful one," Caedmon continued. "So far, you've used those talents of yours to get yourself into trouble. But my mother always taught me to keep an eye out for useful men, and I'm not going to let your abilities go to waste. So here's your choice. Make it right now, or I'll make it for you. Either I call the guards back in and hand you over to be punished the way you should be, or you agree to start working for me."

"Government work?" said Heath. "Sounds deadly. I'm not sure I want to keep this hand just so I can use it to handle paperwork."

"Choose," Caedmon said stonily.

"What would it pay?"

"Plenty," said Caedmon. "But you won't keep any of it. Every oblong you earn goes to the people you stole from. You'll be given food, clothes, and a place to stay, and you'll report to me. And I warn you right now: If you steal again, if you take so much as a loaf of bread that isn't yours, it'll be your head instead of your hand. Understood?"

"Oh dear," said Heath. "Servitude. And I spent so much time and effort avoiding it."

"You'll get used to it," said Caedmon. "Do we have a deal?"

"Can I have these manacles taken off?" Heath asked. "Pretty please?"

Caedmon sighed and removed the bolts that held them closed. Heath rubbed his wrists and stretched gratefully. Then he held out a hand. "My hand," he said. "I'd prefer to keep it away from the reeve, so you can take care of it for me."

Caedmon took the hand and tugged it briefly in the universal sign of trust and agreement. "I'll have Hafwen find you a room. Also, until further notice, you're confined to the Eyrie."

"Now why would I go anywhere?" Heath said innocently.

"Just do it," said Caedmon. "Unless you'd prefer to wear a ball and chain. That can be arranged."

"What, and ruin my pants? I think I'll stay inside. By the way, who was that nice young lady you had in here with you before?"

"That was Lady Myfina," said Caedmon. "One of my council."

"Ah. Brains *and* beauty, obviously." Heath grinned. "You keep good company."

Caedmon rolled his eyes. "Talk to whoever you like, but keep away from Governor Isolde. She's not going to like this at all."

"Keep away?" said Heath. "Certainly not. I plan to tease her at every opportunity."

"Fine, but don't be surprised if Haaek pecks your liver out." Caedmon made for the door. "Come with me. There's work to do."

36

True Northerners

Saeddryn's return to Malvern was a cautious one.

She had reached the walls of the city in a very short time, travelling fast and efficiently and without the need to stop for food or sleep. It was still plenty of time to plan, and by the time she arrived, she had decided what to do. She had to talk to people, but she had to do it carefully. Any one of them might decide to betray her to the half-breed.

She had no fear of being caught, but when she killed the half-breed, she wanted to take her by surprise. But, fortunately, she already knew the best person to speak to first.

She slipped into the city in broad daylight, using the main gates. They were guarded, but nobody had any hope of spotting her.

It was strange to be home again after so long, and after so much had changed, but she was almost relieved to find that it looked just as she remembered. She walked through the streets in the market district, idly listening in to the cries of the stallholders advertising their wares, the arguments over prices and rotten apples. People stood on street-corners, adjusting the hang of their bags or stopping for a chat with a friend. The winter sun was bright and clear, and everything was peaceful. It was as if the trouble in the North were miles away, in another country. These people knew about it, but most of them probably didn't even care that much. It was all far away, somewhere outside their little worlds.

None of them had any hope of seeing the hunter that stalked in among them, sliding from shadow to shadow, taking everything in, preparing for the time when she would strike and set them free from the half-breed Queen's false rule.

She wondered if any of them would ever thank her for it when it was over, but they would. They had to. She was doing this for them. It was the Night God's will, and what she wanted was what was best for her people.

Saeddryn moved on and out of the marketplace, heading for the Eyrie, and the Temple.

Nighttime over Malvern, and the moon rose, thin and bright. The Temple was still incomplete, but the priestesses' quarters at the back of the building had been one of the first things to be rebuilt. All thirteen of the senior priestesses lived there, along with the novices who served under them. None of them were married, and none of them had children. It wasn't exactly forbidden, since their founder, Saeddryn, had had both a husband and children, but it was discouraged. Temple life was strict, and both priestesses and novices were expected to stay indoors at night, to pray and meditate.

Alone in the single room that served as her home, one of the novices was doing exactly that—but she did it quietly, constantly aware of the risk of being overheard. Not that what she was doing wasn't prayer, but it wasn't exactly the kind of prayer her mentors had taught her either.

The young woman hunched over the small, carved stone she held cupped in her hands, and murmured the words to herself—words she herself had invented, and which she recited in secret every night.

"To ye who came to us from nothing, sent by the Night God's grace, I offer ye my loyalty and my soul. Blessed one, heartless one, mighty Shadow That Walks, ye are the master I choose. Watch over me, give me courage, help me to stand up when the whole world tries to push me down, let me serve my people beyond life, beyond pain and beyond hope, as ye did." She took a deep breath, meditating over the triple-spiral symbol cut into the bloodstained prayer stone, and moved on, speaking her prayer for the night. "Great Arenadd, bless me and guide me. I believe in ye with all my heart. Watch over the North, and when the time comes . . ." She hesitated. "Come back to us, Arenadd, Shadow That Walks. Rise again, when yer people need ye. Forgive me, but . . ." She hesitated again—not quite able to bring herself to say what was in her heart, which was that she believed that time was now. But true prayer should come from the heart, shouldn't it?

"Come back to us now," she said. "We need ye now. Our people are troubled, our country's at war. Without ye, we can't protect ourselves from the South. We—"

Behind her, the door slammed suddenly.

The novice looked up sharply, her hand immediately moving to hide the prayer stone inside her silver robe.

"Don't bother, girl, I know what it is," said a harsh voice.

The novice gaped in horror. "High Priestess Saeddryn—?"

Saeddryn moved away from the door and silently strode forward. "Aye, it's me. Teressa, isn't it?"

"That's me." The novice faltered. "Holy Night God, I . . . I'm sorry."

"Don't bother about it," said Saeddryn. "I already know about this little cult ye've started. How many years has it been goin' on, anyway?"

Teressa had gone white. "Er . . . about . . . about nine years, Holiness, but—why are ye here? How did ye get in? I thought— We thought—"

Saeddryn waved her into silence. "I'm not here to kill ye, girl, so calm down. Ye worship the Shadow That Walks, an' ye've been recruiting other people since ye were a child. Did ye think I didn't know about it?"

"Ye knew about it?" Teressa looked petrified.

"Aye, but I didn't see any reason to put a stop to it," said Saeddryn. "It's harmless enough. That's not why I'm here, anyhow."

"Then why *are* ye here?" Teressa dared to ask.

"Because I need yer help," said Saeddryn. "I've come back to Malvern to talk to people, an' ye are the best person to help me do it."

Teressa stood up, pointlessly stuffing the prayer stone into a pocket sewn inside her robe. "Why should I help ye?" she asked. "Ye are a traitor. Ye betrayed Arenadd, and the Queen as well. I should turn ye in to the guards."

"I serve the Night God," said Saeddryn. "Like ye do, Teressa." She smiled. "I heard yer prayer. Ye want Arenadd to come back. Ye want the Shadow That Walks."

"I do," Teressa admitted. "We need his help now, more than we've ever done."

"Ye need my help, then," said Saeddryn, and by way of an explanation she stepped forward and vanished into the shadows.

Teressa opened her mouth to scream, but a cold hand clamped over her mouth and silenced it immediately.

"Be quiet," Saeddryn hissed, reappearing as silently as she had vanished. "I'm the Shadow That Walks now, Teressa, an' now ye've seen the proof. An' trust me; if ye betray me, I'll kill ye on the spot."

Teressa was breathing hard, but she didn't try to cry out when Saeddryn let her go. For a moment, she just stood there, staring in wonder, but then she flung herself down at the old woman's feet.

"Master! Shadow That Walks!"

"That's better," said Saeddryn. "I'm Arenadd's successor, an' if ye serve him, then ye must serve me now."

"I will!" Teressa said immediately, rising to her knees. "What do ye want me to do, Holiness? Anything I can do . . ."

"Stand up," said Saeddryn. Once Teressa had done so, she answered the question. "I need the shadow worshippers," she said. "Everyone ye've recruited. Bring them together, all of them. I want to speak to them."

"At once, Master," said Teressa. "In the meantime, if ye need somewhere to stay, ye can have my room."

"Thankye," said Saeddryn. "How soon can ye bring everyone together?"

Teressa paused to think it over. "It might take a day or so, and I'll have to find out if any of them have a place where we can meet without being seen."

"Work fast, then," Saeddryn commanded. "How many of them are there?"

"A lot," Teressa smiled. "There are a lot of us, Master. Ye'll be proud to see how many."

Saeddryn inclined her head toward the novice. "Well done, Teressa. I knew I was right to leave ye in peace."

"Ye were, Holiness," said Teressa, with surprising firmness. She waited reverently until Saeddryn gave her permission, then hurried out of the room, murmuring prayers of gratitude and joy.

Despite Teressa's promises, Saeddryn had had her doubts about how useful this eccentric little cult of hers would be—but when she saw them all gathered, three nights later in a disused warehouse, she was astonished.

There were more than fifty of them—men and women of different ages and classes. There were no other priestesses or novices, but several of them were clearly griffiners though they had not brought their partners with them. They all greeted Teressa with respect, but it was clear they had never met like this before. Saeddryn, watching from the shadows, heard every word they said.

"What's this all about, Teressa?" one of the griffiners asked. "What's so important? We're running a big risk, gathering like this."

Teressa was wearing her best silver robe, and her face was alight with excitement and pride. "Trust me," she said. "There's never been anything more important than this. Listen with the others, and I'll tell ye everything."

She had set up a box to stand on, and she climbed up onto it now, with a quick glance at where Saeddryn stood hidden. Then she addressed her followers, and they all went silent and listened attentively almost immediately. Even Saeddryn was impressed by the command the novice priestess had over them.

"Everyone!" Teressa said loudly. "Fellow worshippers of the Shadow That Walks! I know this was never meant to be a cult; I never asked any of ye to serve me, and we've never met up like this before. We worship alone, so this isn't a ritual."

"What is it, then?" asked the griffiner who'd questioned her before. "Why are we here?"

"Because something incredible has happened," said Teressa. She smiled beatifically. "I always said that one day something like this would happen—that if we were patient and faithful, then the time would come when we could serve the Shadow That Walks. Well, now that time has come."

There was a stirring from the others.

"He's back!" a woman shouted. "The great Arenadd has come back to us!"

The others took it up and started to exclaim in great excitement, but when Teressa spoke again, they went quiet, all eager to hear what she had to say.

"No," she said, provoking a ripple of disappointment. "Arenadd hasn't come back. But someone else has. There's a new Shadow That Walks. Arenadd's successor. And she's here, now, to talk to all of ye."

The crowd broke up in excitement again. The last of their attentiveness disappeared, and they surged forward, asking eager questions. Some started to move around, searching among their fellows as if they expected to find their long-awaited leader hiding among their own number.

But then Saeddryn stepped forward into the light, and absolute silence fell.

Teressa, taking her cue, stepped down off her platform and let Saeddryn take her place, and the assembled shadow worshippers fell back—half in awe, and half in fear.

"*I* have come," Saeddryn said loudly. "I am Saeddryn Taranisäii, the High Priestess of Malvern. I'm the Shadow That Walks."

"Prove it!" a man dared to shout.

Saeddryn growled and pulled her dress open, quite unembarrassed, to show the deep scars that ran down her body. Several people gasped or groaned at the sight of them.

"Don't ye dare question me again," Saeddryn said coldly as she covered herself up again. "I'm the Shadow That Walks, an' the Night God has sent me here, just as she sent Arenadd, to do her will."

"What is her will?" Teressa asked.

"To kill the half-breed," said Saeddryn. "And place my son Caedmon on the throne. He's the rightful ruler, and the Night God has chosen him."

"But Queen Laela is the rightful ruler," one of the griffiners said doubtfully. "She's King Arenadd's daughter."

"She's an imposter," said Saeddryn. "Arenadd would never

father a half-breed. She lied and seduced him, then she killed him and stole his throne. Now I've come to punish her and set the North free."

"The North *is* free," said the skeptical griffiner. "Isn't it?"

"Free!" Saeddryn laughed harshly. "Listen to yerself. Living in the Eyrie has made ye soft." She looked upward, to where the holes in the roof let the starlight through. "I fought for this country when I was young," she said. "By Arenadd's side. We set our people free together. An' who did we fight? Who was here then, in Malvern's Eyrie, crushing ye all into the dirt, an' selling ye as slaves?"

"Southerners," a woman in the crowd spat.

"Aye, Southerners," said Saeddryn. "An' where did this half-breed brat come from? The South. She's a Southerner; she's not one of us. She killed my daughter an' my husband, an' she had me killed as well because I stood against her. I defied her. Now there's only one true, living Taranisäii left, and it's Caedmon. That's why I'm here. He sent me."

"The Queen's not a Southerner," said the skeptical griffiner. "She's one of us. She's got her tattoos now—she went through the ceremony in the Temple. She went to Amoran and freed our people there. A Southerner wouldn't do that."

"A trick," Saeddryn said dismissively. "A way to get us to trust her before she killed the King." She glared at the man who, to his credit, didn't flinch. "If ye don't believe me, then listen now. Listen, an' I'll tell ye what will happen if the half-breed isn't removed." She pointed southward. "They'll come back. The Southerners will come back over the mountains from where we drove them back into the South, an' they'll come because the half-breed will bring them back. She'll hand the North back to them because she's in league with them. She's one of them. They sent her here as their spy, to destroy us from within!" Saeddryn spoke hard and forcefully, not caring that there was no proof to any of what she was saying. Ugly rumours would only strengthen her cause.

The shadow worshippers muttered among themselves.

"I'll believe it when I see it," said the skeptical griffiner. "But not because I don't trust you, Saeddryn. It's only that I trust Arenadd more, and if he trusted Laela, then so do I."

"Do whatever ye want," said Saeddryn. "Ye'll see I'm right, sooner or later."

"Well *I* believe you," said a woman in front of her. "Because you've come in the Night God's name, and the Night God wouldn't lie. Would she?" She gave the skeptical griffiner a sour look.

"She's right!" others shouted.

"The half-breed is in league with the Southerners!" some added. "She'll send us back into slavery!"

A good number of them turned to Saeddryn now and bowed low.

"What do we do now, Holiness?" they asked. "What can we do to help?"

"Spread the word," said Saeddryn. "But don't tell anyone I'm in Malvern. For now, I have to stay hidden."

"Why?" asked Teressa. "What are ye going to do?"

"What's the plan?" someone else put in.

Saeddryn paused a moment before answering, looking down on them all. Their faces were upturned to look at her, their eyes all alight with faith and excitement. They believed in her.

"My son is coming," she said. "To claim his throne. But I'm going to strike the first blow. In the meantime, I want ye to do what ye can. Tell other people the truth that I've told ye. We won't meet up again like this; it's too risky. Don't let yerselves be caught, because if ye are, then the half-breed will have ye killed, an' I won't come and save ye."

"And what will ye do, Holiness?" asked Teressa.

Saeddryn smiled horribly. "Once everything is ready, an' the word has been spread, an' Malvern is ready to welcome its true King, I'm going to the Eyrie, and I'm going to kill the half-breed. I'll cut off her head and throw it from the top of the Council Tower for everyone to see."

Several of the assembled shadow worshippers cheered or shouted savagely.

"Kill her, Holiness! Kill her for us!"

"I will," Saeddryn promised. "Ye have my word as a Taranisäii."

There was nothing more that needed to be said after that, and Saeddryn felt the meeting beginning to break up, as people talked rapidly among themselves, making plans for how they were going to spread her claims and discredit the usurper. They didn't come to try to speak to her personally—too intimidated, perhaps.

Teressa the novice, though, stayed nearby, and murmured to her, "What about me?" she asked. "Is there anything I can do?"

"No, Teressa," said Saeddryn. "Ye've done plenty. I owe ye for this. Keep out of it from now on—it's best if ye don't get caught."

"Yes, Master," said Teressa. "And thankye for coming here." She smiled proudly. "Now I can say I've seen two Shadows That Walk."

"And if everything goes well, ye'll never need to see another," said Saeddryn. "Once the half-breed is dead and Caedmon is crowned, I won't be needed any more."

"No," Teressa said passionately. "The Shadow That Walks will always be needed."

Saeddryn nodded appreciatively at the look on the girl's face. "Good, Teressa. Faith is the greatest gift ye can have. Never let it go."

"I won't," Teressa promised.

"Now . . ." Saeddryn turned away. "It's time. Send everyone away, and let them begin. Ye can go back to the Temple, an' say nothing to the others. I don't trust them any more."

"I understand," said Teressa. "But will ye still want to use my room—?"

"No," said Saeddryn. "I'll find my own place to hide."

"How will I find ye?" asked Teressa.

"Ye won't," said Saeddryn. She smiled horribly. "No-one finds the Shadow That Walks. And no-one ever sees her coming. Not until it's too late."

37

Growing

Kullervo's pains continued for most of the voyage to Maijan. He rarely left his and Senneck's quarters, and spent most of his time sleeping. When he was awake, however, at Senneck's insistence, he took advantage of his state and exercised, lifting and lowering a lump of lead someone had found for him. The effort made his arms ache just as badly as his back and legs, but he kept at it anyway, driven by his absolute trust in his partner. Inva, whose many skills included healing, visited and applied various soothing ointments, which helped to ease the pain. Trained to be silent and discreet, she made no comment on his condition, and in fact only really spoke once, a month out to sea.

"The messenger dragon reached our ship. Prince Akhane is visiting Maijan and will be waiting for us there."

With that, she put the lid back on the jar and left without another word.

As Maijan drew steadily closer as the weeks went by, and the weather became hotter and hotter, Kullervo finally began to improve. The pains eased off, and moving became easier. He continued to exercise, more vigorously now that it hurt less, and a contented Senneck, watching him, said, "My work is done. You are ready."

Kullervo smiled at her with real gratitude. "I know. I can feel my magic gland now. I couldn't before, but now"—he touched his throat, in the hollow just below his voice-box—"there's a swelling just here; I can feel it if I press down. It really has got bigger."

"Yes," said Senneck. "And when you transform again, you will feel it even more. If need be, you will even be able to open your throat wide enough to display it. But you should not do that."

Kullervo nodded proudly. "I can't wait!"

"But do wait," said Senneck. "Do not change again until you are fully recovered; to use magic now would be dangerous."

"I understand." Kullervo lay back peacefully. Sleeping was much easier now.

As his strength returned, he became more active and spent more time on deck; but he didn't enjoy the suddenly glaring sun or the attention of the crew, all of whom stared at the hump on his back and his broken teeth. Kullervo acted as if he didn't notice it. Stares were something he'd lived with all his life.

Finally, nearly three months after the initial pains had begun, Kullervo found himself nearly pain-free and, more or less, fully recovered. But by now, he hardly recognised himself. He was puzzled to find that, all of a sudden, he had to stoop to get through doors. His shoulders had become wide and muscular from the exercise he had done. His hands looked big and powerful. More astonishingly, his wings had grown as well. They were longer now and felt more strongly rooted to his back. They weren't bald any more, either, but had sprouted long, tawny feathers and looked almost ready for flight. His tail had grown fur, and feathers as well. He cut those off; they made it impossible to hide the tail in his trousers. He couldn't bring himself to cut the wing feathers, however, and resorted to binding them up with Inva's help. She must have been let in on his secret by Laela, or had ridiculous levels of self-control, because she scarcely reacted to the sight of them. But Kullervo thought he noticed a new level of respect from her once she had seen them.

Senneck took in his new physique—he had no problem with stripping in front of her—with obvious pleasure and satisfaction. "Look at you now!" she exclaimed, flexing her talons. "Look what magnificence I have made of you! When I last saw you unclothed, you were thin and scrawny, like a newly hatched bird. Now you are big and strong, as a male should be. I did not expect this to happen, but I am very pleased that it did!"

Kullervo felt himself blushing. "It feels weird. I don't feel like myself any more."

Senneck blinked slowly. "How can you not feel like yourself? You *are* yourself."

"I don't feel like my body belongs to me any more," said Kullervo, cautiously prodding his deepened chest. "I'm not complaining," he added hastily. "It's just . . . odd."

"You will become used to it," said Senneck.

"I'm sure I will." Kullervo shrugged and grinned. "I'm used to having my body do odd things. I should be able to deal with this." A speculative look crossed his face, and he turned sharply and punched the wooden wall of the stall. It juddered under the blow, sprinkling wood dust onto the floor. Kullervo cringed and rubbed his knuckles.

"You see?" said Senneck. "You are powerful now! Imagine how well you will do when there is danger."

Kullervo pulled his trousers back on, suddenly troubled. "I don't want to hurt anyone."

"You must."

Frowning, Kullervo came closer and rubbed his shoulder against her chest, griffin-like. "I suppose . . ."

Senneck nibbled his wings. "When the time comes, you and I shall fight side by side, and we shall be unstoppable."

"But we won't have to," said Kullervo. "The war's going to end. We're going to end it."

"Indeed we are."

They lay together in companionable silence for a while, Senneck grooming Kullervo's wings with surprising gentleness.

"I am becoming ready to mate," she said abruptly, breaking the silence.

Kullervo froze. "You are?"

"Yes. Soon it will be time for me to choose a male. I am not too old for that! It has been too long since I have mated."

"Who are you going to choose, then?" asked Kullervo, in an odd voice.

Senneck yawned. "Skarok, of course. Normally I would

have nothing to do with that young fool, but my time has come, and there are no other males here for me." She stopped her grooming. "Stay here and sleep in my warmth. I am going above to fly."

She walked out and above deck, leaving Kullervo to lie very still where he was, staring blankly after her. His nose was full of her scent, and he could feel her warmth still embracing him.

Silently, not moving or changing his expression at all, he felt tears roll down his face.

Senneck emerged into the open air. She stretched her wings, shivering them as the muscles loosened. She had been contented, but now her throat pulsated irritably. Heat had built in her loins, spreading tense energy through her body. The mating urge had risen up unexpectedly while she was resting, and it made her jittery and angry with undirected lust. She rubbed herself against the mast, bumping her head and flanks on the rough wood and purring frantically. Her talons caught on the planking beneath her, and she dragged them backward, leaving a row of grooves.

Shaking herself vigorously, she darted off, almost prancing around the deck. Her wings unfurled, and she hurled herself into the air.

The wind, moving over her back and belly, helped to cool her down but did very little to soothe the mad energy. She flew with all her strength, beating her wings recklessly. The wounds she had collected in the fight for Warwick ached—they had healed on the surface, but underneath it seemed the damage still lingered. She ignored it, and began to swoop and turn in the air, dodging and banking to avoid imaginary enemies. She had always been an agile flier, and without a human weighing her down, she was fast.

She flew like this for some time, easily keeping up with the slow-moving ship. There were other griffins in the air with her—all females. Senneck, aggravated by the sight of them, flew aggressively at the nearest one. The other female rolled out of the way. Screeching, Senneck attacked the others as well, driving them away. None of them flared up in response, and it was lucky that was the case because if any of them had done so, an ugly fight would have broken out. A griffin on heat wanted nothing except to mate or kill, and failing one, most would happily choose the other.

Unable to vent her urges through combat, Senneck came in for a rough landing on the deck. Huffing and snorting, she looked around quickly for anything that moved. There were humans there, sensibly hurrying off out of her sight. She ignored them.

At last, a scent hit her nostrils that made her bristle and hiss. It was the rich, musky smell of a male.

Skarok.

The younger griffin came toward her, stiff-legged, with his head held high and his wings out to make himself look larger. Tail lashing with controlled excitement.

Senneck turned to him and lowered her own head in what looked like submission. Encouraged, Skarok came closer. Step by careful step. He rasped a deep, throaty, lustful rasp.

When he was one step away from her—one step away from mounting her and making her his—Senneck rose up and smacked him across the face with her talons.

Skarok sprawled on the deck, squarking in shock. Before he could get up, Senneck came forward and began to lunge at him with her beak wide open. He made some attempts to fight back, but Senneck was bigger and more powerful. She hit him several times, tearing out clumps of fur and feathers, and in moments he was up and beating an undignified scrambling retreat. Senneck chased him until he had clumsily thrown himself into the air. She stayed on deck, screeching madly after him.

Once he was out of reach, she lay down on her belly, snorting.

She felt calmer now, but when Skarok came back later, chirping meekly and looking for another chance, she chased him away with just as much ferocity as before.

This was the way of griffins. Her heat would last for three more days, and during that time she would continue to tease him with flirtation followed by aggression, drawing out the torment until she decided to relent and submit to him. Normally, this would be a strategy to attract as many males as possible so that they could fight it out, and the strongest would win the right to mate with her. As it was, she followed the ritual out of instinct—and spite, since in all honesty she did not like Skarok and did not think he was a particularly worthy mate, and as far as she was concerned, this was a good way to teach him a lesson. If he persisted long enough, she would eventually give in.

Persist was exactly what he did. As the next few days dragged by, each one hotter than the last, Skarok returned again and again. Senneck slept up on deck, too antsy to cope with her nest below, and wallowed in the savagery of her mating urge.

She rolled, she purred, she hissed at humans and other females, she went to the bows and sent out an unearthly mating call several times a day. When Skarok came near, she would sometimes sit on her haunches with a hind leg raised, coyly showing off the female part she might let him near, maybe this time . . .

But every time Skarok gave in to his desire, every time he came too close, she would snarl and screech and hit out at him, and when he finally did lose his temper and fight back, she beat him down mercilessly, leaving him bloodied and humiliated.

Caught up in the game of courtship, she had almost forgotten about Kullervo. He did not appear on deck, and in fact hadn't so much as shown his face since she had spoken to him in their nest. If she had spoken to Inva, she might have found out why, but she didn't. Kullervo might have been her partner, but for now that didn't matter, and neither did he.

If she had spoken to Inva, she might have found out that Kullervo hadn't been on deck at all and, in fact, hadn't even left the nest once. Or eaten anything. Or even said a word.

On the third day, Senneck finally felt her mating urges beginning to die down. On that day, she finally tired of her games as well. She sent out the call again, and sure enough Skarok patiently returned. He looked wary now, obviously expecting very little.

Senneck bowed her head toward him, wings tilting upward,

and huffed softly. When Skarok ventured closer, she lifted her tail, flicking it invitingly.

Skarok came on, hesitating every few steps, tensed to run if she attacked. But this time, she did not move.

He reached her safely, and when she did not lash out, he lowered his beak toward her neck. Still no attack, and he began to groom her, with surprising gentleness. Senneck closed her eyes and purred.

Growing bolder, Skarok moved closer—standing over her in the dominant position—and ran his beak through her feathers with increasing strength. In response, Senneck tilted her head and nibbled at his chest. Her purr warmed and deepened.

"At last," Skarok murmured, his old confidence coming back.

Senneck let him move over her body, scratching her with his talons just hard enough to make her shiver. It had been such a long time since she had felt the touch of a male . . . but even though it was as thrilling as she remembered, she felt the slightest hint of self-disgust. To be reduced to this, submitting to some scrawny youngster she despised, one who would not give her any help or status in return . . .

It occurred to her then, gently and sadly, that she had never in her life mated with a male she truly desired. There had never been a male of the kind she had once longed for, a male who was big and solid and self-assured. Her first mate had been not much different from this one—thin and leggy and with the false confidence of youth and uncertainty. If only . . .

Skarok had come alongside her, rubbing his flank against hers. Senneck pushed back, still willing enough, twining her tail with his and rasping sensually. Skarok began to bite at the nape of her neck, preparing to mount, and she tensed in anticipation.

A snarl broke in on them. It was low, it was piercing, and it was full of rage.

Senneck and Skarok broke apart instantly, turning to face the threat, and there was the very last thing either of them had expected.

A griffin. A male griffin. Not a very large one—one much smaller than Skarok, in fact. He was barely the size of a half-grown youngster. But his shoulders were heavy and solid, his paws and legs proportioned like those of an adult. And if he was smaller than Skarok, there was so much hatred burning in his yellow eyes that the skinny griffin found himself squaring up to him in response, his own beak opening to hiss back.

The stranger, whose feathers were grey mottled with black, stepped forward with his head and chest low to the ground and his tail waving from side to side, stalking. His wings opened, making him appear to double in size, and he snarled again.

Skarok reared up, extending his talons. "Leave now, weakling, or die!"

The other griffin rose up, too, pathetically small next to Skarok, but there was no uncertainty or fear in him at all. "You will not touch her!" he screamed. "Leave her alone!"

Senneck, watching in bewilderment, tensed when she heard the voice. It sounded wrong. Too light. Too high.

Too familiar.

Skarok didn't seem to have noticed anything. He was ready to mate, he had been challenged, and that was enough. He made a sudden rush at the other male. It was one meant to impress rather than seriously attack, all open wings and flailing talons, but it was dangerous all the same.

The other griffin, rather than retreating, tensed back and sprang. His smaller size gave him an unexpected advantage, as he dove under Skarok's talons and hit him in the belly, beak first. Skarok stumbled back, but the other griffin had not had the sense to dart out of reach after striking, and Skarok took the opportunity and struck him in the back with his talons, hurling him onto the deck.

The other griffin got up, snorting, and lunged at him. Skarok was ready, and the two males began to grapple with each other, talons tearing through fur and feather, beaks aiming for heads and necks.

Senneck stood back and watched. This was a mating fight, and she had no part in it but to wait for the victor. But even though she knew that, she couldn't shake off her bewilderment. None of this made sense. Where had this other male come from? They were too far away from land for him to have flown over, and there were no other ships in sight.

And anyway, he looked . . . looked like . . . ?

But no. That was ridiculous. Impossible. He wouldn't . . . couldn't . . .

But the more Senneck watched, the more she heard the stranger's wrong-sounding voice, the more certain she became.

He had grown. Grown bigger, sleeker, more well-proportioned. The head was a more proper shape now. But he still had too many talons on his forepaws. His beak was still undersized.

He was still Kullervo.

And he was losing.

Surprise and sheer anger might have given him a head start, but as the fight went on, it became more and more obvious that Skarok was going to win. Kullervo was much too small, and even if his griffin shape was now more complete he had still spent much more time looking more or less human. And he was not a real fighter in any shape.

Skarok threw his weakening foe down, again and again, biting him cruelly on his soft belly. He was attacking not to kill or seriously wound—after all, this was not a territorial fight—but simply to win.

But no matter how many times he fell, no matter how battered he became, Kullervo would not give in. Every time Skarok knocked him over, he got up again, his beak chipped, one eye swelling, but his determination intact.

"You . . . won't . . . touch her," he gasped. "I won't . . . won't let . . ."

Infuriated, Skarok began to attack more savagely, bashing Kullervo's head onto the deck. Kullervo looked up appealingly at Senneck. "Senneck! Help . . . help me . . ."

Skarok reared up onto his hind legs. *"Coward!"* he screamed. "To ask a female for help in this—!" His words broke off into an incoherent screech.

Senneck, however, started toward them. "Kullervo!" she called. "Stop this! Stop now! Fly away!"

Kullervo raised his head, not even seeming to notice the infuriated Skarok. "Senneck . . ."

"Go!" she said again.

Common sense wouldn't get through to Kullervo, but Senneck's voice did. He scrambled upright and ran away, launching himself clumsily into the air.

However, Skarok wouldn't stand for this. His rival had

dared to attack him, then had humiliated him by refusing to give in—and by breaking the oldest law of all, and asking the *female* to help him.

Utterly outraged, and frustrated beyond all reason, he forgot about Senneck and went in pursuit, flying after the cowardly runt as fast as he could.

Dazed, aching all over and still weakened by the transformation, Kullervo had no chance. He flew around the ship in a pointless circle, now truly afraid, but got barely any distance at all. Skarok bore down on him and, swooping on him in midair, struck him a blow between the wings that unbalanced him and sent him tumbling out of the sky.

Kullervo panicked, beating his wings hard to try to recover, but Skarok came on, grabbing him in his talons and shaking him violently before letting go. Kullervo rolled over several times, unable to stop himself. Disoriented, not knowing which way was up, he lost all control and fell into the sea with a deafening splash.

Griffins feared water, and now Kullervo found out why.

In water, wings were worse than useless. As he tried to swim, they caught in the current and dragged him backward, tossing him about like a leaf. He kicked out with his paws, but they were all but worthless here.

Bright light hit his eyes. He squinted as he tried to stay afloat and saw the ship ahead. It was moving away, taking its shadow with it.

When he saw that, Kullervo simply gave up. He could not swim, not to keep up with that, and even if he could, there would be no way to get back on board. Realising it, letting the knowledge settle down on him like a great weight, he relaxed and let himself float, drifting away into the endless ocean. It was easier this way.

The salt water splashed into his face. He closed his eyes against it and tilted his head, pointing his beak upward to help himself breathe.

Something hit him, hard, in the neck. The impact shoved him under, and water poured into his beak. He struggled hopelessly, feeling the talons in his shoulders, and realised that Skarok had still not been satisfied. He had come after him one last time, to push him down and drown him.

The talons hooked in his flesh, pulling mercilessly upward. Kullervo's head broke the surface, and as he coughed and breathed again he found himself skimming through the water, legs dangling. The griffin holding him flew higher, laboriously dragging more of his body into the air. Was Skarok going to lift him up, then drop him again? Was that it? Was he going to torment him before he killed him?

Anger coursed back through Kullervo's body. Death was one thing, but nobody was going to toy with him.

He forced his wings to unfurl, and began to beat them again. They felt heavy, and sprayed water back into the ocean, but he kept going, harder and faster, knowing that the more he beat them, the faster they would dry. Sure enough, despite the wetness making the feathers shrink and bend, he managed to catch some air. As his legs lifted out of the water, followed by his tail, he flapped with all his might, helping his captor lift him higher. Ahead he could see the ship, its deck now almost within reach. He kept trying to fly, thinking that if he could break free, then maybe he could get back to safety.

But even if he was out of the water, his wings would not work properly. They needed to be fully dried and groomed as well. Breaking free was out of the question.

The other griffin flew higher, not letting go. The railings of the ship passed below, then they were descending at last.

Kullervo's paws touched the deck, and as the talons released him, he scrambled away, turning to face Skarok one last time . . .

But it was Senneck there. Senneck, her underbelly dripping, blue eyes glaring at him. "Go to your nest," she snapped. "Dry yourself."

Kullervo's fear left. "Thank you—"

Senneck hissed at him. "*Go!* Go now, before you humiliate me any further, Kullervo."

Every word cut him far more deeply than Skarok's talons ever could have. Head bowed, he turned and limped away.

He returned to his nest and flopped down on the straw without bothering to groom. His wet feathers didn't matter, and his wounds didn't matter either. Nothing mattered any more. Not now.

Kullervo laid his head on his talons and did something no

griffin could do, something that came from the human heart that lived inside him no matter what his shape became. Silently, Kullervo Taranisäii cried.

He must have slept eventually. Vile dreams came to him when he did. But what made them worse was that they weren't dreams, not really. They were memories. Vague, ugly memories.

He was struggling in the sea again, and the sea became a pool. A still pool, filled with a reflection of a hideous face. It wrapped itself around him and dragged him down into itself, embracing him with its ugly reality. Above him, he caught a glimpse of something else, something bright and beautiful that wavered in his vision for just a moment. He strove toward it, reaching out to try to touch it, but the pool closed over his eyes, shutting it away from him forever.

The face stared straight at him, not snarling or mocking but looking at him with a pity that was far worse. Eyes yellow and slanted, head flattened, misshapen feathers stabbing out of the forehead like tiny arrows. Horrible and deformed, full of misery. Full of longing for what it could never have. What he could never be.

He woke up in pain, feeling damp and hot. But he was not alone. Something big and warm touched his back. He felt the heartbeat thudding softly in time with his own, and a great grey beak moved over his wing and flank, grooming him almost delicately.

Senneck.

Kullervo lay there passively and let her groom him, too ashamed to even say her name.

She had noticed he was awake. "Are you well?"

"I'll recover," he replied in defeated tones. His throat felt raw.

"You should not have done that."

"I know. I promise I won't ever do it again."

"You did not need to fight for me," Senneck told him sternly. "I was in no danger. Skarok thought you were challenging for the right to mate with me! But you did not act as a true griffin would. You are lucky he did not kill you for it."

Kullervo shuddered. "I'm sorry. I just couldn't bear the thought of . . . I didn't want him to . . . to . . . not *that*. Not with you. But it doesn't matter," he added quickly. "Not now. I'm sorry. Please just forgive me. What I did was stupid."

"It is only natural that you were jealous," said Senneck. "I am your partner, after all. I confess that when Erian lusted after a female, I, too, was jealous of her."

"I was upset," said Kullervo.

"You did not like Skarok?"

"No. I mean . . . I didn't think anything about him much. He's just some griffin. I just didn't . . . when you told me he was the only male here and you had to . . ." Kullervo shook himself. "But it's too late now anyway."

"Too late for what?" said Senneck.

"Too late," Kullervo repeated. He closed his eyes in a hopeless kind of way, and added softly, "Too late to stop it. He won, so I know you must have . . . you know."

"Mated with him?" said Senneck.

Kullervo couldn't stand to use the word. "Yes."

Even that felt like a struggle.

Senneck snorted. "I did not mate with Skarok."

Kullervo stilled. "You—you didn't?"

"No. He came back to me in triumph, and I spurned him and struck him in the face. He had tried to kill my human, and that is something I will not forgive. If I had not had to rescue you, I would have wounded him badly. If you had died, I would have killed him. As it was, he went away, humiliated and disappointed."

Kullervo could scarcely breathe. His chest felt crushed. "You didn't . . . ? And you're not going to . . . ?"

"My heat is ending," Senneck said brusquely. "The urge will be gone soon. Skarok lost his chance. If I wanted to, I could mate with him regardless, but I do not want to. He is a fool and beneath my dignity to pair with."

Kullervo's voice finally ran out altogether. He lay there, feeling paralysed.

"Thank you," Senneck's voice came from above him, like the voice of a god. "You embarrassed me, but you stopped me from mating with Skarok, and I did not truly want to let him have me. The mating madness was on me, but now that I can think clearly, I am glad I did not . . . he would have mocked me with it forever. Now, I shall mock him."

Kullervo said nothing.

Senneck nudged his head. "Kullervo? Are you sleeping?"

Silence. Kullervo could feel his heart fluttering, but no matter how hard he tried, he couldn't make himself speak.

"Kullervo?" Senneck began to sound concerned. "Kullervo, speak to me. Are you hurt? Shall I tell Inva you need healing?"

Kullervo managed to breathe in, and his voice came back. "Senneck," he said.

"Yes?"

"Senneck, I"—every word felt like a struggle—"I—I fought Skarok because—because I was jealous. I couldn't . . . couldn't stand the thought of another male touching you."

"I understand, but you must control yourself," she said gently. "I am a griffin, and I must be allowed to mate when I choose. We are not made to be celibate."

"No," Kullervo burst out. "No, it's not like that. I love you, Senneck. That's why . . ."

She stood up abruptly, turning to look down at him. "What?"

Kullervo wanted to run away, but he knew it was too late now. He'd said it. "I love you, Senneck," he said. "I always have."

"Love?" Senneck repeated. She sounded quite blank.

"Yes," said Kullervo, desperate now. "I love you like a male would. Does. You're beautiful, and you're brave, and I don't want any other female but you."

"Love," Senneck said yet again, as if the word were giving her some trouble. "I do not . . . that is not something that we . . . that is not a word I know."

"Humans love," said Kullervo. "They fall in love. That's how they choose their own mates, that's why they marry. To stay with the one they love forever."

"But I am not human," said Senneck. "This thing . . . 'love' . . . makes no sense to me."

"It doesn't just have to be between male and female," said Kullervo. "Parents love their children, and brothers love their sisters. Worshippers even love their gods."

Senneck blinked. "I have seen how humans pair for life . . . Erian once tried to tell me . . ." She looked at Kullervo again.

"This means nothing to me. And besides, you are not . . ." She trailed off.

Kullervo stared at his talons. "I know love. But I've never been loved. Not by anyone. When I was a child, I saw people around me, I saw parents holding their children, I saw lovers holding hands. But no-one ever held me. And if I reached out to them, they wouldn't reach back.

"When I flew North, I didn't really know why I was going. I thought my mother might be there, but I didn't really know why I wanted to find her. I knew she wanted me to die. But now I know why. I wanted to find her so I could reach out to her, so I could try to make her love me. But she was dead, and so was my father . . ." He shivered, and dared to look up again. "I've never . . . I've never been interested in human females—women. They just don't look beautiful to me. I've never seen one and wanted to touch her the way I want to touch you. When you touch me, when you groom me, when you talk to me . . . that's when I feel so right, like everything is perfect as long as you're with me. I think that's love. I think I love you."

Senneck only stared at him, utterly uncomprehending.

Kullervo couldn't meet her gaze. "I've become my father," he muttered. "My evil father. I love a griffin, gods have mercy on me. What will I do next? Will I become a murderer . . . will I kill again, and love it? Oh, gods, no. Don't let me be him. I don't want to be him . . ." Tears ran down his beak.

"Kullervo." Senneck came closer and rubbed her cheek against his head. "Be calm. Do not say these things. You are upsetting yourself for no reason."

Kullervo relaxed. "Just promise you'll stay with me, Senneck. I know I'm too young for you anyway. I won't do anything you don't want me to. I don't think I can be a father anyway. Mules are sterile, and so am I."

Senneck crouched down by him and began to groom him again. "Rest now, Kullervo. I will take care of you. Skarok is gone, and I shall not leave you again."

"Do you promise?"

"Yes. I promise."

38

The Diary and the Darkness

"—Passed unanimously. The Master of Taxation was very pleased. Afterward—"

Laela turned several pages.

"—woke up and found her dead beside me. Of all the horrible things that have happened in my life, that was one of the very worst. I wish—"

Another page.

"—visited Fruitsheart with Iorwerth—"

And another.

"Yesterday, I returned to Malvern after a visit to Guard's Post. Skandar and I flew on beyond it to just past the mountains. It was the first time we had seen Southern lands in at least ten years. I was unexpectedly surprised to see they looked so much like my own territory. The sight of enemy lands and civilisation so close gave us both a terrible urge to keep going in the hopes of finding a fight, but while pillaging some pathetic Southern village was horribly tempting I had to admit it would be childish. Guard's Post was in good shape, anyway, and that was the main thing. I must remember to visit it again soon. I can't risk letting it weaken."

Laela listened to her father's voice speak on for a while, then, growing bored, moved on.

Oeka's promise had been right. No matter what page of the diary she opened, every one read itself out loud to her. The voice had been growing fainter over the last few days, however, and she had begun to search through the book more thoroughly, fearing that it might stop altogether. Yorath had vanished without a trace and did not reappear even when she tried to have him summoned. Nobody seemed to know where he was. With him gone, she had nobody else around whom she trusted enough to read the diary to her.

In a way, the book had been keeping her company, but in all honesty, it only made her feel even lonelier. Hearing her father's voice like this was just a constant reminder of how much she missed him.

She missed the way he would smile with his eyes, the way he seemed to know everything that was going on. She missed what she had sensed in him—the terrible vulnerability that hid under his cool, neat exterior, the feeling he had given her that in a way he grieved as much as his victims for all the crimes he had committed. And even though one of the greatest of those crimes had been against herself and her family, part of her still refused to hate him for it. He had shown her the silent, lonely heart he kept hidden away from the world, and in a way she felt she had been entrusted with it, as if it was his greatest treasure.

And now she was discovering that the diary matched its creator, as in between dull accounts of the day-to-day duties of rulership, she found hidden pieces of insight. Sometimes, even in the middle of some dry description of law-making and finance, the text would take a sudden turn into something that read almost like a confession.

The only hard part was finding it.

However, Laela wasn't just going through the diary to indulge herself. If Saeddryn now had the same powers her father had had, then the more she knew about them, the better. And nobody could tell her more about them than Arenadd himself.

So she leafed through the pages, listening to snatches of different entries, searching for the knowledge she needed. The only trouble was that Arenadd himself seemed reluctant to write about them, as if his "condition," as he called it, frightened or upset him too much. Or maybe he just didn't think about it much. Or, Laela thought suddenly, or maybe it had occurred to him that someone else might read his diary one day, and he didn't want that person to know too much.

Keep goin', she told herself. *He didn't tell yeh all his secrets right away when you knew him. Why would he start now?*

She turned another page and listened to his voice yet again.

"Caedmon left Malvern today, along with Shar. I don't think he plans to return any time soon. It was my fault in a way, but maybe it's better this way. A few weeks ago, I wrote about poor Sionen. The girl was half my age, but she loved me all the same. I suppose since I looked like I was her age, it made no difference to her.

"After she died, Caedmon confronted me. I could tell that he had been crying. He was mad and wild; he screamed at me and outright accused me of murdering Sionen. He had been secretly in love with her himself, the poor fool. He didn't have to tell me that. His claim upset me, and I flared up in response. I think that if he weren't afraid of me, he could well have attacked me on the spot. In the end, Skandar drove him away.

"After that, he avoided me for a long time and didn't return to his lessons with me until I commanded him to. When we began to practise combat, he lost his head. He was never able to land a blow on me, and I think it had always secretly made him angry. And now that he believed I had killed the woman he loved, he went mad. He snatched up a real sickle and came at me. I honestly think that he really did want to kill me. I quickly disarmed him, and he responded by attacking me again, this time with his fists. In the end, I knocked him down and sharply reminded him of who I was and what the consequences of his actions could be.

He stormed out without a word, and, today, I was informed that he has left Malvern for parts unknown. I know perfectly well that he hates me now; most likely he also left because he thought I might have him arrested if he stayed."

Laela listened to all this, wide-eyed and fascinated. She had never met Caedmon and didn't know that much about him. Iorwerth had hinted that he'd fallen out with Arenadd, but what she was hearing now was far more serious than she had ever imagined.

"What a terrible mess my family has become," Arenadd's voice continued. "First Saeddryn, and now this. I had put all my hopes in Caedmon; when I look back through this journal, I see constant references to how proud I was of him and how much progress he was making. He was my apprentice, my heir. I always told him that if anything ever happened to me, he would be King, but what he didn't know was that I had secretly planned that one day, when I thought he was mature and ready for it, I would abdicate the throne in favour of him. I may be immortal, but I know I can't rule forever, and Caedmon could have been a great ruler.

"As it is, now that I know he won't forgive me and come back to finish his training, my plan is ruined. I have publicly destroyed the documents naming him as my heir, and so far I have not chosen a replacement. But I hinted to Saeddryn that if I found no Taranisäii worthy of that position I could choose someone outside my own family. Great leadership is not an inherited trait, and simply being a Taranisäii is not enough to make someone worthy of Kingship.

"Saeddryn, of course, is not pleased with me at all. She thinks I am losing my touch—and possibly my mind as well. The woman is impossible. Maybe I shouldn't have made her High Priestess; she spends far too much time worrying about what the Night God thinks and wants and doesn't have the humility to just ask me. I think it annoys her that I won't take a more active role in the Temple, but in all honesty I have no use for religion. Let the imaginary version of the Night God comfort ordinary people; only I have touched her, and only I know how cold her skin is. Her love is even colder. I may not know much, but I do know that the only kind of love a human being needs or truly benefits from comes from other humans.

"How can someone so cut off from us, so unable to understand what really drives us, how can someone like that know us well enough to love us properly?

"Oh, Caedmon. You've let me down. You've let us all down. If you only knew how disappointed I am in you. If you only knew how much like a son you felt to me."

Laela closed the book thoughtfully. No insight into Saeddryn's powers, but plenty of insight into the sad state of the Taranisäii clan. No wonder there had been so much coldness between Saeddryn and Arenadd. And no wonder someone had tried to assassinate him. So far, there was no proof that the assassin had been sent by Saeddryn or anyone in her family, but if they weren't behind it, then she, Laela, would eat her own boots.

She put the diary aside. "Who would've thought big families could get so complicated? Thank gods I got a sensible upbringing."

Thinking sadly of her foster father, she made for the door.

Someone had propped a chair under the handle.

Laela's neck prickled. She turned, looking around quickly. There was nobody else in the room, and the only other entrance led into Oeka's deserted nest. She went in there, but there was no-one in there, either.

"What the—?"

She went back into her own room, and there was the chair, innocently blocking anyone from opening the door. Nobody else had come in, and if they had, there was no way they could have left again. And Laela definitely hadn't put the chair there herself.

Her hand went to her belt, where she had taken to keeping her father's sickle.

It wasn't there.

Laela searched frantically, but the weapon was nowhere in sight, and she would surely have felt it fall out of her belt.

"All right," she said aloud, straightening up in the centre of the room. "This ain't funny. Come out, whoever yeh are. Don't make me come lookin', because when I find yeh, I'll kick yer teeth in."

Silence.

"Oeka?" Laela ventured. "Are you playin' games with me again? I told yeh not to. C'mon, this ain't funny."

No reply, and nothing moved.

Sensing danger, Laela went toward the door to remove the chair. As she reached out to touch it, something slammed into her side-on. She fell hard, and before she had a chance to get up, her attacker was on her. A hand grabbed her by the hair, wrenching her head sideways, and as she threw up a hand to defend herself, pain split her wrist.

Pure fighting instinct took over. She kicked upward with both feet, hitting something that lurched away and, moving with a speed that astonished her, she rolled away and got up.

Half-crouched and ready to attack, she paused for the

fraction of a heartbeat to look, and saw something that put ice into her blood.

Saeddryn. Saeddryn, snarling and savage in a way that made her look horribly familiar. Saeddryn, black-clad, holding Arenadd's sickle, her dead eye exposed and vile.

In the instant Laela saw her, she knew that she was looking at death.

But the half-breed Queen was made of sterner stuff than that.

She hurled herself toward the door and wrenched the chair away, turning in the same movement to swing it as hard as she could. Saeddryn, already behind her, gasped as a leg hit her in the stomach. Winded, but not seeming to care much, she rushed in to attack.

Laela had not had much practice in fighting. But what she did have was the tavern-brawling, rough-and-ready, improvised combat that came from her foster father Bran, and from her own, unsophisticated, tough spirit. She had been made to punch faces and kick groins, not dance with a sword, and it worked perfectly well.

She put her back against the wall and used the chair as a combination of weapon and shield, blocking the sickle and keeping Saeddryn out of range by jabbing her in the face with the legs. When Saeddryn came in low to attack under the chair, Laela smashed it over her head.

Saeddryn fell onto her face and scrabbled away, crying out in rage and pain. Laela came after her, not giving her any room to move, and began to kick her, stomping on her hand so hard that she felt bones break under her boot. Saeddryn screamed and lost her grip on the sickle, and Laela snatched it away.

But Saeddryn was not finished yet. She rolled sideways, and vanished into the shadows.

Panting, Laela darted over to the fire-place, where the light was strongest. Blood had run down over her hand, making the sickle sticky in her grip. She wiped it quickly on her dress. "Come out, then, yeh withered bitch," she growled. "I'm ready."

"Ye shouldn't have done that," Saeddryn's voice said. It came out of nowhere and sounded hollow and chilly.

Laela spat on the carpet. "Why, ain't yeh happy? Yeh

wanted to be like Arenadd, didn't yeh? Now yeh got broken fingers just like him. Lucky ole you."

Saeddryn said nothing. She didn't seem keen to come out of the shadows.

Laela thought fast and decided her best bet was to keep her busy so she couldn't come up with a plan. "You sure yeh wanna go up against me, Saeddryn? After what I did to the last one of your sort? You wanna know what really happened to Arenadd?"

Silence.

"I killed him," said Laela, which was more or less true. "Yeah, that's right. The stories are true. I killed Arenadd. Real nasty, it was. After what I did, all his bones broke an' he started bleedin' until he turned white as snow. I stood there an' watched him die. Horrible way to go, but he deserved it. Is that why yer here, then? Did yeh wanna go out the same way? Well? Do yeh?" She sneered.

"That's enough," Saeddryn said at last, icy as her predecessor. "Don't try an' fool me, half-breed. I know the truth. Ye have no power. Yer nothin' but a peasant brat my cousin pulled out of the gutter to amuse himself."

"That's rich, comin' from you," Laela shot back. "'Cause I heard some story about you being some peasant from a tiny village in the middle of freezin' nowhere when you was my age."

Saeddryn stepped back into the light. "I'm a Taranisäii," she said. "My blood is pure."

Laela made a rude gesture at her. "Yeah, well, you can take yer fancy breedin' an' shove it where the sun don't shine. Now, are yeh gonna come get me or what?"

Saeddryn charged. Laela had prepared herself while she hurled her insults, and now she lunged forward, holding the chair out in front of her, intending to push Saeddryn back with it and trap her against a wall or the floor.

But Saeddryn had done with fighting like a mortal. In mid-run, she dove head first—straight into Laela's own shadow.

As Laela turned, trying desperately to defend herself against an enemy she couldn't see, the chair twisted and tore itself out of her hands, so powerfully it made her arm give an audible crack. The sickle, which she had tucked into her belt again, was yanked out by an invisible hand. Unarmed, she kicked out blindly and hit nothing.

Something hit her on the back of the head so hard, it made coloured lights explode in her eyes. She stumbled and recovered, but then another blow came, and another, and after that the fight was more or less over. Cuts appeared on her arms and shoulder. A stab-wound opened in her forehead, making blood run into her eyes. She tried desperately to fight back, wrapping a hand around her throat to protect it. But how could she hit an enemy she could not see—an enemy who was impossibly fast, impossibly strong? Saeddryn pressed in on her, slicing up her hand, then grabbing her wrist, wrenching it away to expose her throat.

Laela shoved at her, and screamed. *"Help! Help me!"*

And then Saeddryn screamed. The hand holding Laela's wrist let go, and as Laela staggered away, she saw her enemy fall out of the shadows and onto the floor, where she began to writhe and tear at herself. She screamed again, garbling meaningless words, then got up and began to run around the room, smacking into the walls and furniture as if she couldn't see them at all. Near the archway that led to Oeka's nest, she stopped and began to bash her head on the wall, over and over again.

Bleeding and shaking with shock, Laela stared. "What the—?"

Do not be afraid, said a voice in her head.

Laela started. "Oeka!"

The illusory image of the griffin appeared in the middle of the floor, wavering a little before it stilled and became more solid. *You are hurt.*

Laela ignored her and looked toward Saeddryn. The old woman fell to the floor, sobbing incoherently. "What in the . . . ?"

You have nothing to fear from her now, said Oeka.

"What did you do to her?" Laela exclaimed, unable to look away from the awful spectacle.

Struck into her mind, said Oeka. *I have unbalanced the part of her that tells her where she is. She cannot tell what part of her life is happening now; she is lost in her own past and cannot escape.*

Laela blinked slowly. "Uh . . . what?"

I have driven her insane, Oeka said dispassionately.

As if that were a signal, Saeddryn got up. She was shaking, and her eye bulged with terror, staring straight at Laela.

Do not be afraid, said Oeka. *She cannot see you any more.*

"Right." Laela ran to the door and opened it, yelling for the guards. They came running through the audience chamber, where they would have been able to see and stop any normal intruder. When they saw the blood and wounds on the Queen's body, they looked shocked. "Milady!" one said.

Laela pointed back into her room. "Grab her, yeh idiot," she snapped.

The guards, well trained, entered and made straight for Saeddryn. As they approached, however, she seemed to wake up in some way. She turned and ran straight through the nest, staggering this way and that. Laela ran after her, along with the two guards, but they were too late. Saeddryn reached the ledge outside and stepped off it into the void.

Gone.

Off in Skenfrith, Heath sauntered along a corridor in the upper levels of the governor's tower, humming a tune.

In all his life, he could never have imagined that something like this would ever happen to him—and he had a very good imagination.

His goals in life had always been simple. He loved money. But more than that, he loved power. Not the sort of power that came from governing others, though. No, Heath enjoyed a more subtle kind of power: the power of knowing what other people didn't and the power of making them believe whatever he told them.

Heath was a born liar. He was also very clever, and he knew it. He'd noticed that he was smarter than everyone else when he was a boy, and from that moment on his brain had become his favourite toy.

The thing was, as he had discovered, a lie *didn't* have to be completely believable for people to believe it. It could be as outrageous or preposterous as you wanted it to be. The real trick wasn't coming up with something plausible; it was making people want to believe it.

And so Heath had created his own personal credo, and it had served him well. Dress neatly, always smile, and be confident. Dominate with confidence. That was his motto, or would have been if he'd ever bothered with mottoes. He never had, though. So-called "real" work was for suckers; Heath had the gift of making people do whatever he wanted them to, and, for the last ten years, he'd swaggered happily through life, taking what he wanted and somehow managing to be admired for it.

Even now, it hadn't changed.

And they'd *caught* him! They'd kicked his door down and hauled him off to prison, and he'd begun to think that maybe, just maybe, the game was finally up. But he kept smiling anyway, kept on treating the world as if he owned it, and even as a newly minted convicted criminal, his faithful credo had kept on working.

Forget punishment; even in the face of being mutilated for life, he'd turned the situation to his advantage. Now he was living in a griffiner tower, mingling with some of the most powerful people in the city, and even if he wasn't allowed to leave, nobody dared lay a hand on him. Not now that he was one of Lord Caedmon's friends.

Making friends with the young griffiner had been easy. The man was obviously feeling isolated, and no wonder, and in his situation, a friendly face and a cheerful voice was just what he needed.

And then there was that very attractive young woman who worked alongside him. Heath's smile widened slightly at the thought of her. Lady Myfina, oh yes. Watching her with Caedmon was a lot more amusing than it should have been. Heath kept wondering when Caedmon would finally stop making a fool out of himself and just tell Myfina how he felt. Much longer, and Heath might just get tired of waiting and have a try for her himself.

Chuckling at the thought, he reached the door he had been making for and opened it.

Caedmon looked up as he entered and greeted him with an open smile. "Heath! Hello! What are you up to?"

Heath grinned back as he strolled over and made his usual bow. "Coming to have a word with you in fact, milord. If you're not too busy."

"No, no, of course you can talk to me." Caedmon got up from his seat, putting aside the paperwork he'd been looking at. "What's up?"

Heath ran a finger over his moustache. "Now . . . I've been thinking this over for the last day or so, and it's occurred to me to make a couple of observations."

"Yes?" Caedmon prompted.

"First of all," said Heath, "I can't help but notice that your mother doesn't seem to be around any more."

"You didn't know she was here," said Caedmon, immediately tense.

Heath winked. "Didn't I?"

Caedmon relaxed and laughed. "All right, then, what of it?"

"I know she's left," said Heath, more seriously. "And I know where she's gone as well, and why, so let's not waste time over that."

Caedmon's eyes narrowed. "Oh yes? And what do you *know*, Heath?"

"I know she left nearly a month ago, and I know she was heading for Malvern. I also know she went alone." Heath put his arms behind his back. "Yesterday, I overheard certain people whispering. There are rumours that Lady Saeddryn isn't quite herself any more."

Caedmon's expression did not change. "And what do you mean by that?"

Heath had finally lost his smile. "The people who cared for her in Fruitsheart came here with you. Lady Saeddryn somehow managed to come all the way to the city on her own, in the snow, in no time at all. She also has scars all down her body from wounds she couldn't possibly have survived. That tells me a lot, milord."

Caedmon said nothing and only waited for his friend to continue.

"So she's gone to Malvern," Heath concluded. "Sent by you to kill the Queen. And don't worry; I haven't told anyone."

Caedmon folded his arms. "So what does this have to do with you?"

"Well," said Heath, smile reappearing. "The other observation I had for you is that, even though I've been employed by you for nearly two weeks by now, I haven't actually been asked to *do* anything. So now that I have something in mind that I could be useful for, I've come to suggest it to you."

"Which is?" said Caedmon.

Heath came closer. "Let's not pretend here, milord. Your mother should have reached Malvern a long time ago by now. If she's as fast as I think she is, she must have reached it before I even came here. But we've heard nothing back. And trust me, if the Queen were dead, the news would be all over the country. Lady Saeddryn went to Malvern, and she's disappeared. If she's a prisoner, then you need to know about it. If the Queen has her, that changes everything. In any case, *we need to know.*"

"I know," said Caedmon. "What are you going to do about it, then?"

"Simple," said Heath. "I'll go to Malvern. I'll be your spy."

Caedmon stared. "You'll what?"

"Go to Malvern," Heath repeated. "Nobody knows who I am, and you know how good I am at finding things out. And I have people in Malvern who can help me. Believe me, nobody lives the life of a scumbag like me without making a few useful friends." He grinned.

Caedmon frowned back. "How do I know you won't just run off the moment I let you go?"

"You don't," said Heath.

"Then why should I let you?"

Heath shrugged. "If you don't give me permission, I'll go without it. Why not just keep it simple? I'm no use to you here."

"I'll think about it," said Caedmon.

"When should I expect an answer?" Heath pressed.

"Soon."

Heath nodded. "I'll go and pack."

Heath had known perfectly well that Caedmon's "wait and see" had only been for show, and he was right. Within less than a day, he had permission, and the moment it arrived, he left Skenfrith without waiting to say goodbye. He was used to leaving quickly and quietly. He also knew how to leave without being noticed although he'd never had to sneak out of a city that was being guarded as carefully as this one. It was the whole reason why he'd lingered on in Skenfrith in the first place—and therefore the reason why he'd finally been caught. Under normal circumstances, he would have moved on well before the authorities tracked him down. War, he decided, was a pain in the arse. The sooner it ended, the better. And he, Heath of no fixed name and no fixed abode, would help see to it.

In the face of that, a few guards were nothing.

Before he did anything else, he took the opportunity to pay a visit to the house he'd rented—the same one where he had been arrested. Naturally, by the time he levered a window open and climbed in, his possessions had all disappeared. Probably sold to pay off the money he'd stolen. What a waste.

But they hadn't found everything.

Listening all the while for any sign of danger, Heath slipped into the bedroom that had been his. The bed had been stripped, but he flipped the mattress over and slit it open, and sure enough, golden oblong tinkled onto the floor. He scooped them up, scarcely able to believe that nobody had had the brains to check the mattress. The mattress was the *first* place anyone would hide money. Maybe he'd stitched up the hole too neatly.

The mattress money, though, was nothing. He'd only planted it as a decoy in case anyone caught him.

The money under the floorboards was a decoy as well. They'd found that, all right. They must have decided to insult him by assuming that was everything.

Shaking his head sadly, Heath opened the drawers in the now-empty cupboard and lifted out the false bottoms. Gold and silver gleamed seductively underneath. He pocketed the lot—careful to hide a few oblong in his boots just in case.

Having money in his pockets again made him feel much more confident. Complete, even.

With that out of the way and a new spring in his step, he headed for the pantry. No food in it, of course, but the old, broken, and obviously empty wine barrel was still lying on its side in a corner. He opened it and took out the bundle hidden inside.

With that done, he made a quick search of the rest of the

house, where he pocketed a few odds and ends before sneaking back out and into the city.

He went to the marketplace next. A smile and a wink to a certain female stall-holder gave him more than enough time to steal a small bag of flour, and with that hidden in his pocket, he slipped into an alleyway, hid behind a garbage heap, and set to work.

A very short time later, a sad, ragged old man came limping out the other end of the alley. His hair was grey and hung over his face, and he walked with a pained, hunching motion, supporting himself with a crutch. He looked so weak and pathetic that he attracted several pitying looks and even a few offers of help as he crossed the city, heading for the main gates.

They were open, and various carts and other travellers passed in and out without too much trouble though a group of guards stopped most of the larger wagons to search for anything suspicious. Caedmon hadn't completely closed down the city, then. He probably wouldn't until the last moment. No sense in starting a siege before there was anyone to do the besieging.

As it was, nobody paid any attention to the poor old man as he shambled through the gates and away.

It was a long walk to Malvern, but he didn't have to go very far before a trader offered him a ride, which he accepted. Sitting on the back of the cart full of wooden goods, Heath sat back and relaxed. Of course, if he'd wanted to, he could have just shown the guards the letter from Caedmon, which ordered anyone loyal to him to help the bearer, but that would have been too easy. And nowhere near as fun.

39

A Hero's Face

Heath travelled steadily on toward Malvern over the next few days, switching his mode of travel and changing his disguise several times in the process. Sometimes he walked, sometimes he rode with whoever was going in the right direction. Sometimes, he was the old cripple, sometimes he was a simple farm boy off to seek his fortune, sometimes he was a middle-aged father going to rejoin his family in Malvern. Every persona came with plenty of good stories to tell and a voice chosen for the outfit.

When he reached Malvern, he chose the old beggar again to get in. Best be as unthreatening as possible.

He hadn't visited the place in nearly a year—his policy was to wait a good chunk of time before coming back to an old hunting-ground—but it hadn't changed much. The last time he'd been there, Arenadd had still been King. He'd even seen the old man once—"old" being a relative term. As far as Heath could tell, he hadn't looked old enough to sell milk in the marketplace. But he'd been ruling the country for almost twenty years at that point, so Heath was prepared to take that in his stride.

The only real difference that he noticed now was that there were fewer griffins flying over the city than he remembered. That must mean that the unpartnered weren't back yet. Interesting. What was keeping them away so long?

Mulling this over, Heath set out to pay a few visits. He had left several stashes of money and other supplies around the place, and he was pleased to find that many of them were still there. The canvas bag in the canal was the hardest to find—it had been one of his better ideas.

He left them where they were, taking a little money from each one to refill his pockets, then struck out—slowly—for an undistinguished group of houses down in the grubby south end of the city. He shuffled along a particular street, looking vague and asking passers-by for money or food if they could spare it. Since this was a poor district, he got very little in the way of return, but that was all to the good.

Part-way along, he pretended to stumble, stood there shaking his head dumbly for a moment, then moved toward the nearest door, apparently at random.

He knocked on it with his stick.

It opened, and an old woman peered at him. "Yes? Who are ye?"

"Could ye spare some food for a poor old man?" Heath wheezed.

She looked slightly annoyed. "What, do ye think this is a charity? I never saw ye around here before—are ye lost or somethin'?"

"Of course!" said Heath, in grateful tones. "Thankye, kind lady, I'll be gone before ye know it." With that, he elbowed his way inside without further ado, with as much confidence as if he'd just been invited in.

The old woman turned on him. "What the—? Get out! Go on, shoo!"

Heath hustled her away from the door and shut it. Ignoring her protests, he barred it as well.

Then he relaxed. "Whew!"

The old woman looked nervous. "Now just stop there a moment—I'm sorry if I was—ye can have somethin' to eat, just sit down."

Heath grinned. "Thanks! You don't mind if I just tidy myself up, do you?"

Without waiting for an answer, he took off the ragged blanket he'd been using as a cape and put the crutch aside. Straightening up, he removed the false hump and shook the flour out of his hair and beard.

"There!" he said as he dusted himself down. "I feel fifty years younger."

The old woman's face slackened. "What . . . ?"

Heath smiled at her and reached down to touch her shoulder. "Hello, Mum."

She cried out and lunged forward, hugging him. "Hennie! Oh sweet moon, it's really ye!"

Heath pulled a face. "Ugh. Five years away, and I still can't stand hearing that name."

She let go and put her head on one side. "Oh? What are ye callin' yerself this time, then?"

"Today it was Mabon. Last week I think it was Pedr. Names get old if you wear 'em too long."

"So ye always said," said the old woman.

"But you can call me whatever you want," said Heath, with a gentleness in his voice that nobody else had ever heard.

When she smiled, her eyes showed the same brightness as her son's. "I'm so glad to see ye again, Hennie. All this time I had no idea if . . ."

"I told you I'd be fine."

"But ye never came back t'visit, never sent me a letter, never—"

"Mum, you can't read."

"I would've found someone t'read it to me!" she said sharply. "Where have ye been?"

"Everywhere," said Heath, truthfully. "I just came back to Malvern today. You're the first person I visited."

"Came back just to see yer old mother, eh?"

"Not quite. Mostly, but not completely."

"Oh?" She looked keenly at him. "What are ye up to this time, then?"

"Let's sit down," Heath suggested. "I'll take that food if it's still on offer, too."

Shaking her head and muttering with exaggerated annoyance, she let him sit down by the fire and fussed about with bread and cheese and some cheap wine, which she warmed up over the fire.

The food was poor, and the wine wasn't much better than alcoholic vinegar, but Heath ate it as if it were just as good as anything he'd had in the governor's tower with Caedmon. For him, it was a taste of home. Not something he'd tasted in quite a long time.

His mother watched him eat, not saying anything much. She was obviously hiding just how happy she was to see him again, and Heath let her keep it hidden. It was just her way.

"I think you'll be proud of me," he said once the food was gone.

"Will I?" she said at once.

"I think so." Heath nodded. "Your Hennie's gone up in the world recently. Oh yes—before I forget, this is for you."

She took the bag of money and looked at its contents with astonishment. "All this? For me?"

"More, if you want it," said Heath. "And there'll be even more to come, believe me."

She looked up, full of sudden suspicion. "Hennie, what have ye done? What are ye mixed up in this time? Just tell me the truth." Her voice was laced with despair.

Heath held up his hands. "It's all right. Mum, it's all right. I'm fine. I've got a new job."

"What kind of job?"

"I'm working for someone rather important," said Heath, relishing the suspense.

"How important? Who is he?"

"Lord Caedmon Taranisäii."

His mother gaped. "*What?* What the—? Hennie, this is *not* funny. How dare ye come here with this stolen money an' feed me lies like that? Lie to other people, lie to yerself, but how could ye lie to yer own mother?" She threw the bag of money on the floor and actually aimed a blow at him.

Heath dodged it. "Mother!" he said sternly, seeing the tears on her face. "Stop that right now and calm down. I am *not* lying. Look at this." He took Caedmon's letter out of his shirt, and showed it to her.

She squinted at the paper, then looked up at him. "What's this? What's it say?"

"It says, 'By order of Lord Caedmon Taranisäii of Malvern, all those who are loyal to the true King of Tara are commanded to give the bearer of this letter whatever he needs and to protect him from the usurper and her minions.' " Heath pointed to the bottom of the letter. "See there? That's his seal. I watched him put it there myself."

His mother looked at the letter again, then back at him. "Hennie, are ye bein' serious? Is this . . . is this real?"

"Yes. Mum, I'll slit my own throat if this is a lie. It's not. I know Caedmon Taranisäii. And his friend, Lady Myfina, and the governor of Skenfrith, Lady Isolde—she doesn't like me much."

The old woman said nothing.

"I shouldn't be telling you this," Heath continued. "If anyone in Malvern finds out about me and this letter, and why I'm here, then I'm a dead man. But I came here anyway because I had to see you, and I told you the truth because I trust you."

"Oh . . . oh *Hennie*!" His mother let out a sob and hugged him again.

He patted her on the back. "There, there. It's all right. I wouldn't have believed me, either. I don't think even I could sell a lie like that."

"Tell me all about it," she said, her eyes shining with tears. "Tell me *everything*. I won't tell a soul."

"I know," said Heath. He took a deep breath and began to do something he hadn't practised in a very long time: He told the truth. All of it.

"You're right," he said. "I'm a criminal. Or was. I spent the last seven years making money by lying to people. I kept moving around to keep ahead of the law until I got stuck in Skenfrith. I was there when Lord Caedmon and his friends came and took charge, and I decided to stay a while longer rather than be caught trying to leave. I got careless. I was caught."

"And then?" his mother prompted. She didn't look very surprised by any of this.

"And then I was taken to see the governor, Lady Isolde. And Lord Caedmon was with her. I recognised him straightaway, of course. Young man, not very experienced. But cleverer than he looks."

"Yes?"

"Yes," Heath nodded. "Anyway, long story short, he took a liking to me and decided my mind was too useful to waste. So he let me off as long as I stayed with him and did whatever he needed from me. I've been living among griffiners for the last two weeks."

"Didn't they punish ye?"

"Not really. I wasn't allowed to go anywhere or own any money, but I had fun. I'm telling you, Mother, griffiners know how to live! And Caedmon—I made a point of getting close to him. He's a good man. And his friend Lady Myfina—" Heath whistled.

His mother chuckled. "Watch it, boy, or ye'll be in trouble again."

"Oh, I don't know," Heath shrugged. "Last time I got into real trouble, I came out better off than before."

"Why are ye here in Malvern, then?" asked his mother.

"On an assignment," said Heath. "To find out what's going on."

"A spyin' mission, eh?"

"More or less."

"What's it pay, then?"

"Nothing," said Heath. "Only in virtue. Caedmon's making me pay back all the money I stole. At this rate, I should be out of debt by . . . oh, in about two hundred years."

"This is incredible, Hennie." The old woman turned serious. "Ye're playing a part in history. Ye'll be in them books up at the Eyrie one day."

"If I live long enough," said Heath.

"Ye will."

"I plan to."

"I don't believe it!" the old woman cackled. "My son, fightin' the good fight against that half-breed bitch, standin' up for the real Taranisäiis—yer father would be so proud!"

"I hope so," said Heath. He stifled a yawn. "It was a long trip to get here. I'm exhausted, honestly. Anyway, tomorrow I'll be going off to talk to some people and do some listening, but if you don't mind, I could do with a place to sleep—"

"Of course," she said. "Stay as long as ye need. But listen—"

"Yes?"

"I've been seein' a bit of yer old friend—Mostyn. Remember him?"

"Short man?" said Heath. "Pimples on his chin?"

"Aye, that's him. Pimples have got better, though."

"What about him?" said Heath.

"Ye should go see him. I've talked to him a bit, an' it sounds like he's made some interestin' new friends, if ye know what I mean. I think they might be able t'help ye."

Heath nodded. "Thanks. I'll go and look him up first thing in the morning."

He was lying, of course. But she didn't need to know that.

Elsewhere in Malvern, somewhere in a dark place, Saeddryn lay on her side and stared at nothing. She had been lying that way ever since she had come to be there, paralysed by shattered bones and crushed organs.

By now her body had long since repaired itself, but still she hadn't moved. Her eye was glazed, her mouth open. Only her mind was active, but there was no coherent thought left in it.

Old memories played themselves out around her, as real to her as if they were still happening. But they came in bits and pieces, never settling into a whole. She didn't know where she was, or when, and there was nothing for her to grasp hold of that might let her think or even realise what had happened to her.

Eventually, one memory in particular strengthened and grew bolder in her mind.

Saeddryn's eye focused on something only she could see. Very slowly, her mouth twitched into a smile.

"Arenadd," she whispered. "My Arenadd."

Even in her madness, she was not alone. Somewhere near but far, in a place no living thing could reach, the Night God watched over her warrior.

Beside her, Arenadd watched, too. His face was as dispassionate as his master's. "Won't you help her?" he asked.

I cannot, said the Night God.

Arenadd glanced at her. "Well then," he said. "It looks like you've lost, Master."

The Night God showed no anger. *She may be healed,* she said. *But without a partner, she will need help.*

"From who?" Arenadd asked dryly. "You?"

I will find a way, said the Night God.

"You always do," said Arenadd.

Incredibly, the Night God smiled at him. *Your cynicism is amusing. Do you truly believe you understand me? That you can predict me?*

"I've got a pretty good idea by now," Arenadd said, with a sly glitter in his eyes.

No, said the Night God. She turned away from Saeddryn's ravaged form and focused her attention on Arenadd. *No, you do not know. You have much to learn, little shadow. And I must teach you now.*

She descended on him, seeming to grow larger with every moment. As she reached out for him, Arenadd's world-weary calm drained away, and his face grew pale with fear. "No . . . not again! Leave me alone!"

The Night God encircled him. *You are mine forever, Arenadd Taranisäii.*

Lost in the void, there was no-one to hear his cry.

About the Author

K. J. Taylor was born in Australia in 1986 and plans to stay alive for as long as possible. She went to Radford College and achieved a bachelor's degree in communications at the University of Canberra before going on to complete a master's in information studies. She currently hopes to pursue a second career as an archivist.

She published her first work, *The Land of Bad Fantasy*, through Scholastic when she was just eighteen, and went on to publish *The Dark Griffin* in Australia and New Zealand five years later. *The Griffin's Flight* and *The Griffin's War* followed in the same year and were released in America and Canada in 2011.

K. J. Taylor's real first name is Katie, but not many people know what the *J* stands for. She collects movie sound tracks and keeps pet rats and isn't quite as angst-ridden as her books might suggest.

Visit her website at kjtaylor.com.